Dead on the Vine

By JM Harvey

Dead on the Vine

ISBN-13: 978-1500634636
ISBN-10: 1500634638

Cover design by Brandi Doane McCann

Edited by Lana Baker

CHAPTER 1

Everyone liked Kevin Harlan, even the person who beat him to death with a rusty shovel.

Until the morning Kevin's battered body was found in my vineyard, I had known him only as a good neighbor, but before his killer was finally stopped the secrets of his unhappy life and brutal murder would almost destroy everything and everyone I loved.

My name is Claire de Montagne but don't let that put you off. My name may be pretentiously French, but my ancestry is actually loud-mouth Italian mixed with a splash of drunken Irish and I am as earthy as the grapes I grow. I am fifty years old, the mother of one grown daughter and the owner of and slave to twenty acres of cabernet grapes perched on a rocky ridge that overlooks Napa Valley and the town of St. Helena.

My vineyard was originally planted by a banker who bankrupted himself trying to 'return to the soil.' He had named the vineyard Stony Farm, a name I changed to Violet Vineyards, not because grapes are purple, but because I love all things purple. One look into my kaleidoscope-purple kitchen would give that away. Purple tea-towels, purple curtains, lavender trivets, violet pot holders and framed prints and paintings of grapes overwhelm the walls, shelves and counters. Only the huge bay window that looks out on the rows of manicured vines and the valley beyond is unadorned. I love purple, but I love the view of the vines and the hills even more.

I am married…in a way. My husband, Roger, and I have an arrangement: he keeps his distance and I don't kill him. I've seen him only a half-dozen times since our daughter, Jessica, graduated from high school, and every time he was shorter, fatter and balder. And the woman on his arm was younger. I can't honestly say why I don't divorce him, except that I am by nature a loner. An absentee husband whom I despise suits me better than one sitting across the breakfast table slurping coffee. His reasons are much the same. As long as Roger has a wife, none of his mistresses will expect an engagement ring, his family fortune remains intact, and he remains free to chase the next young thing in spandex.

Roger comes from money and I come from a lack of it. Perhaps that's why our marriage lasted, in the truest sense, only five years. I was frugal and he was flamboyant. I wanted a home and a hearth, and he wanted to party until he dropped. My purchase of Violet Vineyards was the knockout punch to our already reeling relationship. More specifically, it was my refusal to use his money or have his name on the deed. For a down payment I used the small estate my parents left me in their passing. For that reason my parent's wedding

3

photo hangs over the fieldstone fireplace in my small tasting room and no picture of Roger has ever blemished my walls...

My daughter and my wines are the joys of my life, and the biggest source of tension. In all fairness, Jessica is bright, beautiful and healthy, and for that I am thankful. She teaches at the Bishop Lynch daycare center in Napa where she is the favorite of the children and the staff. But her emotional relationships and the chaos they wreak on our lives have been a battleground for Jessica and me since she was fifteen and sneaking out to see the captain of the junior high swim team. I was relieved when she moved out to attend college but, unfortunately, she didn't stay out. Every time I turn around she's back on my doorstep with a suitcase in her hand. It was during her latest two month 'visit' that Kevin Harlan was found dead in my vineyard.

CHAPTER 2

I was up at 5:30 that Monday morning, planning my day. I intended to supervise the cutting back of lateral canes before checking the rootstock planted earlier that spring. Then I was going to sample the 2008 Vintner's Reserve Cabernet that we'd be issuing the following week. After that I had a dozen smaller chores to take care of and several calls to make to restaurants and distributors.

I was sipping a cup of coffee and smoking my first cigarette of the day when Victor Gonzalez, my vineyard foreman, charged in the back door and skidded to a stop.

I was a mess. The previous evening, Stanley Kostyol, my daughter's ex-boyfriend, had stopped by at 2:00 A.M. after an overdose of beer at one of the local taverns. Jessica pleaded with him to leave while I hovered in the background gripping an empty wine bottle by the neck, waiting for an excuse to crack Stanley in the forehead. Stanley was maudlin and angry in turns, pacing across the driveway in the glare of his truck's headlights, doing a cut-rate Brando impersonation. When I had had enough, I called the sheriff. That got his attention. He squealed off in his pickup, screaming 'I love you!' at the top of his lungs. I guess that loving feeling wore off, because he was back an hour later to throw a brick through my living room window. By then Jessica was in hysterics and I was ready to grab a shotgun and hunt the little bastard down.

This wasn't the first incident in their long and torturous relationship, but I was determined that it would be the last. I filed a complaint and an arrest warrant was issued. Stanley had been a troublemaker since high school. I even suspected that he was the person who had broken into Jessica's car in St. Helena two weeks before Kevin's murder and stolen her gym bag. Jess preferred to believe it was a juvenile delinquent. A juvenile delinquent who leaves the XM Radio player but makes off with sweaty workout clothes? Until then all of Stanley's crimes had been junior-league vandalism and DUI's, but that night I had sensed depths of violence in his words and actions that frightened me for my daughter's safety.

As bad as I might have looked in my rumpled pajamas, my short silver hair pointing in every direction, every wrinkle on my face deepened by lack of sleep and aggravation, eyes bloodshot, Victor looked even worse. He was dressed in blue jean cut-offs and a faded Led Zeppelin T-shirt. His long stringy hair was down in his face, but did not conceal the panic in his eyes. His face was beaded with sweat despite the chill of the early morning and his hands were shaking.

Victor has been my foreman since 1999. A hippy of the old school, he wears his hair long and favors jeans and flip-flops over slacks and pressed shirts. He's an outspoken advocate for the migrant workers who pick fruit for the farms around the Valley, a fact that has made him unpopular with many growers. I have seen Victor calmly address hostile council meetings and growers' forums, ignoring the angry stares and whispered hatreds as he pointed out the poor living and working conditions, but his cool demeanor was lacking that morning.

"Claire," he panted, looking over his shoulder and out the door. "Jesus Christ!" He swiped at his mouth with the back of his hand and shook his head. "I can't believe this. Jesus!"

I was out of my chair and moving before the second 'Jesus' was out of his mouth. My first thought was that someone was hurt. So many things can happen to people on a farm or vineyard. Every year people are maimed or even killed. Machinery designed to harvest, crush and press grapes can do the same to human flesh.

"Kevin's dead," Victor exploded, shoving his hair out of his eyes. "I can't believe this!"

I tried to step past Victor to the open door, but he grabbed me by the shoulders.

"Don't," he yelled, spraying me with spittle. I barely noticed. My mind was grappling with what he had said. Kevin Harlan dead? I had seen him yesterday at a Growers' Lunch in St. Helena. It wasn't possible!

"We need to call the cops!" Victor's boney fingers dug into my shoulders. "The wine cellar door was kicked in. He must have caught them breaking in!"

"The phone's right there," I croaked around the chunk of fear lodged in my throat, pointing at my cellular lying on the kitchen table. I pried his hands off and tried to step around him. "Call the—"

"Don't go out there, Claire." Victor grabbed me by the arm and jerked me to a stop. "You don't need to see that."

"Victor," I snapped. "Let go of me and call the Sheriff. I'll be right back." I never argue with men when they're trying to protect me, I just ignore them. I had to see for myself. Not out of morbid curiosity, but in hopes that Victor was wrong. What if Kevin was only badly hurt, perhaps barely alive? I'm not a nurse, but after raising a child, tending to her scrapes and breaks and also caring for the workers in my vineyard, I knew I could be more help to Kevin in the vineyard than on the phone.

Victor stopped arguing. He's used to taking orders from me. As he fumbled with the phone, I grabbed the first aid kit out of the cabinet above the sink and ran out the back door and across the patio shaded by a trellis of wisteria dripping with lavender flowers.

6

It was a beautiful day. The sweet-purple smell of the wisteria permeated the air touched with a taste of sea salt blowing up-valley from the Pacific. Mist clung to the green vines with their pale clusters of grape flowers and the rising sun forged miniature rainbows between the rows. The sky was a cloudless blue from mountaintop to mountaintop, but the valley below was shrouded in a sea of fog with treetops, rocky crags and the roofs of wineries and homes jutting through. The unreality of the situation shook me. Death seemed so out of place with the beauty surrounding me. It couldn't be true.

Then I saw Kevin.

He wasn't alone. Near him stood three Mexican day workers in stained jeans and T-shirts who had been hired to thin the grape-flower clusters and prune back the vines. They were staring at the body, their expressions more curious than horrified. They didn't know Kevin Harlan. For them it was like rubbernecking an accident on the freeway, but we who had lived close to the always-smiling young man would feel his loss for a long time to come. Especially Victor. He and Kevin had been drinking buddies since Kevin had moved out here to rebuild the vineyard his grandfather had planted in the fifties.

Victor was right, Kevin was dead. I could see that from twenty feet away. The back of his head was almost flat and caked with drying blood. He was leaning back against the sagging top wire of the grape trellis, his arms draped over it, holding him up. His knees were splayed, ankles crossed. His head was bowed forward as if in prayer, his face streaked with blood. As I got closer I caught the glint of a tiny gold crucifix on a broken chain lying at his feet. Blood-splattered vines poked out around his legs and across his chest. He looked like a mutilated scarecrow. Only the fact that I knew him made the scene horrifyingly real.

I had known Kevin's parents since forever. In fact, my father had leased twenty acres of Chardonnay vines from Kevin's grandfather forty-five years ago when land was still cheap in the valley. While Kevin and I hadn't been close friends (the age difference made that difficult) we were good neighbors. Our many conversations had been about growing conditions, market prices, tonnage and vintages. In my mind I saw him, lean and tanned, working in the fields beside his men, drinking cold beer with them under the overhang of the barn he had converted into a home. Kevin was a generous and friendly young man that half the women in the county lusted over for his dark good looks and reserved charm. Last November, he had helped unclog my drip lines, laughing it up when Victor and I were splattered with purple juice. We drank several bottles of good wine that day in front of a blazing fire. Perhaps if I had been younger I would have been like the drooling tribe of females who eyed him

7

like a rare sirloin, but he was my daughter's age, and the son of high school classmates and therefore not an eligible bachelor but a child.

I looked at the first aid kit in my hand and almost broke into hysterical laughter. My hands were trembling and my breath was caught in my throat. Tears stung my eyes. I crossed myself and whispered, "Mother of God have mercy on your son."

"Senora," a man spoke in my ear, spooking me so bad that I dropped the first aid kit and hopped three feet.

"Why don't you return indoors," the oldest of the Mexicans said in accented English. "This is not for a lady to see." He was in his sixties, maybe older, with kind brown eyes surrounded by sunburned wrinkles.

I nodded dumbly, stooped and picked up the first aid kit, wondering why the tears didn't come, why the horror I felt wasn't translating itself into an emotional outpouring. Shock, I guessed. It was then that I thought of my daughter. Victor had said that the wine cellar door had been kicked in, and the door between my kitchen and the cellar is never locked. So, whoever broke in had access to my home! I hadn't seen Jessica that morning and my blood went cold with fear. A fear only a mother knows. The irrational fear of unknown dangers that can rob her of her children.

"Senora, the old man spoke again. "I will walk you back." He put his rough brown hand on my forearm.

"Oh, no," I whispered, barely hearing him. I broke away and ran for the house, leaving the old man staring after me. I told myself that Jessica was okay, that I was acting crazy, but the dead man on the grass was proof enough that I wasn't. I ran through the open kitchen door in time to see Victor replacing the phone on the kitchen table and my half-awake daughter entering the kitchen through the dining room door.

"Thank God!" I grabbed her in a ferocious hug.

Her eyes filled with fear. She grabbed my forearm and her nails dug in.

"What's the matter?" she demanded. "What's happened?" She was dressed in a baggy T-shirt and white knee socks. The T-shirt and her face were both wrinkled by sleep. "Is it Stanley? Is he okay?"

At the mention of her boyfriend's name my grief flared instantly to anger. After all he had done to ruin her life, he was still her first concern.

"I'm sure that cretin's fine," I snapped. "But Kevin Harlan's dead. Murdered. He's hanging out there with his head bashed in."

"Kevin?" she gasped and I was instantly sorry. I started to explain, but Jess wasn't listening. She shoved me aside and bolted out the kitchen door before I could say another word.

"Jess!" I yelled, but she was already racing down the row toward Kevin's corpse.

The Mexican men looked up in alarm. Two of them backed away while the gentleman who had spoken to me stepped forward, hands raised to block the aisle. But, Jessica didn't make it all the way to the corpse, she stopped short halfway down the row. I ran up behind her and put myself between Jessica and Kevin.

Jessica shuddered, turned away from me and vomited into the clover, heaved and vomited again. She tottered, eyes streaming tears, throat gulping on strangled sobs. "Oh, Mom," she said and dropped into my arms, almost knocking me off my feet. I tried to hold her up but she slipped through my hands and hit the ground just as Victor ran up.

"What happened?" he panted. "Is she all right?"

"She fainted. Help me get her up," I said, my own legs feeling rubbery. Together, we hauled Jessica to her feet. Her eyelids were fluttering and she was breathing shallow and fast, almost hyperventilating.

Victor and I carried her between us, dragging her feet through the clover. She started to come around as we pulled her up the kitchen steps. We put her in a chair at the kitchen table where she slumped, still breathing too fast for my liking.

"Jessica," I said, shaking her gently. "Are you okay?"

She nodded once, stood on her own, then doubled over and retched. I started to sit down beside her but stopped short when I heard a car rolling across the gravel drive out back.

"That'll be the police," Victor said. "I'll take care of Jessica if you'll talk to them." He and Jess are very close. With all the late hours we put in at Violet, Victor spends almost as many nights under my roof as he does his own.

"All right," I said with a dead-weary sigh. "I'll talk to the police." I would rather have stayed with my daughter and made sure she was okay, but the vineyard was my responsibility, not Victor's.

I stood, taking one last look at Jess, then stepped back outside. Already the mist had begun to burn off, revealing the patchwork of farms and wineries and the town of St. Helena in the valley below. A hawk screamed in the woods above Violet Vineyards, and another was circling a few hundred feet below, but still several hundred feet above the valley floor.

The Mexican workers had walked up from the vineyard and were standing at the head the rows, in the shade of a row of twenty almond trees planted to protect the vines from the harsh winter winds. They were looking at a battered gray, mud-caked Jeep Cherokee that had just pulled up.

It wasn't the police. It was Samson, my cellar foreman and master wine maker, and the biggest reason that Violet Vineyards cabernet is a respected wine both in Napa and abroad. Only the year before, we had taken a silver medal at the International Tasting Competition, where some of the greatest palates voiced their appreciation.

Samson arrives every day promptly at 6:30, dressed in one of a number of hopelessly style-less suits complete with 1950's vintage skinny-tie and a sweater vest. Samson is pop-eyed with a receding chin, a nose like a red horn bulb, a grouchy disposition, and a big place in my heart. He came to Napa straight from Greece in the 1940's to work in the vineyards. Over the ensuing decades he became a master winemaker working on commission for some of the most prestigious houses in California. But more importantly, he was my father's best friend and I'm proud to say he's one of mine. Now, semi-retired, he works solely for me on a percentage-of-profit basis.

"De Montagne," he said testily as he climbed out of the jeep. "What are these men doing standing around? If there is no work for them, they should go home." He is forever watching the bottom line, concerned that I am too generous with the temporary laborers, and the permanent staff of two, including himself. I insisted on our profit sharing arrangement after he refused to take a wage, a percentage of the business or any other form of payment. Samson thinks of himself as my surrogate father and guardian.

"There's a problem—" I began, but he cut me off.

"I know. The nights are not cool enough and the days are too warm, but no reason for men to stand idle. There is work to do," he added, casting his eyes over the vineyard. "The 2009 cabernet needs racking, but, of course, that is for *me* to do *only*. But I cannot do *everything*. I see that the compost has not been mixed into the soil as I suggested. I see cutting that needs to be done. I see... What is that?" His eyes had fallen on the motionless figure of Kevin Harlan, forty feet away. Samson is old, but there's nothing wrong with his hearing or eyesight, a fact that many a chastised worker could attest to. "A joke of some foolish kind?"

"Samson," I cut in, "it's Kevin Harlan—"

"Well, I can see it is Harlan, but what is he doing leaning on the trellis like that? He will break the new canes. If he wants to break canes, he can go to his own vines."

"He's dead, Samson," I replied. "Murdered."

"Murdered?" He spoke the word as if he had never heard it before, but then it was a word neither of us had used in reference to someone we knew. It was a word for gangsters and drug dealers, for the streets of LA or New York, not for a stony hillside vineyard in Napa. "Here?"

"I don't know." I replied honestly, just as a sheriff's cruiser pulled in behind Samson's old Jeep. Two more followed.

"This won't be good for business," Samson muttered as I stepped toward the foremost police car and the emerging figure of our Sheriff, Ben Stoltze.

10

CHAPTER 3

I grew up with Ben Stoltze, back when St Helena was a tiny farming community, the local winemakers made cabernet that sold for two dollars a jug and most grapes were grown for the table. Times have changed, and so have I, but I swear Ben still looks like the roughneck right tackle I remember from the high school football team. Ben is an attractive man, tall and a bit stout, with wide shoulders and bowed legs. His face is deeply tanned and lined from too much sun. He looks more like a cowboy from a cigarette ad than a policeman. His stiff-as-straw blonde hair is always tousled and his suit is always rumpled, but he possesses an aura of quiet competence.

After high school, while I was entering into a marriage soon to go sour, Ben went to Southern California on a football scholarship. He lasted two semesters before he returned to Napa and joined the police force. I don't know why he left college, and I never asked. We weren't that close. The last time I spoke to him was at our thirty-year class reunion two years ago. Not long after that his wife Sarah, a charming woman who had raised three attractive, well-mannered sons, passed away from colon cancer. I had attended the funeral along with three hundred others. Ben had looked bad that day, drained and confused, and I was sad to see that he still wore the shadow of that expression.

Ben walked over, his rundown cowboy boots crunching gravel, his eyes straying to Kevin Harlan's body. Behind him came two detectives dressed in suits and ties, one tall and carrying a camera, the other fat with a tomato-red face. The heavy one had a hand thrust into his waistband in a futile attempt to adjust his too-tight pants. Behind them were a pair of deputies in khaki uniforms.

Ben stopped beside me as the other officers continued purposefully down the row.

"Claire," Ben said, glancing at me for a split second with sun-faded blue eyes, then back at Kevin. Ben nodded at Samson.

"Hello, Ben," I replied, crossing my arms to hide my shaking hands.

"You find him like that?" Ben nodded at Kevin.

"Victor did," I replied.

"Better get Victor out here, I'll need to talk to him. When'd he find the body?"

"A few minutes before he called you," I answered, watching the tall detective snap photos of Kevin's corpse. The detective looked young for the job. He had blue-black hair cut in a bristly buzz-cut and his suit looked expensive. The fat detective was several years older, balding with a curly black fringe of hair. His clothes looked cheap, and slept in. Neither man inspired my confidence.

"Hola, cómo está?" Ben called to the three Mexican men as he walked their way.

They watched Ben's approach with hesitant smiles. Many of the migrants who work the fields have a natural aversion for the police. These men, I assumed, were legal immigrants. If they weren't they probably would have bolted before the police arrived. I personally don't care, legal or not. Not because I want cheap labor (I pay a fair wage) but because I find fault with the policy of drawing an imaginary line in the sand and expecting millions to live in poverty on one side while we prosper on the other. Most of the migrant workers are at least half Native American and have more right to be here than I do.

"This is bad," Samson said as Ben spoke to the three men. "A body dead on the vines? That will hurt sales plenty, let me tell you." He shook his head.

"I'm more concerned about Kevin," I snapped. "Not a profitable concern, I know, but—" I didn't finish because I couldn't. If I had, I would have started crying and I'm not much for public tears. Before Samson could say anything further I headed for the house, leaving him staring after me in confusion.

I flopped into a chair at the kitchen table, held my head in my hands and thought about Kevin. My life would be less rich for his loss. We'd shared so many good times. The harvests and crushes, the planting and tastings. Even the bad times seemed precious now. The times when equipment failed or the rains didn't come or came in a flood. It was then that I thought of Laurel, Kevin's wife.

"Oh, no," I said as Victor walked in from the dining room.

"What?" Victor asked, anxiety carving deep lines in his face. "What's the matter?"

"Laurel," I said. "She doesn't know."

"Oh," Victor said. Laurel was a cold and beautiful woman who had married Kevin seven years ago. Many nights I had listened to them argue inside their converted barn, which is less than two hundred yards from my home. With me, she was saccharine sweet and full of complaints. Either my workers were lying under 'Her' almond trees and crushing 'Her' grass or the smell of freshly picked grapes in the gondolas was just too much and could I have them moved downwind? It was never ending. With Victor she was snotty and hot-tempered. One day last fall, during the height of the crush, she had ordered Victor to have one of the pickers move his pickup off the road in front of her house. She would have told the picker herself, she rudely explained, except she didn't "speak wetback." Victor calmly told her she didn't own the road and she countered with a threat to call immigration if it wasn't gone in five minutes.

12

Kevin was apologetic after these incidents, but it did put a damper on our relationship.

"Ben or one of the other cops will tell her," Victor replied shortly.

I nodded, but felt like I wasn't showing Kevin the respect he deserved. No matter how bad it made me feel, I wasn't going over there to deliver the bad news. If she and I had been friends I would have insisted on being there. For the first time I was almost grateful she was such a witch.

We were interrupted by a tapping at the kitchen door jamb. I turned to find Ben Stoltze's frowning face thrust through the still open door.

"Need you out here, Victor," Ben said. They needed no introduction - Victor's family has been in the valley longer than Ben's or mine. Longer than any Anglo. More importantly, both Ben and Victor are natives of the Valley and remember a time when everyone knew everyone. And everything about everyone.

"Coming, Ben," Victor replied and Ben disappeared.

"Jess is doing fine," Victor told me as he trailed Ben outside. I nodded my thanks, but I assumed he was lying. I doubted that Jessica had recovered so quickly from the shock of seeing Kevin's corpse. I knew I hadn't.

I followed Victor to the door and stopped there. Out in the vineyard the detectives were measuring something with a roll-up tape measure while the deputies duck-walked around Kevin's body, combing through the short clover with their fingertips. Kevin was still hanging from the trellis, mimicking the cruciform shapes of the sturdy rootstock from which the grape canes grow. Ben, Victor, Samson and the three Mexican men were standing on the patio talking in Spanish. Ben had a small notepad and a stub of pencil in his hand. It was a scene straight out of a television police drama.

I waited for a break in the conversation before I spoke. "I'm going to take a shower and change clothes. I'll be back in fifteen minutes."

"All right," Ben replied. "I want you to come with me to the Harlans. I'd like somebody the widow knows there when I give her the bad news. Then we'll need to talk."

"Great," I said, and Ben shot me a look. I didn't care. "Ten minutes," I said grudgingly and went back into the house, cursing under my breath, mentally asking Kevin to forgive me.

I've never been one of those women who take two hours to do their hair and another two to dress. Maybe it's because I never have time, or maybe I just can't be bothered. My two indulgences in the feminine grooming vein are bubble baths and perfumes. There's nothing like a long soak with a good book and an even better glass of wine. And the smell of fine perfume can put me into a rhapsody as great as sipping one of my own wines.

13

I was rinsing under a hot jet of water when I remembered Victor telling me about the broken cellar door. The thought set my heart racing and I was out of the shower in a flash, still soapy and dripping. I pulled on jeans, ratty tennis shoes and a purple sweatshirt, ran a comb through my hair and headed downstairs.

I took the stone steps from the kitchen to the wine cellar two at a time. The cellar vault is actually a cave cut into the hillside where the natural temperature controls of the earth keep it cool. A thermometer at the rear of the cellar reads a constant temperature of fifty degrees, summer, winter or fall, while the front of the cellar, where the fermenting tanks are located, hovers between seventy and seventy-five degrees.

The cellar was built by the bankrupt-banker and with one look you can see where his money went. Three thirteen foot tall, 6,000 liter stainless steel tanks take up a large part of the front of the cellar. These tanks are the primary fermentation vats where the must (crushed grapes, including some of the stems, seeds and skins) is allowed to go through its first fermentation, which takes two to three weeks. Stainless steel piping brings the must down from the de-stemming/crushing machine located on the open-air crush pad thirty feet overhead.

The tops of the tanks have pneumatic lids, but for red wine we leave the tops open throughout the primary fermentation process. The stems, seeds and skins float in a cap on top of the juice, to which we add yeast cultures. This cap is punched down twice a day to keep the skins in contact with the wine as the yeast converts the grape's sugar to alcohol. Most people don't realize that grape juice is clear and that red wine draws all of its color and much of its flavor from the skins.

Beyond the tanks, in the cool darkness of the cave, are rows of large oak barrels fire-toasted on the inside to encourage oak flavors in the cabernet. This is where the secondary fermentation process takes place. This usually takes several months to a year, sometimes longer. During this time the wine is racked (siphoned off the top) twice, leaving the lees (sediments) behind. The wine is then racked into smaller oak barrels where it ages until it reaches maturity, usually a year or two. The decision on when to sell is made by me on a vintage by vintage basis.

In the cellar, Samson was perched on top of a ladder leaned against one of the fermentation tanks. A hose was unwound across the floor and Samson was rinsing the inside of the tank with a mixture of water and sterilizing solution. He does this once a month between harvests to keep the tanks clean. Otherwise, any microorganisms or bacteria in the tanks would find its way into the flavor of the wines. And moldy cabernet isn't a big seller.

"The sheriff is still outside, and no work is being done," Samson paused long enough to complain, then went back to rinsing. Nothing can take Samson's attention from winemaking for long, not even the murder of a neighbor. His life revolves around wine and grapes. Violet Vineyard cabernet, Victor and myself are his only friends, and I'm pretty sure I don't rate as high as the cabernet. This suits Samson. He needs no company, has no interest in news or gossip. He doesn't even own a television, but he's on the mailing list of almost every wine magazine and newsletter in the country. If it isn't wine, it isn't worth knowing, is his general philosophy.

"Samson," I said. He didn't take his eyes off the swirl of water in the tank, but I knew he was giving me perhaps ten percent of his attention. "Have you noticed anything damaged or out of place?"

"What?!" His head snapped around and he almost fell off the ladder. "Why would that be?" He turned off the hose and his eyes probed the dark recesses of the cellar as I explained about the cellar door being kicked in by whoever killed Kevin.

"Damn that Harlan," he spat, one of the most insensitive things I have ever heard from my gruff old winemaker, but I didn't rebuke him. I was just too stressed to worry about Samson's rotten attitude.

Samson climbed down, cursing in Greek, and began roving over the cellar. He looked behind an aging winepress coated in a fine layer of white calcium, and under and around the primary fermentation tanks. He lifted the dusty canvas covers off of the bottling machinery and the destemmer and tried the door handle on the small cave where I keep my private stock of wine. He walked back into the vault, past rows of oak barrels, looking at and under each one. He reached the end of the cave and came back to where I stood looking at the broken lock on the cellar door.

"Everything is fine," he said, eyes still peering into the dark corners of the cellar. "It should have been locked. Every night!" He said, poking the air with an emaciated finger.

"It was locked. They kicked it in," I sighed.

"A stronger lock must be bought! I keep records here. Valuable information!" He hurried on his skinny legs to a rickety desk shoved into the far corner of the cellar where he doodles on notepads and chews on cheap cigars that he never lights. He pulled open the top drawer and rummaged through a mess of useless papers and free promotional pens.

"Samson, not many people read Greek," I tried to reassure him.

"There are translators at the university," he reminded me as he took an ancient stub of cigar from the drawer and stuck it in his mouth. Chomping angrily on the withered stogie, he held a yellowed piece of paper at arm's

15

length. I left him there, muttering, squinting at his spiky scrawl, and went to meet Ben.

CHAPTER 4

The Medical Examiner's antiseptic-white van was parked on the grass of my back yard. Two technicians in white coats with 'County of Napa' shoulder patches embossed with a bunch of grapes were transferring Kevin's body to a stretcher. Ben was still talking to Victor, but the three Mexican workers were working on the far side of the vineyard, thinning out the flower clusters and cutting away lateral shoots and leaves to provide the clusters with filtered sunlight. It's a delicate balance, too much foliage and the grape crop will be reduced significantly while taking on an earthy quality, too little and the grapes will not receive the nutrients they need from the leaves. In addition, it is important to cut back old wood and make space for the new canes that will provide next year's crop. It takes practice and a trained eye, so I was a little concerned that they had started without Victor. But now wasn't the time to worry about the vines.

"I'll get back with you soon," Ben said to Victor as I approached. Victor nodded, then hurried over to join the workers.

"Ready?" Ben asked me, raising one eyebrow.

"No, but I'm not likely to ever be," I replied honestly.

"Can't be helped," Ben said with a shrug. "Gotta be done."

I wanted to yell, "Not by me!" but I held my tongue. There was no sense in making this harder. Instead I mentioned the broken lock on the cellar door.

"Victor told me about that. I told Doug to check it out and I'll have Midge dust for prints." We walked side by side toward the weathered gray barn with its freshly shingled roof and bright copper window frames. Kevin had refurbished the barn over two years of rain-days and evenings while he planted rootstock and grafted fruiting vines from sunrise to sunset. During that time, Laurel had stayed in a small apartment in Yountville. Money was tight, even though the forty acres Kevin was farming were worth two million dollars on the current market. In Napa the Harlans were considered 'land poor,' a condition I was familiar with myself. Every penny I had was tied up in the vines.

A glance around the Harlan's place revealed the love Kevin felt for this spot. And the sweat he had expended on it. He had planted fifteen acres of cabernet sauvignon five years ago and the young vines in their neatly trellised rows were already reaching maturity. Kevin had laid the stone foundation for his pressing room this summer with help from Victor and Michelle Lawford, a tireless, burly woman with a man's haircut and mannerisms, who day-labored for the Harlans. Michelle, better known as Mike the Dyke by the cruel wits in the valley, was one of Stanley Kostyol's friends, but I didn't hold that against her. She was as sweet and shy on the inside as she was gruff and tough on the outside. And she knew her vines, which is the highest compliment I can give.

Kevin had hoped to make his own wine in the next year or two, but for the time being he had been selling his crop to Dearborne Vineyards to be used in their medium priced cabernet. The money from Dearborne had allowed Kevin to make much-needed improvements to the vineyard's drainage. Just last week he had terraced and prepared ten acres of trenches for new vines with a rented backhoe. Kevin had big plans and the ambition and drive to see them through.

What would happen to his work now? Did Laurel have the tenacity or the desire to continue, or would she sell the property? It had been Kevin's dream to build the winery, to grow the best grapes and devote his life to bottling great wine. Laurel seemed more interested in the status she achieved by being a vineyard owner. I never saw her lift a finger around the winery, unless it was to point out some grievance.

"Hate this part of the job," Ben muttered as we walked down the narrow stone path that fronted the barn. A heavy growth of hibiscus and roses gave the barn a picture-postcard quality. "Especially after Winter. The Harlans have had a pretty rough time since they moved up here. Hell, that case still keeps me up at night," Ben added, reminding me of the awful ordeal the couple had endured just over a year ago when their daughter, Winter, was taken from Laurel at gunpoint.

Winter had been a sparkling three-year-old with her mother's looks and her father's natural charm. She'd been a sickly child, always down with the flu or some other ailment. But she had spent every minute she could in the fields with her father, brightening all of our lives in the process. Her abductor, a convicted child molester named Buford Logan had been caught two weeks after her abduction, a week before Winter's badly decomposed body had been found. She had been buried under a partially caved-in bank of the Napa River not far from where Buford worked as an auto mechanic. I recalled that time period with a shudder - the news reports, the televised manhunt and the reward money fundraisers. Kevin and Laurel had been devastated, though Laurel managed to keep her composure better than Kevin. Suddenly I felt guilty as hell for thinking so many snotty things about Laurel. If anything, she deserved sympathy and compassion, not spite.

Ben buttoned his jacket as we stepped on a five-foot by five-foot granite slab that made up the barn's threshold.

"A damn dirty business," he said wearily. He used the brass knocker. We waited for a couple of minutes before Laurel opened the door.

We had obviously gotten her out of bed. I was surprised to see that she had slept in her makeup, which isn't very good for the skin. She was dressed in an ankle-length white cotton gown that covered her from neck to toes and would

18

have been considered modest on a nun. That surprised me; Laurel always dressed in clothing that flatteringly revealed her figure and bordered on lewd. Then I noticed the black fishnet hose poking out of the bottom of the granny gown. An odd ensemble

There was no denying it, Laurel was beautiful. Blonde, five-foot-eight, anorexia thin (the current trend in female beauty) with dark eyes and full lips. She looked fantastic even with her hair in a tangled mess and her eyes ringed with mascara. But, more than beautiful, she was sensual. All of her postures and gestures, even in the most informal of conversations, seemed charged with sexual tension. That had made her no friends among the women in our circle of winemakers, but it had won her admiration and amorous pursuit from the men, married and single alike.

I could see that Ben was struck by Laurel's beauty. He stood up straighter, squared his shoulders and sucked in his stomach. He probably wasn't even aware he was doing it. Laurel worked on men's hormones like the moon works on the ocean, though her gravitational pull centered on only one region of their anatomy, bypassing their brains all together.

Laurel looked at Ben and then turned to me, puzzled and still half asleep. Her eyes narrowed when they hit me. Animosity is hard to hide, and Laurel's made me extremely uncomfortable at that moment. I shouldn't have come, I thought. She needs a friend right now, not a feuding neighbor. But, Laurel didn't have any friends I was aware of. I'd do my best. For Kevin's sake.

"Mrs. Harlan, I don't know if you remember me, I'm—"

"I remember you, Ben," Laurel interrupted. Even her voice was seductive, throaty and soft, though still fuzzy from sleep. She stepped into the doorway and panned her eyes over the front yard. "Is there something wrong?"

"Could we come in, Mrs. Harlan? I need to speak with you," Ben said gravely.

"Kevin's not here," Laurel replied, brow furrowed. "He's down on the lower terrace," she explained.

"Yes Ma'am," Ben replied apologetically. "But could I speak with you for a moment?"

"Of course," she said, stepping aside. "How rude of me. You'll have to excuse the house, today is cleaning day so it's a mess."

Ben mumbled something in reply. Laurel led the way down a short hall into a huge open area at the back of the barn that was the Harlan's living/dining room. The barn's ceiling was insulated with a coated sheeting painted pale blue, but the old hand-hewn beams had not been refinished. The furniture was country-chic with lots of flower print upholstery and mass produced folk art. The kitchen was separated from the living area by an L-shaped bar lined with stools. Chintz covered the windows and wallpaper roses bloomed everywhere.

19

Ben stood until Laurel and I had taken seats facing each other, me on a long sofa covered in yellow roses and Laurel in a matching armchair, then he sat beside me, hands nervously kneading his knees.

Ben cleared his throat, and looked around the room and out the huge plate glass windows Kevin had installed along the back wall of the barn. The view of Napa valley sprawling below, stark browns and black slopes bleeding into the lush green and brilliant wildflowers of spring, was dazzling. In the far distance I could see the silver shimmer of the Napa River.

"Mrs. Harlan—"

"It's Laurel, Ben," she said with a strained smile.

"Laurel," Ben began self-consciously. "I'm afraid I have some bad news." He paused. "I'm sorry to tell you this, but Kevin was killed earlier this morning. He was found on Claire's property."

Laurel was motionless for a second, then shook her head. "No," she said. "Not Kevin."

"He was murdered. I'm very sorry, I know how hard this is," Ben said in a pained voice.

At that moment I was so uncomfortable I wanted nothing more than to disappear.

"No," Laurel said in a voice so empty it sounded like a bad recording. "You're wrong, Ben." She stood and walked unsteadily to the windows. "He's down there," she pointed, "working in the new rows. It must be someone else. One of Mrs. de Montagne's men." With every word she sounded more and more like a scared child making up fairy tales about a dead parent actually being shipwrecked or kidnapped.

Ben went to her and squeezed her shoulder. "There's no doubt that it was Kevin." Ben looked pleadingly at me. Reluctantly, I rose and joined them.

Laurel was staring down the slope at where Kevin should have been. We could see only the far edge of the freshly plowed terrace and the valley beyond. The rest was blocked by a row of hedges dressed in new leaves.

"Laurel," I spoke softly. "I'm afraid Ben is right. I saw Kevin this morning. I am *so* sorry." I didn't know what else to say.

Laurel put a palm on the glass and shook her head. "Not Kevin," she whispered and the tears began.

I put my arm around her shoulders. She turned and hugged me tight as sobs wracked her body. Her red-lacquered fingernails dug into my shoulders and her tears were hot on my neck. I held on to her, patting her back and making the little noises you make, and crying right along with her.

"I'll make coffee," Ben said and made a hasty retreat.

As Ben hid in the kitchen, I led Laurel to the sofa and sat her down beside me. Between sobs, Laurel moaned Kevin's name. I did my best to soothe her

20

and by the time Ben was back, a long ten minutes later, with a pair of steaming cups, Laurel was huddled in the corner of the sofa with her knees drawn up and a wad of Kleenex in her hand. All of her seductive qualities and most of her beauty had deserted her. In her grief she was pitiful.

Ben cleared his throat as he put the cups on the coffee table. He sat in the chair Laurel had vacated and leaned toward her, elbows on knees.

"I'm very sorry Mrs. Harlan, but I have questions I have to ask," Ben began. "It won't take long, I promise."

Laurel dabbed at her tears and sniffled before nodding, eyes squeezed tightly shut. "I'll try, Ben," she whispered.

Ben nodded. "Can you tell me the last time you saw Kevin?"

"Last night. I went to bed early. Kevin still had things to do. We argued—" Laurel broke out in fresh tears and hiccoughing sobs. I scooted down the sofa and she grabbed my hand in a strangle hold. She continued after a moment, her already reddened face flushing even deeper. "I said some things…Oh God, I screamed at him, I, I—" her fingernails cut into my palm and I tried not to wince.

"He never came to bed?" Ben asked after a respectful pause.

Laurel sniffed again and wiped her nose before replying, "I took a sleeping pill. I don't know, but his side of the bed doesn't look slept in. He—he might have slept on the sofa—I—I just don't know!"

"That's okay. I only have one more question and then I'll let you rest. Are you aware of anyone that might have profited by your husband's death? Any enemies?"

"Everyone loved Kevin. Everyone!" She covered her face with her free hand and sobbed. Fresh tears sprang up in my eyes. I pitied her the days to come, the deepening knowledge of loss, the replaying of harsh words spoken. All the recriminations and self-abuse that haunt those left behind.

Ben rose from the armchair, smoothed his slacks and ran his fingers through his hair. "I'm afraid I'll have to come back tomorrow and ask some more questions, but this should do for now." Ben looked pointedly at me, but Laurel was still clutching my hand like a lifeline. I didn't have the heart to break contact.

"I'll be along in a minute," I told Ben as I took a tissue from the open box and wiped my eyes. Once again I was glad that I never wear makeup. At this point it would have been pooled around my chin.

"Okay," Ben thrust his hands in his pockets, nodded at me and disappeared down the hall. I heard the front door close quietly. At the soft 'click' of the latch, Laurel looked up at me and I swear I saw cool appraisal in that look, not grief. She squeezed my hand briefly and released it.

21

"I'm surprised you came with Ben," She said as she wiped her eyes. She stood, crossed the room and stared out the window, her back to me. "We're not exactly the best of friends."

"We're neighbors," I told her simply and she nodded without turning to face me. She didn't say anything for a long moment, but when she spoke again it was in a husky voice so intimate it evoked images of overwrought bedrooms and perfumed air.

"I suppose I should thank you for that," Laurel said. "For the performance, I mean," she added, combing her tangled hair with her fingers. "Maybe I should applaud? You are quite the actress, Claire. Holding my hand, comforting me. Holding back the hate to play the role." Her words bounced off the glass and back at me. "But I suppose that was for Ben."

For a moment I was too shocked to speak. Laurel had changed from grieving widow to evil witch as quickly as Dracula turns into a bat. But, after years of hating her, I was able to bounce back quickly.

"Ben is an old friend. Nothing more," I said through my teeth, more for Ben's sake than mine.

"He is quite the man," Laurel said, turning to face me. "Quite the man," she repeated looking at me coolly. "I don't blame you a bit."

"Laurel," I said, breathing deeply to keep control. "I don't know what the hell you're talking about. And I don't want to know."

Laurel sighed and shook her head wearily. "Maybe it's the shock of Kevin's death, but I'm *tired* of playing games with you, de Montagne. I know you hate me," she held up a palm as if I might refute that claim. "And the feeling is completely mutual."

I fought the urge to cross the room and shove the widow through the window. I could imagine the scene, Ben rushing in with handcuffs. Flashing lights and Miranda warnings. It might have been worth it, but going to jail for beating up my neighbor's widow would be a sad way to make the newspapers.

"You overestimate your importance to me, Mrs. Harlan," I said crisply, forcing my most gracious smile. "What you saw was not an act, but genuine emotion. I can't fault you for not recognizing that since you possess so little of it." I didn't give her time to reply. I about-faced and headed for the front door. As I closed it behind me, I heard her low and infuriating laughter.

Ben was standing in the yard absentmindedly rolling a newly sprung rose bud between his fingers. He joined me as I stomped across the yard.

"How's she doing?" he asked. "She all right?"

"I'm sure she'll be fine," I replied shortly.

Ben gave me a searching look, but said nothing more about Laurel.

22

"Any ideas, Claire?" he asked, shuffling his feet through the grass as we climbed the hill to my kitchen door. "Kevin mention any problems with anyone?"

"No, but we weren't that close. What Laurel said is true, to the best of my knowledge. Everyone loved Kevin. He was terribly sweet—" I had to pause or I would have started crying. "Victor was much closer to him," I finished.

The white coroner's van was gone from the back yard, but the detectives were still standing in the row where Kevin's body had been found. A tall woman with kinky brown hair dressed in a white lab coat had joined them. She was kneeling where Kevin had been found, picking at the grass. There was a stack of paper bags beside her on the clover. She looked up and waved at Ben, who waved back and kept walking.

"Yeah, Victor told me the same thing. Which gets me absolutely nowhere."

Ben opened the door and followed me into the kitchen. He stopped on the threshold and looked around, taking in the industrial stove and refrigerator and the overwhelming amount of purple. His eyes stopped on a framed photo, a close-up of a grape-stained foot. The foot was mine, a souvenir from my one trip to Burgundy.

"Like purple, huh?" He said, pulling out a chair and easing himself into it.

"Hate it," I replied with a tight smile. "Coffee?"

"Love it," he said, smiling genuinely for the first time that day.

"Think she's involved?" Ben asked in a falsely off-hand manner while I spooned coffee into a filter.

I thought about that for a second. Laurel was a rotten human being, but could she have killed Kevin? And what would be the motive? If she had divorced him she could have forced him to sell the property and been a very wealthy woman. Of course, she'd be even wealthier if he was dead. But beating him to death? No, Laurel would be a poisoner. A sneak killer.

"I don't know," I told him, leaving out my speculations.

"Don't think much of her do you?" he asked, but didn't give me time to reply. "Any fighting between the two?"

"Of course." I put the filter in a 1920's art deco style coffee maker that I had picked up at a flea market. It's a chrome globe with a red handled spigot that's as beautiful to look at as it is functional. "All married couples fight."

"Anything out of the ordinary? Any violence?"

"Not that I know of." I took two cups down from the cabinet over the sink. They were purple, of course. I set them on the granite countertop, then cocked one hip against the counter, facing Ben. The water began to bubble and spit in the pot. "Remember, they were starting a vineyard. That isn't cheap or easy."

"Has it gotten worse lately?" Ben asked, fiddling with a purple bordered note pad I kept on the table.

I shrugged. "Can't say. Do you think she did it?" *I* sure wouldn't be surprised. Especially after the psychotic conversation I had just had with her.

Ben blew out a long breath and slumped into the chair with a shrug. "Husband or wife's always the best bet. Whoever clubbed him meant it to be permanent. He took a hell of a beating."

I shivered involuntarily.

"Mind if I smoke?" he asked, already reaching into his coat pocket.

"I'll join you," I said and took my pack off the table. We both lit up. Ben was smoking Pall Malls, unfiltered. I guessed he wasn't too worried about tar or nicotine. Not that I was one to make judgments, especially with a cigarette between my lips.

"Do you know what they used?"

"Not yet," Ben said, leaning back and loosening his tie. My kitchen chair creaked a warning. "Notice anyone hanging around that shouldn't be? Not just strangers, maybe somebody coming to see Laurel when Kevin isn't around, or vice versa?"

"No," I answered. I put his cup under the spigot and opened the tap. "Cream or sugar?"

"Black's fine."

I set his cup on a coaster, filled mine and joined him at the table.

"How's Jessica doing?" Ben asked, changing the subject.

"Jessica is fine. Her choice in men sucks."

"She's still seeing Stanley, I hear."

I smiled bitterly. "I guess you read the report I filed last night." Ben nodded. "He's nothing but trouble," I said.

"It's a shame they won't let us make their decisions for them," Ben agreed with an ironic chuckle. "My youngest has decided he's gay. Told me last week. I didn't know what to say. He asked if I still loved him. Of course I do. But I don't know how to deal with it, that's for sure."

"Love him, everything else he has to work out on his own."

"Yeah," Ben said, staring into his coffee. "I take a wait and see attitude about more and more things the older I get."

Just then there was a tapping at the door. It opened before I had a chance to answer. It was the bristly haired young detective.

"I'm going to take a look around the cellar, Ben," he said without looking at me.

"Okay. Find anything out there?"

"Murder weapon, maybe," the detective replied tersely. "Rusted-up shovel under that willow tree. Blood on it. Looks fresh. Barnes is bagging it for the lab." The willow he referred to was one with special memories for me. Winter Harlan had helped me plant it just weeks before her death. It sat twenty feet

24

from the end of the row where Kevin had been found. It seemed both prophetic and depressing that the murder weapon should be found there.

"Keep me posted, Doug," Ben said. The detective disappeared, pulling the door closed behind him.

"Doug Priest," Ben said, nodding at the door. "Been on the force a couple of years. Got a degree in Criminal Science and everything. Barnes is his partner. You probably know him. He issued you a couple of speeding tickets when he was in uniform." Ben grinned at me, and then continued straight-faced, "I'm afraid we're going to have to go through the cellar, Claire. Can't be helped."

"You're welcome to," I replied without hesitation. I felt a shiver of fear. Tonight I would arm the burglar alarm, something I'd done only twice since I'd had it installed. But even with that, I knew I'd find it hard to go to sleep. I thought of the pistol I kept in the bedside drawer, but that didn't drive the fear away. I was almost as appalled by the idea of shooting someone as I was by the idea of getting shot.

Ben stubbed out his cigarette, slurped another mouthful of coffee and stood.

"I better get back to the station," He said, straightening his hopelessly wrinkled tie.

I walked with him to the door. He stopped on the patio and turned to me.

"It was nice seeing you, Claire. Despite the circumstances. We don't see much of each other anymore."

"You spend too much time working," I answered, smiling. "You need to take a break now and again."

"Look who's talking," he chuckled. "How often do you get off this hill?"

I shrugged. "Too much to do."

"Ain't that the truth? Well, see you, Claire."

Ben walked away, shoulders slumped, head hanging, looking every bit his age. Before he made ten feet the female technician appeared at the head of the rows and trotted over yelling Ben's name in a surprisingly deep voice. She was slightly built, but tall and wiry with brunette hair chopped off short and a serious face deeply lined, though she couldn't have been too far out of her twenties. She was wearing a grungy white lab coat and cats-eye glasses with black frames.

Ben waited for her. I should have gone inside, but I couldn't resist the urge to eavesdrop.

"What's up, Midge?" he asked. "Taking up jogging?"

"Ha! I'd have to quit smoking and drinking, and that ain't likely. Dougie wants me to vacuum the whole row. All we'll get is dirt and leaves. I'd do it, if ten people hadn't already walked through the scene, but we'd have hell trying to sort the mess out. I did a fifteen foot circle around the body."

"Detective Priest doesn't like to be called Dougie," Ben said with a smirk.

"It's better than what I call him behind his back. So, what should I do?" She glanced at me, gave me a wink, and looked back at her boss.

"You know better than me, Midge," Ben said, "So do it. I'll handle Doug."

"Roger that," Midge said, a wicked smile curling her lips. "See you at the station."

"Get what you find sent to the labs today," Ben yelled as she trotted away. He noticed me standing there.

"Midge Tidwell," he said. "Our forensics specialist. A damn fine deputy too."

"I thought forensic people were doctors?" I asked. "I've never heard of one that was a deputy. But that's probably from watching too much TV."

"We don't have that kind of money. Wish we did. All deputies are given basic training in evidence gathering, but Midge has had more training than most. Got an eye for the details, and she doesn't mind staying late." He looked at his watch. "Well, gotta go."

Ben climbed in his car and waved at me again. He backed out of the drive and I went back inside to finish my coffee, thinking about how much I had enjoyed seeing Ben, despite the circumstances. He was right, it was too bad that the old crowd didn't get together unless we were burying someone.

CHAPTER 5

I poured myself another cup of coffee and lit another cigarette. So much for my promise to cut down to three-a-day. I'd be through the pack by nightfall if I didn't slow down.

I was feeling restless and out of sorts. When I feel this way I have one remedy: work. Victor and the men were thinning the clusters, so I decided to join them. I slipped on a pair of gardening gloves covered in purple pansies, grabbed a set of pruning shears and headed outside.

They were already through with the first row and were spaced out on the second. I made a cursory inspection of the work as I walked toward Victor. They were doing a good job. Very little foliage had been removed, but the vines had been trimmed down to two flower clusters per shoot and I could see that the renewal spurs would receive enough sun to mature into fruiting canes for next year's harvest.

A fresh breeze came up from the valley. Coupled with the warmth of the sun on my shoulders and the view of the valley, it revitalized me a bit, but all I had to do was look at the spot where Kevin had been killed and my mood slipped back toward depression. I stopped one row over from Victor, and began to clip.

This was the kind of work I liked, and the main reason that I bought the vineyard in the first place. I am happiest when I am busy in the rows or working in the small vegetable garden on the south side of the house. Flowers have never been that interesting to me, probably because I can't eat them.

Victor appeared at my elbow as I reached the middle of the row, so absorbed that I didn't notice him until he spoke.

"Ben gone?" he asked, absent-mindedly rearranging the vines.

"Yes, but the detectives are in the wine cellar."

"Laurel and Hardy."

"You don't like them?" I asked, my hands busy in the vines.

"Don't like their attitude. They treat Latinos as if they're illegal aliens. It gets old."

"Are you okay?" I asked like a mother hen. "I mean, if you want to take the day off, I'll understand." I was worried about Victor. He and Kevin had grown close in the last few years, and I know how hard it is for Victor to make friends. He's one of those people who everyone respects and admires, but he's so serious that people find it hard to nurture a personal connection. Once you get below the surface, however, Victor is one of the funniest men I know. After two glasses of wine he'll have me rolling on the floor with laughter at his sarcastic remarks.

27

"I'd rather work," Victor replied.

For thirty minutes we worked side by side without a word, which is another thing I love about Victor. He doesn't fill silences with idle prattle.

We had reached the end of the row when Victor asked, "What's for lunch?"

"Damn it! I forgot about that." I stopped clipping. Victor has assured me that I'm famous among the field workers around the county for my homemade lunches. I think he says that so I'll keep cooking instead of offering cold cuts or pizza.

"Pot luck, I guess," I said. I tucked the clippers into my back pocket, blade down and tugged off my gloves.

"There's always peanut butter and jelly," Victor said with a smile and a flash of his normal charm. "On Wonder bread."

"Not in my house," I vowed. "I'll whip up something. Don't expect too much."

"Not for me," he said, sadness sweeping away his smile. "I'm not hungry. But," he nodded at the three men working one row over, "I told them you're a fantastic chef, so they're expecting some gourmet type grub. Perhaps chilled gazpacho, followed by Cornish game hen seared over mesquite and Bananas Foster for desert."

I laughed despite the gloom of the morning and shook my head as I tucked my gloves in the pocket with the clippers. "If I have to cook, you have to eat. I'll open a good bottle of wine, maybe a Stag Leap Zinfandel. We could all use a drink, and I want to taste their new vintage. June's told me good things about it."

"Open two bottles," Victor called after me as I headed for the garden to gather vegetables.

CHAPTER 6

I didn't know what I'd be making for lunch, but I knew it was going to be heavy on tomatoes. I had started the plants in the barn in January and moved them outside as soon as I dared. Now I had tomatoes coming out of my ears. The garden isn't very large - a small plot of herbs and a twenty by twenty plot of salad greens, onions, tomatoes, peppers and cucumbers with a quarter row of zucchini thrown in - but it was almost more than I could handle. Believe me, when you're running a vineyard and trying to keep expenses down you stay very busy. And very tired. But when I cut into a juicy tomato or pepper it's worth all the work.

Speaking of work, I made a mental note to make time to pull weeds in the next couple of days. The thought of an afternoon on my knees in the garden made me groan. I had to remind myself how good the tomatoes were going to taste.

I grabbed one of the plastic boxes that we use to transport the grapes from the vines to the gondolas, and filled it with tomatoes, a pair of green bell peppers that looked fantastic, and a yellow onion that was kind of runty. From the herb garden (calling it a garden is charitable, it's more of an herb thicket) I picked a handful of thyme, a bunch of parsley, some oregano and basil. I carried the lunch supplies to the kitchen, reveling in the smells of the fresh herbs and bell peppers wafting up from the box. I was on the back steps when I spotted Michelle Lawford, Kevin's hired helper, standing at the edge of Kevin's rows. She was staring out into the valley looking alone and forlorn. But she always did.

Though Michelle was a very sweet woman. I liked her as much for her parentage as for herself. Michelle's father, Josh, had been in my class at Napa, and Michelle was almost the image of Josh. He had been a fire-hydrant shaped giant of a boy who played defensive tackle in a bungling but extremely serious way. What I remember most about him was that he had the gentlest eyes, always half hidden by a cantilever of messy brown hair. We'd been in 4-H together, where he'd rarely spoken, and when he did he'd watch his feet and stumble over the words. A shy smile and a wave was the most you could have hoped for, but he'd been well liked by everyone that knew him. He had married a woman twice his age just weeks after our high school graduation, scandalizing the valley.

Josh's wife owned a horse farm high in the Mayacamas, in the wildest part of tangled scrub and slag-shale slopes. People said that Josh married the farm, not his wife, but the few times I had run into the shy couple they had seemed well suited and happy. They were both gone, as was the farm. The farm was the victim of the Lawford's self-imposed isolation. They were deeply in debt by the time they were killed in a prop-plane crash on their way to a horse auction in Montana. Michelle had been forced to sell, but she'd never left the valley. She had been working part-time with Kevin for the last three years, a somber but smiling presence. At least she had been in the year before Winter's abduction. Lately a sad and haunted look had been the norm.

I set the box down on the stones, waved at Michelle and crossed the yard to her, my tennis shoes squeaking in the dewy grass. She watched me with a flickering, nervous glance. I smiled at her and she smiled back and stuffed her callused hands into the pockets of her plaid jacket. Her round face was tear-wet.

"Hi, Michelle," I said. "You okay?"

"Hey, Mrs. de Montagne," she said. "Yeah, I'm okay." She looked down slope, toward my rows where Victor had just cranked up the Rototiller and was working it between the rootstock. "Victor should let the tiller bite a little deeper."

"You've been listening to Samson," I laughed.

"Always," she replied seriously.

"You poor child," I said and laughed again, but quit when Michelle didn't join me.

"Samson knows," Michelle said.

"Not as much as he believes," I corrected. "But he is a genius, so we'll cut him some slack."

Michelle grinned and nodded. "He is a little nuts."

"How is Laurel?" I asked, knowing that Michelle had a friendly relationship with Kevin's wife. Laurel treated Michelle like a pet, and Michelle reciprocated by heeling like a dog whenever Laurel spoke. Rumor was that Michelle was in love, or at least lust, with Laurel. Whether true or not, that was not my business.

"Mrs. Harlan is resting," she said, throwing a nervous glance at the converted barn. "She was crying and throwing things—" Michelle sucked in a breath and stopped talking.

"That's to be expected," I said, reassuringly, though my sympathy was for Michelle, not Laurel. "Kevin put in a lot of work here," I said, letting my eyes wander the freshly planted rows. Michelle nodded but didn't add anything, and I searched for something else to say. We were interrupted by Laurel Harlan who poked her head out the rear door and called Michelle like you would call a stray puppy. Michelle bobbed her head at me and hurried to her patroness. The pair disappeared inside. I went back to the kitchen. It struck me again that Kevin was gone, that I would never see him again. Never call early morning

30

greetings across the rows. Never share worries when the forecast predicted frost or a heat wave. I tried to shake those thoughts off with work.

After unloading the vegetables, I headed for the Sub-Zero refrigerator that the banker had been thoughtful enough to build into the kitchen, praying that I had some Italian sausages in the freezer. I was in luck - there were two sausages wrapped in aluminum foil. I took them out of the foil, wrapped them in a couple of paper towels and put them in the microwave on low-defrost. While the microwave hummed, I washed the vegetables and chopped the onion and bell pepper into a ¼ inch dice, then peeled and smashed a couple of cloves of garlic. In a frying pan I heated extra virgin olive oil, then cut the tops off five of the tomatoes and hollowed them out, removing the flesh and seeds.

Already the smell of the sausage thawing had my mouth watering, and I wished that it wasn't too early for a glass of wine. 'Oh, what the hell!' I thought and pulled a bottle of Stag Leap Zinfandel from the wine rack in the coolest corner of the kitchen. I popped the cork and let the wine breathe while I took the sausage out of the microwave. The oil was hot in the pan so I tossed in the onion, garlic and peppers and poured a glass of the Zinfandel as the vegetables sizzled.

The wine was excellent, full bodied with marvelous fruit flavors. The aroma was pleasant, without the heavy oak flavor I had noticed in earlier vintages. I crumbled four pieces of bread, made fresh yesterday, and spread them on a piece of wax paper to dry.

By the time I added the sausage to the vegetables I was starting my second glass of wine. It didn't help push the image of Kevin Harlan hanging dead in my vineyard out of my thoughts. Through the kitchen window I could see the police still searching. I stuffed the tomatoes with the sausage, breadcrumbs and vegetables, covered the tops with thin slices of fresh mozzarella and popped them in the oven.

I was taking the first peek at the stuffed tomatoes, which were bubbling nicely, when detective Priest came in through the wine cellar door.

"Something smells good, Mrs. de Montagne," he said, closing the door behind him. "Ben gone?" Priest had a brown paper bag in his hand, and a look of sneaky triumph. Up close he was older than I had thought, maybe thirty-one or two, and handsome in a cold, impersonal way. He had dark blue eyes, thick lashes, chiseled features, and perfect, store-bought teeth. His skin was unblemished, hair perfect. He was as pretty as a Ken doll, and as characterless. His tailored blue suit was unwrinkled and dust-free, despite his sojourn through the vineyard and wine cellar. His shoes looked Italian and were probably as expensive as the suit. Priest obviously spent a lot of time and money on his appearance. But where did the money came from? The Napa County Sheriff's office didn't pay that well. Not my business.

31

Despite the fact that I dislike pretty men, Priest's appearance didn't affect my opinion of him. But the way his eyes clung to my hips as I turned from the stove made me instantly uncomfortable. I still look good for a fifty-year-old, and I admit to being flattered by an appreciative glance from a younger man, but Priest's look wasn't flattering, it was appraising and slightly leering. The kind of look a chronic philanderer gives the new maid.

"Yes, about an hour ago," I said, stepping away from the stove and picking up my wineglass. "Did you find something?" I asked, glancing at the bag in his hand.

"Maybe," he replied with a wink. His eyes panned over my kitchen with the same look of appraisal he'd given my body. I would have bet that he could have told me the net value of the entire room's contents.

"I'll know after the lab geeks do their job." He came further into the kitchen and stopped, his eyes on a small abstract painting by Nell Ellison. It was a collage of green, red and blue with the suggestion of fish intertwined. I had bought it years ago at a street fair for a hundred dollars. Since then Nell has achieved a lot of success. I couldn't afford to buy her work today.

"Nice Ellison. My Dad has two larger pieces. But the color scheme is all wrong for in here. He chuckled as he turned to me, his eyes panning over the purple curtains, pictures, towels and miscellany. "Then again, can you call 'purple' a color scheme?"

I didn't find it funny. If he had made a better impression on me I might have laughed politely, but his manner of easy arrogance was getting under my skin.

"I choose art that I love, not as an accent for a sofa or a rug." I said and turned to the sink. Feeling his eyes on my backside, I began to tear the lettuce into small pieces.

"Um hum," he said indulgently. "Nice place you have here, pretty expensive, though?" His voice held a question that I ignored. "You de Montagnes are like royalty in this valley. Can't drive a mile without passing something you own."

"My maiden name is Falconè, detective. My parents were farmers, and though the de Montagne's do have money, none of it is mine," I said without turning.

"Heard that name too. I know a lot about this valley. *A lot.*" He added. "You'd be surprised."

"Do you know who murdered Kevin?" I rudely asked.

Priest chuckled and I glanced over my shoulder at him. He was still looking at the Ellison. "Working on that," he said. "You know Harlan very well?"

"Not very," I replied, piling the cleaned lettuce in a violet bowl.

"How long have you been neighbors?"

"Five years, but his parents owned the property for thirty. It used to be planted with olive and almond trees."

"You have any problems with the Harlans?"

I wasn't going to say anything ugly about Laurel to Priest. He could meet her and decide for himself. "No, Kevin was the best neighbor I ever had. He was always ready to lend a hand."

"He have a girlfriend, boyfriend, anything like that?"

"I didn't know him that well, but I don't think so. Kevin wasn't that type." For some reasons these questions, which had seemed appropriate when Ben asked them, irked me coming from Priest. I had to remind myself that he was just doing his job. But he didn't have to enjoy it so much.

He laughed as he crossed the room to the stove and picked up the spatula. "We're all *that* type," he said, scraping at the remaining flecks of sausage and peppers clinging to the bottom of the pan. "Given the chance." He was standing so close to me I could feel the heat coming off of him. The smell of his cologne was expensively nauseating. He turned and gave me a steady stare that probably made his girlfriends in college swoon. It made me want to gag.

"He never tried anything with you?" The suggestion in his voice wasn't lost on me. It wouldn't have been lost on the most backward eight-year-old.

I returned his look with a cold stare, "Are you trying to insult me?" I asked, "Or are you always this crass?"

"Uh huh," he said with a nod and a knowing smile, as if that decided him about me. "Just questions I have to ask, Mrs. de Montagne. A woman as attractive as you must be used to unwanted advances."

"You'd be surprised how infrequently that happens," I replied. "And Kevin certainly never said or did anything rude. More men should follow his example."

"Just a question," he repeated, holding his palm out as he backed away. "Has Ben already asked all this?"

"Most of it," I replied as I spread the tomato wedges on top of the lettuce.

"Then I won't take up any more of your time." He turned up the wattage on his smile. "I do need to speak to your daughter, however." He pulled a small leather bound pad from his jacket pocket and flipped to an inner page. "Jessica," he read and snapped the book closed.

"Is that absolutely necessary?" I asked, unable to hide my exasperation. "She was asleep when it happened, and she barely knew Kevin."

"I'm afraid so. Sorry," Priest said, still smiling.

"Let me get these out of the oven and I'll call her down," I told him as I slipped on an oven mitt. The tomatoes' skins were starting to shrivel and the cheese was bubbly and browned..

33

"Wow," he said and I could feel his damp breath on my neck, "those look fantastic. Any chance of a lunch invitation?"

I gave him a fake-polite smile. "I'm sorry, but I wasn't expecting guests. I made only enough for the men and myself. Next time." I hoped there never was a next time. I had already seen more of Priest than I cared to.

"Rain check," he said. "Now, Jessica?"

"I'll get her," I said, glad to leave him behind.

I walked through the dining room furnished in antique English barley twist furniture, and through the sitting room, where a sheet of plastic was taped over the broken picture window. I seethed internally as I looked at the glass scattered over the floor, but tried to calm myself before heading up to Jessica's room. Whatever she might decide, Stanley had been in my home, on my property, for the last time. If I saw him again, I'd do him great bodily harm. I made a mental note to call a glazier and have the window replaced. A thousand dollars down the drain.

Jessica was lying across her bed reading from a piece of notebook paper and crying when I pushed through her door. She stuffed the letter under her bosom as I came in, and looked guiltily at me. She tried on a wan smile that didn't work with the tears.

"Hey, mom," she said and the thoughts of Stanley and Jessica's torturous love affair were banished by that starburst of love only a mother can understand. She was such a good person, caring, thoughtful, considerate. I was very lucky in so many ways, but her choice in men was as bad as my own. How many nights had we sat up dissecting Stanley down to the last greasy particle only to have Jessica go back to him the next day? But what could I do? I was her mother, not her jailer.

"The detective wants to speak with you," I told her, crossing the room and reaching down to smooth her hair. She pulled away and stared up at me with startled eyes.

"Me?" she asked. "Why? I don't know anything. I was asleep." She sat up on the edge of the bed, slipping the letter into her front pocket. It was probably a note from Stanley, the window smasher. "What does he want?" She seemed far more alarmed than was appropriate. She shoved hair out of her eyes and tugged at her wrinkled T-shirt. She looked haggard, no makeup, tangled hair, but still incredibly attractive. I wished she was less so, her life might have been a little less complicated.

"He's talking to everyone," I said, trying not to sound exasperated. "Just come down and talk to him so he can leave. And when he's gone, we need to talk," I added with emphasis.

"About what?"

"Stanley, my window, et cetera. You better get cleaned up and get downstairs. The detective is waiting." I turned and walked away, leaving her door open behind me. Already I was feeling guilty for my brusqueness. It's so difficult to walk the line between mother and friend. But, I think the broken window had pushed us across that boundary and deep into nagging mother territory. Hey, I might not be as imperturbable as June Cleaver, but I bet June couldn't make an excellent cabernet sauvignon!

Priest was sitting at the dining room table when I came down stairs, chewing on something while he scribbled in his notebook. He stopped chewing as I breezed past him.

"Jessica will be right down," I told him, and headed into the kitchen.

The first thing I noticed was a small piece of cheese and sausage missing from one of the tomatoes. Instantly, I saw red, realizing what Priest had been chewing on. I had the insane urge to grab the tomato, take it into the dining room and mash it right in his face! Instead I took a deep breath and poured another glass of wine. It wasn't worth getting worked up about it, I told myself, but I couldn't help it. I thought of mentioning it to Ben, but it would just sound petty. Better to let it go and make sure I never had the jerk in my home again.

Victor and the workers came in as I finished my third glass of wine.

"Smells great, Claire," Victor said as he passed me on the way to the tasting room. The three Mexican men were close behind him.

"Two minutes," I replied. I got out dishes and silverware and opened another bottle of wine. From the dining room I heard a murmur of conversation then strained laughter from Jessica. Priest was turning on the charm, sharing something funny on this most unfunny of days. That darkened my mood even more. He was just the type of man I didn't want Jessica involved with.

'Well, we'll never see him again,' I thought thankfully. Little did I know that I would be seeing a lot more of Doug Priest than I cared to.

CHAPTER 7

The police left around 5:30 after promising to send an hourly patrol by the property for the next few nights. Samson wanted to stay the night, but I didn't need his grousing and complaining. He went home in a huff. Victor, after making a dozen calls to find a replacement, trudged off to a pool tournament with the reluctance of the truly grieving. He plays on a team called The Diablos Rojos with several men who work for Cab Creek Cellars. If I hadn't felt it necessary to talk to Jessica and get our living situation ironed out, I would have been there with him, drinking ice-cold beer. I could have used the distraction.

Jessica and I made dinner together that night, something we normally enjoy more than the actual eating. We both love to cook, and more than once our dinners have devolved into a competition of who could come up with the most bizarre, but still edible, dishes. And I was still finding dried tentacles of spaghetti hidden behind cookbooks or stuck to the walls of my kitchen from an evening two months ago when dinner had turned into what we now call the 'Infamous Pasta Rumble.' I had accepted defeat when she threatened me with a ladle-full of cold tomato sauce cocked like a catapult and aimed at my head. But that night after Kevin's murder was devoid of laughter and fun. Neither of us spoke more than 'Pass the—' or 'Where's the—.'

I put together salads with cold chicken breast while Jessica mixed up red wine vinaigrette with herbs. I caught her dabbing at her eyes more than once, but said nothing. I assumed she was upset over Stanley. After all, she had been a senior in high school when Kevin began his work next door and barely knew him. Still, Jessica had seen our neighbor dead, hanging on the vines covered in blood and gore. That was certainly excuse enough for tears. I thought about letting her off the hook about Stanley, but I just couldn't. I felt compelled to discuss it now while plastic sheeting still hung where my window used to be.

We ate in the kitchen. At least I ate. Jessica just shoved her food around the plate. I struggled with how to begin, but could think of no segue or smooth opening gambit. Finally, I just blurted it out.

"I intend to press charges against Stanley," I informed Jessica. "I'm not letting him get away with this."

"I'll pay for the window, mom," Jessica said without looking up from her plate. She speared a piece of chicken, ferried it half way to her mouth and then put it back on the plate.

"He'll pay for the window," I corrected. "And he'll do it in jail."

"Stanley wasn't angry at you. He was pissed off at me. Just let me handle it."

36

"Well, my window wasn't angry at anyone. And I've had enough of Stanley," I folded my napkin and took a sip of wine. "I'm not going to tell you how to live your life," I began and Jessica snorted a disbelieving laugh. "I'm not," I repeated indignantly, "But I don't want him here again. Ever."

"We agree on that much, anyway," Jessica said, poking at her lettuce. "I broke up with Stanley a month ago." She wiped a slow trickle of tears and put her fork down. "I've had enough," she said. "I'm not really hungry." That was an understatement; she hadn't eaten anything. She started to stand, but I stopped her.

"Sit with me for a minute," I said. She dropped back in her chair and I proceeded with caution, unwilling to drop the subject. "You've broken up before," I gently reminded her. "But you always take him back."

Jessica shook he head. "Not this time. I don't love Stanley," she said, voice thick with the tears. "I—I, God, I can't talk about this right now." She shoved back her chair, but made no move to rise.

"I understand," I told her, reaching for her hand. I gave it a squeeze. "You and Stanley have been together for six years. That's not an easy thing to walk away from."

Jessica pulled her hand away and hugged herself. She shook her head. "It's not Stanley," she said. "It's—" she shivered and hugged tighter, hunching her shoulders so that her hair fell around her face.

"Is it Kevin?" I asked, scooting my chair around the table, closer to her. "I know. It's awful. I can't believe it myself," and that's when my own tears started. All the events of the day finally gang-tackled me and I was weeping into my plate. I grabbed my napkin and tried to mop them up.

Jessica's shoulders shook, and I could hear her choking back sobs. She huddled even tighter in her own embrace.

"I know, baby," I said and put my hand on her shoulder. "I even feel sorry for Laurel."

Jessica's shoulders went as taut as the grape trellis wires in the vineyard. "You don't understand," she whispered. She pulled away from me. "You can't."

"But I do, babe," I said. "Kevin was a very sweet man. Someone we saw every day. But we'll survive." Jessica looked up at me and her expression was so pitiful that my heart almost broke with love for her. I could see how much the murder was affecting her. But maybe it was more than that? Maybe it was fear? I know that I was feeling the first nibbles of worry in the pit of my stomach as night drew on. I almost wished that I had let Samson stay over. Almost.

Jessica stood, still clutching herself, eyes downcast. "I can't do this," she said in a tearful voice. "I'm sorry, mom, I just can't," she turned away from me and started to leave.

"Jessica," I said. "You can talk to me. I understand." I began but Jessica was walking away, down the dark hall, shoulders slumped. I stood and started to follow her.

"Jessica," I called to her as she reached the foot of the stairs, "come back."

She stopped and shook her head. "Mom, please."

"Jessica—"

"Damn it!" she screamed. She shoved her hair out of her eyes and knotted her fingers in it, clutching her temples with her palms. "Just leave me alone," she yelled. "Please, for once, just leave me alone. For once, just mind your own business!" She ran up the stairs while I stood there with my jaw hanging slack.

Her words hit me as hard as a kick in the stomach. Jessica and I have always been friends, always shared our troubles and our tears. Never had I seen her as dejected as she was at that moment, and yet she was shunning me. I started to follow, but stopped on the second step. What would I say? My hurt feelings were already turning to anger. I'd just make things worse.

Reluctantly, I went back to the kitchen and cleared the table, nursing my bruised ego and worrying about my daughter. I felt like stomping upstairs and reminding Jessica that she was living in my house. If she wanted to be left alone she should move out. But I didn't want to fight with her, I wanted to help. But she had made it clear she didn't want my help. Very clear.

"Oh, Christ!" I gasped, feeling another kick to the gut as a thought hit me. Maybe Jessica was pregnant? That would explain her moodiness in the past two weeks and her tears tonight.

No! There had to be something else. Anything else. Please! I was jumping to conclusions, but the thought lingered.

When the dishes were loaded in the dishwasher, I lit a cigarette, poured the last drops from the bottle of wine and went into the living room, trying to ignore the broken window. Trying to forget my injured feelings. Trying to rid my mind of the nagging image of my daughter pregnant with a future prison inmate's child. It didn't work.

I finished my cigarette, set the alarm and double-checked the padlock and chain Victor had rigged on the inside of the wine cellar door. I drew the line at getting the revolver from my bedside table. I tossed the wine bottle in the recycle bin before heading upstairs to bed. The light was off in Jessica's room. In the darkened hall outside her door I felt the first shivers of fear. Had I locked all the doors? Would someone climb through the plastic sheeting covering the living room window? I tried to put that out of my mind, but found myself listening to every creak and groan of the house, to the rustle of the wind slipping through the almond trees outside.

After washing up and brushing my teeth, I undressed in the dark bedroom and slipped into a pair of sweat pants and a raggedy old T-shirt. I don't shop at Victoria's Secret anymore. The older I get the more comfort means and the less fashion makes sense. If I had a lover, I ruefully thought, I might feel differently.

Still anxious, I went from window to window on the second floor, drawing aside the drapes to look out over empty fields, trees and rocky slopes bathed in the watery light of a quarter-moon. The south side of the house was quiet. All the lights were off at the Harlan's. I wondered if Laurel was asleep, or if she had gone to stay with friends or family. I honestly hoped she was doing okay.

I crawled into bed, pulled the purple coverlet up tight to my chin and stared at the ceiling, thinking of Kevin. Sleep was hard to come by that night. I finally dozed off around 3:00 A.M., but was back up the next morning at 6:00, as usual.

CHAPTER 8

I was tired and grouchy, and my mouth tasted like stale wine and cigarettes. Victor was in the vineyard with the three men from the day before, thinning the flower clusters. I made a pot of coffee and lit a cigarette, wincing at the sunlight flowing in through the kitchen window. I was on my second cup when I heard Samson's jeep pull up. I didn't bother to go say good morning - I was too tired. I'd see him later. I wanted to taste the 2008 Vintner's Reserve that we were bottling this week.

The 2008 Reserve was a special bottling of five-hundred cases reserved from the initial bottling of the 2008, which had been completed six months before. At that time Samson and I had selected the finest barrels for longer aging, a first for Violet. In years past, we had been too desperate for operating capital to reserve any wine. I was confident that our decision would pay off, but nervous too. Thinking of the bottling reminded me that I had to check on my cork and capsule order, which was two days late. The capsules are the foil wrappers that cover the cork and the neck of the wine bottle. I had ordered a pale violet with embossed grapes and I was anxious to see them. I made a note on my pad and picked up the newspaper.

The news wasn't good. Kevin's picture was on page one. I quickly flipped to the agricultural section. The article about Kevin wouldn't tell me anything new, and I just didn't want to read it.

The Agricultural page didn't brighten my mood. The problem of the Glassy Winged Sharp Shooter, a pest that carries Pierce's disease, was growing. Having lived through the re-planting of 50% of my vines after Phylloxera (an aphid that attacks rootstock) infected my vines in the 1990's, the thought of another catastrophe made me shudder. The article stated that the federal government was promising twenty-three million in funds to help control the disease, but that didn't make me feel much better. I needed to do some research and find out how I could combat this threat without spraying chemicals. I'm not an organic grower, but I try to be environmentally conscious.

Jessica trudged off to the daycare center at 6:20. She looked tired. Neither of us mentioned the previous night, but there was a tension between us that made me sad and reminded me of those tough teenage years.

I went down to the cellar where Samson was racking the 2009 vintage from thirty-gallon, heavily toasted French oak barrels into twenty-gallon American oak barrels with a milder flavor. We rack the cabernet (draining off the wine while leaving the grape solids, sediments and spent yeast cultures behind) several times between secondary fermentation and bottling. When I

40

joined Samson, he had the smaller barrel drawn up on a dolly, a clear plastic hose with an aspirator connecting it to the larger French barrel. Two glasses and a wine thief (a clear glass tube used to draw wine off the top of a barrel for tasting) were sitting on top of the thirty-gallon barrel. A dot of red at the bottom of one glass let me know that he had started without me.

"Oversleep, de Montagne?" He grouchily asked without looking up. "Or is today a holiday I am not aware of?"

"It was a long night," I said without explanation.

Samson used the thief to draw off a sample of the Cabernet and place it in the clean glass. I took the glass and held it up to the light. The wine had a rich color, and a silky texture. I could see some sediment, but we were a long way from fining the wine, a process in which we add a small amount of clay called Bentonite which bonds with the sediment and spent yeast cultures and carries them to the bottom of the barrel. I stuck my nose in the bell of the glass and took a long whiff. The smell of berries was even more pronounced, undercut by aromas of tobacco and citrus. 2009 was shaping up to be almost as good a vintage as the 2008, which had been a banner year for Violet.

I took a sip, slurping it in quickly so that the wine hit my entire palate at once, then held the wine on my tongue as I sucked air across it, almost gargling. Not very lady-like, I know, but it is the best way to taste. You're supposed to spit the wine out, but I rarely follow that protocol unless I'm sampling a lot of wine. The wine was full bodied on the tongue with the strong tannins of an immature red. I emptied the glass.

"Good, eh?" he asked, peering at me from under wiry gray brows. "I think we will have no problem selling this, yes?"

"It's fantastic, Samson," I agreed, knowing how important praise was to my old friend. I had commented once, five or six years ago, that I thought a batch of cabernet from the lower slope had a grassy quality and he had sulked for days. That didn't change my opinion, and he eventually agreed with me, grumbling under his breath about the 'uneducated American palate.'

"I think it will do," he said, pleased and struggling not to show it. "Not so good as the 2008, but," he shrugged, "I think it will sell." He adjusted the hose lower in the barrel, keeping the end just below the surface of the wine so that the sediment was left behind.

I put my glass down on the barrel. "What about the 2008 Reserve? I wanted to try it this morning."

"I tasted it yesterday," Samson said with a sly grin. "It is the best we ever make."

"You didn't wait for me?" I teased. "You know what they say about drinking alone."

41

"I know what I say; that it is more wine for me." Samson drew the hose out of the barrel and tapped the wood facing with his knuckle. "I will rack the rest into a carboy," he said. The carboys are five gallon glass bottles used primarily in the racking process, but also for secondary fermentation at some wineries. "I bottled four and a half liters for you," he said, nodding at the front of the cellar. Six bottles, sans labels, but capped in violet foil with the words 2008 V.R. handwritten in gold marker were sitting on his dusty desk beside an antique hand-operated corking machine so splattered with wine juice that its lever was sticky-black. I had worn my hands and forearms out on that corker the first year Violet Vineyard sold wine, when Victor and I boxed only forty cases and Samson was still working full-time at Sonoma Valley Winery. That had been an ordeal of late nights and little sleep. The following year, with four times as much wine to be bottled, I had purchased a used Monoblock corker and filler using every bit of profit from the first year, though we had still done the labeling by hand. Four years ago I invested in the rest of the Monoblock line by buying a bottle sterilizer, pump and labeler. My life got a lot easier but my bank account still hadn't recovered.

"I just want a taste, Samson. Do I look like I need a drink that badly?" I laughed.

"For your lunch with the ladies," he reminded. "Tell the lovely Marjory that I send my compliments," he grinned as he wound the hose into a loop. Marjory is one of the Grande Dames of Napa Valley, and a friend who I can barely stand at times due to her endless gossip and snotty remarks. In other words, she makes me laugh at people I like and then I feel guilty about it. Marjory is active in the Vintners' Association, an avid supporter of a dozen charities and the object of Samson's romantic daydreams.

"Damn it!" I had completely forgotten about the Lunch, a monthly get-together organized by Marjory and attended by most of her female friends, the majority of whom I detest. But I work with many of them on charity events or wine-related activities and they never bat an eye at the rising price of Violet Cabernet. Oh the suffering I endure for a buck! "I'll take four bottles. You can put the others in my cellar."

"Yes, your Highness," Samson said and bowed. I ignored him. He'd probably drink the bottles himself.

I looked at my watch, and muttered "Damn it," again. I had two hours to get dressed and make it to Bistral in Napa, a new bistro that everyone was raving about. I wondered if they had a good burger?

"I would be glad to take your place," Samson offered, "or perhaps I could just entertain Marjory?"

"I'll give her your regards," I assured him. "Dirty old man."

42

"I am like the wines I make," Samson boasted as I grabbed four bottles. "I get better the older I grow!"

Samson wheeled the dolly with the freshly filled barrel back into the far reaches of the cellar as I climbed the stairs to my kitchen. Leaving the hand-lettered bottles on the kitchen table, I went upstairs to change, wondering if I should skip the Lunch. In my current state, short on sleep and long on problems, I didn't think I'd be very good company. But I did want to hear what the ladies thought of the 2008.

I took a pale blue summer dress from the closet and a straw hat to save me the trouble of doing my hair. I slipped on sandals and in less than forty-five minutes I was behind the wheel of my Mustang, which I affectionately call Sally after the old Wilson Pickett song, whipping down the Mayacamas Mountain road with the top down, taking in the scenery at seventy miles an hour.

CHAPTER 9

One thing I can say for the town of Napa is that despite the influx of tourists and wineries it has maintained its small town charm, if you can overlook the traffic jams. Trees line the streets, fronting small antique shops, trendy restaurants and restored office buildings dating from the early part of the century. Half a dozen bridges cross the landscaped Napa River, and the whistle of a paddle-wheeled steamboat often fills the air. A great spot for a day-trip, or to settle down and enjoy what's left of small-town California. If you have the money.

Bistral was a new California-French (whatever that means) restaurant located on the ground floor of the Napa Register Building, one of the oldest and best preserved structures in the First Street District of Napa. I parked at a meter and checked myself over in the rearview mirror to make sure I didn't have bugs stuck in my teeth. My hair was a mess. I gave it a quick finger-comb and plopped the straw hat down on top of it.

There was quite a bit of foot traffic on the sidewalk, mostly pale tourists sporting the bright pink of new sunburns. They all seemed to be smiling. They'd probably already had one too many trips to the tasting table. There weren't many cars on the street, but it was Wednesday, so most of the locals were at work in San Francisco.

Leaving one bottle of my cabernet under the front seat, I took the other three and headed inside. Marjory drank enough wine as it was, I didn't intend to encourage her by bringing in four bottles. Besides, there would be only seven of us today. And the City of Napa would not appreciate seven drunk ladies crashing through the Historic District.

Bistral was a bright, airy place with lots of potted plants, high ceilings and wrought iron furniture. Paintings by local artists adorned the walls, complete with discreet and exorbitant price tags. The restaurant was full of chattering, smiling people oohing and aahing over the food. Most were tourists and business people in suits and ties. I spotted my table, a group of women in sundresses picking at green salads.

Marjory spotted me and waved. I waved back and shook my head at the maître d' as he returned from seating a pair of serious-faced gentlemen in matching gray suits and drab ties. The ladies looked happy to see me, probably because I was carrying three bottles of wine. By the end of the lunch they'd have a low-grade buzz and the conversation would turn catty. And that's when my stomach would begin to churn. God, I hated these things!

"Hello, ladies!" I said, pulling out my chair and sitting down beside Marjory Brennan, a plump, melodramatic brunette who wears too much

44

makeup and enough jewelry to send her to the bottom of the ocean. She's constantly rolling her eyes and talking with her hands. She isn't bad looking, but I honestly didn't see what Samson was so enthralled with. Marjory had been married to a lawyer in San Francisco who had won a huge settlement on a copyright infringement case and been served divorce papers that evening while celebrating with his mistress. After the final decree, Marjory moved back to Napa and bought a home surrounded by Zinfandel and Chardonnay vines. I have to admit that her snobbery gets on my nerves, but she's a laugh waiting to happen, especially when she's had a few glasses of wine.

I said hello to everyone and accepted a quick kiss on the cheek from Marjory, accompanied by an overdose of Obsession cologne. All of the ladies at the Lunch are cut from the same expensive and gaudy cloth. They look elegant and sophisticated, but with a searching quality that makes me wonder if they are really happy. Most of them are married or divorced from very successful men, but the money they have presents as many problems as it solves. When you don't need to make a living, or even lift a finger to feed or clothe yourself or your children, it leaves too much time for introspection. And that leads to self-pity or elitism. Sometimes both. That's one of the reasons I'm glad I'm kept too busy for social games or nitpicking. I listen and smile in the right places, then go home, put on jeans and a T-shirt, get dirty in the garden and have a cold beer with the men. Most of the ladies at the table find my lifestyle incomprehensible, but indulge me. Probably because my last name is de Montagne, even if only by marriage. Did I mention they were snobs?

"Oh, how wonderful!" Marjory gushed as I set the bottles on the table. "Is this the 2008 Reserve you've been going on and on about?" she asked, greedily reaching for the nearest bottle.

"Yes. Hope you like it." I replied as I spread my napkin in my lap. "I think it's our best."

"And how much will it be selling for?" Marjory asked, holding the bottle up to the light. Leave it to her to get right to the bottom line.

"Six-fifty a case, less to my friends." I smiled. "So put your orders in now."

"I'll take four cases," she said. "You can have Samson deliver it," she added with a wink. I made a gagging motion and Marjory laughed her ear-puncturing cackle.

"Samson is quite the man," Marjory informed me.

"Speaking of quite a man, I heard about what happened to that delightful Harlan boy." Janice Brighton said softly. Janice was the newest member of the group, and the nicest of the bunch. I wondered how long she would last with these piranhas?

"Oh, God!" Marjory sighed, rolling her eyes to the ceiling. "That was a man! What a waste!" I cringed. I had known Kevin's murder would be a hot topic, but I wasn't ready to talk about it. Especially not with these she-devils.

"I'm sure he'd agree," I said, my sarcasm lost on Marjory.

"Tell us what happened," Marjory demanded. "All the details." She shoved a horde of gold bangles up her fleshy forearms and plopped her elbows on the table.

Briefly I explained what I had seen in the vineyard, without graphic descriptions. There were many oohs and ahs and shaking heads, and I would swear I even saw a tear glimmer in Marjory's eye. By the time I was finished the waiter had opened the first bottle and poured.

"I suppose Laurel inherits," Marjory said.

"You think money was the motive?" Linda Tate asked. Linda is a bleached blonde with a pinched look about the mouth and deep-set black eyes. While some women grow old gracefully, gathering dignity and poise, Linda had merely grown bitter as grape pumice. She eyed every twenty-something woman in a short skirt with equal parts envy and hostility. Linda had married my sixth grade boyfriend, Dave Tate, who had run to fat and taken to smoking repulsive cigars in the years since he became a Vice President at Stalwart Distillers.

"There are better reasons to kill a man," Marjory said with a wink at me.

"I wouldn't be surprised if *that woman* did it." Brenda Perry, wife of Napa's premiere pediatrician Dr. Lincoln Perry, hissed from the far end of the table. "There's something missing in that woman, and not just her underwear."

Marjory laughed, having already drained her wineglass. "You're just saying that because she slapped Lincoln's face at the Founder's Day Dance." Part of the reason Marjory is so much fun is that she never hesitates to make a comment like that, it's also part of the reason I avoid her as much as possible. I can't help but laugh at her cruel remarks, but the laughter always leaves a shameful taste in my mouth.

Brenda flushed and set her wineglass down so hard it sloshed red splatters on the tablecloth. "You don't know anything about it, Marjory, but when did that ever stop you from talking?"

"Touché!" Marjory exclaimed with a shrill cackle. She refilled her glass, stopping just short of the rim. "I only wish Lincoln had socked her in the mouth."

"He should have," Brenda grumbled.

"She's always been nice to me," Janice said with a shrug.

"Lucifer would be sweet to you!" Marjory announced after gulping down half her wine. "He wouldn't have a choice. You'd kill him with kindness."

46

"I hear she was a lesbian," Linda Tate said, looking significantly around the table. "In college."

"If she is, she hides it well!" Marjory said with good humor. "She's slept with half the men in the valley. If you believe the rumors, which I always do. Hell, I start most of them!"

"I said she *was* a lesbian, Marjory. Back in college," Linda replied snottily, leaning aside to let the waiter remove her salad plate.

"You're either a lesbian or you're not, it's not something you dabble in," Marjory said. "You mean she's bisexual."

"I meant what I said," Linda replied stiffly. "But maybe you know more about it than I do?"

Marjory laughed loud and long. I couldn't help but smile and the rest of the ladies joined in. Thankfully, the subject was dropped right there.

The conversation moved on to Janice's upcoming trip to Europe. She briefly outlined the itinerary as we drooled. I've been to Europe before, but Roger had been with me, flirting with every hostess and hatcheck girl, so some of the charm had been lost. It sounded like Janice and Gerald would have a much better time.

The conversation drifted. Wine prices. The outcome of the last Wine Auction. And finally the Wine Train, a restored steam train that offers gourmet dinner and lunch excursions and stops at wineries along its route for tastings. The hue and cry, meetings and accusations over the Wine Train had died down years ago, but there was still no shortage of people who found the noise, the traffic problems and the tourists too much to bear. Personally, though I have never taken a trip on the rails, I find the train charming.

The lunch went on as usual. All of the women praised my wine and drank too much of it. I must admit that the cabernet was fantastic. One of the downsides of owning a vineyard that produces only thirty-five hundred cases of wine a year is that I very rarely get to drink any of it. Partly because the demand for it is so high and I don't want to turn people away and partly because I can't afford it!

As we were finishing desert, I was surprised to see Ben Stoltze, Detective Priest and two men in expensive suits enter the restaurant. Bistral didn't seem like the kind of place Ben would choose. It was too pretentious for him. I pictured him taking his meals at one of the local cafés or more likely at one of the fast-food chains.

Ben saw me and waved, which drew Priest's attention to our table. He favored me with an arrogant grin that made me want to wash his mouth out with soap. The four men sat down and ordered as our waiter began to clear the refuse, and the ladies dug into their purses to pay the tab.

"And how is dear, dear, Samson?' Marjory asked. "Still as spry as ever?" She gave extra emphasis to the *'spry'*, adding innuendo that couldn't be missed. Marjory was a bit tipsy. Her face was flushed and her eyes had the glassy-sheen of a bear in heat.

"He's fine," I replied. "He sends his regards."

"I bet he does!" Marjory replied with a half-drunk laugh. "Give him *my regards,*" she added. "And the key to my bedroom!" That cracked her up, and she had to hurriedly swallow some wine to clear her throat. I hoped she wasn't planning on driving herself home.

We had the usual hugging session as we all dropped bills on the table. I did a quick mental count, and saw that the waiter was going to end up with about a dollar tip, so I lingered until it was just Marjory, Janice and I, then slipped a twenty under my plate.

"You are coming to my *fete* Saturday, aren't you?" Marjory asked, looking me right in the eye, leaving me no room to maneuver. I had been putting off RSVP'ing until I could think of an excuse. Now my chance was gone.

"Of course," I said, swallowing my dread. Marjory would have what she considered the cream of society at her party, which meant boredom accompanied by two-hundred people I didn't want to see. And the obligatory string quartet.

"And, Claire, you'll bring that darling old gentleman with you?" She lifted her eyebrows and grinned crookedly. A remnant of salad was stuck in her teeth.

"He wouldn't miss it," I assured her. "But I take no responsibility for his actions."

"I'll be responsible for *those,*" she assured me, weaving slightly as she picked up her Gucci bag. "Just make sure he's there."

Janice excused herself and headed for the bathroom. Marjory walked with me to the front of the restaurant where we paused for final farewells. I hugged her and was about to leave when Ben Stoltze walked over.

"Good afternoon ladies," He said. Ben was wearing a gray suit with a rumpled red silk tie held down by his 4-H pin. He smiled apologetically as he spoke to me.

"Can I have a moment, Claire?"

"Take more than a moment, Ben," Marjory admonished in a voice too loud for the emptying restaurant. "Do it right." She roared laughter, letting everyone know how drunk she was. She took one step back and then one forward, eyes out of focus.

I flushed, and Ben looked uncomfortable. Our eyes met briefly, and I swear his ears turned bright pink before he hurriedly looked away. 'God, how cute!' I thought and blushed a little redder.

48

"Come along Marjory," Janice Brighton appeared, giving Ben and me a long-suffering smile. "I'll drive you home." She took Marjory's elbow and guided her toward the door.

"Ver' nice of you," Marjory said, looking at a spot two feet above Janice's head. "'Need a nap." She laughed again, said a loud, breezy goodbye to all the restaurant's patrons, and staggered outside, Janice holding on for dear life.

"How are you, Ben?" I asked, slinging my purse over my shoulder. I caught a glimpse of Priest still sitting at the table with the two men, sipping a cup of coffee. Priest was watching me and wearing a smile that made my skin crawl.

"Fine. How're you holding up?" he asked. His eyes wouldn't meet mine and his ears were still red at the tips. "That Marjory's quite the joker," he said.

"Ignore her," I said, trying to change the subject.

"Let me walk you to your car," Ben offered, pushing the door open. Before exiting, he turned toward his table and held up one finger. Priest nodded in reply and Ben followed me out.

"Great," I said. "I've got something for you, anyway." I had intended to take the leftover bottle of cabernet home and enjoy it later, but Ben was a good friend and his hangdog expression made me want to cheer him up.

The temperature had gotten unseasonably hot while we were eating lunch. The sun was at its highest point, beating down on the faces of the buildings and glaring up from the gray sidewalk. I immediately broke into a sweat, which inspired a longing for a nice cool shower, jeans and a T-shirt.

Ben shuffled along beside me, eyes on the sidewalk, saying nothing as we neared my Mustang. The meter had run out, but just barely.

"Lucky you didn't get a ticket," Ben commented as I unlocked the door and dropped my purse on the passenger seat.

"That's okay," I laughed as I dug under the seat and grabbed the hand-lettered bottle of Vintner's Reserve cabernet. "I've got connections." I winked at him as my hand found the bottle. I pulled it out and closed the car door.

"A gift," I said, handing the bottle to Ben, "not a bribe."

Ben smiled, but he looked pained. "You might not be in a giving mood after you hear what I have to say."

My smile evaporated. "What is it, Ben?" I asked.

"Well," Ben began. "I should let Priest handle this, but he has the impression you don't like him very much."

"I don't like or dislike him," I told Ben, "I wouldn't waste my time."

Ben laughed. "That's what I thought. Well, there's no easy way to go about this, so let me just spit it out. I'm gonna need you and Jessica to come in to the office and be fingerprinted. Samson and Victor too." He watched my expression, looking for a reaction I suppose, but his request didn't seem out of line to me. After all, the murder *had* happened in my vineyard and Victor *had* found the body.

"Did you find fingerprints on the shovel?" I asked, curious at the progress of the investigation.

Ben nodded slowly. "Some partials and one good palm print. The blood on the blade was Harlan's." I shuddered at the image.

"I'll go over right now if you like. But why would you think that I'd be upset? I don't have anything to hide."

"Well, I probably shouldn't tell you this, but I've known you a long time, Claire." He looked at me intently for a moment, seeming to inspect my face for signs of poor character, then sighed and ran his fingers through his already messy hair. "Saw Stanley Kostyol this morning."

"Oh," I said.

"Had a wreck on the freeway. Drunk. He's in the hospital. Out on bail. His parents don't have sense enough to let him sit in jail for once," Ben continued while he looked across the street at an antique store that was spewing junk out its door and across the sidewalk. "Reason I mention this is that Stanley admits to throwing the rock through your window, but he says he saw Jessica in the rows with Kevin. Says they were arguing."

"What? Jessica and Kevin? Impossible," I said, shaking my head. "This is just more of Stanley's crap, Ben. Jessica broke up with him and now he's trying to hurt her any way he can. I'll wring that little bas—"

"Claire," Ben cut me off, holding his hands up, palms out. "I don't know all the facts, and I'm not accusing Jessica of anything—"

"You know Stanley Kostyol better than I do, and you know what he's like. He's a little bas—"

"Calm down, Claire," Ben cut in again, and he was actually grinning at me as I fumed and spat. "I just need Jessica's prints, we'll compare them and that will be the end of it."

"Have you compared Stanley's prints?" I asked, as a man in cut-off Levis and ugly rawhide sandals glanced at me, letting me know that I was talking too loud.

"Yeah. No match." Ben assured me. "Like I said, we can have this cleared up tomorrow afternoon. Our evidence technician, Midge, is out today. How about two o'clock tomorrow?"

"Fine," I replied, wiping sweat off my forehead with the back of my hand. Not very ladylike, but I didn't care, I was too irritated with Stanley. Would we never be free of that idiot?

"Want your wine back?" Ben asked.

I had to laugh. "No, but save it for us to drink together. By the time this mess is sorted out I'll need a drink."

50

"You and me both. Well, I better get back there before Priest pisses the DA off. Nothing like lunch with a pair of lawyers to ruin your digestion. Every move we make is a violation of someone's civil rights. County's hired a team of lawyers to watch over the department. Waste of money, if you ask me. People will sue no matter what I do." Ben sighed, and looked back at the door to Bistral, but made no move toward departure.

"You don't sound too happy in your work, Ben."

"Ha! That's an understatement. I'm not running for reelection. Maybe I'll start making wine, give you some competition."

"I've got enough of that already. But it's an idea. It's never too late to change careers." I was happy to have left the subject of Kevin's murder behind, and I was enjoying my conversation with Ben. Maybe I was enjoying it a little too much, I thought suddenly. Ben was an attractive man, despite the slight paunch above his belt, with a physical presence that inspired trust mixed with a little boy quality that was endearing. But I'm afraid I was feeling something more than trust and friendship. I was sure he would make some woman a very happy wife when he was ready, but it wouldn't be me. After all, I was a married woman, sort of, and though Roger made a hobby out of cheating on me, I had never broken my vows to him, though I confess I don't really know why. I guess I had submerged that part of myself in my work, but Ben had me wondering if that was such a good idea.

"Well, I guess I'll see you tomorrow," Ben said reluctantly. "How about a cup of coffee sometime? I mean socially, not as the sheriff or anything. Just friends, you know," he stammered around, sounding as out of practice as I felt. God, it was charming! And flattering.

I blushed. His asking me out, even just for coffee, reminded me of high school, and a younger more vibrant part of my life. And the way he was looking at me and blushing led me to believe he felt the same way. A pair of middle aged folks nervous as school kids. I almost laughed.

"I'd like that," I replied, my own voice a little quivery. "Maybe lunch?"

"That's even better. I'll be looking forward to it. See you, Claire," he gave me a wave and walked down the sidewalk toward Bistral, dodging a young woman pushing a two-seater stroller occupied by twin baby girls.

"Have fun!" I called after him, and he waved again.

It was only when I sat in the car that I allowed myself the satisfied smile every woman wears after being asked out by an attractive man. I was definitely looking forward to lunch and to hell with Roger.

CHAPTER 10

When I arrived back at Violet, I was relieved to see the glazier from San Francisco on a stepladder measuring the gap where my picture window used to be. I parked on the gravel beside his truck and walked over. By then he was picking broken glass out of the frame, dropping the shards into a plastic bucket. He was wearing thick black gloves and a blue uniform, the pants drooping to reveal an unflattering view of his hairy derrière. I said hello and he flicked me a glance, grunted and nodded. He was old, dried up and skinny as a starved dog. He went back to wiggling a ragged bayonet of glass free from the frame without speaking. I asked him when he'd be finished and he grudgingly told me the window would be replaced that day then reminded me that he needed a check. Everyone *wants* a check and so few want to *give* you a check. Bleakly pondering my checking account's downward spiral, I left him to his work and went around the crush pad and down slope to the back yard.

Victor had a crew of six working that day. They were sitting under the almond trees drinking soda and eating pizza from cardboard boxes spread on the grass. Victor got up as I approached, wiping his hands on his jeans. I said hello and nodded at the men.

"How's it going?" I asked Victor, stepping into the shade and bending down to grab a piece of pepperoni pizza. I know, I had already had lunch, but it smelled too good. Besides, with all the physical work around the vineyard, I never have to worry about my weight.

"Pretty good," Victor replied, scanning the vines with a proprietary eye. "Doing some training and tilling the aisles. With so little rain, I thought I'd turn over the clover on the rows that look stressed." We plant cover crops, usually clover or mustard, every spring to encourage beneficial insects and also to use up any excess water that would be absorbed by the vines. Grapes have the best flavor and highest sugar count when they receive just enough water to survive. Too much water and the vines overproduce, creating a large crop of low-grade fruit. Too little water and the crop yield will be low. We till the cover crops when the spring rains end to eliminate their competition with the grapes.

"Good idea," I took a bite out of the pizza. Bad idea. I'd bet the box was just as tasty. I forced myself to chew and swallow, making a mental note that tomorrow's lunch would have to make up for this cardboard repast.

"Did you have someone work more mulch into the rows?" I asked, knowing that Samson would be checking.

Victor rolled his eyes. "It's plenty deep enough, but we've started doing it anyway. Anything to keep that old coot off my back." Victor loves that old coot almost as much as I do, and Samson feels the same way about Victor.

"Ben wants to see us down at the station in Napa tomorrow. He wants fingerprints to compare with some they found on the shovel," I said, changing the subject.

"They find out anything?" Victor asked.

I shrugged. "Ben didn't say." I dropped my slice of pizza into a plastic bag that already contained refuse. "He said the shovel was definitely the murder weapon. Since it's one of ours, I guess they need to eliminate us."

"I don't think it's ours," Victor said. "I don't leave them lying around."

I shrugged again. "Where else could it have come from?"

Victor shook his head, not believing it, but it seemed like a trivial matter to me. We have a dozen shovels on the place, and I didn't know where half of them were.

"I'm going to tell Jess. I need to do some work in the garden this afternoon. The weeds are about to choke out my lettuce."

"Okay," Victor replied, still looking thoughtful. "I'll have some of the guys help Samson set up and sterilize the bottling line. He can walk them through it, but he ain't gonna like it. If you hear him screaming, just ignore it," he added with a smile.

I was chuckling as I walked away. Samson and Victor are always harassing each other, and it's funny to watch. The eventual winner of this long-running mock-argument was still to be determined, but Samson usually gets the last word in. There's something to be said for tenacity.

Jessica was home from the daycare center and at the computer in the alcove in the tasting room talking on the phone when I walked in, paying her rent by handling Violet's customers. She waved at me and held up one finger. She looked tired, but she was doing her best to sound chipper and businesslike with whoever was on the phone. I was proud of her for helping out. Room and board aren't free around Violet. I poured a cup of coffee and sat down on a bench at one of the two tables in the room. Both tables had been made for me from raw timbers by a 'chainsaw artist' in Yountville and have a rustic pioneer look to them. They aren't very comfortable, which is nice when the tourist season is in full swing. Give a tourist from Des Moines a comfy chair, a glass of wine and a view and he'll be there for weeks. The benches encourage their posteriors to move on to the next winery.

"We'll be shipping next week. I'll call with a firm date when we get the bottling underway." Jessica said as I shook out a cigarette and lit up. She watched me light it, wrinkling her nose. "The case-cost *is* correct." She listened, then laughed, though it sounded forced, "The best costs the most." She listened and chuckled again, "Changing the price on your wine list right now would probably be the best idea." She listened for another moment, "I can only let you have five cases—" She stopped abruptly, making a face, flipped back through the account ledger and ran her finger down a page. "Because you're such a good customer, and a great guy," she rolled her eyes. "I can let you have two more, but that's it. Great. Talk to you soon. Bye." She hung up the phone, sagged in the chair and ran her fingers through her hair. "I wish you would hire an accountant. It's going to take weeks to get the numbers squared away. Samson says we'll be bottling tomorrow, is that right?"

"Should be," I replied. "Barring the unforeseeable."

"You better bar the unforeseeable. I've made commitments." She read down a list of the people she had spoken to that afternoon and we talked briefly about deliveries, the sad state of the account books and the schedule for the upcoming bottling. But, finally, I had to tell her about the fingerprints and my conversation with Ben.

"Why do I have to go?" she asked in surprise. "I never touched that shovel. I have to work tomorrow, and there's tons to do here," she glanced at the ledger book open on the small desk. "I just don't have time," she said shaking her head as if that closed the subject.

"It's just a formality, Jessica. But—" I hesitated to mention Stanley's accusation, but Ben certainly would. Better that she hear it from me. "Stanley says he saw you with Kevin in the rows the night he was killed."

Jessica's head snapped up and her hands froze in her lap. "Stanley said that?" she asked as she stood and paced away from me, shoulders bunched. "It's not true," she said as if I might believe it. Her eyes got misty.

"Of course not, Stanley's just trying to get even. I don't think Ben believes it either, but he has to check it out. We'll go down tomorrow and that will be it."

Jessica didn't say anything. She sat back down at the computer, offering me only her profile. "Stanley," she said and shook her head. "Poor Stanley." She wiped at her eyes, crying again.

That was all I needed to hear. Poor Stanley! Poor drunken, violent, lying Stanley. We should start a charity just for him. I managed to choke down my opinion.

"I've got to talk to Samson. Why don't you finish up what you're doing and come to the cellar. I want your opinion on the 2008 Reserve," I added, trying in vain to keep the exasperation out of my voice. What was Jessica keeping from me? "You're not pregnant?" I asked as I opened the door to the cellar.

"Mom!" Jessica spun around to face me. "No!"

"Promise?"

"Mom! I'd tell you if I was pregnant."

I nodded mutely, wondering if that was true, and headed downstairs.

CHAPTER 11

After a change of clothes, I went down to the cellar. Samson was sitting at his desk, making notes in his spiky Greek scrawl. He looked up as I reached the bottom of the stairs, then back at the notebook. Beside the desk was a clear plastic bag filled with a couple of thousand new corks, and by the door was a stack of cardboard boxes for the bottles that would hold the 2008 Vintner's Reserve. The bottling machinery was set up in a row, all of it connected by the narrow conveyor called a worm. The line is mostly used equipment, but in remarkably good shape, probably because of Samson's constant maintenance and cleaning. The bottle washer is the newest piece, bought with the profits from 2006. It uses a sterilizing solution to rinse the bottles then pumps inert gas into the bottles to keep the wine from oxidizing. The filler machine is next in line, a tall machine with twelve rotating nozzles and clamps to hold the bottles in place, then comes the corker, and finally my pride and joy, a model SH-ADH labeler. The labeler is capable of labeling three-thousand bottles an hour, but since the rest of the line can only fill and cork five-hundred bottles an hour, it's never been run at full throttle. The whole line takes up only twenty feet of the stone floor, but would be the center of the frenzy when we began bottling.

"No labels?" I asked, stepping over to the boxes and beginning to count.

"This afternoon." Samson said, his attention still on the notebook. "They promised, but what does that mean? Nothing. But the capsules and corks are here. The capsule color is *awful*. I am *sick* of everything purple, de Montagne."

One of the foil capsules was lying on his desk and he picked it up and handed it to me. I loved them. Violet and gold. I handed it back to him without comment, avoiding a discussion that would go nowhere.

"I guess I could get the labeler and the cork hopper filled," I said unenthusiastically as I finished counting the empty bottles. There were 6,000 bottles total, enough for the tiny five-hundred case run we were making of the Reserve.

"I already did that," Samson replied while giving me the evil eye. "But I thank you for *all* your help."

"How many men are we going to need?" I asked, ignoring his sarcasm. I'm used to it.

"None, I think. Tommy and three of his friends have volunteered," Samson replied, pushing the notebook away and swiveling toward me. Tommy was Samson's newest protégé, a graduate student at UC Davis who worshipped the old winemaker. And Samson likes to be worshipped. He's had a dozen young people like Tommy follow in his footsteps over the years. Many of them have gone on to great success, thanks in part to Samson's tutelage.

"And how many bottles did you promise them to get these 'volunteers?'" I asked, thinking that it would be cheaper, but less fun for Samson, to hire experienced men at an hourly rate.

"Three bottles each, so a case for all." Samson replied. He picked up his stub of cigar and popped it in his mouth. "A bargain. They know what is to be done. And they care for wine."

"Fine with me, as long as they care as much about bottling it as they do drinking it. When do you want to start?"

"I told Tommy to be here tomorrow. Even without the labels, we can get done a lot. We will be ready to ship on Monday, next."

"Sounds good. We need the money."

Samson nodded and chewed his cigar.

"Marjory sends her regards," I told Samson, rolling my eyes to let him know what I thought about that. He grinned around the cigar like the old letch he is.

"You had a good lunch?" he asked, "Did they like the wine?"

"Yes. They loved it. Especially Marjory. She was half-drunk when she left."

Samson clicked his tongue and rolled his eyes. "I like a woman who has fun. Maybe I take her a bottle or two?" he said. "Maybe three? Wine is the life-blood of romance!"

"You have no shame, Samson."

"Shame is for the young, I don't waste time with it. And Marjory..." he rolled his eyes toward heaven, "she is a woman!"

"And you're a dirty old man."

"I was a dirty young man, so it is a wonder that I am a dirty old one? You are jealous. You need to get rid of that Roger," Samson said and spat at the floor. "He is worthless."

I heard the door into the kitchen open and Jessica came down the stairs.

"Samson, could you get the thief for me?" I asked as I crossed to the sink in the far corner of the cellar.

"Ready to be thrilled?" I called to Jessica.

"Sure," she tried a smile that had as many watts as a nightlight. "Hey Samson," she called down the cellar corridor as I gathered three dirty glasses. I seem to be the only one who washes glasses. Every time I want a taste I have to pick through Victor and Samson's dirty dishes. Sometimes I feel more like their mother than their boss.

"Hello, Princess," Samson called out to Jessica, his voice echoing off the cold stone walls. Even from a distance I could see his smile. My parents died when Jessica was six, and Samson never had children, so he has been like a grandfather to her.

"You will like this wine! It is our best yet, I think."

Samson inserted the thief into an opened cask, then winked at Jessica, as he drew off a half a glass of wine and deposited it directly into his mouth with a much-practiced movement. I wondered how much of our wine disappeared that way?

"No glass for me, de Montagne!" He shouted, his voice echoing off the walls. "I am no amateur!" A bead of red juice dribbled down his whiskery chin.

"Wipe your chin and use a glass," I told him. I held out two of the glasses and he half-filled each one. I passed one to Jessica and then handed Samson the empty glass.

Jessica held the glass to her nose and closed her eyes as she inhaled.

"Berries and citrus," she said "Maybe some tobacco. Great nose." She held the glass up to the light coming down from the overhead fixture and stared intently into the deep red fluid. She took a dainty sip and sucked air in across her tongue in a long slurp, exploding the flavors across her palate. Samson and I watched, our own glasses untouched. "Wide on the palate. A great finish, smoky and smooth." She took the last swallow and held her glass out for more.

"It's fabulous. Reminds me of the '84 Landoun," she said, referring to one of my favorite vintages.

Samson was beaming. I sniffed and tasted the wine as Jessica started on her second half-glass. Samson and I knew it was good, but I don't think either of us would get tired of hearing people say it. Especially when it was someone who had a real appreciation for the work and the craft of winemaking.

"Ahhh," Samson said. "You should have no trouble selling this, eh Princess?" he asked Jessica with a wink. "They will kiss your feet to taste a drop!" Samson was in an excellent mood, and I wondered how much wine he had already drunk. Jessica returned his smile with a genuine one of her own, seeming to come out of her funk a little.

"Another glass?" Samson asked me as he reached for the thief and his own glass.

"Not for me," I replied with a shake of the head.

"I'll have another, Sam," Jessica said. "Maybe two!" She laughed. Samson's good humor could be as infectious as his bad humor was oppressive.

"Maybe we empty the barrel!" Samson said. "Maybe two!"

"Save some for the customers," I warned. "Don't drink all the profit."

"Such a worrier, your mother," I heard Samson say as I walked upstairs. "But she knows her wine!"

58

Jessica said something in reply that I didn't hear, and then I was closing the door behind me, still smiling.

CHAPTER 12

Dressed in an old pair of jeans and a denim shirt, I joined Victor in the vineyard. Victor had two of the men tilling the aisles with a gas powered Rototiller while he and the other men were filling the free-standing fuel oil heaters we use on cold nights. The heaters look like rusty tin chimneys on top of rustier buckets. They stand at the end of every other row, even when not in use. In California we used to use wood-burning smudge pots, but pollution concerns in the 1980's forced a change for the better and the smudge pots were outlawed, though the idea of burning fuel oil still makes me wince at the environmental cost. I hadn't watched the weather forecast this morning, which is unusual for me because in the wine business you live and die by the weather, but they must have called for a cold night. The vineyard sits on an alluvial fan of volcanic rock that is covered by a thin layer of topsoil, so frost is a real worry in the spring.

As I walked down the row, enjoying the sunshine on my face and the mixed aromas of wisteria, pine trees, grape flowers and freshly turned soil, I noticed a Sheriff's cruiser pull up in Laurel's driveway. As I watched, Priest climbed out. He waved at me and I made a face and kept walking. He disappeared inside the house. I guessed he was there with follow up questions for Laurel. Or maybe to make a pass at the widow? I wouldn't put it past the greasy little preppy.

I stopped by Victor and watched him pour a quart of fuel oil into the heater. He stood and stretched, grimacing, hands on his lower back.

"I guess they're predicting a freeze?" I asked, casting my eyes over the neat rows of green vines.

"Yeah. You sleep in today?" Victor asked with an easy smile. "I didn't think you *ever* missed the weather."

I shrugged a reply.

"There's only a slight chance, but better safe than… By the way, what's for dinner?"

"Spaghetti a la Claire," I said, turning my face up to the sun and closing my eyes, the low-grade buzz from the wine making me drowsy. It really was a beautiful day. I could almost feel good about pulling weeds. Almost.

"Easy on the garlic," Victor said. "Last time I ate your spaghetti people avoided me for days."

"You're sure it was your breath and not your personality?"

"One can only hope," he replied with a grin. "Put lots of olives in for me, ma'am."

"Don't call me ma'am, it makes me feel ancient," I said, turning and heading to the garden, wishing for another glass of wine and a cigarette to go with it.

"Ancient? Well..." he grinned and paused a half-beat. "I'll let that one go without comment."

"A wise move. It'd be pretty embarrassing to get your butt whipped in front of the men," I called over my shoulder.

"Woo-hoo, a tough lady!" Victor shouted after me. "And remember, easy on the garlic. For the sake of my social life!"

I spent three hours kneeling in the dirt, the afternoon sun burning my back through my blouse, and only got done half the work I'd intended. But the lettuces looked better without weeds haloing them, and the peppers that had been looking wilted enjoyed a drink from the hose, so I was feeling pretty self-satisfied as I gathered green peppers, onions, tomatoes and a handful of basil, oregano and thyme for dinner. As an afterthought I grabbed a sprig of fresh mint. About a gallon of iced tea sounded like heaven, I was so hot.

I had enjoyed the work outside, but I enjoyed being back in my air-conditioned kitchen even more. The temperature had climbed into the low nineties, unseasonably hot for the spring, and I needed a break. Victor was still setting up the fuel oil heaters, but the hired laborers were not in sight. I guessed Victor had sent them in to clean up the production line for tomorrow.

It took me an hour to put together the tomato sauce, and to put flour, water, butter and yeast in the bread machine. With dinner on the way, I lit a cigarette and settled down at the table with iced tea and decidedly girlish thoughts.

I opened the paper and tried to read, but my mind was somewhere else. Mainly on Ben Stoltze. Unseemly for a married woman, but I couldn't help it. I was looking forward to our lunch, but I was apprehensive too. After all, I was a married woman. It was just lunch, I reminded myself, but I couldn't deny my attraction for Ben, and that made me feel guilty. Why? I don't know. I didn't owe Roger anything. I guess it was just that I'd played the long-suffering wife so long that I had started to believe it was my destiny. But I desperately needed change!

Jessica came in, interrupting my daydreaming. She informed me that she wasn't hungry, then took a Neapolitan ice cream sandwich out of the refrigerator and unwrapped it. I didn't argue. If she chose to eat garbage, so be it. She went up to her room, and I lit another cigarette and poured another glass of iced tea. I was still upset about our argument the night before, but at the same time I was wondering how to smooth things over.

The glazier rang the bell then stood disinterestedly staring at the sky and scratching a sunburned forearm while I inspected his work. I had no idea what

I was supposed to be seeing, but the window looked like it had before Stanley broke it, so I was satisfied. The glazier took a fat check, offered no thanks, and drove away in his truck, country music blaring. I went back to the kitchen. A thousand dollars down the drain, and I didn't think Stanley was going to pay me back.

I put water on to boil for the spaghetti and stirred the tomato sauce. The kitchen smelled like a trattoria, and my salivary glands were working overtime. The water had just started to bubble when Samson and Victor came in through the cellar door arguing.

"Fining is not necessary, ever. Americans think wine with body should be fined, and I do it. For sales. But it is not necessary! Never," Samson was insisting, shaking his head on his skinny neck. This was an old argument, and one you'd think they'd be tired of, but you'd be wrong. He and Victor picked at each other endlessly over this and a dozen other topics, each of them holding on to his own opinions like a life raft in a raging sea.

"What about whites?" Victor asked, giving me a wink.

"Do we make whites? No. So what do I care? I'm talking of our wine, and I say fining is not necessary!" Samson clamped his hands over his ears as Victor was about to reply. "Enough! I am hungry!"

"Well, open a bottle of wine and sit down," I cut in, stirring the pasta around in the hot water. "Dinner in ten minutes, if Victor slices the bread."

"I do not trust him with a knife!" Samson bellowed. "He will stab me in the back! Fining!" He stepped to the counter where I had two unopened bottles of Beaujolais. Samson haughtily pushed them aside. "We drink well tonight, de Montagne!" He informed me as he placed two bottles of Violet Vineyard 2006 cabernet (from my private cellar) on the counter and reached for a corkscrew. Samson is tremendously generous with *my* wine. "You can't pass the cheap stuff off on us!"

I groaned, but their good humor was infectious. Tonight, the night before bottling, was the perfect night to celebrate.

"How about we kick your ass at Spades after dinner?" Victor asked while he sliced the bread.

"Only if you two promise not to gang up on me," I laughed. "I'm getting sick of losing." Neither of them cared who won as long as I didn't. We'd been playing for five years and I had yet to win a game. But I was ever hopeful.

Victor grinned. "Then learn how to play."

It was going to be a long night.

Victor, Samson, and I had too much dinner and too many glasses of wine. We stayed up playing cards and groaning over our stuffed bellies until midnight. I lost as usual, cheated by my employees. Neither of them was fit to drive, so I put Samson in the guestroom and Victor on the sofa downstairs. Both men had enough clothes and toiletries at my place to see them through the next day.

Before going to bed, I glanced out the bedroom window as I had the night before. The vineyard was empty, thank God. The sky was cloudless and there didn't seem to be any wind. A perfect night for a frost. The fuel oil heaters rumbled-roared at the heads of the rows, and I was glad we had set them out. I was about to let the curtain drop, yawning wide enough to unhinge my jaw, when I noticed that Priest's police car was parked behind the Harlan house out of sight from the road. All of the barn's lights were off. If I had been a small-minded person I would have thought evil things about Priest and Laurel. Okay, so I am a small-minded person. There was only one reason I could think of for Priest to stay overnight, and it wasn't friendly concern for the widow. Well, those two deserved each other.

CHAPTER 13

I was the first one up the next morning at 5:30 A.M., with a wine-headache. I put coffee on and went out into the vineyard. Mist clung to the vines and shrouded the valley in dense fog. In the light of the waning moon the landscape had an eerie look, like a pen and ink drawing. It was cool enough to make me shiver in my jeans and T-shirt. I checked the temperature on the thermometer tacked to the wisteria's trellis supports. It was fifty degrees. Barefooted, I went down the rows turning off the heaters. All the vines looked fine, without a sign of damage, and since the ground was covered in a heavy dew that was freezing my feet, I knew the weather alert had been a false alarm. Fifty dollars of fuel oil wasted, but I'd do it again in the same situation.

I was coming back to the house, wet clover sticking to my ankles, when I noticed the Sheriff's cruiser still parked behind the Harlan's home. Priest had stayed the night. I wondered if he had gotten lucky? God, I'm terrible, especially after too little sleep. An early-morning nap sounded good, but Samson's crew from U.C. Davis would be arriving at 6:30. Since I had to be in Napa at 2:00 for fingerprinting I had to get lunch underway early. I was thinking pasta-salad and cold cuts. The men would have little time for anything else. I'd have to send Jessica into town for supplies as soon as she got up, meanwhile I needed to gather vegetables for the salad.

The early sun peeked over the Mayacamas Mountains behind me, coloring the craggy peaks purple and gold and giving me a pale, reflected light to work by. I grabbed a plastic grape crate and walked to the garden, enjoying the clear quiet of the early morning, despite my teeth chattering. I needed a bunch of tomatoes, a few onions, peppers, and anything else that looked good. By the time I was finished I had the crate overflowing with enough vegetables to make the king of all pasta salads and my toes were numb.

I was dragging the crate behind me because it was too heavy to lift when I noticed a light come on over the Harlan's backdoor. I immediately stopped moving and crouched in the twilight like a peeping tom. Doug Priest stepped out and stood on the step, looking toward my vineyard for a moment before walking to his car. He didn't see me kneeling beside my produce, but I could hear him whistling, faintly and tunelessly. He climbed into the cruiser, backed up and headed for Napa.

I stood up, brushed the damp knees of my jeans and continued to drag my crate as the sound of the sheriff's cruiser faded in the distance. All was dark again at the Harlan's.

64

By the time Victor and Samson got out of bed, bleary eyed and hung over, I already had the vegetables chopped and the pasta boiling. I took down my two biggest salad bowls, wondering if that would be enough salad for everyone. In addition to the four boys Samson had coming there would be the usual four or five men working the vineyard. And all of them would eat like wolves.

"You kept me up too late," Samson groused as he poured two cups of coffee, one for himself and one for Victor, who flopped down at the table and hung his head in his hands.

"What time is it?" Victor muttered.

"It's your own fault," I said, forcing myself to sound perky, just to rub it in that I was up and hard at work. "Cheaters never prosper."

Samson put a cup in front of Victor and sat down at the table. I had three loaves of white bread to make for the sandwiches. I got the machine going and poured a cup. The morning paper had arrived, so I opened it and flipped idly through the pages with Ben on my mind. We needed to set a date for lunch. The sooner the better, I thought and smiled to myself. I'd have to talk to him after we did the fingerprinting today. I blushed at the thought, keeping my head down so Victor and Samson wouldn't notice.

Samson left the table first, grumbling that he had to get things ready. Victor left a moment behind him, having heard a pickup pull into the driveway. I reminded him to finish tilling the rows and told him that I had turned off the heaters, but the fuel oil would need to be drained, collected and stored. He muttered something about his breath smelling like he had eaten a whole head of Garlic for breakfast and stepped out the back door.

The pasta had finished cooking by then. I drained it, dumped it in the bowls and mixed in the sliced peppers, onions and tomatoes. Fresh olive oil and red wine vinegar laced with spices went in next. I mixed it all together, covered the bowls with Saran Wrap and stuck them in the refrigerator. Five seconds later the timer went off on the bread machine. I put the dough into a pan to rise, loaded up the bread machine again and hit start. With luck I should be able to get all three loaves out and sliced before I had to leave for Napa.

The view out my window as I rinsed the dirty dishes and stacked them in the dishwasher was dazzling. The mist had burned off to reveal the lush green valley below and the blue ribbon of the Napa River twisting across the valley floor. I could tell that the day would be hot, and that reminded me to get the five-gallon drink cooler out of the closet and put water on for iced tea.

I was standing at the top of the cellar stairs, the door open, listening to the hum of machinery, the 'clink' of bottles and the occasional barked order from Samson when Jessica came downstairs. She was dressed in a light yellow sundress and had her hair pinned back. She was quiet, and withdrawn, but she looked much better than she had yesterday. She had taken the day off from the daycare center, and I was glad she did. I needed her help.

I gave her a shopping list and she headed to town, using my car because hers was parked in its usual spot, on the hydraulic lift at the local foreign car garage. She seemed happy for the distraction. When she had gone, I went downstairs to see how the bottling was going.

Samson was walking up and down the row of machines supervising four tan young men in T-shirts and jeans. Three of the boys were running the bottle washer, the filler and the corker while the fourth was putting bottles through the rotating labeler. One of Victor's men was taking the bottles out of the labeler and filling the cardboard cases.

Surrounded by the hum of machinery, the roar of the bottle filler and the 'thunk!' of corks being popped into bottlenecks, I couldn't suppress a giddy smile. This was music to my ears and money in the bank. Picking a bottle out of an open case, I held it up to the light, grinning with the pride of a new mother. No matter what Samson said, I thought the lavender foil capsules were a real success.

Samson came over as I put the bottle back in the case.

"The labels arrived, de Montagne," he said, stopping beside me and casting his eyes over the bottling machinery with a satisfied air. "Everything is well. We should finish in two days, so tomorrow we drink new wine and eat well, but we go to bed early!" His humor had certainly improved since this morning, and I assumed it was because he had his fan club working the line. The young men who work here at crush, harvest and bottling rejuvenate the old winemaker and probably add years to his life.

"I need corks!" A tall young man with wheat colored hair and a tennis player's physique called out, and Samson shambled away. I recognized the student as one of Samson's regulars and waved at him. He grinned and nodded, hands busy moving bottles from the conveyor to the corking machine's tray. Hell, they were all grinning as happily as Samson and I, but looking much younger, fitter and tanned. A regular buffet of athletic young men! No place for me to be when I was questioning the meaning of my marriage. The boys made me much too aware of all I had been missing. I waved at Samson as he rushed to the corker with a sack of corks to fill the hopper.

"I need labels!" Another of the young men shouted as I stepped into the back yard and closed the door behind me.

Laurel Harlan was on her knees in the flowerbeds in her front yard, grooming her roses. Michelle Lawford, dressed in jeans, work boots and a flannel jacket, was leaning on the handle of a shovel nearby, an open bag of cedar mulch at her feet.

66

Laurel looked up at me as I crossed the backyard to join Victor who was draining the fuel oil out of one of the heating units into a five-gallon can. I waved and Michelle gave me a tentative wave back, but Laurel just stared for a long second then spoke a few words to Michelle before going back to clipping. Michelle shot me an embarrassed glance, laid her shovel aside and went to her truck parked on the shoulder of the road.

'What the hell was that about?' I thought as Michelle fired up the truck, made a U-turn and sped down the hill. Laurel being a bitch wasn't much surprise, but Michelle was usually such a sweetheart. I didn't let it ruin my mood; the bottling was under way and soon the checks would be rolling in!

Victor had a gondola hooked to the small John Deere. The gondola was almost filled by the six battered gas cans that we store the fuel oil in. Three Mexican men were working in the vines. Two of them were training cabernet vines, using twist ties to fix them to the trellis wire, while the third was running the Rototiller up the aisles. Everyone was busy except me.

Victor looked up as I stopped beside him. He set down the gas can and removed the siphon hose from the heater's tank.

"You see Michelle over there?" he asked me without preamble. "With her highness?"

"I saw her," I said, looking over my shoulder at Laurel on her knees in the roses.

"She asked about a job," Victor said as he coiled the hose and looped it around his shoulder. "I told her she was over qualified. Only job she'd be interested in would be mine."

"You tell her to talk to me?" I asked with a grin. "She might work cheaper."

"Ha ha," Victor said with a roll of the eyes as he screwed the lid on the gas can. "I told her to check with Marjory. Stuart left her for the top slot at Bealieau last week," he added, referring to Marjory's vineyard foreman. "Michelle said she'd stop by there, but she didn't sound excited."

"She must know Marjory," I said, and Victor chuckled. "I'll call Marjory and tell her about Michelle," I promised. "Remember we have to be in Napa at 2:00 today," I reminded him, changing the subject. "You can head home and get cleaned up if you want. We'll leave a little after one."

Victor stood, placed the gas can in the back of the gondola with the others and wiped his hands on his jeans. The look on his face was grim, and I was sorry that I had to remind him of his obligation and of Kevin's murder.

"I forgot about that," he said. "I guess I better. I'll drain the rest of these and head over," he said, glancing at his watch.

"I'll get them, don't worry about it," I assured him. "Take your time and meet me back here at one. Earlier if you want to eat.

"I always want to eat," Victor replied. "Don't run over anyone," he added as he stepped away.

"I was driving tractors when you were wearing diapers," I reminded him, "and I haven't killed anyone yet."

He laughed as I climbed in to the tractor's seat. I started the diesel engine, drove it twenty-feet down the row, stopped and climbed down. I heard Victor's truck start behind me as I tried to get the cap off the rusty heater's fuel tank to no avail. I got a crescent wrench out of the tractor's toolbox and set to work on it, skinning my knuckles in the process. Oh! The joys of vineyard ownership! The relaxed lifestyle and graceful living! All myths, I'm afraid.

I finished with the fuel oil, dousing myself twice in the process, parked the tractor in the barn and took a quick shower to get rid of the petroleum stink. I was back in the kitchen, sniffing my hands like a terrier, wondering if I could still smell a trace of fuel, when Jessica returned from the grocery store with enough sliced ham, salami, and cheese to feed an army. She set the bags down on the kitchen table with a thump and went back to work at the computer, assuring me she'd eat something later. I'd believe that when I saw it. She is forever fussing over her weight while living on junk food and soda.

I took the time to call Marjory, but, thankfully, she was out. I left a message about Michelle, giving her a glowing endorsement, wondering if I was really doing her a favor. Marjory couldn't be easy to work for. Not my business.

I took the last loaf of bread out of the oven an hour before lunch was served. The day had grown warm and dry, but not oppressively hot, so I set up two card tables under the almond trees and spread white cloths over them. A cool breeze was blowing through the vines and across the freshly tilled soil. It smelled like a promise of a good harvest to me. The spring hadn't been perfect, but it was growing into a glorious summer. Or, at least I hoped so.

Paper plates and plastic cups have never been my style, so I set out the plain white picnic china and a set of red Bakelite handled knives and forks I had picked up at an estate sale in Calistoga. There would be a lot of dishes to be washed, but the presentation was worth it. When everything looked perfect, I ferried out the food and called the men in from the vineyard and cellar.

The field workers and Samson's crew fell on the food like a pack of starving dogs and it was a joy to watch them eat. Samson opened several freshly corked and labeled bottles of wine and my iced tea was virtually ignored. I had a sandwich and a glass of tea, and introduced myself to the men I didn't know. They were a good-natured bunch, but maybe that was because of the wine they were guzzling. By the time the last of them was rubbing his belly and groaning over how much he had eaten, five bottles of cabernet had been consumed along with most of the bread, salad and cold cuts.

With food in their bellies and wine in their glasses, the group was in a very festive mood, cutting up and laughing. It was contagious. If I hadn't had to make an appearance at the Sheriff's office I would have enjoyed hanging out and downing a few glasses of cabernet myself. One of the students had brought along an orange Nerf football. As I headed to the house to get ready for town, the students and laborers started an impromptu game of tag-football, sending the orange ball zipping left and right. Samson was the referee, which meant he stood in the shade with a glass of wine in his hand shouting insults. A perfect role for him.

CHAPTER 14

Victor missed lunch, but he was in the kitchen when I came down from my bedroom. I had dressed in a pale blue sundress and sandals. My hair was done as much as I ever do it and sprayed in place with an ancient can of Aquanet. I was wearing lipstick, but no other makeup. The way Victor looked me up and down almost made me blush. I was sure that he and everyone else would know instantly why I had dressed, even though I hesitated to admit why to myself. I was going to see Ben and I wanted to look my best. But not like I was *trying* to look my best.

"Wow," Victor said, smirking. "Hot date?" He was dressed in faded and frayed jeans and a yellow Polo shirt. His hair was tied back in a ponytail that hung down past his shoulders. I wished I hadn't put on the lipstick. The downside of rarely wearing makeup is that when I do I feel like a little girl playing dress up. Victor noticed my embarrassment. He knows me far too well, and quickly changed his tone from sarcastic to complimentary.

"You look great, Claire, as always. If I were more mature, I'd be asking you out." I noticed that he said 'mature' not 'older.' Smart move.

"Thank you," I said. Thankfully Jessica came in from the tasting room at that moment and spared me further embarrassment.

Jessica didn't notice the lipstick, or if she did, she didn't mention it. She wasn't wearing any makeup. In that, she takes after me. She looked pale and nervous, her face pinched and lined.

"Are you guys ready?" she asked.

"Yes, let's get this over with," I replied, grabbing my handbag.

The three of us trooped out the backdoor and across the yard. The football game was in its waning moments. I could tell because Samson was staring at his watch and looking irritated. He'd get over it. I stopped and spoke to him as Victor and Jessica went to the car. I would have bet anything that Samson had forgotten about the fingerprinting, so I was anticipating a tantrum.

"Where are you going, de Montagne?" he asked grumpily, flicking a glance at me. "Avoiding work again?"

"We're supposed to go in for fingerprinting today. Ben told you, didn't he?"

"Yes," Samson replied with superiority. "And that is why I went yesterday. Some of us plan our time well, others…" He shrugged. "They let these things go undone."

"But Ben said their fingerprint person was out yesterday."

"And that is why I demand that Sheriff Stoltze do it himself," Samson replied smugly. "You must learn to *demand.* Asking gets nothing."

70

"Smart-ass," I said and gave him a quick kiss on the cheek that made him turn crimson. "Have fun," I said as I went to join Victor and Jessica waiting beside my lopsided old garage. We headed for town as the students and laborers went back to work.

Traffic was heavy, but I didn't mind the slow pace. Everywhere I looked there was something beautiful to see. The wildflowers were in full bloom, dotting the green slopes and open fields, and every garden was lush with irises, tulips and roses. The vineyards climbing the slopes along the highway were dressed in brilliant green leaves, pale grape flowers hanging in their dappled shade. Plum, pear and apple trees were budding pink and white. The temperature was in the mid-seventies and there wasn't a cloud in sight. I was only sorry that I hadn't thought to put the Mustang's top down before we left Violet.

Just outside Napa we had to stop at a gated train crossing and wait for the Wine Train to cross the highway, tourists at every window, wineglasses and appetizers in hand. They seemed to be having a great time, and I envied them. The gloomy silence that prevailed inside my car was stifling, especially in contrast with the day. I tried several times to make conversation, but neither of my companions seemed interested. I was relieved to get out of the car when we arrived at the Sheriff's office on Third Street in Napa.

With fifteen minutes to spare, we entered the impressive old building. A vivacious young woman with a bust that would have made Dolly Parton stare and spiky, bleached blonde hair pointed us in the right direction, down a poorly lit corridor to the booking room.

Jessica plodded along beside me and Victor, saying nothing. Victor too was in a somber mood, but I understood his attitude better than Jessica's. After all, Victor and Kevin had been close friends. Jessica's problems with Stanley seemed pretty trivial compared to that. Unless she was pregnant. Why couldn't I shake that thought? Certainly she'd tell me. Right? Right? God, I hoped she wasn't pregnant.

The booking room was a large office with desks scattered about. Bookcases and filing cabinets overflowed. I wondered how they ever found anything in the mess. An old wino dressed in layers of filthy clothing was manacled to a bench just inside the door. He looked up at us, narrowed his eyes, muttered something and licked his blistered lips. He smelled like a dumpster, and his teeth looked like a row of burned out houses. We gave him a wide berth, and stepped to the only occupied desk.

A chubby deputy in a too-tight uniform, shirt buttons stretched to the limits, greeted us with a jaded, "Can I help you?" His eyes locked on Jessica's breasts and stayed there as I spoke.

71

"Claire de Montagne," I introduced myself. "My daughter, Jessica, and Victor Gonzalez. We're here to be fingerprinted." He kept looking at Jessica's breasts, nodding mutely.

"It's about the Kevin Harlan case," Victor spoke up irritably. "We were told to be here, and we are." He locked eyes with the deputy.

"One second," the deputy sighed and swiveled in his chair. The chair groaned and squeaked desperately. He grabbed the phone and punched three numbers. "Doug? Got three for that Harlan case out here." He listened a moment, said "Okay," and hung up.

"He'll be out in a minute," the deputy said, restarting his appraisal of Jessica's cleavage. "You can have a seat over there," he nodded at the bench where the wino was stretching out, lifting his old legs like they weighed a ton.

"Thanks," Victor replied sarcastically. "We'll stand."

The deputy shrugged. "Suit yourself."

We waited five minutes as the deputy shuffled papers and snuck lecherous glances at Jessica. By the time Priest breezed in, the wino was snoring, snot bubbling from one nostril like toxic ooze, and I was ready to give the deputy a piece of my mind, or maybe just a slap across the face.

Priest was dressed in Armani, Gucci and too much cologne. He looked fresh and well-scrubbed, and I guessed he had stopped at home after leaving Laurel's. His expression was stony, eyes cold. He looked at me and Victor, and nodded. His eyes stopped on Jessica, and he favored her with a particularly hostile glare. Jessica looked up for the briefest moment, flushed, and looked at the floor.

"Miss de Montagne," he said to Jessica. "How nice to see you again," his tone implied that it was anything but nice. Jessica muttered something while she twisted her handbag's strap in her hands. I looked stupidly between the two of them, wondering what the hell was going on.

"What a pleasure to see you, too," I told him with as much sarcasm as I could muster, which was a very generous amount. "Is Ben here?" I asked. I wasn't going to deal with Priest unless I had to.

"He's in the field," Priest replied shortly, "but we won't need him. Please follow me." It sounded like the 'please' hurt his teeth.

Priest led us down a vanilla colored hallway. We passed a wide cross-hall and heard a man hoarsely screaming obscenities in Spanish. Priest took no notice, but Victor cocked an ear, smiled and shook his head.

Priest turned into a doorway that had no door and stopped in front of a green Formica topped counter with paperwork racks, a computer terminal and stacks of forms scattered across it. Ten feet behind the counter sat Midge Tidwell, the tall, lanky woman with spiky brown hair who had worked the crime scene at Violet. She was dressed in the same grubby white lab-coat and cat's-eye glasses. Her metal desk was cluttered with stuffed animals and the kind of toys you get with a Happy Meal. The room's one window was covered by blinds thick with dust. Midge looked up from a computer monitor. Her eyes stopped on Priest and she grimaced. She stood and approached the counter, thrusting her hands deep in the pockets of the lab coat.

"Three for prints," Priest said.

"And good morning to you too, Detective Dougie," Midge said in her low voice, so startling coming from such a thin woman. The lab-coat wasn't quite closed and I could see she was wearing a tailored silk blouse and blue linen slacks, both in a decidedly masculine cut. "Three more desperados, I see. What are they, crack dealers? Jaywalkers?"

Priest flushed and bunched his fists reflexively. "Good morning, *Deputy* Tidwell." He said sourly. "This is part of a murder investigation, so cut the comedy."

"The floor show's free, so no complaints allowed. You get what you pay for." Midge flicked a smile at us, then turned a blank face to Priest.

"Print them and bring them to my office," Priest said, struggling to keep his tone professional. He smoothed his tie and turned away.

"Anything else? Bring you a cup of coffee? Rub your back? Dry-cleaning? I'll be glad to play escort just as soon as I change my title from Deputy to hostess." She made a show of pulling her nametag off. "I've got a magic marker somewhere."

"Cut the crap, Midge."

"Why Dougie, I can't believe you said that! And in front of taxpayers, too! Maybe *voting* taxpayers. How risqué!"

Priest started to say something, but Midge cut him off. "I'm not a tour guide, Doug. When I'm done I'll call you."

"I'll be in my office," Priest said stiffly and left.

"Hi Mrs. de Montagne," Midge said, giving me a bright smile.

"Hi, Midge," I said. "How are you?"

"Same thing different day," she replied. "Don't let Doug put you off, he's the worst of the bunch. It can only get better from here." She grinned. Her eyes stopped on Jessica and I saw a flicker of more than friendly interest. She didn't stare, though.

She placed three fingerprint cards on the counter. "This is gonna be messy," she apologized in advance. "There's tissue in the box and soap in the bathroom down the hall. Not that it'll do much good. This stuff is hell to get off. Just rub it on the chairs in Priest's office, that's my advice." She winked at me. "Okay. Let me have your hand. I promise it won't hurt much."

I laughed and proffered my right hand. She took it by the wrist, turned it flat, and gripped my thumb between two fingers. Midge's fingernails were bitten to the quick and dirty with black powder.

"Good set of calluses," Midge said as she rolled my thumb in the ink. "Lots of outside work, I'd guess."

"I'd rather be outside than in any day."

"Not me. I turn red after ten minutes in the sun. Never had a tan in my life," Midge said conversationally as she rolled my thumb on the fingerprint card. She meticulously repeated the same steps with all ten fingers, then handed me a wad of tissue. As Midge worked I tried to overhear a whispered conversation between Victor and Jess without success. What were they being so secretive about? I was really getting irritated. Why was Jessica so upset? And why wouldn't she talk to me?

Midge put Victor through the same process as I vainly scrubbed at my inky fingertips with the disintegrating tissue. I only made the mess worse. A trip to the bathroom was in order, but I'd wait for Jessica to finish.

Victor finished and took a tissue. He smirked as he looked at my hands, now smeared black from the first knuckle down.

"Finger painting?" he asked as Jessica stepped up to the desk and reluctantly turned her hand over to Midge.

"You need to loosen up some," Midge said. "I can't do it if your fingers are locked."

"Sorry," Jessica said softly, eyes downcast.

"That's better," Midge said, rolling Jessica's left thumb in the ink and transferring it to the fingerprint card. Midge seemed to take her time with Jessica, but maybe I was just being overly protective. Finally Jess was finished. She took her tissue and turned toward me but wouldn't meet my eyes.

"I'll drop these off at the lab and let Dougie know you're ready," she told us, fanning Jessica's card with a blank one from the stack. "The bathroom is down the hall. You passed it on the way in."

We trailed out and down the hall. The bathroom was surprisingly modern and Clorox-clean. There were two sinks, and a row of stalls. Jessica and I stepped up to the sinks and turned on the water. I snuck a look at Jess as I lathered up. Her lips were pressed tight, eyes intent as she scrubbed at the ink with a wad of wet paper towels. Most of the ink came off, but a gray pallor remained on both of our hands. I finally gave up.

Jessica had finished washing her hands but was leaning over the sink, gripping the sides as water gushed and splattered. Her shoulders were trembling and I could tell she was crying though hair curtained her face. I said her name and reached for her hand, but she spun away from me, hands clutching her stomach. She bolted for the nearest stall. The door slammed

74

closed and I heard her retching. My own stomach did a seasick roll at the sound.

My first instinct was to go to my daughter, but Jessica wasn't a little girl anymore and vomiting is a very personal thing. I listened to her gagging and heaving, paper towels dangling forgotten from my right hand. After a moment, the vomiting stopped but the sobbing persisted for several minutes. I busied myself, embarrassed to be listening but unwilling to leave. I wiped the sink Jessica had been using then checked my hair in the mirror.

I was running out of things to do by the time the toilet flushed and Jessica came out, her hair plastered to her cheeks. She pushed her hair behind her ears and smiled wanly at me. She was about to speak when Midge Tidwell stuck her head through the door.

"Is everything okay?" she asked, her eyes jumping from me to a disheveled Jessica.

Jessica nodded quickly, flushing with embarrassment and swiping at her eyes with the heel of her hands.

"It's okay," I said to Midge, trying for a reassuring smile that probably came out looking like I was chewing aspirin. "We'll be right there."

"Are you sure?" Midge asked me without taking her eyes off Jessica.

"Yes, thank you," I said firmly enough for her to get the point. "We'll be right out."

With an uncertain nod, Midge disappeared.

"Are you going to be okay?" I asked, taking Jessica's hand and squeezing it. Her palm was clammy. She nodded and pulled her hand away. I handed her some Kleenex. She grimaced at her reflection in the mirror, wiped her red and swollen eyes and straightened her dress. She still looked awful.

"Let's get it over with." She slung her purse over her shoulder and gave me a look of such despair that I almost decided to spirit her out of the jail, and to hell with Priest and this whole rotten business. But that would needlessly complicate a formality that would soon be over. What was wrong with Jess? I was past being mystified, I was growing annoyed.

Midge was waiting with Victor. Victor took in Jessica's appearance and looked a question at me. I shook my head and Victor looked away.

"Are we ready?" Midge asked.

"As ready as we'll ever be."

"Okay," Midge said, looking at Jessica. "I'll break a rule and walk you to Doug's office. This way."

We followed Midge down the hall and around a corner into another corridor lined with closed doors. Priest's office was the third door on the right. A cheap brass nameplate with black lettering was on the door.

Midge banged on the door like an overzealous process server, throwing me a grin.

"Come in!" Priest shouted.

"We're finished, Dougie."

"You done the comparisons? Priest shuffled papers and didn't bother looking up.

"Not yet, I was playing tour guide. Maybe I'll go to work for the zoo." She turned to us and smiled. "One jackass in its natural environment," she announced making a broad gesture at Priest whose head popped up, lips forming an angry reply. His eyes hit Jessica and his expression changed. I could see him reign in his anger, swallow it back. He almost smiled.

"How long is it going to take, Officer Tidwell?"

"Twenty minutes tops for a preliminary match." Priest nodded.

As Midge turned to go, she leaned in close to Jessica. "Don't let him get to you," she said, then gave her arm a squeeze.

Priest's office looked more like someone's den than an office in a police station. His desk was a massive antique made of hand rubbed oak with a matching file cabinet and bookcase. The walls were cluttered with framed diplomas and photographs of Priest with some of California's leading politicians and sports celebrities. A pair of oil paintings of hunt scenes in antique frames took up the largest part of the far wall. The office had a clubby and contrived feel to me. I believe a person's office tells you more about who they want to be than who they are. I gathered that Priest aspired to blueblood elitism, though he pretended to despise it. Mainly, I wondered where his money came from. The furnishings in this office probably cost many times his yearly income. My eyes and my thoughts eventually stopped on a pair of mud stained tennis shoes sitting on the corner of Priest's desk.

Jessica saw the tennis shoes and stopped dead in her tracks. She even stopped breathing for a moment. Priest took in her reaction and smiled, rocking back in his red leather chair.

"Close the door, please." He said genially to Victor. "And have a seat," Priest nodded at a row of three metal chairs facing his desk, obviously placed there for this purpose. If he had been a cat he would have been licking his lips. Whatever was making Priest so affable was making me nervous as hell. Victor sat down on my left. Jessica remained standing, eyes glued to the tennis shoes.

"Where did you find those?" she asked.

"I think you know the answer to that question, Ms. de Montagne," Priest mockingly replied. "Now, take a seat."

"What's going on?" I asked, looking from Jessica to Priest. "Do those have something to do with Kevin's murder?"

"Ask your daughter," Priest said, still watching Jessica.

76

"I'm asking you," I snapped, my nervousness flaring into angry impatience. "Sit down, Jessica," I told my daughter. She complied, moving like she was underwater.

Priest rocked in his chair, smoothed the front of his pink shirt and adjusted the lay of his blue tie. He was enjoying himself.

"You could say that they do. That's Kevin Harlan's blood smeared all over them."

I remembered the brown paper bag that Priest had brought up from the wine cellar. Just about the size of a pair of tennis shoes. "Is that what you found in my cellar the other morning?"

Priest nodded smugly. "Just got the lab results back."

"And what does that have to do with my daughter?" I asked. "The killer was *in* the cellar, he probably dumped them there."

"They're a lady's size nine," Priest said. "What size do you wear, Ms. de Montagne?"

"They're my shoes, mom," Jessica whispered, eyes in her lap. "They were in my gym bag when it was stolen."

Priest rocked forward, and laid his hands on a loose stack of notebook paper with fold-creases. He picked them up and thumbed through them. "Stolen?" he asked. "How original. Did you report this theft?"

"I thought it was Stanley. My boyfr—ex-boyfriend." Jessica explained, looking at me, avoiding Priest's stare, strangling her purse strap. "I didn't want to get him in trouble."

"That would be Stanley Kostyol? The man who says he saw you and Kevin alone in the vineyard the night Kevin was killed."

"Stanley Kostyol is a liar and a criminal!" I blurted. "If you believe anything he says, you're crazier than I think."

"I'm speaking to Jessica," Priest replied calmly, savoring the moment.

"I was with him, but I didn't kill him!" She shot to her feet. "I would never hurt Kevin!"

My head snapped around fast enough to break my neck. "What? You said Stanley was lying!"

"Somebody's lying, and it isn't Kostyol," Priest interrupted. "Sit down, Ms. de Montagne," Priest pointed one manicured finger at Jessica's chair. She shrank into it, a slow trickle of tears starting.

"What was the nature of your relationship with Kevin?"

"She barely knew Kevin Harlan," I said before Jessica could answer. "She certainly had no reason to kill him."

"I was speaking to your daughter," Priest said, eyes narrowed. "But since you brought it up..." Priest picked up a page of the notebook paper and read.

"I miss you so much, Kevin," he read. "I can't stand being without you. It makes me crazy knowing that you're with her. It's signed, Jessica. Enough?" He smiled at me.

I didn't say anything. I looked at Jessica. Jessica stared at the rug, hair hanging in strings around her face, tears dripping into her lap.

"Sounds like motive to me. The bitter fruit of tainted love," Priest prodded, leaning across his desk.

"I was in love with Kevin," Jessica said so softly I could barely hear. "I would never have hurt him. I'm so sorry mom, I wanted to tell you. I just couldn't. I knew you wouldn't approve. I can't change the way I feel." She covered her face with her hands.

"Oh, no," Victor groaned, the first words he had spoken since we entered Priest's office. He put a hand to his forehead and closed his eyes. "Not like this."

I looked at Priest, still trying to recover from my shock. "You don't really think Jessica killed Kevin? Look at her, she's crushed. Where did you get those letters?"

"That's confidential information—"

"Give me a break! Any good attorney would be able to find out in a couple of hours. But I'm pretty sure I already know: Laurel Harlan, wicked witch of the Mayacamas mountains."

Priest's smirk dissolved. "Mrs. Harlan isn't the person I'm concerned with. I'm looking for Kevin Harlan's killer."

"You're looking for a piece of ass!" I roared, wanting to lunge across the desk and knock Priest's teeth out. "And judging by the time you left the Harlan's this morning I'd say you found it." I had stepped over the line, cursing and planning physical violence. And in the police station! But I'm a fighter by nature. When confronted with a problem my first instinct is to throw up my fists and start punching.

"That's way out of line," Priest came half out of his chair and stuck his finger in my face. "Mrs. Harlan is a very nic—"

I cut him off. "I *know* the woman. What size shoe does *she* wear? Has *she* been fingerprinted?"

"Mrs. Harlan was fingerprinted, and she is not a suspect. She-" Priest's angry response was interrupted by a knock on the door.

"Enter," he bellowed, face flushed. I had definitely struck a nerve, and I was petty enough to relish it.

Midge stuck her head in. "Doug," she said, her tone professional. She cast a worried look over the three of us sitting in the folding chairs. "We have a match."

78

"Ah," Priest sighed and his grin reappeared. He steepled his fingers. "Who's the lucky contestant?"

Midge glanced at Jessica. "Jessica de Montagne," she said. "Her prints match the partial at 16-points. No doubt about it. I'm sorry," she added, looking from me to Jess.

"Close the door," Priest snapped. "Don't apologize to a murderer."

Midge closed the door without another word, but with a long sad glance at Jessica.

"You lily-white little prick—" Victor growled, rising and taking a step toward Priest. I grabbed hold of his wrist, restraining him before he did something stupid.

"That doesn't mean anything. The shovel was on my property, and those prints could have been there for months," I said, scrambling for answers. But I couldn't even convince myself.

"Motive, opportunity, murder weapon," Priest said, ticking them off on the fingers of his right hand. "We *definitely* have a winner."

"I didn't kill Kevin!" Jessica spoke up. "I never even—"

"Don't say anything else, Jessica," I told her, reaching for her hand. "We're leaving right now."

I stood, followed closely by Jessica and Victor. My foreman was as tense as a mongoose eyeing a cobra. If we didn't leave immediately I was afraid Victor would beat the snot out of the detective.

"We're not through," Priest said, coming around his desk.

"The hell we aren't," Victor said and stepped between Priest and Jessica. "I've listened to all the crap I'm going to from you."

"Out of the way," Priest demanded, hand sliding under his jacket and behind his waist. He's reaching for his gun! I thought, a trill of fear sounding in my head. The whole incident was spinning out of control, heading toward a violent confrontation.

"Move me, asshole," Victor snarled. Behind him Jessica was trembling. I probably looked just as scared.

"Don't, Victor," I said, stepping in front of Victor who continued to stare daggers at Priest over my shoulder. "We're leaving," I said, looking back at Priest, my right hand flat on Victor's chest. "If you have any other questions you can talk to my attorney."

"Fine," Priest said, flashing a quick grin. "You two can leave. But," he pointed at Jessica, "she's not going anywhere." Priest stepped around me and Victor and drew something silver from under his coat. He grabbed Jessica's right wrist and snapped a steel bracelet around it, clicking it down tight. Before I could even protest, he spun her around and snapped the other cuff in place.

Jessica's purse hit the floor and her eyes went to me, pleading for intervention. I was as stunned and helpless as she.

"Jessica de Montagne, you are under arrest for the murder of Kevin Harlan." Priest pulled open the office door, revealing two Sheriff's deputies in khaki uniforms waiting just outside. I knew then that Priest had intended to arrest Jessica all along. Why else would he have had the deputies waiting?

Priest pushed Jessica through the doorway as Victor and I watched in stunned silence.

"Read her her rights and book her for the Harlan murder," Priest said, and they led my daughter away.

CHAPTER 15

I watched them lead Jessica down the hall. She never looked back. Priest trailed the deputies escorting my daughter, and Victor and I were alone, staring at each other.

"I can't believe this is happening!" I said, a tremor in my voice. "Why didn't she tell me?"

"We need to get her bailed out," Victor said, speaking calmly, though I knew he had to be as shocked as I. "There's a bondsman on Fourth Street I used when a bunch of us were arrested for picketing Dearborne. Jess'll have to be arraigned first, though. That means she'll probably be here overnight."

Oh, no," I shivered, repulsed by the thought. Jessica was troubled enough already, going through the pain of losing Kevin. A pain I had been blissfully unaware of until now. A night in the county jail would only do more harm.

"Where on Fourth?" I said, thoughts whirling in my head.

"Like I said, she'll have to be arraigned. She'll—"

"I heard you," I snapped, then hurried to apologize. "I'm sorry, Victor. I'm upset. No I'm angry! Ready to *scream!* I just want to get her the hell out of here!"

"They're in the 1400 block. An old blue Victorian," he replied. "But until she's arraigned there's nothing they can do."

"You have their number?"

"In my truck. Why don't we go back to Violet and give them a call?"

What he suggested went against the grain. I didn't want to leave Napa without Jessica! I couldn't, wouldn't believe that there was nothing I could do.

"Let's go," I said and strode briskly down the hallway, sandals slapping on the tile, anger fueling me. Victor trotted up, worry deepening the creases in his tanned face. We passed Midge's office. She was behind the counter. Her head came up as we passed, and she started to say something, but I didn't pause. At that moment I had nothing to say to her or anyone else at the sheriff's office. Except to maybe stand on the steps outside and scream "Idiots!" at the top of my lungs.

When I burst through the courthouse's front doors a cluster of Japanese tourists with video cameras were walking by, craning their necks and looking around like they were lost. They were a few blocks from the antique malls and restaurants. This part of Third Street is dedicated primarily to government offices, cut-rate lawyers and bail bondsmen.

We were halfway down the front steps when my cell phone rang, startling me. I stopped, muttering under my breath, angry at the distraction, and dug into my purse for the phone.

"Hello," I yelled into the mouthpiece.

"De Montagne?" Samson asked, his voice crackling and fading. He didn't give me time to reply. "What is going on? The sheriffs are searching the house. Bottling has stopped, all of the men are loafing, watching the damn show!"

"What?! They're searching the house?" I yelled into the phone, and the Japanese tourists looked my way, video cameras panning over Victor and I. I turned my back on them and stuck a finger in my ear to hear better.

"They have a piece of paper that says they can do this. I hear them in there moving things. I hope they break nothing. Bastards told me to stop the line! I have wine to bottle, wine that is oxidizing!" Samson raged on. Priest hadn't wasted any time. The deputies must have been en route while we were being fingerprinted. Damn him!

"Stay out of their way," I ordered Samson, trying to sound calm and in control while a wild pulse throbbed in my temples. "Begin bottling as soon as they leave, or shut it down until tomorrow. Whatever you think best."

"I think I tell them to get the hell out, that is best! Morons! I can't—"

I cut him off impatiently. "Samson, I've got to go now. They arrested Jessica for Kevin's murder—"

"What?!" He spewed a mouthful of Greek curses. "They are crazy men! That little girl could kill no one! I'll tell them-"

"I don't have time for this, Samson!" I yelled, losing control. "I've got to get to a bondsman's office and get Jessica the hell out of there." Even though I believed what Victor had told me about arraignment and bail I couldn't go home knowing Jessica was sitting in a cell somewhere. If nothing else, I could get the paperwork started. I had to *do* something or I'd go crazy!

"I'll come there and—"

"No!" I screamed into the phone then caught myself. Stirring Samson up would only make matters worse. I shouldn't have told him about Jessica. "Just get the line running if you can and try not to start any trouble."

"They are the trouble, not me! Sons of bitches!"

I hung up.

"They can't do anything until she's arraigned," Victor told me again.

"I know!" I shouted at him, gripping my phone so tightly the plastic cut into my fingers. "But I need to do something, and that's all I can think of."

Victor's eyes jumped from my face to a point over my right shoulder. "Look who's coming," he said, "Ben Stoltze, commandant of the Gulag." Victor can be melodramatic when he's angry, but at that moment I felt exactly the same way. I whirled around, stuffing my phone back into my purse. Ben was coming up the sidewalk with a cigarette dangling from his lip. He was smiling, but the smile started to slip as I strode toward him.

82

"Hey, Claire, Victor," Ben said, nodding at my foreman. "Something wrong?"

"Damn you, Ben Stoltze! You know what's wrong!" I roared. "That cretin Priest just arrested my daughter, and your men are tearing apart my home right now!"

"What?" Ben fell back a step. The Japanese tourist's video camera whirred as they stood in a flock, watching the show. I had the urge to go over and knock the camera out of their hands, but that was just misdirected anger. And I had someone to take my anger out on right in front of me.

"For what?" Ben sounded surprised and I knew instantly that Priest hadn't informed Ben. That hardly mattered. Ben was the Sheriff and therefore responsible for everything that went on in his office. And there I was dressed up and even wearing lipstick, for this man who I now wanted to beat to his knees.

"I don't know anything about it. I'll look into—"

"You'll look into it?! You'll look into it?! Meanwhile my daughter sits in a cell for something she didn't do! Why don't you look into why Priest is spending his nights in Laurel Harlan's bedroom!"

"Now, wait a minute Claire," Ben said, getting red in the face, his tone on the edge of anger. He started to lift a finger to point at me, but thought better of it. Wise move - I would have bit it off. He stuffed his hands in his pockets. "Doug Priest is a fine detective, if he arrested—"

I didn't let him finish. "Doug Priest is a creep! You should be ashamed he's on the force!" I yelled at the top of my voice, unable to control my anger any longer. "Get the hell out of my way!" I brushed past, leaving him standing on the sidewalk staring. Victor followed somewhat more sheepishly.

The Japanese tourists scattered like pigeons as I plowed through the group. They pointed and babbled amongst themselves, enjoying the drama. They'd probably show the tape at home and marvel at the crazy lady ranting and raving in front of the police station, speculating all kinds of scenarios. Let them, I didn't care!

Sally was parked in the lot beside the Sheriff's office. Victor caught up to me just as I slammed the driver's door and jammed the key in the ignition. He climbed in, but said nothing. That was probably a good thing. I wasn't in the mood to chat. I was fuming, mentally calling Ben every name I could think of, names I would never say out loud. I couldn't believe he had let that *creep* arrest my daughter! If he had so little control over his department, maybe it was time he retired. I'd be glad if I never saw him again!

"Where's the bondsman's office?" I barked at Victor.

"It's on Fourth Street, right behind the—"

"Just tell me where to turn," I cut him off.

83

"Okay," he replied, looking straight ahead. "Take a right at the next block, Coombs Street, then a right on Fourth, the—"

"Tell me when I get there," I said, jamming my foot on the accelerator, lunging the Mustang out of its spot. I whipped the steering wheel around and burned rubber out of the lot, swerving across the center of the street and punching the gas again. The Japanese had regrouped. Their camera recorded my departure. Ben was watching too, standing on the sidewalk, looking bewildered.

"Take a right here," Victor said, white-knuckling the dash with one hand while hauling the seatbelt strap down with the other. I took the corner, tires screeching, and hit the gas again.

"Turn right at the next—hey, Claire! Slow down!" Victor yelped as I cranked the wheel into another hard right turn. "It's right there in the middle of the block. Slow down or you'll miss the turn!"

I didn't miss the turn, but I did leave a smear of rubber in the driveway. We hit the sidewalk at the middle of the drive and Sally jumped a foot off the ground, slamming back down on the parking lot's pot-holed asphalt. I slid Sally into a parking space, jammed on the brakes, jerked the keys out of the ignition, snatched my purse and was halfway across the parking lot before Victor got out of the car.

"Hold up, Claire!" Victor hollered as he jogged toward me.

"Hurry up!" I hollered back.

The bondsman's office occupied a dilapidated, dingy baby-blue Victorian with a sagging front porch, dead plants in the window boxes and mirrored glass in the windows. The lawn had been paved over with lumpy asphalt and was littered with cigarette butts and bottle caps. A rotten wooden wheelchair ramp and a set of wobbly cinderblock steps led up to a narrow plate glass door with AAA Bail Bonds printed on it in faded gilt.

Victor caught up to me as I reached the front door. I jerked it open and stepped into a dingy office cluttered with grungy plastic chairs and folding tables. The room must have been the home's parlor at one time, but now it looked more like a flophouse's vestibule. A brand new Xerox copier, wanted flyers tacked to a corkboard above it, was the only clean thing in sight. And that included the startled-looking fat man with a greasy comb-over and sweaty face who was sitting behind a desk placed directly in front of the plate glass door. He was the only person in sight, though there were numerous closed doors covered in seventy layers of peeling paint.

"I thought you was gonna crash right into the place." His eyes suddenly brightened with recognition as he spotted Victor behind me.

"Victor! What's shaking? Y'all racing in the Napa 500?"

"Hey Solly," Victor replied, looking askance at me. "We need to see about a bond."

"I can tell that," the fat man said, leaning back and locking his hands behind his head. The chair groaned pitifully and I thought it might snap in half. The bondsmen's shirt's underarms were soaked with sweat and stained brown. He grinned with teeth as yellow as canned corn. "You just commit a crime? That why y'all are driving like maniacs? If so, I can't help y'all 'til they bust ya." He laughed at his own joke, fat jowls jiggling obscenely.

I didn't have the patience for this! "My daughter was just arrested," I butted in.

"Let me, Claire," Victor said, stepping around me and drawing back one of two chairs that faced the desk. "Sit down," Victor said, giving me a warning look. This was a man who helped Victor on occasion, maybe a friend, and Victor didn't want me irritating him. I saw the logic in that and took a deep breath. It didn't help.

I sank into the chair, purse on my knees, and Victor dropped into a chair beside me.

"Got a problem Solly," he began. "Girl just got arrested—"

"My daughter, Jessica de Montagne," I interjected and Solly nodded with sympathy as fake as the veneer on his desktop.

"When?" he asked, reaching for a form. He took up a pen, scratched his nose with it and then wrote Jessica's name.

"Fifteen minutes ago," Victor replied and Solly looked up with a frown, dropping his pen.

"Nothing I can do about it until she's arraigned and bail is set. They won't even have her records or booking report ready for a few hours. What's the charge, anyway?"

"Murder," I said. "Kevin Harlan."

"Murder," Solly repeated, relishing the sound, probably anticipating a high bond and a large check. "Read about the case. She do it?"

"Of course not," I snapped.

"Hey, just asking," he said, holding a hands up. "No offense. We're all innocent until all the appeals are exhausted. Makes no difference to me either way. Anyway, I can't do anything until bail is set."

"I figured that," Victor said, "But Claire wanted to get the paperwork started. What's the drill on something like this?"

Solly leaned back in his chair and locked his hands behind his head. "She'll be booked, printed, photographed, then put in a cell. Her case'll be on the docket and she'll be set up with an arraignment time. If she's lucky that'll be tonight and we'll have her out by morning. As long as you got the money," He added looking at me. "But since your name is de Montagne, I know you'll come up with the cash. Worst case scenario she'll see the judge tomorrow morning or afternoon, and we'll have her out by 5:30."

"Is there any way we can speed it up?" Victor asked.

"Not through me. Tomorrow morning's best I can say. Bail will be high but not astronomical if it's her first offense."

"She didn't do it," I reminded him, and he smiled, which made me want to pop him in his sweaty chin.

"Is this the first time she's been arrested? Convicted?"

"Never arrested," I told him. "Never."

"Bond should be around two-hundred thousand. Little lower, little higher. I'll need a check for ten percent." He leaned forward, cracked his knuckles and dropped his hands on his desk. His nails were dirty and long. "I'll have a deputy let me know when she gets on the docket. I'll call you and we go from there."

"Twenty-thousand dollars?" I asked, stunned by the amount. I had that much in savings, but not much more. This would wipe my personal finances out until the Vintners Reserve was shipped and the checks came in. It didn't matter, though. I'd auction off a kidney if I had to.

"That's right," Solly said. "Little higher, little lower." He shrugged, "depends on the judge and the evidence they got. A lot of times they won't even set bail on a murder case, but this being her first time and all, they should."

"Well," Victor looked at me with a 'what now?' expression.

"I guess we'll go back home," I said as the phone in my purse rang. "Excuse me," I said to Solly as I dug in my purse, found the phone and punched Accept without checking the caller ID.

"Hello?" I said, thinking it was probably Samson calling to report on the deputies.

"Why hello there, darling," a familiar voice purred in my ear. The voice was cheerful and prep-school nasal, complete with imitation-English accent. I made a face and squeezed my eyes shut. It was the last person I wanted to speak with. My husband, Roger de Montagne.

"Hello, Roger," I said. "What do you want?"

"And how are you, my dear?" he asked. "You sound a little put out? Things not going your way?"

"What do you want?" I repeated, debating whether to mention Jessica's arrest. I guessed I had to, but the thought made me wince. Jessica had been my responsibility for so long that I didn't want his interference now. I had handled diapers, chickenpox and menstrual cycles, I was prepared to handle bailing Jessica out.

"To get our lovely daughter, who takes after her mother, by the way, out of jail, of course."

"How did you find out?" I asked, though I shouldn't have been surprised. The de Montagnes have a grapevine that includes judges, senators, councilmen and police officers. A well paid grapevine.

"I heard this morning that they were going to arrest her for that Harlan boy's murder. Mother called."

Roger's mother is the family patron and CEO of de Montagne Enterprises. She is a ruthless businesswoman, a doting grandmother, and an unforgiving, unrelentingly fault-finding mother-in-law. She and I have never gotten along, mainly because I speak my mind and don't kiss her broad butt, but she could have called me and warned me about Priest. Instead, she had allowed her personal animosity for me to interfere. A typical de Montagne back-stabbing.

I got up, held a finger up to Victor and Solly and stepped outside. I shielded my eyes from the sun with one hand as I talked.

"She could have called me!" I shouted. "What is wrong with that woman? Is she insane?"

"Now, now, dear, let's not get into personalities. The important thing is that we get Jessica out of there. Mother—"

"That's exactly what I'm doing, Roger," I cut him off. "I'm sitting in a bondsman's office right now. I don't have time for this."

"Is it one of those squalid little places clustered around the jail like ticks on a dog? Tell me, are they as grim on the inside as they look on the outside? How does it smell? Like unwashed feet? That's what I always imagined."

"If you're so interested, let's trade places." I said, unable to suppress a smile. I hate to admit it, but Roger's bantering tone and bemused attitude were having their usual effect on me. He's always known how to make me laugh, how to ease any tense situation. That was part of the reason I had fallen in love with him, that coupled with his good looks and charm. It wasn't until we were married that I realized that an attractive shell was all he was. He has no goals and no aspirations beyond the next party or dinner. He informed me once that it was 'a sign of good breeding to be absolutely useless and dependent on your ancestors' money,' and he had lived up to that with gusto.

"If it's as horrible as I imagine, I don't think I'd fit in. As a matter of fact, I think you should flee the place immediately and wash off the lower class stench."

"Roger," I said, squinting at my watch, "I have to bail Jessica out. That place will be too much for her right now."

"Ah, Jessica, my little hot-house flower," Roger said with a smile in his voice. "Fear not, fair lady, the courageous knights of Fine, Fine and Morgan are at the rescue as we speak. Our lawyers will scale the walls of justice and retrieve the fair maiden within the hour."

"That's not possible," I informed him. "She hasn't been arraigned yet—"

"That will be happening in moments, I assure you, or Judge Robert Phelps will lose his biggest backers, namely de Montagne Enterprises. Mother lit a fire under the good judge and he is absolutely quivering to be of help."

The relief I felt couldn't be put into words, but it irked me that Roger could step in and with a few phone calls, handle everything. In Napa, Roger and his family know all the right buttons to push. And how much money to slide into the hand waiting under the table. I hate the manipulations and backroom deals, and I was ashamed to be benefiting from them. But if it got Jessica out of jail I would deal with my bruised ideals later.

"Sounds like you have it all worked out," I said sourly. "I appreciate your help."

"It was nothing, but if you really want to thank me, how about dinner tonight? The Palm?" Roger asked smoothly. "You love the Champagne Brie soup, and they carry your excellent 2006 cabernet. I called to check."

I laughed out loud. "Do you ever stop?"

"Only for red lights and beautiful women. What do you say? I'm in New York, at the Ritz at the moment, but I'll be in St. Helena by six."

"I really shouldn't," I said, annoyed at the wistful tone in my voice. But I really do like the soup. "There's so much going on."

"Which is why you need a break. I've made reservations for eight. I'll be there, the wine and the soup will be there, will you?"

"I'll take a rain-check," I said. Like for the day *after* I die, I mentally added.

Roger's sigh sounded genuinely disappointed. "I'm going to hold you to that, darling."

"I guess I'll wait and pick Jessica up," I said, thinking aloud and trying to change the subject.

"I wouldn't," Roger said. "Mother drove down with the lawyers."

"Witch," I muttered.

"She likes you just as much as you like her," he assured me. "My money's on you in a fistfight, though."

"Jessica doesn't need the added stress," I said with rising irritation. "Your mother—"

"Is getting Jessica out of jail," Roger cut in smoothly. I had nothing to say to that.

"Well," I said, lamely. "Have her call me tonight or in the morning."

"Of course my dear," he cooed. "I only wish you cared as much for me as Jessica. I remember when first we married—"

I hung up. I'd had enough conversations with Roger to last a lifetime. I just plain wasn't interested anymore. And if he took offense, well, that'd be great! I stowed my cell phone in my purse and stepped back inside. The men stopped talking and looked up at me.

"I'm sorry to have taken up your time," I said to Solly. "But we won't need a bond apparently." I looked at Victor, "That was Roger. The de Montagnes are handling it. He says she'll be out in an hour."

Solly had been smiling when I entered, but it vanished when he realized I wouldn't be writing him a check.

"Called in the big guns?" He said. "I guess if ya got the clout ya don't have to follow the rules. Nothing new there." He sighed heavily and shuffled paper around on his messy desk. "More power to ya, though. I'd use it if I had it."

"Sorry, Solly," Victor said as he rose. "Nice talking with you."

"Always good to see ya, Victor," Solly replied without looking up from his paperwork. Then he laughed and glanced up at us, suddenly back to good humor. "Nicer when you got a check in your hand, though!" He laughed at his own joke, belly shivering with loose fat.

"Nicer for you," Victor grinned back. "Take care."

"Do the same. And good luck Mrs. de Montagne," he added to me.

"I appreciate that, Solly, and I'll keep you in mind if I need a bond," I said as I stepped out the door Victor was holding for me.

"Do that!" Solly yelled as the door swung closed behind Victor and me. "Tell your friends. Hell, tell your enemies!"

CHAPTER 16

When we were inside Sally, I stuck the keys in the ignition, closed my eyes and melted into the seat. Victor sat beside me, staring through the windshield, looking thoughtful and worried.

"I need to apologize to you, Victor," I said. "For acting like a crazy lady."

"No need to apologize," Victor replied, still looking straight ahead. "That'd stress anybody out."

"It was just such a shock. I never had a clue about Jessica and Kevin. They barely spoke around the Vineyard. It just doesn't make any sense," I explained with exasperation. "I never would have guessed." But it did explain why Jessica had been so upset. At least she wasn't pregnant!

"They met at the Fitness Factory," Victor said, naming the local meat-market fitness center. "A few months after Winter was killed."

"What?!" I yelped, twisting in the seat to face Victor, banging my knee on the steering wheel in the process. "You knew about them? You knew and you didn't tell me?!"

Victor cocked one leg up on the seat and faced me. He shook his head tiredly. "I didn't know until it was over. Jessica told me one night last month after you went to bed. We were drinking and it slipped out. I didn't think it was my place to tell you. Besides, it was over."

"Kevin never said anything to you?" I asked incredulously, rubbing my sore knee. They had been best friends after all, and I didn't think men were very good at keeping their conquests quiet.

"If he had I would have kicked his ass," Victor said with a flash of anger. "If he was looking for a fling there were plenty of women that would have been glad to have him. He didn't have to mess around with Jess. She's like my sister! If nothing else he should have had more respect for me."

"And for his wife," I reminded him.

"Ha!" Victor laughed without humor. "She was banging half the guys in the Valley. He didn't owe her a *damn* thing. Kevin told me she even had an affair with a cop while we were still searching for Winter."

"Not even her," I said, unwilling to believe it. No mother could do that. "How did he know?"

Victor shrugged. "He didn't say, and I didn't push it. Then I found out about him and Jessica. I didn't have a lot to say to him after that."

"You never confronted Kevin about Jessica?"

"Jess made me promise I wouldn't, but I came close more than once. It really pissed me off. But they were adults, so..." Victor shrugged again helplessly. "It takes two to mambo."

"This is like a bizarre soap opera! You think you know what's happening around you, then you get blindsided. You should have told me after Kevin was killed. At least then I would have been prepared."

"I promised Jess," he reminded me. "Besides, like I said, it was over months ago," irritation crept into Victor's voice. "Kevin had already moved on."

"Moved on?" I said. "Like, to someone else?"

Victor nodded. "Marta Valdez. I saw them together in town a few times." The name meant nothing to me.

"Does Jessica know?" I asked.

Victor shook his head. "I wasn't going to tell her. What was the point, anyway? Maybe I should have."

I sighed and shook my head. "No, you did what any good brother would do." I reached over and squeezed his hand. "Jessica needs to take responsibility for herself."

Victor avoided my eyes. "It's hard for her. She doesn't think she's lived up to your expectations."

"So she has an affair?" I asked heatedly. "And that's my fault?"

"I didn't mean it that way," Victor explained. "I'm just telling you how she feels."

I sighed again with all the anxiety and frustration of a single mother. And I have to admit, a little guilt. What Victor said was at least partially true. But what parent doesn't have high hopes for their daughter? And, besides, I was the safety net that she fell into when things got tough. Who wouldn't resent that? It was just too complicated to think about at that moment, so I changed the subject.

"Roger asked me to dinner," I told Victor.

Victor grinned. "How is he?" he asked. "Still the same?" Victor likes Roger. Almost everyone likes Roger, there's nothing there not to like. But there isn't much there to respect either, and that's where our problems began.

"Exactly the same," I assured him, making a sour face. "He'll never change."

"Dinner would be interesting," Victor laughed, "as long as he kept the knives out of your reach."

"That's not very nice," I said. "I'd be the perfect lady. Besides, I'm not going." Victor just nodded. He knows how I feel about Roger.

"It might be fun," Victor said, stretching his legs as he twisted forward in his seat.

"Wanna go?" I asked, only half-joking.

"No way," Victor said, shaking his head. "I ain't his type and he ain't mine."

"And I feel the same way about it," I said.

91

"I know a good attorney," he grinned. "Divorces for ninety-nine dollars and ninety-five cents."

"Nothing's too good for me," I replied dryly. I turned the key and Sally jumped to life. I put her in reverse and backed out much more sedately than I had pulled in.

I headed for Highway 29 and home, wondering if Samson had gotten the bottling line back up and running, and how big a mess the Sheriff's deputies had made of my house.

CHAPTER 17

Samson was standing beside his jeep when Victor and I pulled up. There were no signs of the students, Sheriff's deputies, or the field crew. I parked Sally in the garage and Victor and I walked over. Despite the angry old scarecrow of a winemaker awaiting me, I had managed to dial my own anger back a couple dozen notches and was determined to keep it there. Jessica was probably out of jail by now, the immediate crisis resolved, and my mind was threatening to short out on thoughts of Kevin and Jessica, murder, lust, and revenge. I couldn't think straight and I couldn't do anything about any of it! What I could do was address a pressing desire for a tall scotch and a half a pack of cigarettes. And Samson would be wise not to stand between me and my addictions.

The sun shone down from a sky as blue as topaz, dramatically lighting the rocky slopes of the mountains, bringing out the bright reds, blacks and drab tans of the rocky slope Violet Vineyard straddles. The day was so clear that I could see the gray-yellow pall of pollution hovering over San Francisco at the head of the valley. In Napa, though, birds sang in the trees, insects whirred. And Samson was fuming.

"I shut down the line!" He started shouting, hands planted on his bony hips. "The police have no respect for wine! And where is Jessica? If they keep her, I will go down there! Son of bitch!" He shook a knobby fist. "Ben Stoltze, son of bitch!" His voice echoed off the stone face of the wine cellar. "Son of bitch! I tell you, de Montagne, these people—"

"Samson," I cut him off. "Watch your blood pressure. Jessica will be out within the hour."

"My blood pressure?" he roared. "Those who make me angry should watch for it! If young I was...ah, to hell with them! The storm troopers realize their mistake? Too late for the bottling! But they care? I ask you—"

I put my hand on his forearm and squeezed. "Samson, calm down."

"Don't blow a gasket, old-timer," Victor chimed in with a laugh. "The wine can wait. Just turn off the taps, no problem."

"Turn off the taps?! What do we have, a brewery?!" Samson exploded. "Wine oxidizes, idiot!" Samson's threw up his hands and shook his head, still muttering but running out of steam.

"Hey, the American palate stinks, right? So, who'll notice?" Victor said cheerfully.

"You will notice," Samson threatened, shaking a fist, but his volume had dropped. "I should drain the lines into my own glass, is what I should do. I could use a drink. Many drinks!" He grinned like the merry lunatic I love so well.

"And now you're talking sensibly," I spoke up. "A long awaited event, but much appreciated. Just drain the lines and top off the wine pump chamber. That should keep the air from causing any damage."

"To the wine cellar!" Victor exclaimed, one finger in the air. "After you, fair lady," he said to me with a bow and a flourish, then jumped in front of me to get through the door. Some gentleman. But he was sure lightening the mood.

"I want to look around the house first," I begged off. "You two go ahead."

"They took things from Jessica's room," Samson said, spitting the words out, instantly angry again. "Boxes and bags. I ask how they have the right, and they waved a paper in my face. A paper! Like that makes it right! I tell you is like the secret police-"

"What about the rest of the house?" I butted in, picturing furniture overturned, drawers pulled out and dumped.

"Nothing, I think. It looked the same when they left. But count the silver! I trust them not at all!" Samson followed Victor to the cellar door.

"Save a glass for me!" I yelled at them from the kitchen stoop.

"If there is to be a glass for you, it will be so. If it is not in the stars, well…" Samson stepped through the door and slammed it closed.

I dumped my purse on the kitchen table and took a quick look around. Everything was where it should be. Almost. There was a subtle skew to every object; nothing was exactly as I had left it. As I wandered from room to room, noticing chairs and bric-a-brac turned at odd angles, drawers not quite closed, neatly stacked papers shuffled into disordered piles, I grew as angry as Samson. I got even madder when I reached Jessica's room.

The police hadn't been as neat in her room. Posters had been pulled from the wall. Her drawers were a jumble of wadded up clothes. Her closet had been rifled and there were gaps in the rows of hanging garments that made me think several articles were missing. Her bed had been stripped of its sheets and quilts and then hastily reassembled by uncaring hands. Grinding my teeth in frustration, I began to put things back in order.

I made the bed, refolded the clothes, straightened the closet, then stood in the middle of the room and looked around. The posters were crooked, so I spent another fifteen minutes pulling out tacks and sticking them back in. When I was done, everything looked pretty much as it had before the police and their search warrant. By then, all the relief at Jessica's release had evaporated from my system and I felt like I might cry. I wouldn't give Priest the satisfaction! My low-grade distaste for the man had blossomed into pure hatred. I assuaged myself for the moment with my knowledge that Jessica was innocent and would be proven so. After all, that's how the legal system works. Right? The innocent go free and the criminals go to prison. Most of the time.

In my own room, I laid fresh clothes on the bed and hopped in the bath, taking a good long soak. I stayed in there over half an hour and felt much better for it. I dried my hair, wrestled it flat, put on a sweatshirt and jeans, and headed for the wine cellar.

As I breezed through the living room I noticed my message light blinking on the answering machine. Reluctantly I pushed the PLAY button.

There were two messages. The first was from Marjory, wondering why I hadn't called and told her about Jessica. As if I would call the biggest gossip in the county and offer up my problems for display! She can resist relating a juicy story like a cat can resist tuna casserole. With a groan, I promised myself that I would call and give her the condensed version.

The second call was a bit of a surprise.

"Hey Claire, it's Ben," Ben Stoltze began, his voice a low bass rumble. "You probably don't want to talk to me, but I really want to talk to you. Please, give me a call when you get this. Don't worry about the time, I don't sleep much anymore anyway. 665-7712." He hung up.

"Great," I sighed. "I don't need this," but I was already reaching for the phone. I wanted to hear what he had to say, wanted to yell and scream at him as he groveled and apologized. Then I wanted him to tell me it was all a big mistake and everything would be all right. Then everything could get back to normal. I hoped he'd stick to the script. For his sake.

I dialed the number. It rang only once before Ben answered.

"Hullo?" He said, sounding half-asleep.

"Hello, Ben," I said, cool as an Alaska breeze. "You called?"

"Claire, uh, oh, just a second." He covered the phone and cleared his throat loudly. It sounded like coal going down a chute. That reminded me how much I needed to quit smoking. It also reminded me to get up and tread my way into the kitchen, take a Marlboro out of my purse and light it. Oh willpower, wherefore art thou?

"Claire," Ben said as I put the lighter's flame to my cigarette. "You okay?"

"No," I said with a puff of smoke. "Is that all you wanted?"

"Hey, hey, hey," he said. "Don't be like that with an old friend."

"Friend," I repeated.

"That's right," Ben replied. "Old friend."

"A friend who had my daughter arrested." I said. "Friends like that I don't need."

"I don't have any control over the DA, Claire. He looks at the evidence and decides to file charges or not. I enforce the law, I don't make it."

"Do you think Jessica killed Kevin?" I asked, stomping my way back to the sofa. "If you do, you're as big an idiot as Prie-"

"Claire," Ben cut me off, "I barely know Jessica, but the evidence looks pretty damning. I'm not saying she's guilty. Hell, enough suspects are crawling out of the woodwork to make Angela Lansbury cringe."

"Did you know they were going to arrest her?" I asked, holding my breath, hoping he would say 'No.'

"Yes, and no," he replied with a sigh. I heard him light a cigarette and inhale. "I knew she was the prime suspect, but it happened a lot faster than I thought. If I had known the warrant had been issued I would have talked some sense into Priest and the assistant DA. There's still a lot we don't know, and, at least to me, it looks like it might be more complicated than a lovers' spat."

I sat and tucked my feet up under me. "Wait a minute, Ben. You're the sheriff and you're telling me you didn't know a warrant had been issued?"

"Tell me about it," he replied. "It's common knowledge that I'm not running for another term, so I'm a lame duck. Everyone's jockeying closer to the new power-base, whoever they think that might be. Kissing ass in all the right places. They don't need my approval for a warrant, but it would have been nice to be informed, anyway." He sounded weary, but I wasn't going to cut him any slack. He was the Sheriff and he should act like one!

"So, you're retiring and you can't be bothered to make sure the right person is arrested for murder?" I asked with rising irritation.

"I didn't say that. I promise that I'll do everything I can to make sure the *right* person goes to prison. Whoever he or she might be."

I wanted nothing more and would expect nothing less. If I thought there was the slightest possibility that Jess had killed Kevin I wouldn't have been half as angry as I was. But the whole thing was ludicrous!

"You know Priest is with Laurel," I told Ben. "Sleeping over, and I don't think it's a pajama party."

"No," Ben said, sounding like his jaw was clenched tight. "No, I didn't know that. But it shouldn't surprise me. The woman has a thing for cops."

"What do you mean she has a thing for cops?" I asked, thinking instantly of what Victor had told me about Laurel's affair with a policeman.

Ben didn't say anything for a long moment.

"I shouldn't have said that," he sighed. "This isn't the kind of thing I'd like to discuss over the phone. And if you weren't such a good friend I wouldn't be speaking to you about it at all. Hell, I could get reprimanded just for calling you." Ben laughed, but it sounded forced.

"You're retiring anyway, right?" I reminded him.

"True." He laughed. "Where are you right now?"

"At home. Why?"

"How about meeting me for a beer?" Ben asked. "I could meet you at Shaky's in an hour. Got anything better planned?"

"I was thinking of going to bed early. I have the bottling to finish, and Kevin's funeral is tomorrow morning."

"You're going to the funeral?" Ben sounded surprised.

"And why shouldn't I?" I asked.

"'Course you should," Ben hurriedly said. "How about that drink?"

"You'll tell me what you meant by 'she has a thing for cops?'"

Ben sighed and let the silence lag. "I'll tell you," he agreed grudgingly.

"Thirty minutes then. Are you sure Shaky's is still open? I haven't been there in twenty years." Shaky's was a popular burger joint when Ben and I were in high school. A weathered-gray building built in the 1800's, Shaky's slouched disreputably in a small pecan grove off Silverado Trail, five miles past Redwood Road, at the foot of the Mayacamas Mountains. Back then it had a half dozen rickety tables, always crowded with high-schoolers and college kids home for the weekend, a splintery counter fronted by rusty metal stools, and a juke box that stole more nickels than it played records. Shaky, the owner and head grouch, who was pushing sixty when I was a kid, had been a grumpy and vulgar old man who's chief asset was that he was too hard of hearing to complain about the juke box volume. "I can't believe that place is still standing."

"I eat there four or five nights a week," Ben said with a laugh. "I'm on a greasy burgers and fries diet."

"Doctor recommended?" I asked, surprised and annoyed that my anger at Ben was slipping away. I was looking forward to seeing him. And to picking his brain for anything that might help Jessica. And, no, I didn't feel guilty about it!

"The lettuce and tomato are,' he replied. "I think of it as 'beef salad on a bun.' That's how Shaky writes it on the ticket, just in case I need proof that I'm eating right."

"He can't still be alive!" I exclaimed, grinning like an idiot. "He must be a hundred and ten."

"Ninety-five, and damn proud of it. Still sharp as a rusty nail and about half as nice."

"I can't believe it." It was almost like finding a piece of my childhood trapped under glass.

"So, you'll come?"

"Make it an hour and a half," I told Ben. I wanted that drink with Samson and Victor. The three of us needed to discuss the schedule for tomorrow, what would ship and what would wait.

"How flattering for me," Ben said. "Drive carefully. Or at least keep it below eighty. I've got a half dozen cruisers out tonight on DWI patrol."

"Thanks for the warning. See you there." I put the phone down and headed for the cellar, grabbing my purse, my cellular phone and the shipping manifests on the way.

Victor and Samson were sitting at Samson's desk, their feet propped on the battered surface, wine glasses in their hands. The bottling line sat silent, open cardboard packing cases, foil capsules and broken corks scattered about the floor. Samson had removed the bottles from the worm and placed them back by the sterilizer. The pump looked clean and I assumed they had already drained the lines. A gallon jug of cabernet was sitting on the desk by Samson's left foot and they both had full glasses.

"I was just telling Samson that Roger asked you out," Victor said, grinning.

"Roger is a fool, and she is proof!" Samson said, slapping his feet on the floor and standing. "If I was a young man I would dance you off of your feet!" He bowed at me. "And a privilege it would be!"

"Thank you. Now pour me a glass of wine."

Samson grabbed the bottle and blew into a dusty glass. I guess that passed for washing to a lifelong bachelor.

You two are cutting into our customer's supply," I said, taking the glass from Samson.

"To hell with them! Are they here? No!" Samson took a swallow. "But we will save them a little."

"You're both spending the night," I told them, not asking, but ordering.

"Perhaps I call Marjory and have her drive me home," Samson said, flopping back in his chair and putting his feet up.

"As long as you're not behind the wheel, go where you like," I said. "But spare me the details." I put my glass down on the table, still half full.

"About tomorrow…" I began, riffling through the shipping manifests. Victor groaned and Samson muttered a Greek curse. I ignored them both and got down to business. By the time we were done, a half-bottle more of the wine was gone and an hour had passed. I would have to hurry to meet Ben. I hoped the sheriff's patrols would take a date with Ben as an excuse to speed! Did I say date?

"Well, I'm off. Stay out of trouble, you crazy kids!"

"Where are you going?" Samson asked as he reached for my half-full glass. I told them that I was meeting Ben for a drink. Samson made some nasty comments about our sheriff, but Victor was curiously quiet.

"Drive careful," was all he said as he poured another glass of wine. "And tell Ben I said hello."

"Tell him I said to go to Hell-o," Samson chimed in as he polished off my wine.

I walked to the garage in the sun's fading light. Long shadows crossed the lush green vineyard and draped the rocky slope that falls away into the valley. The trees were inky outlines against the paler sky. The smell of wisteria was a delightful perfume. I couldn't help looking toward the Harlan's as I crossed the yard, and I wished I hadn't. Priest's car was parked out back and a dim, flickering light, which had to be candles, glowed from the living room windows. I shook my head. Here I was married to a rake and I was faithful, but the merry widow was entertaining gentlemen just three days after her husband's murder! Could she be using Priest? Trying to divert suspicion? Could she have killed Kevin herself? Three days ago I would have said no, but now? I wasn't sure. I would have loved to intrude on the lovers right now and give them a piece of my mind. Instead I tossed my bag on Sally's front seat and pushed in the lighter before I started the car. Sally purred to life on the first turn of the key. I took a cigarette out of my bag, lit up and almost shuddered at the first deep inhale.

CHAPTER 18

It took me ten minutes at sixty-five to make it to the dirt turnoff to Shaky's. The place looked the same as I remembered. A paintless gray ruin, every wall, window and door about five inches out of square, porch sagging into the dust, and all of it shaded from the moonlight by hundred year old pecan trees. A garland of Christmas lights (red and green chili peppers) had been strung across the eaves, the only improvement I noticed. A half-dozen farm trucks were parked at a half-dozen angles in the dirt lot, all coated with dust, most of them crew-cabs with extended beds and all the options. Farmers are the worst for buying decked out trucks and farm equipment and then complaining that they 'just ain't gonna make it this year.' Beside the trucks, Ben's shiny-clean county car looked like a gazelle sleeping with rhinos. I parked Sally beside Ben.

The night had turned cool and I didn't have a coat. I shivered as I walked to the screen door. The porch boards squealed and sagged under me, but held up long enough for me to pull the screen door open and step inside.

It was like a time warp. Shaky, balding, stooped, wispy hair a snowy white on top and nicotine yellow at the edges, was at the counter, resting his weight on skinny forearms. Ben was on a stool opposite Shaky, a beer at his lips. A dozen men were seated at the rickety tables I had used thirty years ago. The scarred tops held the graffiti of a half-dozen generations. Most of the men wore jeans or overalls with give-away feed caps on their heads and plastic cups of wine in their hands.

Ben put his beer down and waved me over. I recognized a few of the men sipping wine. Many were friends of my parents, two were friends of mine. I smiled and nodded at the people I knew and got a lot of smiles and nods in return. I thought a couple of those smiles looked knowing, but who can say? Anyway, a little gossip wouldn't do me any harm. Probably get more party invitations. Shaky's patrons went back to their drinks and conversation as I dropped onto the stool beside Ben.

"Claire Falconè," Shaky wheezed with emphysema lungs. "How're ya?"

"Hey, Shaky," I said, so flattered that he remembered me I felt sixteen again. "It's de Montagne, now."

"The names change, but the girl remains the same. Just as beautiful as you were in bell-bottoms and platform shoes," Shaky looked at Ben. "Still keeping lousy company, though."

"I always ran with a rough crowd," I said, grinning along with Ben.

"What'll it be?" Shaky asked, reaching for a dirty rag. He wiped down the counter in front of me. It looked dirtier when he was through. "Got some of

that Violet Vineyard Cabernet back here. My own stock, but what the fu –
excuse me, not used to ladies in here –I'll share it," Shaky winked at me, "But
your boy can stick to beer. He ain't the sophisticated type."

"I'll have a beer, too, thanks," I said, setting my handbag on the counter
and opening it to get my billfold.

"Hey," Ben said, waving a hand, "I'm buying."

"The hell you will!" Shaky shouted, drawing looks from the tables. "A
beautiful girl comes in and you swoop down like a buzzard after a sick calf.
How ya know she isn't here to see me? I'm old, but I got style, something you
lack." He reached below the bar and pulled out a bottle of MGD dripping ice-
water. "On the house."

"If style's what you got, I hope it ain't catching," Ben said and sipped his
beer as Shaky opened my beer and wiped the bottle down with the dirty rag.
Between his and Samson's cleaning techniques I was lucky I'd never come
down with blood poisoning.

"Hey Shaky, another round of the Merlot," a rail-thin old man at the end of
the bar yelled and Shaky drifted that way, shuffling his feet and throwing me
another wink.

"You'll have to excuse Shaky, he's his own best customer," Ben said.

"He's adorable."

Ben snorted. "I remember him running Roger and me out of here with a
broom handle one night after a game with Mendocino High. He put a knot on
my forehead that I still feel on cold days."

"I forgot you and Roger were friends," I said. Those days seemed so hazy
now. It was hard to believe so many years had passed. The bitter-sweet smell
of nostalgia was in the air and I loved it. But that wasn't why I had come here.

"Always a lot of fun, Roger." Ben sipped his beer.

I didn't say anything to that.

"So," I began, "Why do you say Laurel has a thing for cops? Not personal
experience, I hope?"

Ben flushed pink. "Good old Claire, straight to the point," he said, running
his fingers through his already mussed hair. It made him cuter, god help me!" I
don't know how much of this I should tell you. Kind of unethical." Ben sipped
his beer.

"I think I have a right to know. You'd do whatever it took to prove your
own child's innocence."

"If they were innocent," Ben replied mildly. He carefully placed the bottle
back down on the circle of condensation it had created.

I went from warm and fuzzy to angry in a heartbeat, but I tried not to let it
show. I had come here to get information, not to get even.

"You think Jessica did it?"

"Noooo, I'm saying that with de Montagne money Jessica's chances of going to prison are pretty slim. I like you, but it bothers me that the rich can afford better justice than us poor folk."

Now I let my anger show. "I have nothing to do with that, but I won't sit here and say I'm ungrateful. If I thought there was *even a chance* that she was guilty, I would have turned her in myself. But I know my daughter, and she is *not* a killer. She's being framed, from the tennis shoes to the shovel. Someone is using my daughter as a scapegoat."

Ben nodded and half-smiled. "I believe you would turn her in. Same old Claire, tough as leather."

"Keep on saying 'old Claire' and you'll see how tough I am in the parking lot," I said. "So, are you going to tell me what I came here to find out, or are we going to finish our beers and say goodnight?"

"Those the only options?"

"Tonight, they are."

"Well," Ben said, then took a slow sip of his beer. "I wouldn't normally share anything about an investigation, but the way this has been handled irks me. It's an end-run, and that makes me suspicious. Add that to what you say about Doug Priest spending his nights at Laurel's and…well, it stinks."

At the far end of the bar Shaky said something that made two old farmers laugh. One of the farmers shot me an embarrassed glance, blushing, apparently afraid I'd overheard the joke. I was glad I hadn't.

"Understand me, I'm not saying they were wrong to arrest Jessica, just premature," Ben explained. "When you rush, people get hurt that shouldn't."

"Victor told me that Kevin suspected Laurel was sleeping with a cop when Winter was missing. Is that what you meant by she has a thing for cops?"

Ben went rigid. "Not that again," he said, then looked up at me sharply. "What else did Kevin say? Did he accuse anyone?"

"No, he didn't," I replied. "What did you mean 'not that again'?"

The tension left Ben's body. He sighed and looked at me ruefully. "My big fat mouth," he said then half-turned on his stool. "Another beer, Shaky," he called down the bar. Shaky brought it over, glanced at my half-full bottle, then returned to his conversation.

"You remember Hunter Drake?" Ben asked and I shook my head. "He's two or three years older than us, but a Napa native. He was the lead detective on the Winter Harlan abduction." Ben sipped his beer again. "He retired after they caught Buford Logan. Buford confessed to killing Winter and dumping her in the Napa River."

"Was Drake sleeping with Laurel too?"

102

"God, no! Nothing like that. You gotta understand, Laurel was out of her head with grief and Hunt was working eighty hours a week. They were both stressed. Neither of them are bad people. It was just a misunderstanding."

"A misunderstanding about what?" I prompted. Ben blushed and I wondered why. Not for long.

"Laurel said Hunt was harassing her. Sexually. I spoke to him and he blew up. Called her every name in the book. By then he was on suspension for drinking on the job. That's no secret. I took over the case."

"Did you think he was lying?" I asked. I pulled out my cigarettes and lit up.

"No. Hunt's a professional, no bullshitting around with him. But he *was* drinking. I'd like to believe it was just a big misunderstanding. I had to file a report, though, and Hunt took early retirement. His wife dumped him and that was about the end for old Hunt. He took to drinking hard, almost killed himself one night 'bout six months ago out on Mayacamas. Had to cut him out of the car. Not a scratch on him, though. Luck of the lush."

"That's why you said she had a thing for policemen? Sounds like she was trying to get Hunt fired."

Ben rubbed his face with one big hand. "I feel like a damned gossip.

"It goes no farther than me," I assured him. "Just a couple of friends passing the time."

"All right. Hunt told me Laurel was sleeping with a cop. That he confronted Laurel and that's why she made up the charge. Hunt thought Laurel was afraid he would tell Kevin."

"He never did?" I asked, looking around for an ashtray. There was none, so I flicked the ashes into the neck of Ben's empty beer bottle.

"Would you tell a man whose daughter is missing, probably dead, that his wife is fooling around?"

"Probably not."

"Everything was so screwed up that I gave them all the benefit of the doubt. And what if she was sleeping with a police officer? If she was, I bet it had more to do with comfort than sex."

"I bet!" I laughed derisively.

"Seriously," Ben said, stern-faced. "Kevin wasn't talking to anyone. Wouldn't even let Laurel touch him. He couldn't even identify his own daughter! Kept screaming that it wasn't her. Doctor Perry finally had to sedate him. You're a mother, imagine going through all of that. Imagine having to identify your daughter's mutilated body. Mrs. Harlan was distraught. It almost killed her."

"Who was the policeman?" I asked.

"Won't tell you that," Ben said, shaking his head. "I wish I hadn't mentioned it in the first place."

103

"Is he still on the force?" I persisted.

"That either. Like I said, it's all rumor."

"Was it Doug Priest?" He was my number one contender.

Ben went still for a moment. He looked at the bar top as he replied. "It was rumor, Claire. I won't let a good officer be slandered. Not even by you."

"Then it *was* Priest. And he's at it again. And Laurel is using him to frame my daughter. He might ev—"

"Drop it, Claire," Ben said flatly without looking up. "Whatever Priest is doing isn't against the law."

I let it drop - it didn't seem like I had much choice anyway. "On the phone you said that there are other suspects?"

Ben laughed. "God! You just come here to pump me? My charm have nothing to do with it?" He sipped his beer then wiped his damp hands on his pants leg. "Can I have one of those?" he asked, pointing at my cigarettes.

"Sure," I pushed the pack toward him. Shaky came over and I ordered another beer. He set it down while Ben sucked in a lungful of smoke, sighed it out and slouched against the stool's metal back.

"I thought you were gonna kill me this afternoon," Ben laughed.

"I was tempted to hop the curb in my Mustang and put the pony emblem against your backside." I told him. "How many other suspects are there? Kevin didn't seem the sort to make enemies."

"Doesn't mean anything. Pleasant personality often hides a very sick mind."

"Do you know something about Kevin that I don't?" I asked, my interest piqued.

"Just that he had several affairs," he replied evasively.

"That's all?"

"So far. I'm going to check out everything."

"You personally?" I asked. I'd feel a lot better with Priest out of the picture. Or at least in the background.

"Yeah. At this point I better."

"Well, I'm glad to hear you're on our side, anyway," I said. I stubbed out my cigarette and sipped my beer.

"Hold up there, Claire. I'm not on anyone's side. In fact, I feel obligated to tell you that you make the list of suspects. Right below Jessica."

I almost spit beer across the bar. "What?"

Ben was grinning, showing a tiny gap between his two front teeth. Something I hadn't noticed before. Kind of sexy, but maybe that was the two beers talking.

"Priest calls you a potential 'Murdering Mother.' That's his term. He even compared you to that Texas cheerleader's mom. The woman who tried to open a spot on the squad for her daughter by killing another girl's mother?"

"I know who you meant," I said testily. "I don't live under a rock."

"Touchy," Ben smirked.

"I can't believe that jerk is on the force. That *my* tax dollars pay for the car he drives to Laurel's every night." I sputtered. "The man is drunk on his own power and the myth of his charm."

"Thank you, Dr. Laura," Ben chuckled. "A thumbnail sketch of the perfect politician. I'd love to see you tell Priest that to his face."

"Don't think I won't!" I told him.

"One thing I'd never accuse you of is withholding an opinion."

Ben's laughter died in a cough that sounded like his lungs were shredding. He gasped and wheezed as I watched with concern. "Damn cigarettes," he said when he had it under control. He cleared his throat, sipped some beer and went on, red-faced and slightly out of breath. "I need to quit smoking. Priest thinks he could be the next Sheriff. I think he's too young, but other than that he could win. He's got charm, like you said."

"A charm with as much depth as the veneer on motel furniture." I changed the subject. "Is Laurel Harlan a suspect?"

Ben shook a cigarette from my pack and lit up. That would help his cough. "Officially, no. No obvious motive. She'd filed for divorce, but Kevin wasn't contesting it. By all accounts he was relieved it was over."

"Unofficially?" I persisted.

"She's numero uno on my list," Ben admitted. "Spouse always is." He looked at the clock behind the bar. "It's getting late, Claire, and we both have to get up early." I nodded and dropped my cigarettes in my purse. I made no move to leave, sensing that he had something else to say.

"Well," he said, "you've asked a lot of questions—"

"And got very few answers," I inserted with a small smile

He smiled back, but seemed ill at ease.

"Now, I've got a question. When this is over, we still on for lunch?"

I almost laughed out loud. I thought he was about to grill me, but instead he asks for a date. I went through several shades of blush, from flustered-pink to embarrassed-red in ten seconds. My hands went dewy and my heart kicked up. I had felt like this in Shaky's before. With Roger, on our second date. Better not to think of that.

"Of course," I said, putting a hand on Ben's forearm. In Ben's eyes I saw something that frightened and thrilled me—desire. "You're not getting out of it that easily, buster."

Ben grinned and winked at me. "Until then," he said.

105

"Until then."

"Walk you to your car?"

"Sure." I was aware that we were talking in monosyllables, the ease of earlier conversation having evaporated.

We said goodbye to Shaky, and he made me promise to come back soon, a promise that I would be glad to keep. It's not often you get a chance to revisit your past.

We walked in silence to the car and Ben opened the door for me.

"Drive safe," Ben said as he closed the door.

"You too," I told him, cranking down the window. The smell of dust and green fields filled the car. A farmer's sachet. The moon had crested and was dipping toward the mountains, painting the mountains a solid shade of smoky-gray.

"I'll keep you posted," he called. I nodded and started Sally up.

Ben turned out of Shaky's right behind me, his headlights bright in my rearview mirror. I left him when I turned off on to Mayacamas and headed home. I watched him pass my cut-off, waving on the off chance he might be looking.

CHAPTER 19

My headlights cut a bright tunnel along the asphalt road enclosed by trees and weed-choked fences. I kept my speed down to a reasonable sixty-five, ten miles over the limit, worn out and sleepy now that my anger and frustration had been replaced with relief that Ben would make sure the real killer would be caught. And he better do it soon if he wanted a date!

My house was a dark cut-out against the paler black sky. Not a single light was shining. The Harlan home was dark too, except for the dim glow of a nightlight brightening a window on the south side. Priest's car wasn't there. Maybe Laurel went to his place? New anger welled up inside me at the thought of the pair of them together. I was growing more certain that Laurel had murdered her husband and framed my daughter. Who else could have gotten Jessica's shoes? And the shovel? Who but a neighbor had that kind of access to my property and home? And who but Laurel had motive? Then she shakes her ass at Priest and my daughter becomes public enemy number one. Men are such idiots! And Ben had the nerve to get irritated about the de Montagnes throwing their weight around!

I had managed to get myself good and mad by the time I parked Sally in the dilapidated shed I call a garage. I stepped out into utter darkness, cursing myself for not leaving on the rear patio light, but that didn't magically make it come on. I exited the garage, feeling suddenly uneasy. It was too quiet. Living in the mountains I'm used to the quiet of nature, the rustle of animals in the brush, the whir and chirp of insects and the flutter of wings from birds and fruit-bats, but this was an unnatural silence. It was like every animal for a hundred yards was holding its breath. A chill ran up my spine and I stopped dead outside the shed's open door, my heart kicking up to a disco beat.

I peered into the shadows that draped the house and reached long arms into the brighter, moonlit vineyard. The rows of grapes swayed like feathered ghosts in the cool breeze that was draining down the mountain slope into the valley. My eyes panned down the rows and over the sweep of lawn that ended in a ragged-edged drop-off, then beyond that to the mountainside that cascaded down, covered with scrub brush, trees and boulders, to the yellow and white lights scattered across the valley floor. How many nights had I stood in the darkness and drunk in this view like a healing tonic? Now that same view made me cringe in the dark under the eaves of the garage. I tried to laugh it off, to step toward the house, but my feet remained rooted. Something was wrong, I could feel it.

I've always thought that the idea that you can feel someone staring at you is absurd. How can you feel a pair of eyes? Now I wasn't so sure, because that's exactly how I felt. Maybe not exactly. It was more a feeling of not being alone, if that's a feeling at all. The silence reinforced that feeling. The night creatures are only silent when they are disturbed. Maybe the noise from my car had silenced them? But I had cut the engine five minutes ago. By now the sound of insects and rodents should be rising back to its wilderness crescendo.

I let my eyes continue their anxious jitterbug over the barn, the house, the Harlan place, and back to the rows of cabernet. My ears strained so hard for sound that they began to feel hot. Nothing.

The whir and click of insects began to rise again around me. Something scurried down the rocky slope, fast and almost silent. A bobcat? Squirrel? Raccoon? Murderer? I shivered. Was I being paranoid? Had Kevin's murder shaken me so badly that I was frightened to be in my own backyard? You bet! I won't even try to deny it.

Well, I couldn't stand out here forever. Then again, there was no reason to give up caution at this point. The inner argument raged, until the thought came that someone could be sneaking up on me now. If someone was out there, they must have seen me pull into the garage. They would know where I was. That got me going. I was halfway across the lawn, moving at a frightened walk, starting to feel ridiculous, when I heard something behind me. I froze, then turned fast and froze again. A perfect target for a shovel wielding murderer. My eyes fixed on a pocket of shadow at the end of the row where Kevin's body had been found. The spot was fifty feet away so I couldn't make out much. And there's nothing unusual about shadows, but, I thought the sound had come from that direction…and that shadow looked wrong…

"Please, not again," I breathed, as my heart raced. I tried to explain away what I was seeing. Maybe it's just my imagination, I thought. Or something left by the workers? My eyes stayed glued to the shadow as my inner alarm jangled. Nothing moved and I was beginning to feel like a scared kid hiding under the bed. Purposefully, heart thudding, breathing fast, I took two steps toward the shadow.

The shadow moved! A shape rose from the ground like a graveyard specter, a black form on a black background. I gasped a frightened, "Oh!" as the shadow turned to face me.

I could see it was a man, tall and trim with dark hair, but I couldn't make out the features.

"Hey Mrs. de Montagne," he called in a gravelly rumble. He came toward me, walking at a leisurely pace. I stayed frozen, unsure what to do: run, scream for help or yell "Freeze!" But, he wasn't acting like a killer. Still, I held my purse by the strap, ready to use it as a club. One thing was for sure, I wasn't running.

"Who the hell are you, and what are you doing here?" I hollered, trying to sound tough and ready for anything.

"Hunter Drake," he said. "Former deputy sheriff," he added as he came closer. "Why am I here? Well, that's hard to explain."

He stopped about ten feet off, hands jammed into his jean pockets. He was a little over six-feet tall, trim, about my age with sun-browned skin and dark brows over deeply set eyes. He grinned now, a little sheepishly.

"You must be Claire de Montagne," he said. He didn't offer his hand and came no closer.

"You should be more careful, Mr. Drake," I warned, trying to sound stern while curiosity ate away my fear. "People get shot trespassing."

"Sorry about that," he said with a shrug. "I didn't want to wake anyone."

"What are you doing out here?" I asked again, conscious that I was alone with a stranger just thirty feet from the spot where Kevin had been killed. But, as weird as it sounds, I felt no fear. Something about Hunter Drake had struck a calming chord with me. I liked him instantly. Call it woman's intuition. He was really good looking too. I hate to admit it, but that probably had some influence.

Hunter didn't answer directly. "They found Kevin Harlan over there?" he asked, nodding back over his shoulder.

"That's right," I replied.

"You find the body?"

"My foreman did. Victor."

"Pretty bad, huh?" he asked, looking me straight in the eye. He had great eyes, even in the dark.

"Yes," was all I said. All I could say. His question brought the bloody image freshly to mind and I shivered.

"Cold?" Hunter asked and I shook my head. For a moment we stood silently. I cleared my throat and shifted my bag to my shoulder.

"Are you going to tell me what you're doing here?" I asked again and Hunter laughed.

"Like I said, I don't really know. I worked Kevin's daughter's abduction. When I heard he was murdered it got me thinking. So…I came out here."

"Got you thinking what?"

"About coincidences," Hunter said.

"Coincidences? What about them?"

"I don't believe in 'em," he said, looking over his shoulder toward the rows so I could barely hear him. "Two murders in the same family? A year apart?" He shrugged. "Stranger things have happened."

"I have a coincidence for you," I told him. "I was just talking with Ben Stoltze and your name came up. And now you're here."

109

Hunter laughed. "You just made me a believer." He didn't ask me why or how his name had come up. Most people would have. His failure to ask made me curious. He seemed so calm and collected, not the drunken has-been that I imagined from Ben's description. Did I mention he was good looking?

"My daughter was arrested for his murder," I told Hunter.

"She do it?"

"No!" I said indignantly. "Of course not!"

"Did you do it?" He continued.

I stood with my mouth hanging open for a second. "No." I finally said. "I didn't."

"Know who did?" he asked.

"Didn't you say you were retired?"

Hunter laughed. He had a good laugh. "Guess it hasn't took."

"Ben could give you more information than I could. And, he'll probably tell *you* more than he has *me*," I added with a touch of annoyance.

Hunter shook his head. "Wouldn't count on that," he said. "Ben keeps his opinions to himself. More than's good for him."

I didn't say anything to that. I wanted to ask him about Laurel Harlan and the adulterous cop, and about his forced retirement, but what Ben told me was in confidence. If I asked Hunter those types of questions he would know where the information came from and I could end up losing Ben as a source and as a friend. I couldn't take that chance. But the question was burning a hole in my head.

"Feel like coffee?" I asked.

"Got anything stronger?"

"Scotch?" I said uneasily. Hunt had a drinking problem and here I was about to serve him liquor. I didn't see any way of avoiding it without being rude.

"My favorite type of wine," he said, grinning. "Lead the way."

Hunt fell into step beside me and we walked to the kitchen door. I was conscious of his eyes roving over me surreptitiously. I was flattered by it, mainly because I was checking him out too. What was happening to me? No men for almost twenty years and tonight drinks and conversation with two. I opened the door with my key and ushered him in.

Hunter's eyes traveled over the room and his smile grew. "Ya gotta love purple," he said, eyes sparkling as they fell on me and lingered. Blushing, I ditched my bag on the table and went down the hall to the bar.

"Ice?" I called out.

"Straight from the bottle," he called back.

I poured two fingers of Glenlivet into two lowball glasses and carried them back to the kitchen. Hunt was already sitting down, legs crossed at the ankles, one arm hooked around the back of his chair. I put his drink down in front of him and sat facing him.

Hunt took a sip and raised his eyebrows. "When you say scotch, you mean it."

"Glad you like it," I said as I sipped my own. The fiery liquid burned its way down my throat and warmed me up after the chill of the evening air.

"Hits the spot," Hunt said, looking into my eyes again. I held the look for a second before looking away. I could feel a heat in my cheeks that had nothing to do with the scotch.

"Known Ben long?" Hunt asked.

"Forever," I replied. "We went to school together."

"Must have been a few years behind me," Hunter said with a nod. "You good friends?" he asked casually, but his meaning wasn't lost on me.

"Yes," I said a little too slowly and he looked away. He cleared his throat and fumbled in his jacket pocket, producing a pack of cigarettes. He shook one out and put it between his lips before looking at me again.

"Sorry," he said, coloring slightly. He started to tuck the cigarette back in the pack.

"You can smoke," I said, reaching for my purse and taking out my own cigarettes.

"Nicotine and scotch," Hunt said," my kinda woman."

"Pretty skimpy requirements," I said.

Hunter laughed and leaned across the table to light my cigarette. His coat slipped up his arm and I saw a USMC tattoo on his forearm. He flicked the lighter and I leaned in and inhaled. Hunt smelled of cheap, spicy cologne. He leaned back and lit his own cigarette.

"You have dinner with Ben?" he asked.

I shook my head. "Just a beer at Shaky's."

"Shaky's, where if the grease don't kill you the owner's breath might," Hunt commented, flicking ash into a purple bowl I was using as an ashtray.

I laughed.

"Noticed that picture over there," Hunt said, nodding at the window ledge behind the sink. "Harlan's little girl, isn't it?"

"Winter," I said sadly. "Kevin took it."

"Spoke to Kevin a couple weeks ago." Hunt took drag. "Seemed pretty down. I don't think he ever got over losing that child."

"I don't guess he did," I agreed. Much of Kevin's carefree exuberance and lust for life had died with Winter. He had channeled his energy into the vines. "What did you two talk about?"

Hunt looked uncomfortable. He shrugged. "Talked about the case. About Buford and another little girl Kevin thought Buford killed."

"Another little girl?"

Hunter took a drag before replying. "Gotta understand. Kevin couldn't let it go. Saw conspiracies. Not unusual for a man to react like that. Hard to accept the fact that your kid died to satisfy some sicko's lust. That the murder didn't mean more. Didn't mean anything."

"Who was the other little girl?"

"Parental abduction," Hunter said dismissively. "No connection. But Kevin wouldn't let it go."

"He couldn't, I guess. You know he and Laurel were divorcing," I said, hoping to draw more out of Hunter than I had Ben.

"Divorce might've been the best thing for him," Hunter said. "Think Ben's still down at Shaky's? I'd like to talk to him."

"No, he was heading home."

"Guess I could catch him there," Hunter said, downing the last of his scotch in one gulp. He stood, and I was sorry he was leaving so quickly, but I could think of no way of drawing out the conversation.

"Thanks for the drink, Mrs. de Montagne." He said and stuck out his hand. I stood and shook it. His hand was callused and hard from rough work and I could sense the power in his arm. Whatever he was doing since retiring hadn't made him soft.

"Claire," I said. "Anytime."

"Be careful what you say," Hunter said, holding my hand for an extra five-count. "I might take you up on it."

I blushed again. God, I was way out of practice with this!

Hunter let my hand go with what might have been reluctance. But, maybe I was just flattering myself.

He was halfway through the door when he stopped and turned to face me. Back-lit by the moon, his features were in shadows.

"How well do you know Laurel Harlan?" he asked me.

I felt my face set and my body went rigid. A slew of hostile words hammered on the back of my lips, but all I said was, "I think she killed Kevin."

"Bright lady." Hunter winked. "Coincidences."

"You don't believe in them. Are you sure that's all?" I pressed.

"Well," he said, drawing the word out. "I can't really add anything."

"You mean you won't," I crossed my arms and gave him the 'angry female' glare. It works on men, sometimes. Not this time.

"Not 'til I talk to Ben. All I got is a string of speculations. And an active dislike for the woman."

I nodded, too tired to argue. "Talk to Ben," I said. "And then one of you better talk to me. I'm sick of this 'Don't worry about it little missy, let us men handle it' stuff."

112

Hunter laughed. "I'll get back with you. Gives me an excuse to come back," he added and I blushed yet again. I needed to get out more!

"Be careful," I yelled at his back. He disappeared around the corner of the house.

"You too," he called back. I wondered where his car was? I hadn't seen a vehicle parked on the road. He must have pulled off further up, but why?

"Who knows," I said to the darkness. My weariness was becoming bone-deep fatigue. I couldn't think anymore. The only thing I was certain of was Jessica's innocence.

I got dressed for bed, grateful to slip into a ratty T-shirt and frayed pajama bottoms. I washed my face and brushed my teeth, then climbed into bed and closed my eyes. It was just after midnight and I had an early day tomorrow.

Twenty tosses and turns later, I looked at the clock. It was 2:15.

"Why me?" I groaned as I sat up. I felt wired. There was no way I was going to get to sleep. I got up and stuck my feet into my slippers. I was going to be tired and groggy tomorrow, so I might as well get a jumpstart on my day by going through the shipping manifests.

I passed the guest room door on my way to the stairs. Samson was snoring like a freight train with asthma. He had slept through Hunter's visit. So had Victor. My faithful protectors. They were going to pay for their wine-drinking tomorrow.

I flipped on the kitchen lights and got the shipping forms from the table in the tasting room. I turned on a lamp in the living room and sat on the sofa, feet curled under me, manifests in my lap. The answering machine message light was blinking. I had erased the earlier messages before I met Ben, so this was new. I pushed PLAY.

The hissing silence of an open line played for ten seconds before a muffled voice spoke. It was a woman's voice, I could tell that much, but I didn't recognize it.

"Jessica's fingerprints aren't the only ones on the shovel. There are several unidentified fingerprints that aren't Kevin's or your daughter's." That was all, but it made me sit up straight. I pushed play again and listened all the way through, straining for an identity to go with the voice. It still sounded distorted, but there was a glimmer in the back of my mind.

"Midge," I said out loud. "God bless you." It had to be her. I pushed play a third time, listened and was certain. She had taken the risk of being fired to call me.

The phone call was enough to make me forget the manifests. If someone else's prints were on the shovel, that person must be the killer! Or they could belong to a hired laborer who used the shovel a month ago. Still, it shed a little more doubt on Jessica's guilt, and it made me even angrier with Priest. He

113

hadn't mentioned other prints. Was he deliberately keeping information hidden to make sure Jessica took the blame? I could believe it.

I turned over the top manifest and wrote down four names on the back of it; Priest, Kevin, Jessica, and Laurel, then sat staring at them. The next thing I knew, Victor was shaking me awake at 7:15 A.M. and I had a stiff neck.

CHAPTER 20

"Jess is on the phone," Victor said, holding the handset out to me. I hadn't even heard it ringing. Too little sleep for too many nights.

I took the phone. Victor pointed toward the vineyard and whispered, "Get to work." He was bleary-eyed, but he still had enough energy to joke around. I flicked him away.

After a stretch and a groaning yawn that threatened to unhinge my jaw I put the phone to my ear.

"Hey, babe," I said. "How are you?" I stifled another yawn, rubbing at my eyes. "Everything okay?"

"Mom," Jessica whispered. "Can you come and get me? Right now?"

"What's the matter? Why are you whispering?" I asked, immediately dropping into a whisper myself.

"Everybody's asleep. I want to get out before they wake up," Jessica said. "Can you come? Gram is driving me nuts, and Daddy's just as bad. They act like I killed Kevin. Like I'm a nut-case. Can you come?"

"I'm in my PJ's," I said. "Let me get dress—"

"Please!" Jessica cut me off. "You have to hurry. I'll meet you at the gate. Just come!"

My heart went out to her, in part because I had a good idea what kind of misery my mother-in-law was putting Jessica through. The woman was a nagger and a whiner, not a pretty combination. And to even suggest that Jessica might be a murderer! Her own granddaughter!

"I'll be there as fast as I can."

"Thanks, Mom," Jess breathed with relief. "I'll be out front." She hung up and I got up.

I splashed water on my face and ran a toothbrush across my teeth. I didn't look in the mirror. I wasn't in the mood for a horror show this early. I dragged on jeans and T-shirt, grabbed my purse and my keys and headed out, barefoot and groggy. My right foot was still asleep and tingled and stung with every step.

Samson and his crew were at work in the cellar and the clatter of machinery was music to my ears. Stacked cases were sitting under a tarp by the back door ready for pickup. Victor was tilling the first row with a gas tiller, turning over the clover to expose bare earth. I waved at him and he grinned and shook his head.

"Looking good, baby!" He yelled over the roar of the tiller, confirming that I looked awful. He waggled one hand at waist height. "Hot, hot, hot!"

"You're fired!" I yelled back.

115

"No I'm not!" He eased the tiller forward and got back to work.

My foot was still numb when I climbed into Sally and started her up.

I was at Grandma-wolf's house in just under fifteen minutes, breaking every speed limit. From the road I couldn't see the gothic gray monstrosity Roger's grandfather had built eighty years ago, just trees and shrubs and manicured lawns. The driveway disappeared behind a copse of pines. The gates reminded me of all of the monster movies I had seen on TV. And, if I could have seen the house it would have only reinforced that image. Roger de Montagne II had built for ostentation, not beauty.

True to her word, Jessica was standing in front of the massive wrought iron gates that blocked the asphalt drive. She looked like a hitchhiker who had slept by the side of the road last night. She was wearing the same clothes she'd had on yesterday and her hair hung limp around her face. I pulled into the driveway opening, angling myself to make a U-turn, and reached across to pop the door lock for Jessica. She jumped in like we were robbing a bank.

"Drive!" She said, staring up the driveway.

"What's the hurry, babe?" I asked, slipping the gearshift into drive and looking both ways for traffic.

"Grams just called on the intercom and told me to get back inside. We gotta get out of here before she comes down!" As if by magic a black Rolls Royce swept around the pines and sped toward the gates.

"Maybe we should stick around," I said, watching the Rolls approach through narrowed eyes.

"She'll make me stay!" Jessica's eyes shifted from me to the approaching Rolls. "Just drive!"

"She won't make you do anything," I said. "But, okay." I punched the gas, burned rubber in a neat circle and floored it. The tires squealed and Jessica yelled "Mom!" I ignored her. She had asked for speed… We roared down the narrow road, accelerating fast enough to push Jessica back in her seat.

"Mom!" She screamed over the engine's roar, dragging her seatbelt across her chest. "Slow down!"

I immediately let off the gas, grinning like a teenager. "God, I love this car!" I said to Jessica, who had heard that line a million times, usually right after I scared her to death.

"Great for you, but I've had enough drama to last me a lifetime." Jessica had both hands on the dash. "Just take it easy."

"Sorry, babe. Got a little carried away." I grinned at her, watching the rearview. The Rolls Royce didn't exit the gate. 'Good for 'Gram's,' I thought. She probably recognized my car and knew what she was in for. I had threatened to punch her lights out the last time I saw her, and I think she believed me. She better have!

116

"Just take me home. I need to get cleaned up and get to the center," Jessica said, referring to the daycare center where she worked with preschoolers.

"You think that's a good idea?" I asked. "With all the publicity, I mean."

"I called Sister Evelyn last night and told her I was going to take some time off, but I promised to bring my lesson plan and manuals in for my replacement. If they find one, that is," Jessica said. I was touched that she was more concerned for her kids than herself. She hadn't mentioned her arrest, cried or whined. "Could you run me down there later?" she asked as my heart swelled with pride. Jessica always does that to me. Right when I'm ready to wring her neck she'll do something that makes me want to hug her.

"You got it," I said.

Jessica stared dolefully out the window for the rest of the drive home. When we arrived home, we both got showered and dressed and headed into Napa.

CHAPTER 21

Bishop Lynch Daycare was built as a convent in the twenties, but by the time I was a teenager it had been converted into a youth center. I had many fond memories of dance socials and basketball games held within its faded stucco walls. The bathrooms were ancient, the gym floor creaked and sagged under your feet and the halls smelled of chalk dust. In the eighties the building had been renovated by the diocese and rededicated as Bishop Lynch Daycare. The center's main clientele were the children of the working poor who paid a fee based on income. The renovation had been sensitive to the Spanish architecture and the whitewashed porticos and breezeways remained, along with the ancient oaks that shaded the balding grass of the playground.

I parked Sally in the lot behind the playground and Jessica and I crossed to the rear entrance. Swings squeaked and rattled in the warm breeze and dust hung in the air. Recess had ended only recently and I could almost hear the echo of yelling children and the gallop of sneakered feet. Jessica didn't seem to notice her surroundings. Clutching a sheaf of paperwork and three books to her chest, she walked with steady purpose for the rear doors. Her somber mood wiped away my nostalgic musings and my heart welled with love for my daughter, and pain for all she was going though.

Jessica pushed through the metal fire-doors and I followed her down the main hall. The manila-colored walls were covered with garish finger-paintings and childish depictions of perfect families under incredibly bright suns. Behind closed doors, children laughed and chanted the alphabet. Somewhere a class of children was screaming and squeaking through a rendition of "Jesus Wants Me for a Sunbeam." Jessica's stopped and listened for a moment, then turned and grinned at me. "The little boy bellowing 'Sunbeam' over and over is Octavio. He's five going on fifty." She laughed. It was the best sound I had heard all day.

We stopped at a door midway down the hall. A giant smiley face was taped to the window. Jessica hesitated only a moment as the song died on one last chorus of 'Sunbeam!' from Octavio.

"I'll only be a minute, mom."

"I'll be out here enjoying the art," I said, waving at the brightly covered walls. "No hurry." She thanked me with a smile and disappeared inside.

A chorus of children yelled "Miss Jessica!" and the sound of a tiny herd of stampeding cattle reached me before the door swung closed.

I wandered down the hall, getting a smile or two from the paintings along the way. Some were sloppy, others more methodical. A unicorn grazed beneath a picture of Smokey the Bear complete with jeans and yellow hardhat.

118

Two-inch houses were shaded by two-foot tall trees while families of giants held hands beneath suns that looked close enough to touch. I reached the end of the hall and the door to the faculty break-room. An over-stuffed bulletin board was mounted on the wall beside the door.

Announcements of field trips and teacher's vacation days, a lunch menu and a reminder that the daycare's board of supervisors was meeting Friday night, overlapped and partially blocked each other. Older flyers were buried beneath the current announcements as if no one ever cleared away the detritus. For lack of anything else to do I scanned the announcements, reading them with as much enthusiasm as I read the dental hygiene magazines at the dentist's office.

I was flipping back a two-month old announcement for a teacher's potluck supper when the break-room door opened beside me. A thin faced nun with bright gray eyes that matched her gray skirt and jacket looked startled to find me standing there, almost on top of her. Her expression turned to warm welcome faster than any normal human being's should have. It has been my experience that nuns generally fall into two categories, dour and prim or Flying-Nun understudies. The lady before me was definitely an understudy. When she spoke, her voice held a smile as kind as the one that graced her lips, but the way she addressed me was disconcerting.

"Hello, Mrs. de Montagne," she said, extending a boney but tanned and strong hand. "A pleasure to finally meet you. Jessica has told me so much about you. She's very proud of you, you know."

"You must be Sister Evelyn," I replied, amazed that I was able to so quickly drag the name of the center's director out of my sluggish memory bank. But Jessica had mentioned her many times in the past two years, and my daughter's description fit the woman before me perfectly. Beautiful inside and out, is how Jessica had summed her up. "Jessica's told me a lot about you, all of it good."

Sister Evelyn acknowledged the compliment with a dip of her head and a small smile. "I had been hoping to see you," she said, her hand automatically reaching for the rosary around her neck. She fondled the beads, her expression pained. "Jessica phoned and said that the two of you would be down this afternoon to gather her things." Sister Evelyn's smile faltered. "I wanted to talk to you about that. I was hoping you might help me convince her to reconsider my offer."

"Offer?" I said.

"She's concerned about what the parents might think. And, as an administrator here," Sister Eleven touched my arm, "I have to agree with her. As a compromise I asked her to work in the office with me until all of this silliness is cleared up."

I couldn't suppress a huge smile. "That's very generous," I said, "and an incredibly good idea for Jessica." The last thing Jessica or I needed was her hanging around the house. She needed to be occupied and I could think of no better place. "I'll speak to her."

"If you can't talk her into it no one can." Right! 'Not too familiar with mother-daughter relationships, are you sister?' I thought, but kept it to myself. Sister Evelyn looked at the watch on her wrist, a practical black plastic Timex.

"I'm sorry to hurry off, but I'm taking Mrs. Ingram's Arts and Crafts class for her. She's getting married next week and I'm afraid she's not the most organized person. Some crisis with the caterers has arisen," she laughed and shook her head in the best mother-hen fashion. I could see why Jessica liked her so much; the woman positively radiated patience and caring.

She shook my hand and was off in a swirl of gray skirts. "Tell Jessica I expect to see her tomorrow morning at 7:00." She called over her shoulder and I yelled 'okay' back.

Jessica was still in the classroom. I turned back to the bulletin board and my eyes fell on a flyer with the picture of a young girl's face. I could only see half of the girl's picture, but what I could see was hauntingly familiar. Winter, I thought, and lifted the sheaf of menus and circulars to have my suspicion confirmed. MISSING CHILD was printed in block letter across the top of the page. My eyes drifted down to the picture, my heart freshly crushed by a wave of sadness. But, the girl in the photo, who was just as blonde, cute and adorable as Winter, was not the Harlan's little girl. My eyes went back to the text.

The girl's name was Jenna Valdez. She had been abducted just six days before Winter. A white male in a dark van had been seen in the area just minutes before Jenna disappeared. CALL 911 WITH INFORMATION was block printed below the picture. Across the bottom of the page another phone number was hand written in red ink. The parent's number, I assumed, feeling a pity made deeper by the fact that a similar tragedy had touched my own life, though not in so cruel a way. I was so engrossed in the poster that I didn't notice Jessica until she spoke.

"Jenna was such a doll," she said and I dropped the corner of the overlapping flyers and jumped straight out of my loafers. I landed half in my shoes, my heels pressing the backs of my shoes flat.

Jessica looked at me as if I was crazy.

"You scared the hell out of me," I told her as I tried to slide my right foot back into my shoe. The back wasn't springing back up. Jessica watched, starting to grin. I gave up on the shoes, deciding to wear them like sandals. I wedged my toes down into them.

120

"I called your name. Twice. But, they do say that the hearing is the first thing to go," Jessica shook her head. "Then it's the hips." She gave my hips a critical look. "They look okay, but..." she shrugged. "Who knows? Once they start spreading there's no reigning them back in."

"Speak for yourself. I can still dance you into the dirt. In fact, I bet I could chase you down and give your butt a swift kicking."

"In *those* shoes?" she asked, and gusted with fresh laughter.

"This shoe will be lodged in your nether regions if you keep it up," I warned, but I was smiling myself.

"Whatever," she flicked her hair back over her shoulder and hoisted a bundle of books to a more comfortable position against her chest. Her eyes looked fresh and her cheeks were flushed. The visit with her kids had done her good.

I half-turned back to the bulletin board. "I was reading about this poor little girl. I don't remember hearing about it on the news?"

Jessica's expression went serious and sad and I was sorry I had mentioned it.

"The police said Jenna's father, Ricky, had taken Jenna to Mexico. There was a custody battle. Marta was lost without Jenna. She's from Russia, so she had no one to lean on. Marta volunteered here for a while after that, but she always seemed so sad. I haven't seen her in months."

At the name Marta my pulse skipped. Victor had told me that he had seen Kevin with Marta Valdez. Had they been drawn together by the loss of their daughters? I couldn't ask Jessica. I didn't want to bring Kevin up there at the center.

"How awful," I said.

"Ricky called the sheriff's office from some little town on the coast of Mexico. He said Jenna was fine but that was all. That's what Ben told Marta."

I was at least partially relieved to know the girl was with a parent. I felt awful for Marta, but at least Jenna was still alive.

"I got everything," she said. "Want to stop for lunch at Sonic?"

I made a gagging motion, and told her I had to cook for the crew. As we walked to the car my shoes kept sliding around, threatening to pitch me onto my face.

CHAPTER 22

Somehow I managed to get lunch made as the hum of bottling went on below me and Jessica printed shipping labels and called customers. I love to cook, but I felt cheated out of the fun of bottling this small run. How did I become scullery maid? It was Samson's fault. He had conned me into this two weeks ago with the promise of cheap labor from his protégés. The only consolation was that the lasagna was a hit with everyone. But I probably could have thrown a raw side of beef into the back yard and the men would have been just as happy. Even Jessica joined us at the tables for a few minutes and ate just enough pasta to keep a hummingbird from starving. She was an even bigger hit than the food with Samson's young students. She acted like she didn't notice, a quality attractive women have to learn if they want to avoid embarrassment.

Victor ate very little, looking sober and thoughtful. He left a half a plate of lasagna on the table when he went inside to get dressed. Samson wasn't going to the funeral, no surprise there. The wine had to be bottled! I didn't bother trying to talk him in to going. I didn't need the stress. I left him rounding up his pupils, yelling and cursing in Greek. I also left a mess of dirty dishes and open wine bottles. It would have to wait until after the funeral.

I was heading back inside to get changed when Jessica stopped me under the wisteria arbor.

The wisteria was slowly dropping its purple buds, but the air under the arbor was still cloying. Jessica had plucked a bunch of the flowers and was nervously shredding petals as I approached. I stopped beside her and she spoke in a flash flood of nerves.

"I want to go to the funeral. I know I probably shouldn't, but I feel like I should. I can't stand the idea of Laurel standing over him, knowing that she didn't give a damn about him. I want to be there for Kevin, and I don't care what people say."

"I think you should go," I told her simply. I don't know how Jessica expected me to reply, but I could tell my response shocked her.

"Really?"

"You should go, head held high."

She stood there a moment, looking pensive, still destroying the wisteria.

"You better get ready," I prompted her. "I'm leaving in thirty minutes."

"I just need to change clothes and brush my hair," she said, bustling ahead of me.

"Thirty minutes!" I yelled after her.

Miraculously, we all made it downstairs, dressed in black like three penguins far from home, in under thirty minutes. We filed out to my Mustang and headed for the First Methodist Church in downtown Napa.

The First Methodist Church is a classic New England style saltbox with a high gabled roof and a boxy bell tower. A wide green lawn and a dozen old oak trees surround it. Behind the church is a small graveyard, well-tended and as picturesque as anything in Maine or New Hampshire. I parked in the brand new asphalt lot beside the church with a couple of dozen other cars and we went inside.

The minister and Kevin's family sat at the front of the church. Kevin's closed casket was before them on a dais. I saw Claude and Mozel Harlan, but I didn't speak to them. I didn't want to cause a scene, and I had no idea how they might react to Jessica's presence. Better not to find out. Fortunately, or should I say sadly, they were so engrossed in their grief that none of them noticed our arrival. Aunts, uncles and cousins, many of whom I recognized, were clustered around Claude and Mozel, who looked dumbfounded and shriveled. Only Laurel kept her distance, staying close to the minister, hanging on his every word. We came in right behind Linda Perry who was as well dressed and dumpy as ever. Her husband, Dr. Lincoln Perry, ten years younger and looking sharp in Armani, was with her. He smiled and nodded. Linda sniffed and said my name. Neither of them looked at me, but they took in Jessica with grisly fascination. Everyone wanted a glimpse of the murder suspect.

We took seats in the farthest corner, out of the way and almost out of sight. I waved at a few people I knew as they entered the church, and there was a lot of whispering and curious stares directed at Jessica, who kept her chin up and eyes forward. Slow tears streaked her face. I handed her a tissue and she whispered grateful thanks. The church slowly filled and the service began.

The minister, a young man with long hair, a scraggly goatee and tiny eyes, kept his talk short and to the point, offering comfort and hope to the parents, family and friends without alienating anyone or using the service to convert new parishioners. In all, it took just under a half-hour, then we sang "Rock of Ages" in off-key harmony, and everyone filed out.

Jessica, Victor and I waited until the crowd had dispersed before we stepped out the side door and went to the car. I certainly didn't want to turn Kevin's day of mourning into a circus. That would be an insult to his memory and to his parents.

The three of us climbed in the car and I started the engine and turned on the air-conditioner. The day was warm and balmy, without a cloud in the sky. Not the stereotypical funeral gloom. The silence inside the car was as oppressive as the heat while we waited for the air blowing from Sally's vents to turn cold. It takes a while for the old girl to get it going. Victor finally broke the quiet.

"So," he began reluctantly, "should we go to the cemetery?"

I looked at Jessica.

"I don't want to," she said, dabbing at her eyes. "But I will." She looked the question at me then cocked her head to see Victor in the back seat. He shook his head and then shrugged.

"Let's just go home," I said, emotionally and physically drained. I had seen Kevin's body, his head half caved in, dead eyes staring, and I had watched my daughter being arrested for the crime. All I wanted to do was escape. Neither Jessica nor Victor objected, so I assumed we were in agreement. I backed Sally into the street as the members of the funeral procession returned to their cars. We were gone before any of them had started their engines.

CHAPTER 23

All was silent at Violet when we arrived back a little after 4:00. The tables I had set up under the almond trees were still there, littered with refuse and dirty plates, but there wasn't a sign of Samson's protégés. Samson greeted us at the cellar door, his face beaded with sweat, tie askew and splotched with wine, shirt and pants rumpled. He had a glass of wine in his hand and a satisfied smile on his face.

"There is it," he said, pointing to a spot inside the door that I couldn't see. "Violet Vintners' Reserve, the finest wine in the valley, I dare them to say otherwise!"

"Dare who?" Victor asked with the trace of a smile.

"Them," Samson made a broad gesture with his wine glass, taking in the entire valley and parts of San Francisco. "Them!"

"Fantastic," I said. After the funeral, I needed some good news. "You sent the students home with their wine?"

"I sent them home, to drink and to think. They learned much," Samson said. He took a sip of wine and smacked his lips. "Food of the Gods," he said and took another sip.

"I guess UPS made its late pickup?" Jessica asked, edging past Samson and into the cellar.

"They threw it in the back of the van," Samson snorted. "I told the cretin 'be gentle,' but he knows not the word. I load them myself, in the end. But he will take them off the same way! No appreciation." He shook his head and sipped his wine as the sun beat down on the back of my neck.

"Forty cases go out tomorrow, ten more we'll hold for customer pick-up and that's it," Jessica said. "I'm going to go shower and change," she added before disappearing inside.

"Great," I said, imagining the checks rolling in. If I was lucky, they might just cover the bills. I'd have to go over the accounts and plan the budget for the next season, a chore I was dreading. But another chore suddenly intruded in the form of Samson.

"I told the men that we would clean the machines," Samson said with a smirk. "Actually, I told them that *you* would clean the machines. I would help, but tonight I have a date."

"Excuse me?" I said as Samson stepped into the cellar. I followed my foreman inside. Samson went to his chair, grabbed his jacket and shrugged into it.

"You have done nothing else," Samson said, picking up his wineglass and finishing off the cabernet. "I work and you? You do whatever it is you do.

Tonight, you work and I have fun!" He stepped around me and headed for the door, where Victor was leaning against the doorframe.

"Step aside!" Samson warned Victor imperiously.

Victor bowed him through the door. "Try to keep it in your pants. You old guys gotta be careful."

"Victor!" I exclaimed, but Samson cackled.

"Oh," Samson said as he crossed the patio, "I almost forgot. The corker is jammed. I finish the last case by hand. It must be cleared."

I knew what that meant; a sticky mess of wine and splintered cork waiting to be cleaned up.

"Jammed?" I said. "Jammed?" But he was already gone. I turned to Victor. He grinned at me.

"I don't see why you're smiling," I snapped. "You're going to help me clean it up."

Victor pushed himself off the doorframe. "No can do. Got me a date, too."

"Wait a minute. I have to do this all by myself?" I was sickened by the whine in my voice. "That's not fair!" I almost stomped my foot and pitched a fit. Very mature, I know.

Outside I heard Samson's old Jeep rattle to life.

"And that's why you make the big bucks," Victor said as he turned and stepped outside. I followed him as far as the door.

"You're kidding, right?" I begged. He didn't look back.

"Nope." He waved at Samson, who revved his Jeep and peeled off, kicking up gravel.

Victor climbed into his truck. I just looked at him, hands on my hips. "This isn't fair," I said, but nobody was listening.

Victor backed out and was gone. I closed and locked the cellar door and surveyed the shattered corks, foil capsules and wine puddles littering the floor. The stainless steel machines looked grungy and sticky. Open packing cases, foam beads, long streamers of packing tape and a shattered bottle of cabernet made the cellar look like the aftermath of a New Year's Eve party. I groaned, tempted to just lie down and not get up. Instead, I dragged myself upstairs to get undressed and re-dressed in worn out jeans and a T-shirt. To top it all off, I still had the tables and dishes outside to clean up.

"Why do I always get stuck with the mess?"

I swept the floor and blotted up the spilled wine and then trudged upstairs to the kitchen for a quick cup of coffee before starting on the machines. Jessica was out of the shower and was ferrying dirty dishes from the tables outside to the kitchen sink. She came in, laden with lasagna-splattered plates and forks, as I plugged in the coffee maker and reached for my pack of Marlboro Ultralights.

"Lazy," she said as she placed the dishes in the sink in a messy jumble, forks and knives sandwiched between the plates causing the whole stack to sway and lurch. I shrugged and lit my cigarette, settling wearily into a chair.

"And you are a lifesaver," I told her, blowing a plume of smoke at the ceiling.

"That's a really disgusting habit," she added as she stopped beside me and reached for the open pack. "And I think I'll join you, this once." Expertly, she shook out a cigarette and put it to her lips. She lit up and inhaled.

"I didn't know you smoked," I said, trying vainly to hide my disapproval.

Jessica shrugged. "Sometimes. I don't make it a habit. *That's* disgusting."

"I don't smoke that much," I said defensively, puffing away.

"You smoke every day."

"Yes, I do."

"That's called a habit. Psychology 101."

"Thank you, Doctor. For the cleanup help, not the diagnosis."

"You're welcome for both," Jessica said, her head wreathed in smoke. "That was the last of the dishes. I'll rinse them and load the dishwasher."

I glanced at the swaying pile, the dirty pots and pans on the counter. "Probably three loads there."

"Don't remind me."

"Samson and Victor took off, so I've got the machinery and the cellar to clean. I'll probably be at it all night."

"I'll help," Jessica said. She stubbed out her cigarette only a quarter smoked.

"You are my savior," I told her as I went to the coffeepot. I filled my cup and offered Jess some.

"I indulge in one disgusting vice a day, thank you," she said haughtily. "Now, out of the way."

I stepped aside, put creamer in my coffee and sat back down. 'Oh, what the hell,' I thought and shook another cigarette out and lit up.

"Tsk, tsk," Jessica said without turning from the sink. "Such willpower."

I ignored her. Outside the sun was dipping toward the western mountain. It would be dark soon, and I had a lot to do. Not to mention that I was determined to talk to Jessica about Kevin and all the things she had kept from me. I had hopes that the talk would go well, Jessica was in better spirits today than she had been in months. That surprised me, but then again, it was closure to the relationship, final and irrevocable, and maybe that's what she needed.

But, did she need closure bad enough to kill Kevin? The thought slammed into me at a hundred miles an hour and made me shiver. I glanced at my

127

daughter, transferring dishes from the sink to the dishwasher. No way. Jessica was not capable of beating someone to death with a shovel. I would never believe that.

"You did great at the service today," I told her. Her shoulders tensed and she didn't say anything. "It must have been hard for you."

"It wasn't easy," she said without turning. "I'm going to miss him."

"We all will."

Jessica sighed, turned off the water and dried her hands. She sat across from me, took another cigarette and lit it.

"I guess you want to talk about all of that," she said, looking at the table. "It's been over for months. God, it seems like years ago."

"Is that why you've been so depressed?"

Jessica thought about it for a moment then nodded slowly. "That and Stanley. It was weird. Stanley loved me, I loved Kevin and Kevin was with Laurel. Like something out of a cheap romance novel. Every time I saw Stanley I felt guilty. Every time I saw Kevin I felt depressed. And every time I saw Laurel I was pissed. Not good for the self-esteem."

"It must have been awful," I said.

"Worse. But things got better. After I told Stanley about it, confessed, I guess, and told him we were over, it felt like a weight had been lifted. I still cared about Kevin, but I was too emotionally drained to feel much for anyone. And then he was murdered." She stopped there. "I think I'll have some coffee now." She stood and got a cup from the cupboard, a purple cup, of course.

"Is there any Glenlivet on the bar?" she asked, setting her cup on the table.

"You bet. But didn't you say 'One vice a day?'"

"Today is different," she told me over her shoulder. She came back in a moment with the bottle. She poured some scotch in her cup then looked a question at me. I held my half-empty cup out and she added a dollop of scotch.

"That's better," she said after the first sip. Jessica continued. "My feelings were mixed up after that. I had hoped I was over Kevin, but …I don't know, maybe I thought that someday he would come back to me, but after his murder…well, I knew it was really over. And then I started feeling guilty again."

"Guilty? For what?" I asked, afraid she was about to tell me she was involved in Kevin's death. Then Stanley's name popped into my head. Certainly she wouldn't cover up a murder for her abusive ex?

"Jeez, Mom, calm down. I did *not* kill Kevin."

"I didn't think you did."

"I saw the look on your face," she smiled wryly over her cup. "You looked like a cornered rat."

"Such a charmer," I replied dryly.

128

"You know what I meant. I felt guilty because I didn't feel much of anything. Except maybe relief," she added. "And that was worse than anything. The man I loved, or thought I loved, was dead and I'm relieved because I won't have to deal with hurt feelings? What kind of person does that make me? Don't answer that."

"I'd say a normal one. What you felt was absolutely normal. It's like having a terminally ill relative, only you had a relationship on life support. When the relative finally dies, relief is mixed in with the grief. Relief that the worst has happened and you can deal with it and move on. It doesn't mean you loved him any less."

"It doesn't seem like the same thing," Jessica said, "but it makes sense, in a strange way."

"That's me, sensible in a strange way."

Jessica laughed a little sadly. "I guess I'll survive this, but right now I just feel empty. I don't know what I want to do, and with this hanging over me, well…"

"No need to make big decisions right now," I assured her. "After the police come to their senses and drop the charges—"

"Do you really think they will?" She interrupted.

"Yes," I said with more sureness than I felt. "The truth will come out. It always does." If only I could believe that.

"And then, that bitch," Jessica slid her eyes in the direction of the Harlan's, "will get what she deserves."

"Speaking of that," I began, fiddling with my cup so I wouldn't have to meet Jess's eyes. "Did she know about you and Kevin? Before she found the letters?"

"Found?!" Jessica bellowed. "Found? That bitch didn't find them, she stole them! I never sent those letters. They were in my gym bag when it was stolen from my car."

My mouth flopped open with surprise, which probably seems ridiculous. I had no trouble believing Laurel killed her husband, but I was shocked that she had broken into Jessica's car. "You think she broke into your car to get the letters?"

Jessica made a jerky shrug. "I don't know why she stole my bag. She couldn't have known there were letters in it, but how else could she have gotten them?"

I nodded and sipped my coffee, picturing Laurel skulking along the road, bashing in Jessica's window, grabbing the bag and running for it. In my mental picture she was dressed in the same black crepe and heels she had worn to the funeral, not typical burglar attire. It almost made me laugh. I checked myself with a look at my daughter's grim expression.

"My shoes too," Jessica reminded me. "They were in the bag. She must have planted them in the cellar. She knew all along she was going to frame me."

"Revenge," I said, nodding stupidly.

"On both of us," Jessica nodded back. "Me and Kevin."

I got up and poured more coffee. I'd have to call Ben with this little tidbit.

"So, do you think that's why she killed Kevin? Revenge?" That didn't make much sense if she was divorcing him.

Jessica shrugged again, and her expression turned thoughtful. She picked at her nails, chipping off pieces of pale pink gloss.

"I think there was more to it," she said finally. She dropped her hands in her lap and took another sip of coffee. She added more scotch to her cup, filling it to the rim. "Kevin blamed her for Winter."

"Blamed her? That's insane! The woman is rotten, but she loved that little girl. There was nothing she could have done. He had a gun." It felt strange defending Laurel, but I had to keep the facts straight. This wasn't a witch-hunt. I wouldn't let Laurel turn me into that kind of person.

Jessica nodded, "I know, but he did blame her. Not at first, but lately. He hated her, I think."

I tried to make sense of that. Kevin should have been enraged at the animal doing life without parole, not his wife.

"He said she should never have been there," Jessica added.

"It was after the clothing drive at the PAC, wasn't it?" I said.

"Yes. Laurel and charity don't seem to go together, do they?" Jessica asked with an icy edge. "That's what Kevin thought, as irrational as that sounds. He thought she was meeting someone. Another man."

"That's like second-guessing yourself after a car accident."

"You have to understand how much he loved Winter," Jessica said defensively. "He wasn't thinking straight. And he was drinking."

"When did he tell you this?" I asked.

Jessica hugged herself. "The night he was killed. He had hinted at it before, but he was really pissed that night. I'd never seen him like that before. He was drunk."

"How drunk?" I asked.

"He could barely stand. He was leaning on that shovel. He almost fell once," Jessica stared at the tabletop. "I grabbed the shovel and pulled him back up."

"And that's why your prints are on the shovel," I said. She nodded. "Did you tell the police that?"

Jessica shook her head. "Daddy's lawyer told me to keep my mouth shut."

"Makes sense," I said grudgingly. "Still, it might have been better to tell your side of it."

"That's exactly what I thought! But Mr. Fine said 'Don't help them build a case against you.' Like I was guilty! Gram acted the same way. They all did, watching me out of the corners of their eyes like I might snap. That's part of the reason I had to get out of there."

"Part of the reason?" I asked.

"Gram was ragging on you at dinner last night. She said you had 'brought me down to the lowest common denominator'." Jessica didn't look at me as she spoke, but if she had she would have seen my jaw lock. "I told her to shut her mouth and she dropped her wine glass and ordered me to leave the table. Which I was happy to do."

"Tell me about it," I said wryly, proud of my daughter for standing up to her grandmother.

"I had to get away from them. I'd rather be in jail."

We sipped coffee in silence, and Jessica stole another of my cigarettes. I had another one too. The kitchen was filling up with gray smog, so I opened the window over the sink. What I should have done was put the cigarette out. I was smoking way too much. At this rate I'd be up to a pack a day before I knew it. I kept puffing away, the picture of the mature nicotine junkie, as a cool breeze laden with the damp smell of growing things wafted through the window.

"When you left Kevin was he still in the rows?" I asked.

"No. Stanley threw the brick through the window and I ran around front with Kevin staggering behind me. I saw Stanley's truck burning out of the driveway. You were up right after that and Kevin said he was going home. Then the police came."

"So, Kevin was still alive when Stanley came by," I said, thinking out loud. I cocked one hip against the kitchen counter and blew smoke in the direction of the window.

"Yes."

"Did you see Kevin later, after the police left?"

"No, but he must have come back."

I nodded. "With the shovel."

Jessica nodded. "I guess he was still drunk."

"Why was he in our rows?"

Jessica shrugged. "I didn't ask. I saw him walking down the row and I went to him."

My next question was a hard one to ask, but I had to know. "Why did you and Kevin split up?"

131

The life drained from Jessica's face, and I thought she might cry. She brushed at her eyes with her fingertips, shook her head. "I don't know. He wouldn't say anything definite, only that I was too good for him. He was drinking a lot and working too hard, acting a little wired. But..." Jessica petered out.

"But?" I prompted after the silence had lingered for over a minute.

"But I think it was more than that. He was obsessed with Winter. With Buford Logan. He'd get drunk and talk crazy. He talked like Winter was still alive. I couldn't take it, and I told him that he needed help. A therapist. He acted like I had betrayed him."

Jessica was giving a much more intimate picture of what Hunter Drake had already told me about Kevin's obsession with his dead daughter. I was ashamed that I hadn't noticed any of this. Yes, Kevin had seemed subdued, but that was to be expected, right?

"Kevin went through so much," Jessica continued. "And in the end I think it killed him." I couldn't agree more.

Jessica stood, and shook herself. "I can't think about this anymore. Not right now. I think I'll get the tables inside. And finish the dishes."

"And I better get started on the cellar," I groaned. I hip-pushed myself off the counter, ground out my cigarette and slurped the last of my coffee.

"I'll be down to help later," she yelled over her shoulder.

"That'd be wonderful," I said gratefully. "It's a mess."

"And our two male leads have wandered off into the sunset with other women," Jessica added, giving me a grin.

"Male leads in a cartoon maybe. A bad cartoon," I told her with a laugh and went downstairs.

CHAPTER 24

We use an industrial solvent to clean the machines then we go back over everything with mineral spirits and dry it all down. While Jessica did the dishes upstairs, I got out the buckets and sponges and went to work. I unjammed the corking machine first, pulling splintered corks out with my fingernails, picking and tugging at the crumbling stuff. That took me twenty minutes. After that I went to work on the rest of the machines, scrubbing up coagulated puddles and spots of purple. Every nook and cranny of the pump, filler and labeler were splattered with wine. My passion for purple took a serious blow. I never wanted to see purple again. But I go through this every time, probably because Samson and Victor ditch me with the cleaning every time. By the time Jessica came down I was finished with the bottle filler and was halfway done scrubbing the worm, the conveyor that feeds the bottles down the line. She didn't need to be instructed; she had been teenage slave labor, working for a meager allowance. She grabbed the mineral spirits and started wiping down the filler, drying as she went. With her help, a four-hour job became two. We covered the machines in their canvas shrouds and left them there for the men to store at the back of the cellar. They could do that much!

By the time we finished, we were exhausted and sweaty despite the permanent chill of the cellar. We hit the showers.

Dressed in a bathrobe and frayed pajamas I curled up on the living room sofa, an ashtray balanced on my knee. I lit a cigarette and dialed. It was after ten, a little late to call Ben, but I wanted to talk to him while my conversation with Jessica was still fresh in my mind. I had punched in the first four digits when Jessica appeared at the foot of the stairs, dressed for bed in a rumpled T-shirt and shorts. She looked pale, the dark smudges under her eyes the only color.

"I'm going to bed, mom," she said. "Who're you calling?"

"Ben," I said, flushing a little.

Jessica arched an eyebrow. "Momma's got a boyfriend," she said and laughed, a sound I was glad to hear even if it was at my expense. "Kiss him once for me," she said before heading back upstairs.

I finished dialing Ben's number. On the fourth ring, he picked up.

"Ben Stoltze here," he said irritably.

"Hey, Ben. It's Claire," I said, "How's it going?"

"Hey Claire," he said without enthusiasm. The silence stretched before he spoke again. "Not very well."

"What is it?"

133

Ben cleared his throat. "Had a little conversation with the assistant DA handling the Harlan case, Bill Moyers. You might know him, officious little prick in a sweater vest, a drift of dandruff on his collar? I think he was in school about the same time as Jessica."

"No, can't say I do. What's the matter?"

"He's asked me to back off the case. Actually, he ordered me to."

"What?"

"Looks like I'm done being sheriff before the election even happens. Someone complained to Bill about our relationship and mentioned that Roger and I used to pal around in high school. Conflict of interest. Moyers' words."

"Our relationship? What relationship? Friends?"

Ben laughed bitterly. "Friends. Yeah, you could say that. But more than friends, if you get my meaning."

"What a load of..., Ben, you don't have to stand for this! Everyone knows you're honest. Who the hell does—"

"Let it go, Claire," Ben cut me off. "It's done and it doesn't matter. In three months I'll resign anyway. They can have the whole shooting match."

"You sound like you don't even care," I said, getting angry. "This isn't the Ben Stoltze I know."

"Nope," Ben said and laughed sardonically. "This is a *tired* Ben Stoltze that just wants to be left alone."

"Is that last remark directed at me?"

"Not a bit of it," Ben began, trying to be conciliatory. "You know you're a good friend. But I think it's best if we don't see each other right now. I have three months left and I want to keep my reputation intact. I've worked too hard to retire under a cloud."

"What about Jessica?" I asked, growing hotter by the second. "Without your help Priest will railroad her right into prison." I had been counting on Ben.

"I didn't say I was going to drop out of the case, did I? I said Moyers *ordered* me to. I don't take orders too well. I'm talking about appearances."

"So, what are you going to do?"

"Well, I'm going to keep asking questions and reading the reports that Priest files. I'll keep my distance and not crowd anyone, for your sake more than my own. The private detectives Roger hired are stirring up a real mess. Lawsuits've been threatened and mud has been flung, which doesn't help Jessica in the long run."

"That might not be enough," I said testily. "I called to give you some information. I talked to Jessica tonight and she told me some things."

"She didn't say much at the interrogation," Ben said. "She wouldn't tell them a thing."

134

"Maybe because Priest's a jerk. She told me that the letters Laurel gave Priest were stolen from her car. She told me that Kevin was obsessed with his daughter's murder and that he blamed Laurel and –"

"Hold on a second, Claire. Let me get a pen and something to write on." I heard him shuffling around. "Okay, fire away."

Quickly I ran down all that Jessica had told me, adding what I knew about Marta Valdez and Kevin spending time together.

Ben didn't seem too impressed. "I'll need to pass this on to Doug Priest," he said when I finished. "But I have to do it in a way that keeps you out of it."

"Why do you have to tell *him* anything?"

"He's the lead detective. If I know something that's pertinent I have to share it. That's how it is," Ben explained, annoyance creeping into his voice.

"I could call him," I offered.

"That's not a good idea," Ben said. "Just leave it to me. I can handle Doug. My advice is to stay away from him and Laurel Harlan."

"I guess you're right," I sighed. "I just don't want to be left out of the loop. Jessica's arrest really blindsided me."

"I swear I'll keep you posted. I can't tell you everything, of course. That *would* be a conflict of interest, but I'll do what I can."

"Thanks for your help, Ben," I gave in. But I wasn't giving up.

"You're welcome. If you hear anything else, if Jessica tells you anything else, pass it along to me immediately. Okay?"

"You got it," I told him, then changed the subject. "So, are we still on for lunch? After this is over, of course."

"Not trying to worm out of it, are ya?" Ben asked with a chuckle. "Cause, I ain't gonna let ya. Burgers and fries on me at Shaky's, as soon as possible."

"Oh, big spender," I teased, feeling way too girlish for fifty.

Ben laughed. "I've got four kids, two of them in college. You're lucky I didn't say tuna fish sandwiches at my place."

"Shaky's will be great," I told him. "Be looking forward to it."

"Me too. Good night, Claire," Ben said.

"'Night, Ben," I replied and hung up.

I smoked another cigarette, thinking about Ben. Thoughts that I won't share. But there was concern as well. Ben had been ordered to back off. No matter what he said, that wasn't good for Jessica. She'd be left at the mercy of Priest, more or less. My natural inclination to meddle had me wondering what I could do to spur things on. Three more cigarettes and I still hadn't thought of anything clever. Miss Marple I'm not. I went to bed, my mind occupied with thoughts of murder and the adorably rumpled, ex-football-hero sheriff.

CHAPTER 25

I got to sleep late again. And once again I was up early, awakened by the sound of rain pounding the roof and wind whipping the eaves. I worried about the vines. This much rain wasn't good for them. Samson came in late and grouchy, eyes bloodshot. He grumbled something about Marjory's drinking and headed downstairs to nurse his hangover. Or for a little 'hair-of-the-dog,' more likely. Jessica stayed in her room until early afternoon, then borrowed my battered old vineyard van to go to her grandmother's, rolling her eyes and whining the whole time. Jessica's MG was in the shop, but then it always is. It's a pretty piece of junk her father bought her at age sixteen, and she refuses to get rid of it. Wonder where she got that trait, I thought wryly.

Forced to stay inside by the rain, I handled the FedEx driver and talked to three old clients who wanted cases of the Reserve. I didn't have the cases to spare, but I managed to squeeze a few bottles out of my personal stash. It hurt, but it made them happy.

The rain kept coming but the temperature stayed in the mid-fifties. I lit a fire in the kitchen fireplace and kept it going all afternoon as I went through the accounts, leafed through a vintner's catalogue and scrubbed the floors and counters. Anything to stay busy and keep my mind occupied. It didn't work. My brain was twisted too tightly around Kevin's murder and my daughter's arrest. I wanted to do something, and the inactivity was driving me nuts!

The sun poked through only once or twice during the day, usually right before a fresh downpour. The Valley was shrouded in a ghost-river of mist and my vines hung heavy and wet as the greedy earth sucked up the rain. At 6:00 Samson said goodbye. He was his usually crabby self, bitching about the FedEx driver. He left, still muttering, telling me he'd see me at Marjory's party tomorrow - a party I had completely forgotten about. And I had to go. Marjory would kill me if I didn't.

Victor came in moments after Samson left.

He was dressed in black jeans and a black T-shirt, his hair slicked back and tied with a green, white and red band. He was speckled with rain and smelled of cologne.

"Didn't expect to see you today," I said as he ducked inside. "You look like you're going out on a date?"

"Just came back from one." He waggled his eyebrows and winked. "But don't ask for details, I don't kiss and tell."

"Thank God for small favors," I said, placing a freshly scrubbed pot on a dishtowel to dry. "Coffee or a drink?"

"Tell me what's wrong first," Victor said, drawing a chair back from the table, looking intently at me.

With a sigh, and a shake of the head, I pushed up the window over the sink and lit a cigarette. A gust of cold wind flowed into the cozy room and I heard the rattle of tree limbs thrashing in the breeze. The rain had stopped.

"I am kind of down," I admitted. As I smoked, I told Victor about Ben being told to back off and my belief that Priest was trying to frame Jessica at Laurel's behest. Victor nodded throughout, of course.

"You know what you need?" Victor asked, trying valiantly to be lighthearted. "A break. I came by to see if you wanted to get a drink. I figured you'd be bored crazy by now, what with the rain and all. And it seems I've arrived just in time to rescue you from yourself."

"I'm not really dressed for a rescue," I said, glancing at my jeans and the blue button-down shirt I was wearing untucked. "But, what the hell." I grabbed my keys and locked up.

Rain was dripping from the eaves, but the clouds were clearing. The moon was a thin sliver hovering over the mountains, casting only a sallow light.

"Where do you want to go?" Victor asked as we climbed into Sally. "I was thinking San Cito's over in Calistoga?"

"I was thinking of anywhere else," I said. "The crowd at San Cito's is kind of young for me. And loud."

"You're only as old as you feel," Victor said with a grin as I backed out the driveway and turned down Mayacamas.

"Then I must be a hundred."

"You do need a drink. Where're we going?"

"San Cito's," I gave in. "Smart-ass."

San Cito's was alive with Disco retreads, smoke, and flirting yuppies. Victor looked over the women while I had three cups of coffee with Baileys. It was impossible to talk, and I got bored pretty quick. By the time we left, just after midnight, I had a pounding headache, Victor had been shot down by three women and I had been hit on once, so we were both in a bad mood. To top it off, the rain had started again in the form of a depressing drizzle. I wove back to Highway 29 and headed north with the windshield wipers whapping. We made good time until we reached the outskirts of St. Helena and turned up the Silverado Trail. Brake lights stretched for a half of a mile up the usually lightly-traveled road, ending in a confusion of flashing lights that I guessed were police cars and fire trucks.

I waited as patiently as I could, despite Victor's annoying habit of changing the radio station every five seconds. He finally stopped on a hard rock station and I vetoed it by snapping the radio off.

137

"Hey! That's a good song!"

"It's noise pollution. If you can find something we can agree on, I'll turn it back on."

"The music you listen to puts me to sleep," Victor groused, playing with the latch on the glove box. "What's goin' on up there? Shove the damn thing out of the way already!" We were close enough to see a crumpled white van tangled in the guardrail, its front end suspended over a hundred-foot drop-off into a dark and craggy ravine. Whoever was in the van got lucky. If it wasn't for the guardrail wrapped under the chassis and around the rear wheels it would have toppled over the edge and ended in a fireball at the bottom of the ravine. The van was illuminated by the flashing strobes of a trio of police cars, an ambulance and a fire truck. A few cars had pulled to the shoulder, their drivers standing around talking as a policeman waved traffic through. Two attendants were loading someone into the ambulance. The ambulance's siren yipped twice and the policeman held up his palm to stop traffic. I hit the brake just in time to avoid crashing into the minivan in front of me.

Victor groaned as the ambulance crept into the lane ahead of us. I took the time to rubberneck the wreck, feeling guilty, but unable to resist. The van had purple lettering on the side, but I was having trouble making out the words in the dark. The ambulance's headlights flared across it and the words came clear.

"Oh my God!" I shrieked and Victor jumped. "That's my van!"

"What?" Victor said, then yelled "Hey!" and grabbed the dash as I lurched out of traffic, slipping between two police cars, jarring us to a stop facing the van, my headlights lighting up the wreck. The van looked as if it had been hit by a train. The chassis was buckled. Torn and ripped metal gleamed dully, but I didn't care about the van! My only thoughts were for my daughter. I was out of the car and running across the wet asphalt before what I had said hit Victor. He jumped out of the car a split second before I was blindsided by a beefy Sheriff's deputy cloaked in a yellow rain slicker. He hooked an arm around my waist, pirouetted me through a complete circle and set me back down like I was a little girl.

"Hold up, lady," he ordered then plucked me up again when I tried to dodge around him. He had me around the waist, my back pressed to his massive chest. I kicked and squirmed, my eyes glued on the wreck, picturing Jessica bloody and broken behind the wheel. No one was going to stop me from going to the van!

"Let me go!" I wailed. "Let me go!" I snapped an elbow back at his face. The impact sent pain rocketing up my arm and the deputy staggered, but he didn't let go.

"Stop it!" he bellowed in my ear. "Hold still! Damn it! Stop that!"

138

Victor ran up. "That's her van," he panted. "Her daughter was driving it."

"She's okay lady!" the policeman yelled in my ear. "She's alive. They took her to County." He put my feet on the ground but didn't loosen his grip until I stopped struggling. He put one hand to his lips. It came away bloody. "Damn it. I'm bleeding."

"She's okay?" I panted, feeling weak in the knees. I was soaked to the skin by the cold drizzle. I shivered. "Are you sure? How can you be sure? How?" I was talking fast, the shivers turning to shakes. Victor put his arm around my shoulders.

"She was talking when they put her in the ambulance," the policeman barked. "Christ, this hurts." He wiped blood off his chin. His lip was split.

"Sorry," I said, my eyes returning to the wreck. "I've got to go." I broke away from Victor and sprinted to my car. Victor's boots slapped the pavement right behind me. I was opening the driver's door when he caught up.

"Other side," he ordered, stepping between the car and me. "I'm driving."

I didn't argue. I dove past him and slid across the seat. "Then drive!"

Victor burned rubber backing up, fishtailed around and pointed Sally toward the valley. The policeman watched us go, shaking his head, gingerly touching his lip.

Victor made me proud. He ran every light, and got us to the hospital as they were wheeling Jessica into the emergency room. I leapt out before the car had come to a stop and ran to my daughter's side.

Her eyes found mine as I reached the gurney. I grabbed her hand and asked if she was okay.

"I think my arm's broken," she said, her voice tight with pain. Her left arm was splinted and her face was bruised. Her right cheek was already turning a sick green-yellow. A thin gash dripped blood from her forehead and another marred her jaw.

"Out of the way," the EMS Technician pushing the cart said curtly. "She's gotta go straight to X-ray. The nurses at the desk will talk to you."

"You're really okay?" I asked Jessica, keeping pace with the gurney.

"I'm fine," she said. "Don't worry." I touched her face and they wheeled her through the door.

"She okay?" Victor trotted up behind me.

"She's okay," I said and he hugged me fiercely. His heart was pounding. I patted his back and he let go fast, obviously embarrassed.

"Where they taking her?"

"X-rays."

Victor followed me inside where we were intercepted by a young Asian nurse with a peroxide blonde ponytail and sad brown eyes. She couldn't have been over four-foot-six.

"Ma'am?" she said. "Are you with the girl who just arrived?"

"Yes, we are."

"Could you come with me? I'm sorry, but I have some paperwork," she told us with an apologetic smile. 'Some' was an understatement. By the time I finished signing my name to a hundred documents Jessica was in an observation room on the second floor talking to the same policeman who had tackled me at the wreck. He touched his swollen lip and grinned when Victor and I stepped into the room. He was a good-looking young man in a corn-fed German way. Ruddy and blond, big square hands and feet. The kind of man you liked immediately.

"Got a wicked elbow, Mrs. de Montagne. Oughta take you in for assault."

"I'm *so* sorry," I started, prepared to grovel. He waved the apology off.

"Got two kids of my own. God help anyone that came between me and them. I'm just about finished with Jessica."

Jessica was lying under crisp white sheets, her jaw and forehead bandaged, her left arm in a cast. She looked like the worst end of a fistfight. She smiled weakly. "Hi mom, Victor. Sorry 'bout the van," She said in a cottony-thick voice. Her pupils were huge, and she could barely keep her eyes open. They must have given her something for the pain.

"Don't worry about the van, I'm just glad you're okay."

"Y'all can have a seat, nothing top secret here," the policeman told Victor and me, nodding at two plastic chairs. He turned back to Jessica.

"So, you didn't see the truck up close, but you're sure it was a truck?"

"I'm sure," Jessica nodded. "It came flying up behin' me. Thought she was gonna pass, but she just stayed on my bumper. Scary."

"I'm sure it was," the policeman said patiently. "And then it rammed you?"

"What?!" I said, scooting up to the edge of the chair. "A truck rammed you?"

"Ma'am," the policeman shot me a warning then turned back to my daughter. "How long was he tailgating you?"

"Few minutes. Hours. I slowed down, but she wouldn't pass. I sped up, but she did too."

"And then she rammed you? When the other truck was coming?"

"'S right. She rammed me and pushed me. Righ' at the truck! Then Bam! And I don't remember…"

"Okay, did she hit you once or several times?" the policeman asked while I listened, teeth clenched.

"Severa'," Jessica said, blinking more lethargically. She yawned, and winced. She closed her eyes.

"And then she shoved you at the diesel?"

"Lights 'n my face. Blinded me, then I hit the guardrail."

140

"I notice you keep saying 'she.' Did you get a good look at her? Do you know the person?"

"Didn't see her real good," Jessica said thickly. "But it was Michelle Lawford."

"Michelle Lawford?" I yelped and the deputy shot me a warning look as he jotted down the name. My heart jumped in my chest. Laurel's dogs-body had tried to kill my daughter!? Rage followed close on the heels of shock and disbelief. My hands knotted up and blood throbbed in my temples. I'd kill her! I'd kill them both!

"Why do you think this Lawford tried to run you off the road?"

"She called me," Jessica said. "Asked me to meet her. Talk about Kevin."

The deputy looked confused.

"Kevin Harlan," I said and the deputy dutifully wrote the name down.

"Guy that was murdered?" he said, eyes on me.

I nodded.

"You're sure it was this Michelle?" The deputy asked my daughter.

She shrugged without opening her eyes. "Think so."

"We'll check it out. You're lucky to be alive," he said, folding his pad and pocketing it.

"Don' feel lucky." Jessica said, eyes still closed. "Don'." She snuffled and then snored.

"What was she talking about?" I demanded of the policeman. "She was deliberately run off the road?"

"Yep. Don't know about this Michelle, but I got the same story from the trucker that almost creamed her. He saw a red farm truck on the van's tail. Says it shoved her right in front of him. Lucky they were on that steep grade. Trucker had cut his speed or he'd have plowed right over her."

"Did anyone get the farm truck's license plate?"

He shook his head. "No such luck. Trucker said it was a washed out red. Road rage's is what I figured. Happens all the time."

I didn't argue with him about that. He probably knew very little about the Harlan case, so the names would mean nothing to him. They'd mean something to Ben.

"Sorry about your lip," I told him, smiling sheepishly.

"Not a worry," he said. He touched it and winced.

"Be glad she didn't have her feet on the ground," Victor said, standing to shake the policeman's hand. "She'd probably have taken out a tooth or two."

"Got one a little loose, matter of fact," the policeman said, touching a canine with one blunt finger.

"I am so sorr—"

141

He waved it off again. "See you folks. I'll call when we find out something." He left us alone with Jessica's snoring.

"Road rage," Victor said. "Bullshit."

I sat back down and looked at my daughter. Jail and the hospital all in a matter of days. My poor baby.

A half hour later, a balding young doctor in tennis shoes poked his head in the door. He assured me that Jessica would be fine, and advised Victor and I to head home for the night. I didn't want to go, but Victor needed a ride back to his truck. I kissed Jessica's damp forehead, clicked off the room's light and left my daughter in her drugged sleep.

Later, after Victor went home, when I was lying alone in my bed listening apprehensively to all my home's groans and squeaks, I thought how convenient it would be for Laurel if my daughter was no longer alive to defend herself against the murder charge. I looked at the clock, thinking of calling Ben. It was far too late, or too early, depending on whether you had been to sleep that night. I settled back into the pillows and stared at the ceiling. My daughter could now be dead and Laurel would be off scot-free.

Sweet dreams, indeed.

CHAPTER 26

I called Ben first thing in the morning, got his voicemail and left a two-minute message that was reasonably coherent, detailing last night's events. I dressed quickly, grabbed my purse and cigarettes and was at the hospital before Jessica had slept off the drugs.

Eyes closed, draped in hospital white, she looked wan and insubstantial. Her cheeks were bloodless, the left bruised badly and turning seven different colors of purple. Her lips and eyes were puffy, even her hair looked listless and sad. I spoke with her doctor in hushed voices as she dozed. He told me that after a quick exam she could go home that morning. He handed me two prescriptions and hustled off on his rounds.

"Hey mom," Jessica said weakly.

"You okay, babe?" I asked as I stroked her hair.

"Fine," she croaked. "Water?" she licked her dry lips. I poured her a glass, and helped her sit up to drink it.

"Better," she said, pushing the glass away. She grimaced as she put her cast in her lap and looked at it. "That hurts."

"The doctor said you can leave after he checks you over," I told her. "Let me go to the nurse's station and see if they can track him down."

I found the doctor at the nurse's station, chatting with a young candy-striper with a stuffed bra and too much makeup. He was mildly annoyed at my interruption, but he followed me back to the room and pronounced Jessica fit to leave. We waited a half hour for a nurse to come with a wheelchair, while Jessica groused about not needing one. By the time we finally got into the car and were heading back to Violet, Jessica was grouchy and in pain and my nerves were wearing thin. But I made her tell me what she remembered from the night before anyway.

"It was Michelle," Jessica said. "I caught a glimpse of her. I couldn't swear it in court, but I'm sure. She tried to kill me. God, I'm so tired."

"It's the medication and the stress," I said. "Mainly the stress. It pumps so much adrenaline into your blood it just burns yo—" Jessica's snores cut me off. Guess I had gotten all I was going to. I turned on the radio to NPR. Two commentators were discussing the highest grape prices in years and speculating on what effect that would have on the valley.

"More money, more people," I muttered under my breath. Simple as that.

I got Jessica to bed then made a half dozen trips to and from her room for magazines, ice-water and extra pillows. None of which Jessica wanted or needed. She pointed out that her arm was broken, not her legs.

"Don't you have anything better to do?" she groaned when I poked my head in her bedroom door for the fourth time. She was tucked under her covers staring at the ceiling.

"Not really," I said brightly, fluffing her pillows. "Do you need anything?"

"Peace and quiet," she said. "Isn't Marjory's party today?"

"I was going to skip that." I wasn't going to leave my daughter alone. Someone had tried to kill her the day before, they might try again. With more success. I explained that to Jessica and she rolled her eyes.

"No one's going to come in here with a gun," she said. "Be serious." Actually, I felt pretty confident that Laurel wasn't that stupid. But I wasn't sure enough to take a chance.

"I am being serious," I said. "You were almost killed and Kevin *was* killed. I think I should call your father and get his detectives to protect you for a while." The police weren't going to do anything, that was for sure.

She shot up straight in bed. "Don't you dare! They'd take me to Gram's. I'd rather be at the bottom of that gorge. I'd rather be shot! I'll call Daddy and tell him about the accident, but not about Michelle."

"Jessica—"

"Don't 'Jessica' me," she snapped. "I'm twenty-three years old, I'll make my own decisions." She dropped back on the bed and stared at the ceiling.

"Well, I think I'll stay anyway," I said firmly.

"To stay here and pester me?"

"Well, I don't look at it as pestering…" I smoothed the blanket and brushed hair off her forehead.

"That's what it is," Jessica said, turning her eyes back to the ceiling. "Victor called on my cell a few minutes ago. He's coming over this afternoon. I'll ask him to hang out with me."

"Jessica—"

She hurried on, cutting me short. "It's a beautiful day, mom," she said, turning her gaze to the window. "At least as far as I can see."

She was right, Marjory had gotten lucky. The clouds of the day before were a memory. Outside, the sun was shining down on sprouting fields and blooming vines. A perfect day for an outdoor soiree. I crossed to the window and looked out. The first thing I saw was the Harlan home. I had to bite back the flare of rage. But I couldn't prove Laurel had anything to do with Jessica's wreck. I'd have to bide my time until the police caught Michelle Lawford. Or until I did myself!

"Either go to the party," Jessica ordered, "or stay out of my room. You're driving me nuts."

"You'll call me if you need me?"

"Yes," she groaned. "Go!"

"All right," I said, smoothing her blankets one last time. She kicked them off into a tangled mess on the floor.

"Mom! Please!"

"Well, call me on my cell if you need anything."

"I will. Now go! Have fun!" She closed her eyes and I closed the door.

Ben still hadn't called. I tried him again, but didn't leave another message. Feeling annoyed, wanting to cross the yard and beat the hell out of my neighbor, I went down to the cellar to check on Samson, dreading telling him about Jessica.

CHAPTER 27

Samson was in the cellar wearing a new tie and a slightly less rumpled suit than usual. The tie was shiny yellow and the suit was a sooty gray with a less than subtle red stripe. A green tweed fedora sat on his desk, quite the topper for his ensemble. Somehow I kept from laughing. I didn't tell Samson about Michelle Lawford, only that Jessica had had a wreck last night. I didn't need his ranting today. Besides, he was in good spirits, wanting to begin planning our trip to the French tasting events in the fall. Last year, I had promised that we would attend the most important tasting in the world and he was determined that I not forget. Still, the news about Jessica made him furious.

"And you did not call me, why?!" he asked then launched into a sputtering diatribe in a word-stew of Greek and English about bad drivers before I could reply. He had the certainty of a father that 'his' Jessica could not be at fault. He reminded me that Jessica drove carefully, "not with racecar foolishness, like you, de Montagne." We'd had this conversation before. He gave me the evil bug-eye as my own eyes did a lazy roll toward heaven. Why me?

I cut Samson off when he wound down to cursing humanity in general. I tried to break away, but he merely changed subjects back to the French tasting trip. He waved two brochures, both showing impossibly cheap motor-court hotels located on the outskirts of Paris. Samson is always trying to squeeze the pennies. But when we got there he'd bitch nonstop about the lousy accommodations.

"Decisions must be made, de Montagne!" he yelled at my back as I walked upstairs. At that moment, the only decision I was worried about was what to wear to Marjory's party. I wished Ben would call with some good news. I was starting to suspect that he was avoiding me. If I didn't hear from him soon, I'd take what I knew to the private detectives Roger had hired.

I changed into a summer dress, tried to fix my hair, then gave up and put on a straw hat with a pink band. Samson was still looking at brochures and dreaming about Paris. I dragged him out to his Jeep, shoved a dozen back issues of Wine Spectator off the seat and climbed in beside him. I was worried that he'd pester me to death about Paris, but all he wanted to talk about was Marjory.

"She is such the lady, de Montagne. In everything she does," he beamed at me, taking his eyes off the road for far too long. I white knuckled the edge of my seat.

"Watch the road, Samson."

"Yes," he said testily. "The road." He was silent ten whole seconds then smiled dreamily.

"She is so like a girl," he gushed. "Shy and sweet." I had to wonder if we were talking about the same Marjory? Shy? Sweet? Overbearing and malicious was more apt. And those were her good qualities!

"She's a wonderful lady," I agreed. "And you're very lucky." This comment made him slip into a fugue, and I wondered just how close he and Marjory had become.

"Like a fine wine," he said and I tried not to gag. Thankfully the drive was short. We turned through a rustic wooden arch and drove up the oak-shaded drive. Marjory's vineyard almost encircled the house and winery. The freshly tilled and flowering rows of Chardonnay stretched across thirty acres of sensuously rolling hills like green silk ribbons.

The stone-flagged parking area in front of the long one-story building that was Marjory's 'Mayacamas Vineyards' was half-filled with Mercedes, Lexuses, Lincolns and Jaguars. Valets in red jackets rushed back and forth as people disembarked. Samson bypassed the valet station, drove slowly across the parking area and ramming the Jeep's bumper into a rhododendron shrub loaded with pink flowers. Petals showered down on the hood as we climbed out.

Samson waved off a chubby teenager in a tight red valet jacket who was heading our way.

"I parked it myself," he yelled and the kid skidded to a stop. Samson turned to me. "They can't be trusted," he said.

I looked at the battered, mud-splattered Jeep. "Wouldn't want it to get scratched," I said.

"Scratched? Don't be foolish." He shot a look at the teenager and then whispered to me, "They steal, De Montagne. You should know this. They copy your keys and rob your house!"

I let that go without comment as we crossed the grass toward the house.

A huge white tent had been erected on the lawn beside Marjory's grand home, which had been built in a rustic mega-mountain cabin style. People were sipping cocktails while waiters circulated with trays of appetizers. A string quartet (blech!) was playing classical music. I spotted Marjory under the tent, supervising a dozen waiters who were awkwardly shuffling tables around to make a dance-floor. A stack of six-foot by six-foot hardwood squares stood ready to be fitted together for the purpose. Glittering silver and glassware cascaded to the grass with a crash as one of the waiters stumbled and let go of his side of a table. Marjory threw her hands in the air and started cursing. Samson was right, Marjory was as delicate as a butterfly. If there's a poisonous species of butterfly, that is.

"I need a drink," Samson said, a wary eye on Marjory.

147

"And I'll see if your girlfriend needs any help," I told him as he snagged a waiter and jammed a crab-puff in his mouth.

"'Ell her I b' 'ere in minute," he mouthed around the crab-puff. Classy.

"Claire!" Marjory bellowed as I stepped into the shade of the tent. *"Help!"* She grabbed my hand.

"What's the matter?"

"Everything! The caterer is behind schedule and the bartenders haven't shown up. And they forgot to assemble the dance-floor," she cast a malignant eye on the clumsy waiter who was scrambling around picking up silverware and glasses.

"Why don't you get a drink and talk to Samson," I told her. "I'll get this cleaned up. And I'll get the dance floor put together." And then you and I are going to talk about Michelle Lawford, I thought to myself. I couldn't believe that I had given Michelle a good recommendation!

"I knew there was a reason I loved you!" she yelped. "A drink!" she charged off toward Samson, who watched her approach like a startled deer. She stopped halfway to him and yelled back at me. "Is Jessica all right? I heard about her accident. Poor dear."

"She's fine," I called back.

Kneeling beside the blushing waiter, who couldn't have been more than sixteen, I helped him load a plastic tub with the litter from the grass. I saw Marjory pulling Samson into the house like a cat with a field mouse. He caught my eye and threw up a hand like a drowning man. I waved back, smiling maliciously, and kept picking up silver.

We got the dance-floor situation under control, and I procured myself a glass of Marjory's excellent 2008 Zinfandel, which was growing fruitier and mellower with age. The wine was a little hearty for so early in the day on an empty stomach, so I ate crab-puffs and boiled shrimp to compensate. I mingled with friends and acquaintances. None of them mentioned Jessica's problems with the law, but small talk seemed to wilt in their mouths and they took the first opportunity to bolt. And after I turned my back the whispers flowed as freely as the wine. I couldn't help but catch snatches of conversations.

"A de Montagne in prison? We'll never live to see the day. Her father—"

"…I bet she did it. I heard she had an affair with that Harlan boy—"

"...too pretty for the gas chamber—"

"…all that money—"

I began to wish that I hadn't come, but I smiled brightly and had another glass of wine as the band played and people kept arriving. Marjory was back outside and making the rounds with Samson, who looked proud as a rooster and just a little bit drunk. I tried to mingle, but my heart wasn't in it. I got in a brief but heated argument with Glen Dearborne about the new federal subsidy

148

program. Or, as Glen called it, welfare for farmers. He accused me of being a 'liberal wimpus' whatever that was, then spotted some more conservative friends and dumped me after placing an order for a case of the new Reserve.

Linda Tate, her half-drunk husband Dave in tow, skirted me like I was a typhus victim. Dave threw me a kiss that earned him a few whispered threats. I smiled and waved at Dave, which got me an ugly look from Linda. To hell with Linda.

I needed a lift, so when the band struck up a string version of Wilson Picket's 'Mustang Sally' I ditched my wineglass on an empty table and made a beeline across the lawn to where Samson was arguing with Marjory.

"It is not a wine!" Samson sputtered, one hand squeezing the life out of a glass of red zinfandel. "It is soda pop! Kool-Aid!"

"White zinfandel sells, sweetheart," Marjory cooed, leaning in close. She stumbled and bumped in to Samson, slopping wine across her hand. She licked it off, giving Samson a look that would have made a hooker blush.

"So does cow manure! Will you taste it? White zinfandel is leavings! Left over from a far better red wine! Excrement!" The first white zinfandel was actually the juice from the last pressing of zinfandel grapes fermented without the skins.

"But people like it," Marjory said, leaning in to peck Samson's withered cheek. Samson tried to dodge, but Marjory grabbed on and held him still. She had fifty pounds on my old wine maker.

"People like Big Macs and chicken fingers! Those people have no palate. None!" Samson leaned back as far as he could, but Marjory managed to place a slurping kiss on his chin. "I would pour it out for the dogs before I wasted a barrel on it!"

The band was halfway through the opening chords of the song, so I had no time to waste. I was determined to alleviate my mood, and Samson was going to help whether he liked it or not.

"I'm borrowing him," I told Marjory as I grabbed Samson's wrist and dragged him away.

"As long as you bring him back!" Marjory laughed. "And don't wear him out, I have plans for that old stud!" She winked at me and I tried not to vomit.

"I do not dance, de Montagne," Samson tried to dig in his heels, but I kept pulling.

"You mean you *can't* dance," I corrected, "But you will try. Or we're planting zinfandel and fermenting it without the skins."

"You are sick in the head, de Montagne," Samson muttered, but he quit fighting. He's really not a bad dancer, just a little old fashioned. Ball room manners seem out of date and out of place these days. But I wanted to dance!

149

We reached the dance floor under its billowing white tent and I tugged Samson onto the floor. He stood erect, one hand on my hip, the other clasping my hand, and led me gracefully across the floor, hopelessly out of step with the song. Even on violin and flute, Mustang Sally was a bit up-tempo for Samson. All around us people were shaking their butts and waving their arms while we floated around like the Queen Mary at half-speed.

"This rock and roll," Samson sniffed. "It is undignified. They are dancing like chimps in the circus."

"Hush," I told him. "I love this song."

"You would," he said under his breath. "I am done dancing."

"White Zinfandel," I sang and laughed, enjoying myself for the first time that night. "Or, maybe white Grenache!"

"White Grenache," Samson spat. "That name sounds like a disease."

"Hush," I told him again and, surprisingly, he did.

The song ended and Samson let me go, already looking around for Marjory. Suddenly his eyes bugged and blood rushed to his face.

"What is she doing here? Why has she come?!" I followed his gaze to find Laurel Harlan at the edge of the dance floor talking to Linda Tate. The widow was dressed in black silk from head to toe, a half-veil descending from her pillbox hat. She looked like she had just stepped out of the wardrobe department of MGM where she had been outfitted with the Grieving Widow #1.

"She was not invited!" Samson bellowed and took a step in Laurel's direction. I tried to grab him, but he shrugged me off. I trotted across the dance floor after him, my sandals clacking on the squares of hardwood. I caught up with him just as Laurel looked our way. Linda Tate looked too, and an ugly smile brought life to her pasty face. She whispered something to Laurel and the widow laughed and nodded, her gaze never leaving Samson and me.

It was too late to turn away. I would not shrink from this woman, would not shy away. I linked arms with Samson, keeping him on the side farthest from Laurel, and kept walking.

"Is this a bail-raising party?" Laurel asked Linda, staring me dead in the eye. Linda laughed a shrill, wine-induced bray. The last time I had spoken to Linda, at the Ladies Lunch, she had been bashing Laurel Harlan, and here she was sucking up. But, Linda probably liked me even less than she liked Laurel. That was fine. I despised the pair of them.

"It is not a wake, either," Samson said nastily, trying to veer around me. I banged him with my hip and tightened my grip on his arm. "A widow should mourn, not dance!" I kept moving, passing them without a glance. I would not make a scene at Marjory's party. But seeing Laurel Harlan had my blood boiling.

Laurel threw her head back and laughed. By now, everyone within earshot was looking our way and all I wanted to do was get far from the widow before I lost control of Samson or myself.

"I think Marjory's been feeding your date too much Viagra," Laurel said and took a sip of wine. Linda thought that was hilarious. Maybe I'd punch her instead.

"Marjory is twice the lady as you!" Samson tried to break away, but I kept dragging him. "Twice and more!"

"Measured by weight," Linda said and the pair laughed. Thank God Marjory didn't hear that or Linda might be missing some teeth.

"A pair of crows," Samson spat at the floor. "Crows!" I pulled Samson back to Marjory. He was sputtering and cursing, and steam was about to come out of my ears. Marjory was mystified, but I was too angry to enlighten her.

"Calm him down," I told her and walked away, feeling every eye on me. I held my head proudly. I had nothing to be ashamed of. I walked around the house to the rear patio and lit a cigarette. Laurel's day would come, I'd see to that!

The small rear patio opened on a vista of head-trained grape rows, the aisles brilliant green with mustard plants past flowering stage. The dark, ropy rootstock were covered in new growth flowers and leaves, perfectly pruned and arranged. Marjory ran a tight ship, and made some of the Valley's finest wines. Beyond the rows, the Mayacamas thrust its jagged edge into the twilight sky. Streaks of white could still be seen on the higher slopes where winter never completely gives up. I sipped the earthy Zinfandel and tried to enjoy the view, letting my eyes drift over the landscape as I wondered how early I could politely leave. It had been a mistake coming with Samson, who would probably stay the night if Marjory let him. But, I hadn't imagined Laurel would come to the party or I would have driven myself here and thus ensured my escape. I stubbed out my cigarette, thought about rejoining the party, then lit another one. That's when I saw the truck.

It was parked in the shade of a row of almond trees that separated the flatland vineyard planted with Chardonnay from the undulating hills planted with Zinfandel. The truck was a sun-washed red with white lettering on its door. The front end was half caved in, the headlights smashed, grill jutting out in broken strips. I dropped my cigarette and walked up the rows for a closer look.

The faint smell of mustard rose up from green stalks that rubbed my ankles. The setting sun was warm on my back and birds called from the almond trees. But I barely noticed any of that. All I saw were the streaks of off-white paint that marred the crumpled bumper and fenders of the red truck. The same off-white color of my van.

I reached the truck and circled it to inspect the damage. White paint and bare metal gleamed back at me, surrounded by dusty red. The damage was very recent, the metal rust-free. A flattened trail of grass led to the truck from a dirt track that bisected the rows. The truck was a write-off, but the damage to it was nothing compared to my van. This was the truck that had run Jessica off the road, I was certain. How many red farm trucks could have been wrecked in the last two days? And if it was the truck, that proved that Michelle Lawford was the driver. At least to me. Marjory had been desperate to hire a new foreman. She must have hired Michelle, based on my recommendation! I needed to call Ben and let him know about this. And there was no time like the present.

Taking my cell phone from my purse, I called the sheriff's office and asked for Ben. He was actually in his office!

"Hello, Claire," Ben said tiredly. "Been meaning to call you back. What's going on?"

"Sorry to bother you," I talked as I walked back to the rear patio, explaining about the wrecked truck and its connection to Michelle Lawford. "I think Laurel put Michelle up to it." I looked uphill at the truck. "I think she might even have killed Kevin for Laurel." I added as the thought hit me. But, maybe Laurel did it herself.

Ben hadn't interrupted while I spoke, but he did now and he sounded irritated. "Well, all I can tell you is that Mrs. Harlan called me wanting a restraining order against Michelle. She claims Michelle is stalking her. So you can put a conspiracy right out of your mind. We've arrested Michelle three times for assault. I admit they were all barroom bullshit arrests, but she has a capacity for violence and she's as nutty as a Snickers."

"But the truck—" I said, getting annoyed and discouraged. If Ben didn't believe me where else could I turn?

"Claire," Ben abruptly cut me off. "I'm not saying Michelle didn't run Jessica off the road. Hell, I wouldn't put it past her. But, if she did, she did it on her own, for her own twisted reasons. Mrs. Harlan says she had an unhealthy fixation on Kevin."

"I never saw that," I said testily. And I had worked with the pair, pitching in or asking for help when another pair of hands was needed. Michele had issues, no doubt, but she didn't seem crazy to me. "What does Michelle say?"

"Nothing. We haven't been able to track her down," Ben snapped. "But when I do I'm gonna—" he stopped and took a deep breath. "I'm sorry, I'm a little wired right now. DA's got me jumping through hoops. Roger's private detectives are looking through our files. I'll be glad to pack it in at the end of the year. On top of that, there's this girl who I want to take out and she barely knows I exist," he laughed, but it sounded forced.

This remark seemed inappropriate to the circumstances, but I was flattered anyway. It didn't make me less annoyed. "She knows you exist, believe me," I told him. "And she's flattered. But while this is hanging over my head I can't think of anything else."

"You and me both. He sighed. "Tell you what, I'll send Midge out there to look the truck over. Shouldn't be a half-hour."

I thought immediately of Marjory and her guests. Police cars and questions would be a definite party-ender. Marjory would never forgive me.

"Can it wait until tomorrow?" I asked, then explained about the party.

"Tomorrow morning, then," Ben said. "And quit thinking about Michelle and Laurel. Trust me to do my job and to make sure everyone else does theirs."

"Okay," I lied. If Ben wouldn't follow up my leads, I'd do it myself. What can I say, sitting back and waiting isn't my style. "Talk to you soon."

Ben hung up and I sat there, my butt getting cold and sore from the stone flags, thinking about him. I wished he was doing more, but I couldn't fault him for following his own instincts. 'After this is over,' I promised myself, 'I'm cooking that man dinner.'

"What are you doing out here?" Marjory startled me.

"Marjory!" I jumped six-inches, twisting around so fast I wrenched my back. "Don't sneak up on me like that!"

She had a glass of wine in her hand and a knowing look on her face. "Who were you talking to that you needed so much privacy? A man, I hope?"

"Ben Stoltze," I said, stowing my phone.

"Ooh la la!" Marjory chortled. I could tell she was on her fourth or fifth glass of wine. She was swaying and sloshing. "Our ruggedly handsome sheriff."

"And where is the ruggedly handsome Samson?" I replied.

"Bathroom," she waved toward the house. "Saw you sitting here and figured it was because that bitch was out there acting like Jackie O."

"Laurel?"

"Who else? She cries on demand and sucks up sympathy like a dying plant. I wish I had never invited the Harlans, but how was I to know she'd kill Kevin before the party? And Kevin was so sweet."

"Yes, he was," I agreed, my eyes wandering back to the wrecked truck. "Someone have an accident?" I asked off-handedly.

"Damned lesbian!" Marjory sloshed wine over the patio railing. She was definitely tipsy. "Michelle, my *former* vineyard foreman. She came in this morning telling me it was stolen, wrecked, and returned! Right!" She eyed the truck, pupils like ice picks. "I let her drive it and she wrecks it then lies about it. And lies badly, to boot. On her first day!" She raised an eyebrow at me. "I won't even remind you that *you* were the one who recommended her."

153

"Thanks," I said sarcastically. Marjory shrugged magnanimously.

"When did it happen?" I asked.

"Last night. Fired her this morning."

"The police are looking for her," I told Marjory. I stood and brushed off the back of my dress.

"The police?" Marjory asked, so I told her what I suspected about Michelle. I finished and added, "Ben's sending someone out tomorrow to take fingerprints and look the truck over."

"You really think Michelle tried to kill Jessica?" Marjory asked and took a swallow of wine. Her eyes above the rim of the glass had that gossip-mongering gleam. I didn't care.

"At Laurel's instigation. When the police come tomorrow we'll know for sure."

"Watch what you say, Claire," A woman's low voice came from behind us. Marjory slopped wine across the stone flags as we both spun around.

Laurel, wearing a viper's smile, crossed the patio toward us, spike-heels clicking. In the black outfit with her pale skin and dark eyes she looked positively vampiric.

"Spreading slander could get you sued," she said, raking her eyes over me, smirking. "Your daughter's a liar. And a murderer."

I set my wineglass on the railing. Here was my chance to give Laurel the beating she deserved. Unfortunately, that would only make things harder on my daughter.

Laurel continued, eyeing me sadly. "I'm not the one out on bail. I'm not the one sleeping with other people's husbands. I'm—"

"A murderer," I finished.

"And a low-class whore," Marjory added.

Laurel's eyes flashed on Marjory. "Marjory, Marjory, jolly, old Marjory," she said with a sad shake of the head. "We all screw for a purpose. Some just look better doing it." The widow turned her attention to me as Marjory went three shades of red.

I'm surprised you'd even show your face around this crowd," she said. "All your so-called friends whispering behind your back. Twisting the knife with malicious glee." She smiled and raised her wineglass in a taunting toast. "Of course, that's exactly why I came."

"I'm surprised you have the gall to wear black. You'd look so much better in prison gray," I replied.

Laurel laughed good-naturedly. "Sweet old Claire, never a harsh—" she began, and that's when Marjory punched her in the face.

Laurel never saw it coming. And neither did I. One moment she was talking and the next she was spinning away and falling into an untidy black pile.

Marjory took a swallow of wine, as she frowned at a small cut on her right hand.

"That felt good," she said and took another swallow. "Gonna leave a mark, though."

Laurel sat up. "I'm calling the police," she said thick-tongued. Her lip was split and already puffy.

"Call them from somewhere else, dear," Marjory told her. "You're dripping blood on my patio. I'm afraid I'm going to have to ask you to leave."

"What is this?" Samson came around the corner, stopped and stared at Laurel. "What is this? What has happened?" he directed his question at me, but Marjory answered.

"Laurel is leaving, Samson. Could you be a dear and ask the security guard out front to escort her?"

"Security?" Samson looked uncertain.

Laurel struggled to her feet. "Don't bother. I'm leaving. But you haven't heard the last of this, fatso," she stomped across the patio to the rear door, gingerly touching her bloody face. She slammed the French door behind her hard enough to rattle glass.

"What is this about?" Samson asked again, twenty decibels louder. "Tell me now."

"Marjory decked Laurel," I said. "About five seconds before I was going to."

"Get me another drink, lover," Marjory trilled. "And an icepack for my hand."

I got an icepack from the caterer and rejoined the party, where Marjory busily circulated the story, embellishing it with every retelling. I took the first opportunity to slip away. It didn't do me much good. On every side were those who wanted to hear the story for the first time or retell it to those who hadn't heard it yet.

When dinner was served, I took a seat with Samson and Marjory, who was rehashing the single-punch fistfight for the tenth time, brandishing her bandaged knuckles for emphasis. I rolled my eyes and ordered another glass of wine.

"And tomorrow," Marjory gloated, "the police will come and find out that Michelle was the one driving that truck, the one she used to try to kill poor Jessica de Montagne."

"We don't know that for sure—" I tried to be diplomatic, mainly to shut Marjory up, but Marjory waved me off.

"Oh, she did it, and the fingerprints will prove it!"

I gave up and let her babble.

155

The food was excellent. I had a filet of sole with a buttery sauce and baby carrots and a piece of strawberry pie for desert. By the time the dishes were cleared and the first couples hit the dance floor, dusk had shrouded the valley. Party lights popped on and torches were lit. Everyone was drinking and having a great time. Even I was feeling festive, re-visualizing Marjory decking Laurel. I only wished I had done it myself!

"Fireworks! Fireworks!" Marjory yelled as she wove through the crowd, a wineglass in one hand, towing Samson with the other. "Everyone move to the rear lawn! Fireworks!"

En masse, people rose and followed the queen and her jester around the house where the darkness was broken only by pale squares of yellow splashing across the grass from the house's windows. People laughed and chattered quietly, like the audience at a play before the curtain rises.

Whoosh! A red light streaked from the ground trailing sparks. It exploded in a cloud of yellow steamers. A blue one followed and then a series of white rockets that turned into violet spirals as they descended. The vineyard was splashed with red, blue and green, a kaleidoscope of color that stuttered and faded at first but then congealed into one bright light as more fireworks flew. All around me people clapped, oohed and aahed, craning their necks.

The show lasted for ten minutes, growing in intensity until the sky was filled with colored streaks and falling ash. All around me faces were turned toward the heavens, captains of industry and businesswomen as rapt as any child. The show ended in a blizzard of yellow sparks and flowering red fireworks. The crowd applauded wildly as the last light faded from the sky.

"Is wonderful!" Samson breathed wine fumes in my face. "Incredible!" His eyes were red rimmed. He was drunk. "I have never seen—so wonderful!"

"Samson!" Marjory yelled in my ear. "I wondered where you got off to. Let's get everyone back to the tent. The night is young!"

"Show's over!" she yelled at the crowd, and directly into my right ear. "Everyone back to the tent! Show's over! Show's ov—"

Kawumph! An explosion five times more powerful than any of the fireworks shook the ground, lit up the vineyard like the sun and threw the wrecked red truck twenty feet in the air. It flipped over twice and flopped down into the Chardonnay vines, a ball of fire that immediately set the twisted old vines ablaze. Someone screamed and then everyone was screaming and people were running for cover. Only Marjory, Samson and I stayed stock still, watching her vineyard go up in flames.

The fire department arrived in time to save most of the Chardonnay, but the hoses dragged through the vines and the huge amount of water pumped onto the flames had done their damage. There would be no crop from those vines this year. Maybe not for years to come.

Marjory wouldn't leave the back patio. She sat and watched her vines burn then flood, tears of rage and grief in her eyes. She spoke to no one except Samson, and then only in monosyllables. When the flames were out and the last of the guests had departed, I pulled Samson aside.

My cellar foreman didn't take his eyes off Marjory as he told me he would be staying the night, just to keep an eye on Marjory. He gave me his keys. Any other night I would have stayed as well, but I had Jessica to think about. I kissed Marjory's cheek and she squeezed my hand hard enough to break my fingers.

"Michelle," she said through her teeth. "She did this! Her and that bitch Laurel!" I tried to calm her down, but it was a losing battle. I finally left her and headed home.

I didn't tell her that I thought she was right, but I would definitely tell Ben. Laurel was the only one who knew the police were interested in the truck. She must have called Michelle Lawford and 'Kaboom!' no more evidence.

CHAPTER 28

Jessica was awake when I got home, in her room reading. Victor was on the living room sofa, sound asleep. Some protection! I didn't wake him, just tossed a blanket over him and climbed the stairs. Jessica brightened considerably when I detailed Marjory punching Laurel's lights out, but she dimmed again when I told her about the exploding truck and the ruined vines. She agreed with me and Marjory that Laurel must be involved. It was the only logical conclusion.

"So all of her Chardonnay was destroyed?"

"Seven to ten acres, burned, trampled and doused, so…" I shrugged. Poor Marjory.

"I feel like it's my fault," Jessica pulled a pillow across her chest and tucked her chin in it. "I know it's not, but I can't help it. If I had never loved Kevin—" her eyes swelled with tears.

"That's not true, Jessica," I told her, though I was feeling guilty myself. Marjory had defended me and what had it gotten her? But Jessica and I weren't to blame. "Blame Laurel and Michelle."

Jessica nodded into her pillow, but the tears kept rolling. I kissed her forehead goodnight and crawled into my own bed. The last thing I remember was a replay of Marjory punching Laurel. I fell asleep smiling.

Samson called at six the next morning, waking me from a fitful sleep. He told me he was going to spend the day with Marjory looking over the decimated vines.

"There will be no crop this year," he said. "The ground is waterlogged and the vines are wilting. Heat and flood." Heat and too much water are the enemies of any good winemaker.

"Want me to bring your Jeep to you?" I asked, wiping sleep from my eyes.

"You will pick me up later?"

"Whenever you say. Just give me a call. How's Marjory?"

"Sleeping. She took a pill of some kind. Maybe she sleeps for a long time," he sounded like he hoped so. "I tell her men to clean up the burnt wood and the ashes. If she sleeps two hours, it will look much better."

"Give her my love," I told him. "If she needs me, call me."

"I will."

Samson rang off and I climbed in the shower. Clean and dressed, I went downstairs, made coffee and toast and drank the coffee as I smoked and watched the toast grow cold. At 7:00 A.M. I called Ben at home. He answered grumpily on the fourth ring.

158

"Hullo?"

"Hey Ben, it's Claire. Catch you sleeping?"

"Caught me in the shower," he said, his tone lightening. "How's it going? I heard about the fire last night. What happened?"

Briefly, I told him about Marjory and Laurel's confrontation and the truck's explosion. "She's the only one who knew that you were going to have the truck examined today."

"That's a theory," Ben said carefully. "But she wasn't the only one that knew. I knew about the truck. Midge knew about the truck, hell, half a dozen people up here did. Someone could have said something that got back to whoever blew the truck up. And, don't forget, I already told you about Laurel and Michelle. The restraining order?"

"You don't believe it's possible?" I wasn't buying the restraining order a bit; I had seen Laurel talking to Michelle just two days ago.

"Like I said, it's a theory. Sure wrap up a lot of loose ends. I'll pass it along to Priest. And we're still trying to track down Michelle. Personally, I think she could have killed Kevin. She has a thing for Mrs. Harlan. Not a great leap of the imagination to picture Michelle killing Kevin, probably thinking she was helping Laurel. We'll get her, though."

"No leads on Michelle?" Ben seemed almost as determined as Priest to explain away Laurel's possible involvement. But he was just trying to be fair, like a good sheriff. Priest could take some lessons.

"Nothing. Got an eye on her house and everyone in the county is looking for her. Wish I had more to go on, I'd like to get inside her house and poke around. Need a warrant for that. She'll turn up, though. The crazy ones always do."

"I'm sure she will," I said, my thoughts drifting.

"What are you thinking?" Ben asked warily. "I've told you before, Claire, to let me do my job. Just stay by the house and keep your eyes open until Michelle's in jail. I'll send a car by once in a while to check on you."

"In case Michelle decides to finish the job on Jessica?"

"Exactly. Keep an eye on your daughter and I'll keep you posted."

"All right," I lied.

"Gotta go," Ben said and we exchanged good-byes.

I finished my coffee, grabbed a set of hand clippers and went into the vineyard.

Most of the mist had burned off the valley below. The sun was up, and it was promising to be another warm day. Victor waved at me from the top of the tractor. He was mowing the field beside the vineyard. I waved back then strolled the aisles, looking over the green shoots jutting out from the withered-looking black canes selected at last year's pruning. I clipped here, adjusted

159

canes there and generally did nothing that really needed to be done as my mind restlessly rewound the events of the last week. I was thankful that Ben agreed that Michelle was probably involved in Kevin's murder and the attempt on Jessica. But I didn't think she'd done it alone. Laurel had stolen Jessica's love letters to Kevin and given them to the police. Why would she do that if she weren't involved in the murders? There was no good reason.

I looked over at the Harlan's barn. It was dead quiet. Laurel's car was parked out front, but there was no one in sight. No work had been done on the new vines since Kevin's murder and they looked shaggy. His older vines needed a trim as well, and grass was sprouting in the aisles. It's amazing how quickly man's accomplishments can be devoured by nature.

CHAPTER 29

I ate lunch in the kitchen with Victor, who was full of questions about the party at Marjory's. I told the story for the third time and then took Jessica a plate while Victor returned to the tractor. Jessica didn't eat much but that was no surprise. She looked better, though.

I called Marjory at 2:00. It took a while before she came to the phone, but when she did she sounded surprisingly chipper. I asked her about the vines and her mood dipped. Three or four acres would be a total write-off, but Marjory has seventy-five acres under vines so it wasn't going to bankrupt her. When she got on the subject of Samson, I swear I could sense her glowing right through the phone.

"Claire, I've got to tell you how wonderful Samson is. He's really cracking the whip over here," she gushed. "I'm gonna steal that man away from you!" I felt a little trill of jealousy, and then disgust with myself. Samson deserved to be happy, and he could do a lot worse than Marjory. Right?

"I thought you might not be talking to me," I told her. "I feel like it was my fault."

"What?! We both know whose fault it was, and I told your Detective Priest this morning. That bitch Harlan."

"Priest was there this morning? What did he want?"

"To talk about Michelle, or Mike the Dyke, as he called her. Tacky little man, but sexy in a freaky way."

I made a retching noise. "Sexy as the bubonic plague. What did he ask about Michelle?"

"Work habits, attitude. I didn't know much. Name and address, a couple of references."

"Could you give me her address?" I asked on a sudden whim.

"Sure, but why?" I could hear Marjory shuffling paper. "I *had* it right here. Oh, there it is. I was using it as a coaster. Orange juice, my dear, with just a trace of vodka." She laughed shrilly and I wondered how many 'orange juices' she had already downed.

"Just curiosity," I lied.

"Ha! I know you Claire, you're up to something. Just promise me all the juicy details?"

"Promise."

She read off the address and I jotted it down on my purple pad then asked when I should pick up Samson. Marjory laughed, yelled "Never!" and slammed down the phone. I was smiling when I returned to the rows with my pruning shears.

Jessica didn't want dinner, and Victor had another date, so I was stuck on my own. I did laundry and dusted and vacuumed. And every time I walked through the kitchen my eyes fell on Michelle's address. I knew what I wanted to do, but fought it. 'Trust in Ben,' I told myself. But I'm not good at trusting men. Finally, I picked up the pad. The address was in American Canyon, a twenty-minute drive away.

"What the hell," I said to myself. I climbed the stairs to Jessica's room. She was awake, listening to the radio and writing in her journal.

"Hey babe," I called as I pushed open her door.

"Hey Mom," she replied without looking up.

"I've got to go out for a while," I told her as I straightened the coverlet.

"Please, leave that alone," she said, still writing. "You're reminding me of why I had perfect attendance all the way through high school. I couldn't stand the way you fussed over me if I stayed home sick."

"Ah, a daughter's love, all I could hope for," I said with a roll of the eyes. "I'm going to arm the alarm before I leave. If you hear anything, call the police or Ben Stoltze. I scratched Ben's home number on a pad beside her phone. "Got it?"

"Got it," she said. I kissed the top of her head, locked up and went to my car.

The sun was dipping and the valley below was already sliding into the gloom, but the green and gold hills were brightly lit and as soaked in color as an impressionist painting. I tore my eyes away, started Sally and headed for American Canyon.

American Canyon would be just another suburb in most parts of California, but in Napa it has all the cachet of a slum. That's just snobbery, really. There are some very nice areas in American Canyon. Unfortunately, Michelle didn't live in one of those. The house she shared with two other vineyard workers was in a neighborhood of clapboard ranch-houses with orange asphalt shingles and tiny yards that backed onto a concrete drainage canal. The home had been painted white about a hundred years ago, but had turned a dingy gray streaked with orange from the cheap shingles. The front yard hadn't been mowed or watered in years and was choked with foot-tall weeds and crabgrass. Two half-dead pine trees, more brown than green, were the only landscaping. The windows were dark and the oil-stained driveway was empty, which didn't surprise me. Michelle's friends probably weren't the type to appreciate the police dropping in unannounced looking for Michelle.

A party was shaking the foundation of the house two doors down. Cars choked the narrow street and throbbing rock music filled the night. People

162

were hanging out in the front yard, laughing, smoking and drinking in the meager glow of a porch light. A few heads turned as I drove slowly past, mainly guys checking out the car. I should have driven Samson's Jeep. I made the block and passed the house again. If Ben had men watching for Michelle, I didn't see them. I pulled to the curb one block down, killed the engine and the headlights and lit a cigarette. As I smoked, I watched the street in my mirrors. A car stopped at the party and two people got out. There was a lot of yelling and cheering for the new arrivals. The music jumped five decibels as the front door admitted the couple. The rest of the street was dead quiet.

I had made no plan before I left the house other than to look over Michelle's home, but as I sat smoking an idea formed, an idea born of my natural stubbornness and take-charge attitude. Ben had said they didn't have enough evidence for a search warrant, but *I didn't need one*. I wouldn't break in, I decided, I'd just look in the windows. Probably. My hands started sweating as soon as I made the decision. I almost argued myself out of it, but I had come all the way here.

I took my old metal flashlight out of the glove box and slid out of the car, easing the door closed behind me, feeling a trace foolish. Miss Dick Tracy, I thought derisively and almost laughed. I crossed to the sidewalk and walked back to the corner.

The cross street dead-ended at an orange and white barricade. Beyond that was a field of three-foot tall weeds with the Mayacamas Mountains thrusting up in the dark distance, purple against the night sky. Already the chill and the damp were getting to me, and I hadn't brought a coat. Fog was drifting up from San Francisco, turning the watery light of the quarter moon into a ghostly opalescence. I skirted the barricade and slipped into the weeds, jumpily looking over my shoulder. No one was in sight.

Twenty-five feet beyond the barricade was a ten-foot deep concrete channel. There was only a trickle of muddy water down the center of the thirty-foot wide ditch, but that didn't comfort me. Every spring people are killed in these channels, which can flood with runoff from the mountains in a matter of seconds. I shuddered as I imagined a wall of water bearing down on me, but there was a more immediate hazard. The slope of the channel nearest the houses was mounded with bursting trash-bags and cast off appliances. It looked like everyone in the neighborhood pitched their trash over the back fence where it festered until the next flashflood carried it downstream. The slope itself wasn't that steep, but a fall into that jumble of wreckage could be fatal. The stench alone was almost enough to kill me. I looked along the channel, thinking that maybe I could walk along the top of the ditch, but the house's chain-link fences abutted the concrete lip of the channel. Unless I was going to start hopping fences, fighting family dogs along the way, I had to climb into the ditch.

"Or go home," I whispered, eyeing the garbage. Glass and ripped metal glittered in the moonlight. From where I stood, there was no easy way down. I flicked on the flashlight and panned it over the mess, breathing through my mouth. One spot, two houses down, looked cleaner than the rest. I flicked the light off and tucked it into the waist of my jeans, grabbed the chain-link fence with both hands and inched along it, walking the top edge of concrete like a tightrope. I slipped once, my foot skidding on something rotten and foul smelling. I didn't look too closely. I lost my grip for a second, banging my knee on the concrete edge, but managed to hook my fingers back through the fence's links. Shaking and cursing under my breath, I hauled myself back up and continued on.

When I reached the gap in the trash I squatted on the lip of the channel, one hand still curled in the fence's links. I heard a shuffling noise and the trash below me rustled. I flicked the flashlight on. A pair of red eyes shined back at me from the grizzled face of an old pit-bull that was enjoying a supper of dirty diapers. My breath caught in my chest and hardened into a rock. The dog growled low in his throat and backed away from me, a stained diaper hanging from his jaws. He retreated to the bottom of the channel, then trotted west, throwing red-eyed glances back at me. I kept the flashlight on him until he loped up the opposite side of the channel and disappeared into the weeds.

I flicked the light off and sat there, sweating, trembling but not with the cold. Where there's one wild dog, there are twenty, I remembered my father warning me as a child. Back then the Valley had been truly rural and packs of wild dogs were not uncommon. Most farmers shot them on sight, but not my father. I had always respected him for that, but at that moment I wished I had a gun.

I didn't want to move, but I couldn't sit there forever. Carefully, I scooted downhill on my butt, kicking loose trash out of the way. The smell was awful and choking-thick down in the ditch where no wind stirred. At the bottom, I flicked the flashlight on, half-covering the lens. The last thing I needed was to be spotted by a nosy neighbor, or worse yet, shot by one.

The middle of the concrete ditch was wet, but clean compared to the slope. I moved down it quickly, counting houses. Rats wiggled through the trash, their beady little eyes glowing red in the flashlight's beam. Some looked as big as the pit-bull, but they paid little attention to me and I returned the favor. I reached the slope behind Michelle's home, dropped to my knees and started to climb, prodding trash aside with the flashlight. Halfway up, my hand came down in a pile of something that made a sick squish. I jerked my hand back, wet and rank. A present from the pit-bull or one of his friends. Thank god I

164

was a mother, or the stench would have made me vomit. I wiped my hand on the concrete as best I could and kept climbing.

At the top of the slope, careful to keep my smelly hand away from my clothes, I clambered over the fence and dropped into the foot-tall weeds of the back yard. The weeds might have been unsightly, but they made good towels. With my hand a little cleaner, I crossed to the rear of the house, weaving through piles of beer cans and past a rusty lawnmower left dead at the end of a swath of shorter weeds. The yards beside me were dark. Only light from a few rear-facing windows broke the night.

I peeked in the first of three windows along the back of the house. A small bedroom with two mattresses on the floor and a third on an old iron bed painted white. Dirty clothes made mini-mountains on the floor. A stack of pornographic magazines filled one corner, and a cardboard box labeled Coors Light supported a lamp with a naked bulb. I flicked the flashlight off and moved to the middle window. A dirty kitchen, but not as dirty as the bedroom. A trashcan was stuffed with frozen dinner and fast food packages. More beer cans, plastic silverware and plastic cups cluttered the counter. But the cheap glass-topped table was clean and the floor looked like someone had mopped it not too many weeks ago.

The third window looked in on what I assumed was Michelle's room. It was spotlessly clean. A white spread was fitted neatly over the bed, piled high with pastel pillows and topped with a lethargic, stuffed Sylvester the Cat. A pink ruffle peeked out below the spread. The furniture was antique-white trimmed in gold, a style they used to call the Little Princess when Jessica was a child. Pictures covered the dresser, mostly snapshots from what I could see, and posters dotted the walls, all of them the fuzzy kitty and Words-To-Live-By type. I didn't see any cosmetics or any other clutter. Still, this room did not fit Michelle's gruff and masculine demeanor.

I was about to flick off the flashlight, thinking that this had been a big waste of time, when I noticed the latch on the window wasn't closed. I can resist anything except temptation. I looked left and right, considering. What the hell. I tried the window, half-hoping it would be painted shut. It slid up easily. Feeling like a middle-aged Nancy Drew, I threw a leg through the opening and climbed inside. I left the window open in case I needed to make a hasty escape.

After listening to the sounds of the house, refrigerator humming, dresser clock ticking, I crossed the room and opened the closet. I recognized the red plaid jacket hanging on the door hook. Jeans and T-shirts were neatly hung in the closet, but there were several dresses as well. Shoes and boots were lined up on the floor. A suitcase was on the top shelf along with a dozen cardboard shoeboxes. I looked at the boxes for a long moment, wondering how far I was going to take this? Not that far, I decided. I'd just have a quick look and be gone. I moved to the dresser and opened drawers. Everything was neatly folded, and the drawers looked full. Well, that made one thing certain, Michelle hadn't left for good, or if she had, she had abandoned everything.

I played the light over the pictures arrayed on the dresser. Family photos, a work-group shot of Michelle and her peers crowded around a gondola of grapes. Michelle sitting with Laurel at some club, their heads together, grinning blearily. Michelle had her arm around Laurel's shoulder. Next to that picture was a photo in a cheap metal frame that was wreathed in black crepe paper. A photo I recognized, because I was in it. I had a copy of it in my kitchen. Winter Harlan and me kneeling by a freshly planted willow tree, our hands covered in dirt. Kevin and Laurel were in the background grinning, looking suntanned and happy.

What was Michelle doing with that picture? I picked it up and that's when I noticed that a smaller photo had been taped to the glass in the corner of the frame. It was a photo clipped from the paper. At first glance I thought it was Winter, but it wasn't. I had seen the identical photo on the bulletin board at the Bishop Lynch daycare center. It was Jenna Valdez. Once again I was struck at how similar the two girls were. But what the hell was it doing here? This was getting crazier and crazier. How did Michelle know Jenna? Or was Michelle so seriously messed up in the head that logic no longer applied?

A knock on the front door made me jerk to attention and I lost my grip on the flashlight. I grabbed for it as it fell, juggled it one-handed for a five-count, the beam jumping over the walls and rear window, and finally snatched it to my chest, gasping with fright. I turned the flashlight off, put down Winter's picture and crossed to the bedroom door on jittery legs. I held my breath as I eased it open a crack. Down a narrow hall I could see a broken-down sofa in dingy plaid and beyond it the front door. Someone aimed a flashlight through the door's tiny window and I hopped back, clutching my flashlight like it might leap out of my hand again.

"Open up in there!" A voice drowned out my panting. "I see you back there! This is the police!" A hand rattled the doorknob as I tip-toed at top speed to the open window and clambered through. How long before the policeman circled the house? My breath was coming in gasps and that added to my panic. I tried to close the window but it jammed, cocked at an angle in the frame. The policeman pounded on the door again.

"Open up! Michelle Lawford!" \

Forget the window! Tucking the flashlight into my jeans, I ran across the yard, hurdled the dead lawnmower and straddled the fence. In my haste, I lost my grip on the fence and fell in a heap on the concrete slope on the opposite side. Before I could catch myself, I was sliding backward on my belly into the

166

fetid darkness. My shirt went up over my head and the flashlight almost got away from me. I tried desperately to roll over, but that sent me into a blind spin that ended when I came to a jarring stop at the bottom of the slope, slamming my thigh into the corner of a rusted gas range. Clenching my teeth against the pain, I jerked my blouse down and frantically looked up slope. No one was there. Yet.

I pushed myself up and started walking fast, covered with the slime of decomposing trash, my hair clotted with it. I didn't dare go to the middle of the channel this time; I would be too easy to spot. Instead I navigated through the refuse at the edge. It was like wandering through a bombed out city at night. My shins and thighs took a beating as I hurriedly stumbled and bounced through the castoffs, afraid to turn the flashlight on. It would be only a matter of moments before the police circled the house and decided to check out the drainage channel. My heart was banging against my ribs and a pulse pounded in my temple.

"Did you find what you were looking for?" An angry voice asked from the shadows and I screamed and went down backward in a sack of lawn clippings. Green shreds bloomed up around me accompanied by the rich-sour smell of a compost heap. Ten feet away a shadowy form was standing beside a refrigerator without a door.

"I asked you if you found what you were looking for?" the shadow demanded.

"Who are you?" I whispered, eyes jumping around for an avenue of escape. How quickly I became like a hunted mouse. Fear feeds on itself. I had to beat it down like a brush fire.

"You just broke into *my* house, so why don't you tell me who *you* are before I stick my boot up your ass? And don't even think about running." I heard the distinctive click-clack of a revolver being cocked. "You can't run as fast as my friend." She was trying to sound tough, but her voice held a tremor. That didn't make me any calmer, I was afraid she might pull the trigger at the first movement I made.

"Michelle?" I said, recognizing the voice, ready to scream for help from the policeman I had just been fleeing. Breaking into Michelle's had been a *really* rotten idea! It was too bad that it took staring down the barrel of her gun to make me realize that.

"Quit wasting my time. What did you take?" Michelle took a hesitant step toward me and the moonlight gleamed off her pistol. She was dirty and disheveled and her eyes were jumping around crazily.

"Nothing! I didn't take anything," I proclaimed my innocence as I gripped the flashlight tightly. "It's me, Claire de Montagne."

She stopped, gun aimed at my forehead. "Mrs. de Montagne?" She said. "What are you doing here?" She didn't sound any less angry, just more frightened.

My mouth went dry. "I, I wanted to talk to you about Laurel," I croaked. "And Kevin."

"Kevin? What? You think I killed him too?"

"I didn't say that—"

"I didn't kill him!" Michelle bellowed. "Why would I kill him?" She bit back what could have been a sob. "You! You told the police I tried to kill your daughter. Laurel told me all about you!"

"Laurel doesn't deserve your friendship," I said, trying to sound like I wasn't about to wet my pants. "She'll let you go to jail for her."

"I told you I didn't kill anyone!" Michelle jabbed the gun in my direction to emphasize her point.

"We both know what you did," I said and started to push myself up. "You're covering for Laurel. For a murderer."

"Stay right where you are! I haven't killed anyone, but I will."

I settled back in the bag of grass. "You can't cover for her forever."

Michelle took a step closer and I could see her face. Her eyes were red-rimmed and puffy. Her skin looked sooty and the hand that held the gun was trembling. "What are you talking about?" she demanded, lowering her voice.

"Tell me about Jenna Valdez and Winter Harlan," I said and Michelle flinched. "Tell me why you have a shrine in your bedroom?"

"What do you know?" Michelle whispered, dark eyes digging into my face. "What do you think I did?"

"Murder," I said simply and tears welled in her eyes. "Laurel's not worth going to prison for."

"How could you know?" Michelle's hand clenched and unclenched around the butt of the revolver. "I kept her safe. I took care of her. I covered her."

What the hell was she babbling about? She covered her? Covered for Laurel? "I know that Laurel's going to let you go to prison for something she did." I said, holding my ground, gripping the flashlight in case I had to smack her.

"She wouldn't. Not after all I've done for her. No," she shook her head jerkily, sending tears flying. "No."

"You'll go to prison for killing Kevin, unless you go to the police."

"Kevin?" Michelle said, eyes narrowing on my face. "Kevin?" She took a step back. "You think I killed *him?*"

"Or helped Laurel," I said, starting to wonder if she might really shoot me after all.

She stared hard at me, lips squeezed tight. She stooped and picked up a two-foot long piece of rusty metal pipe. "Laurel was right about you. You'll do anything to cover for Jessica. I'm not going to jail for your little Princess," her voice had gone up a few octaves. She was on the ragged edge of panic.

"Is that why you tried to run her off the road?" I asked, fingers tightening on the cold steel of the flashlight. "I know you're not the type to do something like that on your own."

"You don't know me! I didn't try to run her off the road! Why would I?"

"Because Laurel asked you to. Because Kevin was having an affair with Jessica."

She took a step toward me, lifting the pipe, and for a second the gun wasn't aimed at me. I took that second, rolled left and swung the flashlight at Michelle's kneecap. It connected with a solid 'thunk!' and Michelle yelped. I hit her again in the other kneecap and rolled away, trailing green clippings.

The pipe clanged on the ground. But she still had the gun. I leapt up and ran into the dark tangle of trash and scrap. I was twenty feet from Michelle, draped in darkness, safe in darkness, when the drainage canal was flooded by the light of a spotlight mounted on a patrol car parked in front of the barricade I had circled twenty minutes ago. A shot boomed behind me and a bullet whipped past my ear. Michelle was shooting at me! She fired again! The bullet slammed into a pile of trash bags just ahead of me. Sludge leaked from the wound. I dove for the ground as a volley of shots from the top of the canal ripped the night apart.

I hit the concrete with my shoulder and pain froze my right side. I grabbed my shoulder, stifling a scream, and rolled against a mound of trash bags, head tucked, knees drawn up, laying in a puddle of something cold and sticky.

I heard Michelle scream, "You shot me!" And then the police were barking orders and sirens were wailing.

I stayed where I was until a sheriff's deputy kicked me with the toe of his shoe and told me I was under arrest.

CHAPTER 30

"Could ya sit kinda forward on the seat?" The skinny, acne-scarred deputy asked me, covering his nose against the stench rolling off me in waves. "I gotta ride in that thing every night."

"Sorry," I said and tried to scoot forward, not easy with my hands cuffed behind my back. I was covered in spots and smears, grass clippings and beer drippings. It felt like insects were crawling over my arms and thighs, and I knew that if I didn't get a bath soon I was going to start screaming. The deputy shook his head in disgust and joined a dozen of his peers who were crowded around the cruiser with Michelle in the back. She was cursing and spitting and kicking the door while the deputies laughed. They stopped laughing when a car pulled up behind me. I tried to look over my shoulder and slid back in the seat like it was greased. So much for keeping the deputy's car clean.

"Quit playing around and take her downtown," a familiar voice snapped and the deputies broke it up. Ben walked up to the car where I was sitting, ducked down, looked at me, sniffed twice and grimaced. "What the hell are you thinking, Claire?" he said and stood before I could reply.

"What's she doing in there?" Ben bellowed at the deputy who wanted to keep his seats clean.

"She was with Michelle Lawford," the deputy said as he trotted over. "Greg told me to cuff her until we worked out what's what. Lawford took a shot at her."

Ben ducked back down. "She shot at you?"

"Yes. Ben, I really need a bath and—" I began, but he was standing again.

"So you got a crime victim handcuffed in your car? A novel way of handling things," Ben snarled. "Tell Greg to get his ass over here."

The deputy trotted off and returned a few seconds later with another skinny deputy with a shock of tangled black hair and a prominent Adam's apple.

"What's up, chief?" Greg asked, eyeing me.

"What's she doing in cuffs?" Ben hooked a thumb in my direction.

"Breaking and entering," Greg said. "Caught her coming out the back of Lawford's. Don't smell too good, does she?" Greg grinned.

"Smells like crap," the acne faced deputy opined. "Sorry Ma'am," he added to me, blushing.

"The truth hurts," I said and Greg laughed. Ben gave him a look and Greg swallowed it, Adam's apple bobbing.

"You break and enter?" Ben leaned down and asked.

"The window was open. I entered," I tried to shrug, not easy in handcuffs. "I didn't *break* in."

170

"Mind telling me what the hell you were doing in there? No, never mind. I don't wanna know," Ben straightened and pointed at me. "Un-cuff her," he said. He walked away with the acne-faced deputy.

"Out ya go," Greg said as he guided my head through the door and helped me stand. "God, you are ripe!" He said, unlocking the handcuffs.

"Compliments, compliments," I replied. I was still jittery from my altercation with Michelle, but I felt better as I watched her being driven away under police power. Maybe Jessica would be safe now.

Half the neighborhood was in their back yards or on the street behind the orange and white barricade. People were drinking and talking like it was a block-party. The crowd parted for a white van with County markings that pulled up as I was chafing my wrists and sniffing myself, trying to identify the strongest of many odors. Something smelled dead. I had to swallow hard to keep from throwing up.

Midge stepped out of the van and crossed to where Ben was standing with Greg. The three of them talked for several minutes before Ben came back to me.

"Do you have a cigarette?" I asked. He patted his pockets fruitlessly, turned and yelled. "Greg! Give me a square!"

Greg trotted over and handed Ben a crumpled pack, then trotted back to where Midge was working her way down the littered concrete slope, a flashlight in her hand. Ben shook out a cigarette for both of us and lit them. I inhaled greedily, closing my eyes with the pure pleasure of it. I had almost died down there, I thought, watching Midge cross to the spot where Michelle was shot. Grazed, actually. I took another shaky drag on the cigarette.

"Doing a little amateur detecting?" Ben asked.

"I just wanted to see if she had left for good. You said you couldn't search the place…" I shrugged.

"So you decided to help me out?" Ben leaned against the patrol car.

"You make it sound so foolish," I said, staring at the ground.

"Just foolish?" Ben said. "I was thinking plain stupid," he shrugged and looked at the stars, "I figure you should make wine and I should catch criminals, but maybe I got it wrong. Maybe I should be crushing grapes and you should be cuffing creeps."

"I need a bath and a drink," I said sourly. "At least I found her," I added.

Ben nodded. "Or, she found you." He flicked his cigarette over the side of the channel and turned to face me. "All joking aside, Claire, I asked you to keep out of this and let me do my job. You could be dead down there right now, you thought of that?"

I dropped my cigarette, hugged myself and nodded. "Maybe, but I can take care of myself," I told him.

171

"You need to be worrying about Jessica," Ben tried another tack. "She doesn't need any more tragedy."

I didn't say anything. Ben sighed in exasperation. "All right. Where's your car?"

Ben walked me back to the Mustang, past the curious stares of the neighbors. He opened the door for me and watched as I took the floor mats and lined the seat with them. I sat down and he closed the door.

"Get a bath and I'll call you tomorrow," he said through the open window. "Gonna need a statement, so be dreaming up an explanation for why you broke into Lawford's house."

"I didn't break—"

He waved a dismissive hand. "Save it for tomorrow. She's gonna have enough problems without worrying about pressing charges against you. Go home."

Ben stepped back and I left American Canyon, watching Ben in the rearview, thinking about what a wonderfully feminine side of myself I had shown him tonight. "A bath," I said out loud. "And a drink." All else could wait until I had washed the smell of dead cat off me.

172

CHAPTER 31

I was only two miles from home when my cell phone rang inside my purse. I dug for it and answered.

"De Montagne," Samson breathed in my ear. "You will come and get me now."

"It's 1:00 A.M., Samson, and you *don't* want me to come get you right now. I smell awful. Let me get cleaned—"

"Come," Samson said in a loud voice.

"Who are you talkin' to, baby?" I heard Marjory ask, her voice muffled.

"It is de Montagne," Samson replied and he sounded irritated. "She is coming to take me."

"You're goin'? Thought you'd spend the night."

"De Montagne, you will come and get me." He hung up on me.

"Samson," I groaned as I folded the phone and dropped it on the seat. Everyone was having trouble with their love life. What had Marjory done to run Samson off? At that moment, I didn't care. All I knew was that my shower was going to have to wait. I made a U-turn and drove back to Marjory's.

The gate was open and Samson was standing at the top of the driveway. He hurried over as I pulled up, but he wasn't going to make a clean getaway. Marjory staggered out the front door as Samson opened the car door.

"Samson!" She yelled as she came down the steps, placing each foot very carefully. "You forgot your wine!" Marjory had a bottle of her Zinfandel in one hand and a half-filled glass in the other. "Hey lover!"

"Son of bitch," Samson said under his breath. "I am going home. The wine will wait."

"Oh, no, that won't do. I gave you a present, you take it." She grabbed Samson's sleeve for balance and ducked down to look at me.

"Hey, Claire! Baby, baby, baby! Something smells awful! She took a step back, slopped wine on the concrete and laughed. "Did you hit something?" She turned to Samson and smiled drunkenly. "I love animals too, but I wouldn't put a dead one in the car," she said and burped. Delicate as a flower.

"Hello Marjory," I said. "How are you?"

"Havin' a little party! Guest of honor's pooping on it. Can't ya spare him for one night?" She winked at me. "Just a few hours?" She linked arms with Samson who turned bloodshot eyes on me for help.

"We've got to go, Marjory," I said, giving Samson a 'You Owe Me' look. "How are the vines?"

"That," she said, "is what I was just talkin' 'bout." She downed the rest of her wine, looked around for some place to set the glass down. She finally flipped it into the bushes. "Gonna find that bitch," she said to me. "Gonna find her and break her neck!"

"Michelle?" I asked, then wished I hadn't.

"Michelle? That loser? I'm talkin' 'bout the bitch that sent her! She might think I hit her last night, but she hasn't seen nothin'!" She shook her fist, then realized she had the bottle of wine in that hand. "That's yours, baby," she said, batting her eyes at Samson. He took the bottle. "Sure you won't stay and finish it with me?"

"I must go. We have work," Samson said, patting her shoulder like she was a stray dog who might have mange.

"You'll call me?" Marjory asked as Samson ducked and hustled into the car. "Tomorrow?"

"I will," Samson replied, eyes straight ahead.

"Toodles, Claire," Marjory waved with her fingers. "And wash that car!"

Marjory watched us drive away. When we were back on the highway, Samson sighed and tilted his head back against the headrest.

"What was that all about?" I asked.

"She is drunk," he said and closed his eyes. "She is crazy! I thank you for coming."

"I warned you that Marjory can be a *strong* drink."

"Marjory drinks too much strong drink. And then she talks! She will not shut up!"

"So, you going to call her tomorrow?" I asked.

"I will call her. She is troubled."

"And rich," I reminded him snidely.

"She smells good too," Samson said, opening one eye to look at me. "Better than you, de Montagne."

"I love you too," I said, deciding right then not to tell him about my evening. He could read about it in the papers.

"Wake me when we are at Violet," he said and five seconds later he was snoring, his beard-stubbled Adam's apple bobbing.

I punched Samson in the shoulder after parking Sally in the garage.

"What is—!" He came awake with a start. "De Montagne," he said. "Where is the Jeep?"

"Where it always is," I said and slammed the door behind me. "Getting senile?" What can I say, I wasn't in the best of moods and Samson's snores had driven me right over the edge of bad-humor.

"I only ask!" He yelled from behind me as I crossed the grass at a brisk walk.

"I only told you!" I yelled back without turning, and that's when I noticed that the cellar door was standing wide open. Samson noticed too.

174

"Damn it, de Montagne! The cellar is open!"

"No, really?!" I yelled at him as I trotted to the door. "I locked it before I left!" The padlock and chain were lying on the grass, neatly bitten in two by a pair of bolt-cutters. I reached inside and flipped on the overhead lights as Samson panted up beside me.

"No," I said and my heart dropped through my stomach.

The cellar had been vandalized. The door to my private storage area was open, the concrete floor in front of it littered with broken bottles and purple puddles. Several of the oak barrels filled with 2010 Cabernet had been bashed in and the wine formed a sticky river flowing toward the front door. The bottling machinery had been uncovered and smashed into mangled metal. The fermenting tanks were the only thing left undamaged. Even Samson's desk had taking a beating. The drawers were open, disgorging pamphlets and shipping manifests.

"Oh, my God," Samson moaned and I turned my shocked eyes on him.

"De Montagne," he said and his lips worked like a fish out of water. "De Montagne," he tried again and then collapsed against me like a sack of potatoes. I tried to hold him up but he slipped right through my hands. His chin bounced off the concrete and he flopped over, his hands clutching his chest.

"Samson!" I screamed, forgetting the wine. "Samson!" I dropped to my knees beside him and cradled his head, feeling for a pulse. His heart was pounding like a horse at full gallop. He was sweating and his eyelids were fluttering.

"Don't die, Samson! Don't die!" I pleaded with him as I fumbled my phone from my purse and dialed 911.

CHAPTER 32

Jessica came sleepily down the cellar stairs before the ambulance arrived. She took one look at Samson prostrate in the doorway and burst into tears. I yelled at her to call Victor and then to wait out front for the police. She ran back upstairs, her broken arm flopping in its sling. I stayed with Samson, holding his hand and talking to him, begging him to be okay, until the EMS technicians arrived and shouldered me out of the way, grimacing at the stench. They loaded Samson in an ambulance and I climbed in beside him. The technician in the back started to argue, but his buddy slammed the rear doors and we were streaking down toward Napa, the technician hooking Samson up to a bevy of machines with computer displays. I tried to stay out of the way, still holding Samson's hand and whispering to him.

"Out of the way!" The technician yelled at me as we swept up in front of the emergency room entrance. The rear doors popped open and I jumped out. They rushed Samson inside with me traveling in their wake. I would have followed him right into the treatment room, but an officious nurse in a powder blue uniform intercepted me.

"What happened?" she asked as she tugged me toward a gurney that was pushed up against a wall. "What's that smell?"

"Trash," I told her. "But, I'm fine. I'm fine." She tried to push me down on the gurney, but I finally convinced her that, though I was filthy and smelled like a dead rodent, I was unhurt. She turned officious then and handed me a sheaf of papers to fill out for Samson. I sat with a half-dozen other people wearing shell-shocked expressions. The woman beside me changed seats, covering her nose. Several people made comments, but I ignored them, concentrating on the paperwork. Having just been there for Jessica, I was familiar with the forms so they didn't take too long. That was too bad, because waiting for Samson's doctor to come and give me news of his condition was enough to drive me batty.

While I waited, I tried to clean up in the public bathroom, but it was no use. The smell clung to my hair and permeated my skin. I would need to burn the clothes and fumigate myself. In the harsh fluorescent lighting my skin looked bleached and spotty. My hair was knotted and clumped. Dark bags half-circled my eyes, my right cheek was scratched and my lip was bloody. I was limping from my collision with the castoff electric range in the drainage channel. No wonder the nurse thought I was an accident victim. I splashed water on my face again and again, but a dreadful lethargy began to settle into my bones. Everything was falling apart. My daughter was a murder suspect with a broken arm, one of my best friends was in the emergency room and my wine cellar was a shambles.

The powder-blue nurse entered the bathroom as I was leaning over the sink fighting the tears, trying to collect myself. She had a set of green scrubs over her arm topped by a towel and a tube of shower gel. I was so grateful I wanted to kiss her prim face. Instead, I asked about Samson. She had no news, other than that he was having tests done now. The nurse gave me the clothes, led me to an empty room and left me to get clean. Hot water and soap never felt so good. Now, if I only had a change of underwear! I tossed my dirty clothes in the trashcan and tied the bag to hold down the smell.

The people in the waiting room gave me the once over, but nobody moved away when I sat down. A trio of women with a herd of sleepy children had arrived while I was showering. Two of the women were crying while the other tried to control a grumpy little boy dressed in footed pajamas who was rubbing his eyes and whining. I leaned back in the chair and closed my eyes. Water trickled from my hair down the back of my neck. I was tired and feeling pitiful. I had insurance claims to file and I would have to talk to the police about the vandalism and the altercation with Michelle.

Anger flashed like sheet lightning through my veins. I knew who had vandalized the cellar. There was only one person that hated me enough. Laurel Harlan. I should have expected something like this. Laurel wasn't one to suffer slights, as Kevin and Jessica had both found out. The woman was unbalanced, but how to convince the police of that? Ben seemed determined to ignore any indication that Laurel was behind Kevin's murder, and Priest was sleeping with the culprit!

I must have dozed off, because the next thing I remember was Victor shaking me awake.

"Victor," I said, rubbing my eyes and stretching. My vineyard foreman looked like he had just climbed out of bed. He was wearing rumpled jogging shorts and a T-shirt and his hair was pointing in ten different directions. I looked past him to the nurse's desk. The powder-blue nurse was filling out paperwork, glasses perched on the end of her nose. "I wonder if they've brought Samson out yet?" I said to Victor as I stood and stretched to tiptoe.

"Just wheeled him upstairs. Said he had a cardiac episode, whatever that is. We can't see him right now. They have him sedated." Victor rubbed his beard-stubbled chin and shook his head. "What the hell happened?"

I told Victor about Samson's collapse, then backed up and told him about my run-in with Michelle Lawford. He had stopped by the house and spoken to Jessica, then come straight to the hospital.

"Police were taking prints and stuff," he told me.

"How bad was the damage?" I asked, preparing myself for the worst.

"Bottling line is trashed. About half of the 2010 is on the floor and your personal stock was hit pretty hard. Looks like they went to town in there. Sorry, Claire," he added, touching my shoulder.

My teeth ground and my fingernails dug into my palms. "She's going to pay for this."

Victor gave me a worried look. "Don't get yourself in trouble," he said. "Let the police handle it."

"Like they're handling Kevin's murder?" I snapped. "I haven't any faith in our sheriff's department, outside of Ben, and he's officially out of the loop."

"Aw, crap," Victor muttered into his cupped hand. "You're gonna do something, aren't you? Something crazy."

"I'm going to do something," I agreed, "But nothing crazy. They won't consider Laurel a suspect until the proof smacks them in the face."

"And you're the one to smack them," Victor said sourly. "I ain't *even* going to try to talk you out of it. But, promise me you'll be careful." He looked at me for a long moment. "What am I saying? Telling you to be careful is like warning the cat not to eat the goldfish. It just encourages you. No more burglaries, can you promise me that much?"

"No more burglaries," I said.

"You're a damn liar," Victor said. "And what the hell is that smell?"

The nurse let us duck our heads in Samson's door at 3:00 A.M. He was asleep, a frail gray skeleton under a white bed sheet. I couldn't help crying. Victor gave me a one-armed hug. We left Samson just in time to meet Midge and Priest in the emergency room lobby.

Midge looked sleepy and tousled, but Priest looked like he had just stepped off the pages of GQ. His shoes were shined and his hair was perfectly combed.

"Mrs. de Montagne," Priest said as he crossed the floor to meet us, Midge hanging back. "How is your friend?"

"He's stable," I said. "Did you find anything?" I asked, pointedly looking past the pretty-boy detective at Midge.

She shrugged. "Lots of prints, but none on the pry bar they used. I'll have to check what I have against the prints you guys gave us."

"Actually," Priest butted in, "we came to talk to you about Michelle Lawford. Let's start with why she took a shot at you?"

"I don't know why she tried to kill me," I said, crossing my arms, suddenly cold in the thin green suit. "She said—"

"Let's find somewhere we can talk alone," Priest interrupted.

"I have some questions about the cellar, locks, keys, etc.," Midge interjected.

"I can handle that," Victor said, giving me a worried look.

178

"I'll be fine," I assured him. He and Midge sat in adjoining plastic chairs and she flipped open a notebook while Priest asked the powder-blue nurse for an empty room. He walked back to me, tried his charming smile. It made me want to puke.

"She said to use the one you showered in?" He raised an eyebrow at me, but I didn't give him an explanation. I led the way to the room.

I could smell my clothes festering in their trash bag cocoon. Priest wrinkled his nose. "These places always smell like death to me," he said.

"Maybe you're just morbid," I replied. He gave me a look, dropped to a seat on the edge of the bed and took out a spiral pad. I sat in the room's one chair.

"Why were you in Michelle Lawford's home?"

"I wanted to see if she was gone for good."

"Guess you found out the hard way," he said, writing on the pad. "What happened? From the beginning. Start with getting out of your car in American Canyon."

Step by step, I walked him through the events of that night, feeling like an idiot, but also a little proud. I had done what the police couldn't or wouldn't do. Without me they might not have captured Michelle. Priest had a different opinion.

"Why don't you let us handle the investigation?" He said after he closed the pad.

"If you weren't sleeping with the murderer I might." I said and his expression stiffened.

"I'm not sleeping with Laurel," he snapped, clenching his fist so hard I thought his knuckles might crack. He took a deep breath and continued. "Do yourself a favor and answer my questions without the commentary. You said that you and Michelle talked before the deputies arrived?"

"That's right."

"About what?"

"Laurel Harlan," I said.

"You're still on that kick?" he asked. "Christ!"

"Michelle admitted that she helped Laurel do something illegal," I said.

"She admit murdering Kevin?"

"No," I couldn't lie. "But when I told her that she'd go to prison if she helped Laurel cover it up she broke down."

"Give it to me word for word, or as close as you can come," he said and I did, closing my eyes and reliving those moments. A cold sweat dotted my brow and I could smell the garbage again. But maybe that was just my clothes.

"That's it?" Priest asked curtly when I had finished. I nodded.

179

"So, Michelle says she didn't kill Kevin, and she didn't try to run your daughter off the road?" Priest asked. "Yep, that sounds like a confession. Guess I'll arrest Mrs. Harlan right away."

"What about what Michelle *did* say about Laurel? That Laurel wouldn't let her go to prison, not after all that Michelle had done for her? That doesn't jibe with the theory that Michelle is a crazy stalker, does it?"

"It fits perfectly. Stalkers often identify so closely with their victims that they imagine a deeper personal connection. A loving relationship."

"Isn't it worth checking out? Or are you just going to take Laurel's word for it?"

Priest stuffed his pad back in his jacket pocket and stood. "I don't take anyone's word for anything. Everybody lies to suit their purpose, and that's exactly what Michelle's doing."

"What about the vandalism? I know it was Laurel getting even for the fight at Marjory's," I said, the blood hot in my cheeks.

"Let me just add that to the list! I heard about the fight from Mrs. Harlan. I tried to convince her to press charges against that drunken idiot, but she wanted to forget the whole thing. She was devastated."

"Not too devastated to come back and blow up the only piece of evidence connecting Michelle Lawford to Jessica's accident," I retorted, but he wasn't listening.

"Just stop for a minute. Stop *right there*. I think you're right, I think Michelle ran Jessica off the road. And I think she murdered Kevin. But, I don't think that Laurel Harlan is behind it." He held up a hand to stifle my protest. "Let me finish. I'm going to tell you something that I want you to promise me will go no farther than this room. Deal?"

After a lead in like that, how could I say no. "Deal," I said to a man I despised.

"We'll be dropping the charges against Jessica," he said and watched my expression.

My mouth dropped open. "What? Really?" I was flooded with relief so palpable that I almost swooned.

"Really," he said with a nod. "So the amateur detective bit stops right here. Got it?"

My relief didn't last long before it was replaced by suspicion. "Why are you finally admitting you were wrong?"

"I'm not at liberty to discuss the case," he said. "Isn't Jessica being cleared enough for you?"

"You have another suspect?"

"More than a suspect," he said, avoiding my eyes. "Much more." I sensed an undercurrent of excitement in Priest, an excitement he was trying to keep in check. He flashed that smile.

"Who is it?" I asked, knowing I wouldn't get an answer.

"I'm not at liberty to discuss the case, but I have received information that pushes Jessica out of the picture."

"What about Laurel Harlan?"

Priest lost the smile. "Laurel Harlan is a *victim,*" He said coldly. "And I'm sick of pointing that out to you. You've got what you wanted, so back off." He stepped to the door and looked back at me. "Laurel will be leaving her home in a week or two to move back to San Francisco. Just stay away from her until then."

Priest tried to slam the door, but it was on a pneumatic hinge. He pulled it so hard that the knob slipped out of his hand and he stumbled, sliding around in his three-hundred dollar shoes. He tried to recover his dignity, throwing me a glare through the slowly closing door. I waved and smiled, wanting to give him the finger.

After he was gone and the door had closed, I sat and thought about what he had told me. I was thrilled that Jessica was officially off the most wanted list, but I can't deny that I was disappointed that Laurel Harlan was being exonerated once again. She was involved, I felt it in my gut. But how to prove it? And was it my place to prove it?

"Yes," I whispered to myself. Kevin Harlan was a friend. I couldn't sit by and watch Laurel ride off into the sunset. And I knew where I'd start, where Kevin had left off. Jenna Valdez and Winter Harlan.

Victor was alone in the lobby when I came down the hall. He stood and we walked out to his raggedy red truck in silence. He cranked the truck and the sounds of Salsa filled the cab. He turned it down and looked at me.

"You okay?"

"No, but I'll survive," I replied, buckling the seat belt and rolling down the window. "Mind if I smoke?"

"If you have to," he said, backing out of the space. "Stinking up my truck."

I lit a cigarette and blew smoke out the window.

"What'd Detective Dickhead have to say?" Victor asked, his eyes on the road.

"That Laurel Harlan is the next best thing to Mother Teresa. But they're dropping the charges against Jessica."

"Really?"

"That's what he said," I replied, taking a drag.

"So, who's the new convict?" Victor cranked down his window and the cab was filed with wind.

"He wouldn't tell me."

"What an asshole."

I didn't say anything, but I was in complete agreement.

"You really think she did it? I mean, you think she killed Kevin?"

"Or had it done. And I think she wrecked the cellar." Just saying the words made me seethe. Insurance would pay for the damage, but that wouldn't replace my carefully collected bottles or the casks of wine that had been destroyed.

"You're not going to let this thing drop, are you?" Victor asked. "Don't bullshit me, either. I know you, Claire."

"No."

"What are you going to do? Talk to the private detectives Roger hired?"

"No point in that." I stubbed the cigarette out on the box they came in and slipped the burnt butt into the pack. I didn't want to stink up Victor's ashtray, but I wouldn't litter either. "They'll be off the case as soon as they hear the charges have been dropped."

"You going to talk to Ben?"

I shook my head. "Ben has enough problems." I said simply. I was thinking of Hunter Drake, the detective who investigated Winter's abduction. He was the only one I'd spoken to who believed that Laurel was capable of murder. What had he said about coincidences? Well, I agreed with him. I didn't relate any of that to Victor; he'd just be more worried. "I'll think about all of that tomorrow. I've got to get the cellar cleaned up."

"No way," Victor said, "You've probably slept ten hours in the last three days. You're going to go to bed. I'll clean up the mess."

"We can't clean it until the insurance adjuster looks it over. And there's paperwork to fill out. And—"

"And, as Vineyard Foreman, I'm authorized to handle all of that," Victor cut in. "And that's what I'm gonna to do. I'll take pictures for the insurance. You're going to take some time off."

I squeezed my friend's shoulder, blinking away grateful tears.

"Don't go all gooey on me," he said, shrugging off my hand.

I took Victor's advice when we got home and went upstairs for another shower and bed without even glancing at the cellar. My body was bruised and battered, and I could still smell garbage in my hair. Fortunately, sleep came deep and dreamless. Too many late nights and early mornings had taken their toll. But that didn't keep me from jerking awake at 8:30 A.M. when my phone rang.

CHAPTER 33

Blearily I fumbled the receiver off the hook and said, "Hullo."

"Mom. It's Jessica. Samson's throwing a fit."

"Where are you?" I asked, shaking off the cobwebs, turning my feet out on the floor. "At the hospital?"

"Victor drove me down. Samson's okay, but he wants to leave. He's fussing at the doctor. Will you talk to him?"

"Who?" I asked, thinking dumbly that she meant the doctor.

"Samson. Are you okay?"

"I just woke up," I replied. "It won't do any good, but put him on."

"De Montagne!" Samson wheezed. "You tell them I must return to Violet. You tell them now!"

"Samson, listen to your doctor." Rubbing my eyes, I walked to my bathroom. I turned on the tap and let the water run in a cold trickle, filling the basin.

"This baby-doctor? He knows *nothing!* I am not needed here, but the cellar—"

"Is being taken care of," I cut in.

"But, I tell him—"

"Samson," I said sharply. "You could have died. Do you understand that? Do what the doctor tells you." I splashed water on my face with one hand, holding the phone clear of the splatter.

"I will do what *I* tell me! Not *you,* de Montagne and not this five-year old!" He shouted. I held the receiver far from my ear.

"I'll be there in an hour, your highness," I said, trying not to laugh. Jessica was right, Samson was definitely okay.

"No reason to insult me! I—"

"An hour, Samson." I hung up on him. There was no way I was going to let him leave the hospital without his doctor's permission, but maybe I could convince him to stay. "And maybe I could ride my flying pig down there," I muttered as I reached for my toothbrush. So much for catching up on sleep.

I dressed in khaki slacks and a white polo shirt with lavender accents and tamed my hair with a pair of hairpins and exited the house through the cellar. No time for coffee today.

The cellar floor had been hosed down and swept. The broken casks were stacked by the door and the bottling line, which looked like a car wreck, was standing in the shadow of the steel fermentation tanks, the overhead lighting glinting off mangled metal. Victor was picking through a pile of broken bottles, setting the labels aside. I tried not to look at the names on the labels. I told Victor that I was going to the hospital and he made a face.

"Samson was raising hell when I left this morning."

"I know," I said, pulling my keys out.

"Want me to go with you?" he asked with obvious dread.

"Not unless you want to." Victor pretended to gag. Well, that answered that. "I'll be back before lunch."

Victor went back to separating the labels for the insurance agent's inspection. I hoped they'd make good on the loss - God knows my premiums were high enough. I headed for my car, wanting a cigarette badly. I was out. I'd have to stop after I saw Samson. The wait promised to be interminable. "Junkie," I accused. Guilty as charged.

The powder blue nurse from the night before was at the main desk. She looked haggard, her pantsuit rumpled and spotted with something brown. She didn't recognize me minus the smell of garbage. I introduced myself and thanked her for the scrubs I wore home that morning. She nodded stiffly, eyeing the paperwork piled in front of her in a preoccupied way. I promised to wash and return the scrubs and she gave me a doubtful look that I ignored. Maybe I wouldn't bring them back. But then they'd probably show up on Samson's bill. I didn't need a two-hundred dollar bright green jumpsuit.

I asked for Samson's room number and she gave it to me and pointed me toward the elevators with a thin smile and a "Take care." She bent back over her work, pinching the bridge of her nose and rubbing at her eyes.

Samson's room was on eight, down the hall from the intensive care unit. He was alone, the curtains open on a sunshine and blue-sky view that he was ignoring. A The Price Is Right rerun was blaring from the TV and Samson was cursing a frizzy-permed housewife who had just bid $3.98 on a box of dryer sheets.

"Four dollars for a pretty smell?" He yelled. "Four dollars?"

The TV picture went to a close up of Bob Barker. "The actual suggested retail is…three dollars and ninety-eight cents!" The woman went wild, ran up on stage and jumped the aging pitchman.

"Bullshit," Samson muttered. He clicked the TV off and dropped the remote. "De Montagne, thank God!"

"Not watching the soaps?" I asked as I dragged a chair close to the bed.

"I am waiting for you," he said, throwing the sheet off his spindly white legs. He turned his feet out of bed and looked toward the closet. He looked pale and gaunt, his face etched with pain. "My clothes, de Montagne," he said, as if I was his chambermaid. "The closet."

"Afraid I might see your skinny backside?" I teased and he blushed and sputtered. "Too bad I don't have a camera. Marjory would *love* a glamour shot."

"Now is no time for fun," Samson groused. "My clothes. Please."

"Lie down, Samson," I said, plopping my purse on the floor. "You're not going anywhere."

"And you are who to tell me this?" He sputtered. "I have work to do!"

"You almost died, Samson," I pointed out.

"I will die when I die!" He shot back. "You and the baby-doctor know everything! How can you know? I know me and I will not to die so soon!"

"Calm down, Samson," I said. It was time to get tough. "I swear if you come home I'm going to sit by your bedside and read to you and feed you soup and check your temperature every ten minutes and make sure you take your medication and—"

"Orders!" He shouted. "I do not take orders!"

"Neither do I," I told him, crossing my arms. "And I'll do what I say."

"I am being punished," Samson muttered, glaring at the darkened TV. "I have sinned against the gods." I stood and tucked the sheet in around him. "I am not afraid of you de Montagne," he said.

"You should be," I told him.

"Leave me be!" He said, slapping at my hands and tugging the sheet into a loose tent. "I will fix it."

I didn't argue. "Don't call Victor. He won't come get you either," I warned.

"Orders," he muttered, eyes focused on the ceiling. If you've never seen a seventy-year-old pout, count your blessings.

"How are you feeling? Really?"

"I am fine," he said, then turned the TV back on. The people on screen were spinning a giant wheel. "Tomorrow you take me home." He said, frowning at the TV. Conversation over. He didn't ask about the cellar, and I was glad. It would be bad enough when he saw the damage for himself, no reason to get him worked up prematurely.

"Where's Jessica?"

"Down the hall," he said without turning his head. "Stanley's room. Son of bitch!"

"Stanley?" I said.

"I told her she should not go. Does she listen? Do you listen?" He shook his head, his eyes on the TV. "Stanley! Son of bitch!"

I stooped over Samson and planted a wet kiss on his forehead. He grimaced and merely grunted when I said goodbye. I left him watching Bob Barker and fumed my way down the hall to the nurse's station thinking black thoughts.

185

Why was she visiting Stanley? Was it just a courtesy? If she was getting back together with that ass she could find another place to live. He'd never set foot on my property again. I stopped just before the nurses' station and took a deep breath. I would not make a scene! I would not!

Sitting on a stool behind the tall desk was a pretty young girl in a pink sweater, blonde hair tied in a bun. She smiled at me tentatively.

"How may I help you?" she asked, getting to her feet, pulling her sweater closed with one hand.

"I'm looking for Stanley Kostyol's room," I said, returning the smile. Just seeing this girl's fresh-scrubbed face dialed my anger back a notch or two. I would not cause a scene!

"812, but he has a visitor at the moment. A young girl," she gave me a significant smile and my bad attitude re-invaded. "If you'd like to wait..." she said, gesturing politely to a pair of plastic chairs.

"The girl is my daughter," I said, too brusquely.

Her smile faltered and she said, "Oh."

"812?" I repeated. She nodded.

I didn't bother to knock. Anyone who throws a brick through my window shouldn't expect courtesy in return.

Stanley was in bed, his chubby face puffy and sallow. A bandage crossed his forehead just above the eyes. He was attached to a heart rate monitor that beeped steadily. Its pace jumped up a notch when he saw me. Good!

Jessica was holding his hand, but she jerked it away and stepped away from the bed.

"Mrs. de Montagne," Stanley said and tried to smile. "I didn't expect a visit from you."

"And you're not getting one," I snapped. "Jessica, are you ready to go?"

"I was just checking on Stanley," Jessica replied, slinging her purse over her good shoulder, wincing as she jostled her broken arm.

"He's alive," I said, looking him over with a jaundiced eye. "Let's go."

Stanley laughed, but it sounded forced and more than a little frightened. "No need to be like that, Mrs. D. I'm sorry about the window."

"Say it with cash," I told him, unsmiling. "Or go to jail. The latter suits me."

He laughed again. "You've got every right to be pissed," he acknowledged generously. "But, hey, my truck is wrecked and I'm in the hospital. Isn't that enough punishment?"

"Tell that to Ben Stoltze," I replied as Jessica came around the bed, eyes on the floor.

"I've got nothing to say to that asshole. I don't need my ass kicked before I go to jail."

186

"What do you mean by that?" I snapped, getting angrier by the second. "Ben is not an asshole."

"Depends on what side of the tracks you're on," Stanley said. "He's beat the crap out of me twice."

"Mom is going out with Ben," Jessica warned him, much to my embarrassment.

"I am not!"

Jessica shrugged and Stanley looked stricken. "I didn't mean anything," he told me. "I was just talking."

"I saw Doug Priest here this morning," Jessica said. "He told me they were dropping the charges against me."

"No shit?" Stanley said from the bed. He grabbed the remote and pushed a button. The top half of the bed started to rise. "That's great!" He really sounded happy.

"Priest told me last night," I told my daughter. "Are you ready to go?"

"Who did it?" Stanley asked, eyes going from Jessica to me. "I mean, who killed Kevin?"

"The news on the radio said Michelle Lawford confessed," Jessica told Stanley and I looked at her in disbelief. Michelle told me that she hadn't killed Kevin, and I had believed her. I could be wrong, but I didn't think I was. Could this be another of Priest's attempts to save Laurel? Was Michelle stupid enough to go to prison for something she didn't do? Stanley butted into my thoughts.

"Michelle?" Stanley exclaimed. "That's a load of crap! She was at the Gimpy Mule, drunk off her ass! That's what I'm talking about. These cops'll frame ya if they can't catch ya." I didn't point out that Stanley *was* guilty of the crime he was charged with.

"You're sure it was the night Kevin was killed?" I asked, interested in what Stanley had to say for the first time ever.

"Yeah. Michelle was f-ed up. No way she got up and went to Violet. She couldn't even walk to the bathroom. Some chick had to help her."

"So, she was there when you left to break my window?" I asked darkly.

"Yeah," he said, staring down at his sheet-covered feet. "And later that night. When I went back to Violet she was still there."

"You came back that night?" Jessica asked. I glanced at her and wanted to shove her out the door. She was looking at Stanley with too much compassion for my taste.

"To apologize," Stanley said, shooting me a glance then looking back at his feet. "I was gonna stop, even after I saw the cops. They'd have arrested me sooner or later, might as well get it over with."

"So why didn't you?" I asked.

"I saw Ben down the road," Stanley said. "I can talk to the other cops, but not him. He's had it in for me since I papered the high school in tenth grade."

"You broke into the high school," I reminded him. "And, besides papering it, you stole five computers."

"That don't give him a right to smack me around," Stanley mumbled. "Asshole." He glared at me, suddenly full of defiance. "And you can tell him I said that. I don't give a crap."

I had heard enough. Stanley was a born liar. Of course he hated Ben, the man who had arrested him a half-dozen times. And how many criminals complain of police brutality? But, what he had said about Michelle rang true. He had no reason to lie for her.

But what about him saying that Ben was down the road while the police were looking at my broken window? I hadn't seen Ben that night. Maybe he was checking up on his men? More likely it was another lie. A pointless one.

"Are you ready, Jessica?" I repeated.

She nodded and waved at Stanley.

"I'm really sorry 'bout the window, Mrs. D," he called at my back.

"You will be," I said snottily and left the room. Let him stew, thinking about jail. That was his future.

Jessica and I stopped by Samson's room before we left the hospital. He told me, once again, to pick him up tomorrow. I replied that I would if the doctor okayed it. That started a cursing fit. Jessica and I exited during the opening chords of the Perry Mason theme song. We headed back to Violet, Jessica whining about her arm itching under the cast.

CHAPTER 34

I got a coat-hanger and straightened it for Jessica and left her in her room scratching away, cooing with relief. I dug out the phonebook and looked up Hunter Drake's address. I admit that I was a little nervous about calling Hunt, mainly because I felt like I was going behind Ben's back. But Ben wasn't listening to me, what else could I do? Hunter was the only person who had listened to what I had to say about Laurel. And he was about to listen some more, whether he liked it or not. I didn't call ahead because I was afraid he'd tell me not to come. And he'd be prepared for me. I wanted answers, so the more off balance he was the better.

I yelled up the stairs to Jessica that I'd be gone for a while, then went to the cellar to ask Victor to keep an eye on her. I wasn't taking any chances with Laurel Harlan. Victor said he'd hang around until I got back and I climbed into Sally and headed for Hunter's, feeling a little nervous. I hadn't given Hunter much thought since our meeting; I had been too distracted. But, at the idea of seeing him again, I must admit that my palms went clammy. Not very dignified for a mature adult.

The drive didn't take long. Hunter lived in American Canyon, not far from Michelle Lawford's home, but in a much nicer neighborhood of well-kept ranch houses with large yards and detached garages. Water sprinklers cast rainbows over manicured lawns and blooming flowerbeds. Elms and oaks shaded the wide street. The street was almost deserted at that time of day. I caught a glimpse of a barefooted woman in a pink housedress hanging laundry up in her back yard. Three women in spandex trotted by as I parked at the curb in front of Hunter's home. The women were trailed by a black and tan dachshund who was panting so hard I worried he would have a heatstroke. The dog gave me a pitiful glance and then hurried on, little legs working double-time. Somewhere a baby bawled, then went silent.

Hunter's home had pale green siding and red brick wainscoting. A large willow tree dominated the green square of lawn. Small hedges lined the front of the house like soldiers ready to march. A white Chevy with round spots on the doors where decals had been peeled off was parked in the driveway. Probably a city car bought at auction. I walked up the sidewalk to the front door and rang the bell.

Hunter's mailbox was filled to overflowing. At a glance, it looked like the 'current resident' variety. The front door opened and he was standing on the other side of a screen door dressed in crease-less khaki pants and a white T-shirt, leather sandals on his feet. Hunter smiled, a bemused look in his dark blue eyes. Only the flushed skin and rough texture of his nose marred his good looks and hinted at his drinking problem. He had a Mickey Mouse jelly jar glass in his hand, half filled with amber liquid. I could smell whiskey on his breath, but he didn't look drunk.

"If you're the Avon lady," he said with a toothy grin, "I'm more than willing to buy perfume, even if I gotta wear it myself." He stuck out his hand. "How ya doing Miss de Montagne?"

I laughed. "Hi Hunter," I said as he pushed the screen door wide. His grip was firm and dry, his hands strong and callused.

"Come on in." He stepped out of the way. "Coffee's in the kitchen," he said, leading the way. He didn't ask why I was there - in fact he acted as if I was expected.

The ranch house's narrow foyer opened onto a hallway that ran straight through the house. The living room was on the left, furnished in Bachelor Primitive; a leather sofa, two easy chairs and a big-screen TV. No pictures on the wall. I followed Hunter past two closed doors and a bedroom converted into a home office to a sunny kitchen occupied by a fifties-style red Formica dinette and four matching chairs. The kitchen was spotless, but what caught my attention, what made me stop dead in my tracks, was the view of the backyard through a pair of huge bay windows.

The front yard and the interior of the house were neat and tidy, but didn't hint at the opulent beauty of the backyard. Azaleas bloomed in five different shades, snapdragons swayed in the breeze and roses dropped petals on the lawn. A goldfish flashed gold and orange in a small pond surrounded by ferns and crowded with white water lilies. I saw two orange trees in full flower and several pink and white crape myrtles. A wisteria loaded with purple flowers filled the far corner of the yard, its ropey vines climbing a wooden privacy fence. If I was a psychiatrist, I could have had a field day analyzing this hidden garden and the prim face that hid it.

"How wonderful!" I gushed.

Hunter shrugged and looked uncomfortable.

"This is incredible!" This was no weekend garden, this was a passion. I stepped closer to the window and noticed that Hunter was building a winding brick walkway. Bricks were stacked in two uneven piles and the sod had been cut in a graceful arc that circled the pond and ended in a concrete patio at the rear stoop. On the patio, several battered steel lawn chairs circled a small mesh-metal table. More flowers filled terra cotta planters. I could imagine sitting there in the cool of the evening having a glass of wine and enjoying the fragrances of the flowers.

"Keeps me busy," Hunter said dismissively. "You take cream? Sugar?"

"Black's fine," I said. He carried two cups to the red table and waited for me to sit down. Gardening skills *and* a gentleman.

190

I took a sip. "Good coffee."

"Grind my own beans," he replied simply, then stared at me until I began to get uncomfortable.

I cleared my throat and he grinned.

"Sorry," he said. "Old cop habit. Most people can't handle the silence. They start gushing. Works better on men. What can I help you with?"

"I wanted to ask about Laurel Harlan," I began, wishing I had a cigarette. I didn't have to wish long. Hunter's expression hardened at the mention of her name and he fished a pack of cigarettes out of his pocket.

"Mind if we step out back?" he asked. "Don't smoke in the house. Not much, anyway."

"I'd love to!" I said. I followed him, carrying my coffee. He left his coffee on the table, but he didn't forget his jelly jar.

Bees buzzed among the flowers, competing with the low drone of a hummingbird circling a red plastic feeder.

"Have a seat," Hunter offered, tucking a cigarette in the corner of his mouth. They were unfiltered, but I didn't care. My lungs were sobbing with desire.

"Can I have one of those?" I asked, as he slipped the pack into his pocket.

He held out the pack and then lit the cigarette for me. I couldn't get over the flowers. Maybe I should give up on vegetables and plant some blooms? Then again, you can't eat snapdragons.

"What do you want to know about Mrs. Harlan?" he asked. "And why?"

"The why is rather involved. Can I ask you a few questions first?"

"Ask," he said without enthusiasm.

"Do you think Laurel was capable of killing Kevin?"

"Everyone was capable of killing Kevin," Hunter said. "We're all innocent until we find a good reason to shoot somebody." That was a pretty bleak attitude, but I let it pass.

"You know what I mean."

"Don't like her much, do you?" he asked with a smirk.

"And you do?" I replied sharply.

Hunter took a moment, like he was deciding how much to tell. "No, I don't," he finally said, "Not from the first time I met her. Didn't like the story she told me about Winter, either."

"Really?"

"Sounded like bullshit. Her description, for one. Most people get a few details right, but not everything. I mean, they'll remember the eyes, or maybe the nose or a scar, something distinctive. But as you go along their descriptions get vague. She was just the opposite. When we finally caught Buford he didn't look much like the sketch. But Laurel identified him."

191

"You thought she was lying about Winter?"

"I thought she was lying about how it happened, and where. She said she was at the homeless shelter dropping off clothing, but nobody remembered her. I figured she was with a boyfriend and left the kid alone. Or maybe she was buying drugs and made up a story to cover that. Possibilities are endless." Hunter lit another cigarette off the butt of the first, leaving the pack on the table.

What Hunter said didn't exactly surprise me. Jessica had told me Kevin blamed Laurel for Winter's death. I guessed Kevin had come to the same conclusion Hunter had.

Suddenly I had a moment of absolute clarity, not easy for my sleep-deprived brain, and several pieces of information snapped together. It wasn't a clear picture, just the corner of a bigger puzzle, but my pulse quickened. That night at my vineyard, Hunter had told me that Kevin was obsessed with Winter's murder *and* the disappearance of another child. That child *must* have been Jenna Valdez, who could have passed for Winter's sister. The same Jenna that was enshrined alongside Winter Harlan in Michelle Lawford's bedroom. And what had Michelle said when she had me cornered in the drainage ditch? "—I covered her up. I took care of her," or something similar. What had she been talking about? What did she mean 'covered her up?' I came to an unexpected conclusion and my breath caught halfway down my throat. What if Kevin hadn't merely blamed Laurel for Winter's murder? What if he believed her *responsible?* I looked up from the tabletop to find Hunter watching me with a bemused smile.

"I can see the wheels turning."

"You told me that Kevin was obsessed with Winter's death, and with the disappearance of another little girl." I began, still sorting it out in my head. Hunter nodded, so I continued. "Was her name Jenna Valdez?"

Hunter eyed me speculatively. "That's right."

"I understand that Kevin couldn't, or wouldn't, identify Winter's body?"

"Happens more than you think," Hunter shrugged. "They don't want to believe. And she'd been out there for a few days. Didn't look too good." I got a quick mental image and my stomach rolled. Hunter dragged on his cigarette, squinting as smoke crawled up his face and into his eye. "Where you heading with this, Claire?"

"So, only Laurel identified Winter," I said. "Is it possible she lied? That the little girl was Jenna Valdez?" Hunter was shaking his head before I even finished.

"You've been poking around, huh?" he said, with an edge of annoyance in his voice. That made me defensive and I quickly told him all I had surmised, beginning with the theft of Jessica's gym bag and ending with the pictures in

192

Michelle's shrine, and what she had said while holding me at gunpoint. Hunter listened without interruption and soon I was running out of steam. And starting to feel a tiny bit foolish. All I had was a bunch of scraps and a few loose ends. But that's why I was there with Hunt, to get a professional opinion.

"Think maybe you should leave it to the police?" he said mildly, but I could see he was interested.

"They haven't done a very good job," I retorted. "They've insisted all along that Laurel's not involved. But this many coincidences? I think Kevin found out the truth about Winter and Laurel killed him."

Hunter dragged on his cigarette. "The truth," he repeated and shook his head. "Pretty strong allegation. From what I read in the paper, the case is closed."

I was talking before he finished. "I don't think Michelle Lawford killed Kevin. I was told she was drunk the night he was killed. Too drunk to drive."

"She confessed. Says so in the Gazette." Hunter sipped his liquor.

"She's covering for Laurel. She'll change her tune in court," I said, not nearly as certain as I pretended.

Hunter shrugged. "Stranger things have happened." He sighed again and shook out another cigarette. He offered me the pack and I grabbed one.

"Kevin was as crazy as you. He thought Winter might still be alive," Hunter said around the cigarette. "I tried to talk some sense into him, but he wasn't about to listen. He thought Jenna Valdez was the one killed by Buford. Kept insisting it wasn't his little girl."

"So you took Laurel's word over Kevin's?" I cut in.

Hunter waved that away. "Hell, no. But Winter's pediatrician, Lincoln Perry, confirmed the ID. Matter of fact, Ben insisted on bringing Perry in because Kevin was so sure the little girl wasn't Winter. I reminded Kevin of that, but he said Perry barely looked at the corpse. That he turned green and rushed to the bathroom to puke. Kind of strange for a doctor, but not criminal. Of course, Winter had been out there for days. It wasn't pretty." Hunter flicked ash on the bricks. "Hell, even Buford Logan picked Winter's photo out of the victim's lineup! So, either everyone is lying, or Kevin's nuts. You make the call."

"What are you drinking?" I asked Hunt, sensing that he was getting ready to shut down and block me out. Men are like that. And they get more stubborn the more you push. Besides, I needed a drink to go with the nicotine I was huffing in.

"Scotch. McAllen twelve-year old. You don't approve?" he asked with a juvenile delinquent smirk.

"I don't approve of not being offered any," I replied and he laughed.

"Be right back." He disappeared inside but was back a moment later with another jelly jar and the bottle. He filled both glasses.

"Sorry 'bout the glasses. Don't entertain much," he said as I sipped the scotch. It burned a smoky trail down my throat.

"I don't believe Michelle killed Kevin. Not on her own," I started in again. "And I think she might have helped Laurel cover up Winter's death."

"Buford Logan killed Winter," Hunter said. "I thought Laurel was involved. Parents kill their kids more than you'd like to know. But my theory, and my credibility, went out the window when Ben caught Buford. Buford confessed to snatching and killing Winter. He took us to the body." Hunter sipped his scotch.

I started to speak and Hunter held up a hand. "They found clothing identified as Winter's and blood and hair samples that were consistent with Winter. By then, Ben had taken over the case and I had bought a case of scotch." Hunter grinned lopsidedly.

"You headed the case until then?"

"I was off the case and retired before Buford was caught. But Ben kept me posted. Ben wrapped it up nice and neat. Good cop." He gulped the last of his scotch and poured another. A double. Already his eyes looked dewy.

"I heard that a Sheriff's deputy had an affair with Laurel during the investigation? Was it Doug Priest?" I had asked Ben and he wouldn't tell me, maybe Hunter would? That was the next link in the chain, Laurel's friend in the department. I was sure it was Priest.

"Don't know what you're talking about," Hunter said, scratching at his chin. "Your daughter's off the hook. Kevin, Laurel, Winter, and Jenna Valdez are none of my business. And none of yours." His words were getting mushy around the edges. He poured himself another drink. "Let the cops do what they're paid to do."

"I've already tried that," I said. I stood and slung my purse over my shoulder. "It got me nowhere. Thanks for the drink. I'll show myself out." I was sorry to have stirred up painful memories for Hunt, but, I was sorrier for Kevin. And I was going to keep stirring up memories until I knew the truth!

"Come back anytime." Hunter drawled.

"Maybe I will," I said, trying to end the visit on a pleasant note. The words came out stiff as boards.

I left Hunter sipping his scotch. I hadn't really learned anything new from Hunt, except that everyone involved with this case was determined to keep me in the dark, but I was starting to believe in Kevin's conspiracy theory. Maybe there had been a cover up of Winter's murder, as crazy as it sounded.

Victor called while I was still gathering myself together.

"Claire, Steve is here doing an inventory for the insurance claim."

"Great," I said, hating the tremble that infected my voice.

"Not great," Victor said. "We're having some problems with pricing."

"Problems?" I said, and my voice was tremble-free. Funny how fiscal problems can erase any emotion from love to rage. "I'll be there in ten minutes."

CHAPTER 35

Victor was standing at Samson's desk with my insurance agent, Steven Hearst, Jr. Steven's father had sold crop insurance in the valley for thirty years before turning the business over to his son. Steven Sr. was a bluff, good-natured, meat and potatoes kind of guy with a hearty laugh and a good-old-boy mentality. Steven Jr. took after his mother. He was thin and stoop-shouldered with a shock of lank brown hair and the annoying habit of tapping his pen against his front teeth. He was doing that as he slowly turned over wine bottle labels stained red, many with bits of green or clear glass still stuck to the back. Neither Victor nor Steven noticed me approaching.

"There's no way of knowing whether these bottles were full or empty when they were broken," Steven said, shaking his head dolefully. He had his back to me, unaware that I was there. What he said sent my temper flaring.

"I'm not in the habit of keeping empty bottles in the cellar," I said, and Steven almost jumped out of his skin.

"Mrs. de Montagne," he said, swallowing hard. "I'm sorry for your loss."

"A loss that is fully insured," I pointed out icily. "A loss which I expect to be compensated for."

"Of course, of course," he said, chewing on his pen now and looking nervously from me to Victor. "It's not me, you understand. It's the agency." He turned and flipped through the stack of labels. "Nothing really outrageous here, though. Some Champagne that's a bit pricey," he tapped a label for 1995 Louis Roederer with his pen, "and some of the Burgundy," he held up a label for a 1965 La Romanee Burgundy and my heart almost broke. I had bought the bottle in a mixed case at auction ten years ago and planned to drink it on some special occasion. None had ever seemed special enough. Now it was gone.

"What's the list on this now?" he asked, his voice dripping worry.

"I'd have to check, but somewhere close to fifteen-hundred," I replied.

"They stuck pretty close to the front door," Victor said, trying to cheer me up. "Grabbed bottles at random, mostly new vintages. Stuff you can replace. Looks like they were in a hurry." That was some comfort.

"That's the only really high-dollar bottle," he said, flipping through the rest of the stack of labels. Hs fingers were already stained purple. "The rest is pricey, but not outrageous. Probably ten-thousand, total. Have to check prices and get back with you."

"So, you'll pay fair value? *Full* value?"

"I'll submit the forms and the company will let us know," he shrugged and fidgeted. "The bottling equipment is totaled. I'll check prices for new machines and send you some quotes. The casks," he said, looking at the stack

196

of four wooden barrels with their fronts bashed in, "will be valued by contents and the barrel themselves. All of this is subject to negotiation, of course." He wouldn't meet my eyes. He stared at the labels, the casks, the damaged machinery.

"So, maybe I should hire an attorney." I said. "And find a new agent."

That brought his head up. "What? No need for that, Mrs. de Montagne! You're a valued customer and I promise you I'll handle everything. I gave Victor a check for the van. Not much, just four-thousand, but it was ten years old." His brown eyes were on me now. Who could stay angry with a man who looked like an overgrown puppy? Besides, I was in a hurry.

"All right then," I said with a sigh and a look that let him know he wasn't off the hook. "Tell your father I said hello."

"I'll do that," he said, smile turned up to ten. "One more question for you, though. Do you have any idea who did this?"

I looked at Victor and he looked at me.

"No," I told Steven, "but I hope to find out."

He nodded, tapping his pen on his two front teeth. "I was so sorry to hear about Samson. He's an icon. Is he okay?"

"An anachronism would be closer to the truth. He'll be fine. As long as he doesn't get worked up over the insurance claim," I said pointedly. "I think we should keep that between us."

Steven looked concerned. Samson's temper was legendary. He started to say something, then stopped. "Well," he said, turning to Victor, "let's go over the numbers?"

"Just a second," Victor said, pulling me to the door by my elbow. We stepped out into the sunshine of another perfect day. The wine train whistle wailed in the distance and I wondered what winery they were stopping at today? And once again I was glad I didn't offer public tastings. It takes up too much time for too little return.

"I've got a date tonight, so you might want to stick around just in case," Victor told me.

"I'll see you in the morning," I said, stifling a yawn, though it was barely 5:00. Victor went back to Steven as I trudged upstairs.

That evening, Jessica and I had a dinner of grilled three-cheese sandwiches with fresh tomatoes and basil. On the side were some of my famous sweet pickles and bagged potato chips. Not very creative, but it was good. I was too tired to do more. And I couldn't get Winter and Jenna out of my thoughts. Around a mouthful of sandwich, Jessica asked me about the vines, and I told her that last year's buds were coming in strong. We talked a bit about the weather and the coming season, and the fact that Jessica would be back at work next week, but it was obvious that neither of us was in the mood for conversation. We finished dinner in a comfortable silence. Jessica went to bed after helping me clear the table despite her broken arm.

At twilight, with my cup filled with coffee and a cigarette burning, I stepped out on the patio. The overhanging wisteria filled the air with purple perfume. The Harlan's house was dark. It was hard to believe that Kevin was gone while his vines were growing tall and full of promise. I sipped coffee and stared, thinking morbid thoughts, wishing someone was here to talk to. Jessica was in bed, Victor was gone and Samson was in the hospital. I could call Ben and tell him what I had found out, precious little though it was. But he had told me to butt out. I put my cigarette out in the grass, then stuffed the butt into the pack.

The valley below my perch was studded with lights, but there were large pockets of darkness where houses and wineries had not yet intruded. I could imagine how peaceful it would have been here a hundred years ago when there were no lights except from candles and fires. A simpler time.

I shook myself, annoyed with my own lethargy. I could sit here and mope, I decided, or I could get back up and do something. But what? My eyes fell on the Harlan's converted barn and I had an evil thought. I went back inside and grabbed my key ring. Kevin had given me a key to his home several years before, at the same time I had given him a key to my own cellar. Neighbors investing in trust.

I crossed the lawn to the Harlan's back door and tried the key. I have to admit that I was a little apprehensive. What I was doing was illegal. But, I did have a key. Feeling like a cat burglar sneaking in a penthouse window, I stepped into the musty silence of an empty home. Even with the large windows, the room was dark. I half considered going back to Violet and finding a flashlight, then thought 'what the heck?' and flipped on the overhead lights.

The living room looked like a cyclone had hit it. The furniture was all gone, but loose newspaper, magazines and litter covered the carpet. Pictures hung at odd angles, mingling with clean white squares where other pictures had been removed. Laurel was gone!

I stepped into the kitchen and turned on that light too. Cabinet doors stood open revealing only a few orphaned plastic plates and cups. Dirty dishes overflowed the sink and an army of wineglasses covered the counter. Laurel had taken only the clean dishes.

I was about to turn off the light when a foil capsule from a wine bottle caught my eye. I stopped and picked it up off the counter. It had a bunch of grapes on one side and the words 2008 V.R. handwritten in gold marker below it. I recognized the foil as Violet Vineyard's, and the handwriting was

Samson's. I'd recognize his scrawl anywhere. The V.R. stood for Vintner's Reserve. This capsule had to have come from one of the six bottles Samson had hand-filled and corked for the Lady's Brunch.

My teeth grated and I saw red. The foil proved that Laurel had vandalized my cellar! It wasn't possible that she had purchased this bottle. This had to be one of the two bottles I had left behind that day and later stored in my private cellar.

I slipped the foil in my pocket, wishing Priest were here so I could exclaim aha! and wave it under his nose. But, he'd have some ready and logical explanation. I almost couldn't wait to get back to my cellar and verify that at least one of the two bottles was gone. That would prove, to me at least, that Laurel was the vandal.

I flipped off the kitchen light and went down the hall to the Harlan's bedroom. I wasn't nervous anymore. Laurel wasn't coming back, that was obvious. Scuff marks from moving dollies marred the hallway's gray plank floor and the corners of the walls were battered and nicked. The movers had been in a careless hurry and I could imagine Laurel shrieking at them to move faster.

In the Harlan's bedroom, women's clothing was scattered over the floor and cascaded from every drawer. The closet had been ransacked. A collection of wire hangers hung at drunken angles. A pile of old shoes and three hats were on the beige carpet. The bed was unmade and another pile of shoes was mounded on the wrinkled sheets. The only area that looked undisturbed was the top of a mahogany dresser. Pictures of the Harlan family stood in a neat row. Most of them were shots of Winter with one or both of her parents. A pile of albums sat on the floor beside the dresser, a thin layer of dust coating the top one. I stooped and picked it up and leafed through it. Pictures of Winter smiling in a ski suit. Smiling in a little red and white jumper. Smiling, smiling, smiling. And as I looked my blood ran colder and colder. Dropping the album on the pile, I walked back through the house, spotting pictures of Winter and her parents here and there. By the time I made a full circuit and was back in the bedroom, it was obvious to me that Laurel had left behind *every* picture of her daughter and her husband. What kind of mother could do that?

My stomach felt like it was filled with rocks. I wanted out of the barn and away from the creepy feeling crawling up my spine, but I made myself slow down and look at everything. I would only get one chance.

I went through closets and drawers, even the bathroom medicine cabinet, but found nothing. I thought about the cellar, but the light switch at the top of the stairs made a futile, light-less click. Without a flashlight, I wasn't going down those pitch-black stairs. After turning off all the lights, I went out the back door, locking it behind me. Full might had settled in. I crossed the lawn to my own property.

"Find anything interesting?" Ben Stoltze asked from the shadow of the wisteria arbor, and I almost jumped out of my skin. He dragged deeply on a cigarette and the glowing ember lit his face a hellish orange. "Breaking and entering, count two," he said.

"You scared the hell out of me!" I yelped. "What do you think you're doing?" I wasn't happy to see Ben, I realized. I wasn't sure what to believe anymore.

Ben heaved his bulk out of the wooden chair and stepped toward me. Involuntarily, I took a step back.

"That's what I was about to ask you," Ben said, stepping too close. I could smell stale cigarettes and the ghost of Old Spice after-shave.

"Just looking around," I said defensively and shuffle-stepped sideways, giving myself more space.

"Looking for what?" he asked, his voice like gravel from too many cigarettes. My eyes adjusted to the moonlight and I could see his rumpled shirt bulging loosely from his pants. He was unshaven and his face was so deeply lined it looked like a river basin. His eyes were bloodshot and I detected the odor of beer and burgers on his breath. I thought jealously, and ridiculously, that he had been back to Shaky's without me.

I shrugged. "I don't know."

"Find anything?" he asked indifferently and flicked his cigarette out into the lawn. It traced a red arc and hissed as it hit the dewy grass. My mouth popped open to let him have an earful about the non-biodegradable properties of a cigarette's filter, but I bit off the complaint. I'd pick the butt up in the morning.

"No," I lied and instantly wondered why I had. I hurried to add, "I noticed she left all of Winter's pictures behind." That didn't prove anything except that she was a rotten human being, but I told him anyway.

Ben grunted at that. "She's really gone, I guess," he said and he sounded almost wistful. My jealousy flared again. I couldn't keep it from showing.

"Disappointed?" I asked, remembering the way he had stared at Laurel that first day when we told her about Kevin.

"Hell no," he said, brow knitted. "What are you trying to say?" Now he was on the defensive. He ran his fingers through his messy hair. "Spit it out."

"Nothing," I said and crossed my arms over my chest.

We stood in silence for a long moment.

Ben turned his eyes on the view of the valley. "Thought it'd make you happy. Mrs. Harlan leaving," he said, patting his shirt pocket and coming out with a crumpled pack of Winstons. He stuck one in his mouth and lit it. The lighter's flare revealed even more clearly the fatigue etched in his face. The lighter winked out and all was darkness and shadow again.

"I'd be happier if she hadn't left so many unanswered questions behind her," I told him. "There's coffee inside," I added, wanting to get out of the chill and out of the dark.

"No, thanks. Can't stay long," Ben replied. "Nice out here, anyway," he cocked his head and sniffed loudly. "My wife always loved wisteria, but our youngest boy's allergic. Shoulda planted one after he went off to college."

"Why'd you come by?" I asked, then added, "Not that I'm unhappy to see you."

Ben closed his eyes and shook his head. "Hunter Drake called me this afternoon."

"Uh-oh," I said. "Guess I made him mad."

"Upset's the word I'd use. He said you were asking about Winter Harlan and Jenna Valdez."

"I asked, and I didn't get any answers," I told him. "Jenna isn't in Mexico with her father, as you know."

Ben nodded. "We made a mistake there," Ben said carefully. "You have to understand what we were dealing with. Hunter was drinking heavily, and his reports reflected that. I did the best I could when I took over the cases." Ben's tone turned heavy with disgust. "It was a mess, and we had a pedophile, a killer, who could have gone free thanks to sloppy police work."

"What about Michelle Lawford? The papers said she confessed to killing Kevin?"

"Yes, she did. Seems that they had an argument that got out of hand. She said she was here to see Laurel when Kevin confronted her. They argued and he hit her. She grabbed the shovel and beat him until he quit moving."

"Argued about what?"

"She wouldn't say. Something to do with Laurel's my bet."

"That's all very neat," I said sarcastically. "Did Priest come up with that on his own?"

"You don't believe it," Ben replied tiredly. "Surprise, surprise."

"I believe Michelle's lying about killing Kevin. I think she's covering for Laurel."

"I can't believe this crap," Ben said, running his fingers through his hair and shaking his head with exasperation. "Like an Agatha Christie novel!"

"Stanley Kostyol told me that Michelle was too drunk to walk when Kevin was killed. And I know there's an unidentified print on the shovel," I felt like wagging a finger in his face. "And I bet it's not Michelle's."

"Stanley Kostyol is a liar and a thief," Ben said with rising irritation. "And Michelle could have wiped her prints off the shovel."

201

"Again, very neat."

"Damn it Claire!" Ben exploded. "The only thing that would make you happy is locking up Laurel Harlan, and that ain't gonna happen! Why? Because she didn't do anything!" Ben snapped his cigarette into the lawn. "The case is closed."

"I'd like to look at that file," I said defiantly. "To ease my mind."

"You don't believe a word I'm saying, do you? You're *not* going to look at the file. You're *not* a police officer, it's *no* business of yours," Ben turned his back on me and stalked to the edge of the patio. He stopped there and faced me, a dark cutout against the lights of the valley. "Let this be, Claire. Worry about Jessica and Samson." He walked into the night without saying goodbye. A moment later I heard his car start and then heard the sound of the engine fade as he drove away.

"What the hell is going on?" I asked the stars, but they just stared coldly back. It seemed that everyone wanted me to butt out. It saddened me to think that I might have damaged my relationship with Ben beyond repair, but it made me angry too. Was Ben so jaded that he would close the case even if he doubted Michelle's confession? I couldn't believe that. Ben was a man of integrity. A man of integrity who probably wouldn't be buying me lunch anytime soon.

Well, if my relationship with Ben was down the drain then there was no reason to drop my own investigation, for that's what it had become. With thoughts swirling, I went to bed.

CHAPTER 36

The next morning dawned clear and cold. A stiff wind was blowing in from the ocean, smelling strongly of salt and seaweed. I had my morning coffee with Victor, who looked tired. He grinned at me lecherously when I asked him how his date went.

"Wanna hear the details? Pretty juicy stuff, I'm not sure you can handle it."

"Keep it to yourself," I told him.

"Jealousy is an ugly thing," he replied as he headed for the back door. "I'm going to finish mowing the field."

"Sounds good to me," I replied, sipping coffee. "What do you think of the vines?"

Victor shrugged. "Looking good. Too much rain lately." It's like that in wine making; too much rain is as much of a problem as too little.

"If you need me, call." He stepped outside and pulled the door closed. I finished my coffee, went upstairs and showered, then went back downstairs in my robe and had more coffee. I took my time getting dressed, smoking too many cigarettes and thinking about Ben. I couldn't deny my attraction for Ben, or the turmoil I felt over running behind his back for information. Had I ruined any chance for something more than friendship? Did I even want something more? And what about Hunter Drake? Better not to think of him. But I couldn't help myself. Despite his drinking and his refusal to help me, I still liked the man. Why, suddenly, at fifty, was I feeling this emotional confusion? Was I going insane, or making up for lost time? Only one thing was certain, it had been too long since I played the dating game; I was way out of practice.

Even as I pondered Ben and Hunter, I couldn't shake the nagging suspicion that the two knew something about Winter and Jenna that they weren't telling me. What had happened to those two beautiful little girls? What was everyone trying to keep me from finding out? What mistakes were made? And did they lead to Kevin's murder? Only one thing seemed certain now; there wasn't a thing I could do about it!

Frustration and anxiety began to give me a headache. I had to find something to keep me busy.

There was wine to rack, the 2012 vintage, but I just didn't feel motivated. I went down to the cellar anyway. The battered bottling equipment still sat in the middle of the aisle. The broken casks were gone along with the broken glass, but the machinery spoke eloquently of the damage done, and the rage behind Laurel's actions. She must have used a sledgehammer. Wires and springs jutted from battered metal. Creases and dents reflected the overhead fluorescent light. I wished I could have the mess hauled off, but until the check

203

came from the insurance agency it had to stay where it was. In a way I was happy that Laurel had focused so much of her rage on the machinery. She had broken only a few casks of the 2010, which revealed her ignorance of her husband's trade. Machines can be replaced, but the wine that was aging in oak could not be. Still, the loss of the thirty-gallon casks meant that a lot of people weren't going to get their promised allotment of wine.

I heard the phone upstairs ring, trotted up the stairs and caught it just before the answering machine kicked in. It was Marjory.

"Claire, dear, how are you?" she asked, sounding tipsy. At 9:00 A.M.

"I'm fine Marjory," I said, rolling my eyes. "What's up?"

"Just wanted to let you know that I smuggled Samson out of the hospital this morning," she said with merry good humor. I could just have merrily wrung her neck!

"*Marjory*—" I angrily began, but she cut me off.

"Don't be mad at me!" She said. "You *know* how he is. I went by to see him and he was getting dressed five seconds later. There was nothing I could do! He's got the cutest little butt," she added in a conspiratorial whisper.

"That's more than I need to know," I told her, about to gag. "Did the hospital release him?"

"Sort of," Marjory said evasively.

"What does 'sort of' mean, Marjory?"

"Well, his doctor wasn't there, and the nurse went into a hissy fit. She grabbed Samson. If she hadn't been a woman I think he would have decked her!"

I groaned and closed my eyes, bracing for a story that was sure to make me angry. "You said 'sort of?'" I reminded her.

"I'm getting there. We had a bit of a tussle. She insisted on Samson filling out some paperwork. I threw my American Express card on the counter and she shut right up. That proves that they just keep you there to run up the bill. I think—"

"How is he?" I cut in.

"He's fine. He's lying by the pool. He wants to come to Violet. I tried to put my foot down, to make him rest, but he won't listen to me," Marjory said.

"Or anyone else," I sighed.

"He wants to see the cellar. Was it as bad as he said?" Marjory asked, and there was as much desire for gossip as there was compassion in the question. She's my friend, but a black widow is a black widow.

"Not as bad as it could have been," I replied, but she wasn't satisfied with that.

"Was it that witch?" She hissed. "I swear she'll pay for destroying my vines, one way or another. My babies," Marjory added with the hint of a sob and I could feel her misery in my own heart. Marjory has five times the acreage under vines as I, but the loss of even one row would be devastating to me. By comparison, the loss of wine and machinery in my cellar was minor. The vines were alive, full of the promise of great things. They were the future, and more precious than a million bottles.

"I don't know who it was," I said evasively. I didn't want her spreading rumors, even if I was sure they were true.

"Well, Samson swears he'll shoot her on sight," Marjory said. I squeezed my eyes shut. That's all I needed, Samson on the warpath.

"Can you keep Samson for a day or two?" I asked, like I was talking about a child. And, in a way I was. If Samson saw the mangled bottling line, the broken barrels and the empty spots in my wine cellar, he'd have another stroke. "He should be in the hospital," I added, guilt-ing Marjory into complying.

"I'll try to keep him away from Violet for a day or two. I can keep him amused that long," she trilled a brassy laugh. "No promises, though. I can't— oh, crap! Samson's screaming at the maid, dear. Gotta go." She hung up. Thank God! I stepped on to the patio, pushing Samson out of my thoughts.

Victor was on the tractor pulling the brush-hog mower through the field that separates the rows from the rocky slope. The smell of fresh cut grass was delightful. He pulled up beside the patio, engine roaring.

"I'm working up a hunger!" he yelled over the racket.

"Sitting on your ass!" I yelled back.

"Love my job!" He grinned like a lunatic and gunned the engine.

"I'm grilling steaks tonight," I yelled.

"Aaaa-rooooo," Victor howled, craning his skinny neck. "Red meat, red meat, red meat," he popped the tractor into gear and sped off across the lawn, engaging the brush-hog's mower blade. With my eyes, I followed the closely-cut path he was making through the field. By contrast, the back yard looked shaggy. I really needed to mow the front lawn too. The idea actually appealed to me, I was so desperate for any distraction. But first I'd get the steaks ready.

In the kitchen, I took down a large glass bowl and poured in a couple of teaspoons of olive oil. I minced three cloves of garlic (Victor would have a fit about bad breath, but he'd gobble it down anyway) and tossed them in the olive oil followed by a half-cup of chopped shallots. A tablespoon of Lee and Perrin's Worcestershire sauce and a dash of ground mustard seed. I took three rib-eye steaks, hand-cut by my favorite butcher, from the freezer and dropped them into the bowl. They were as hard as rocks, but they could thaw in the marinade. I covered the bowl with a tea towel and scanned the refrigerator for inspiration for side dishes.

I had a bottle of homemade raspberry vinaigrette in there and a small block of Maytag bleu cheese that I had been picking at for weeks. I knew there were plenty of ripe tomatoes and red onions in the garden. Voila! Instant salad, and one of my favorite dishes. There were several sweet potatoes in a wooden burlap-covered box in the pantry. I took out three, buttered and salted them and wrapped them in foil, ready for the oven.

With dinner ready to go, I changed into ragged shorts and a grass-stained T-shirt. I popped in on Jessica, who was working on a pile of construction paper, cutting out stars, triangles, circles and squares in a rainbow of shades and piling them in a plastic tub for her kids at Bishop Lynch. It was rough going with just one arm, but she was managing. Her hair was brushed back in a ponytail and she looked fresh-scrubbed, tanned and cheerful. It brought a smile to my face and put a spring in my step. I trotted out to the barn and started up the riding lawn mower. Things were getting back to normal.

There's something soothing about cutting the lawn, especially when all you have to do is ride around in circles sipping on a plastic cup of iced tea. The clean green swaths gave me the feeling of accomplishment while the mower did the work. For a time Winter, Kevin and Laurel were lost from my thoughts. It was a break I needed.

Victor waved when he passed on his way to the barn. He made a skinny muscle and goosed the tractor to show me who had the *real* power mower. I snubbed my nose at him and demonstrated the agility of the small Ford mower by turning several sharp donuts in his path and dodging out of the way as he hit the brakes. He mouthed something that I didn't hear and then I was around the side of the house and out of sight.

By the time I finished with the lawn and my iced tea and had stowed the mower in the barn beside its big brother, Victor was sitting in the shade of the wisteria sipping a beer from my refrigerator.

"Any time you wanna race," he said with a grin. I plopped down beside him, wiping sweat from my face with my sleeve.

"Got any money?" I asked, leaning back and stretching my legs.

"Nope. The lady I work for is a tight-fisted shrew."

"Hardy, har, har."

"Gonna check on food stamps soon," he sipped his beer. My beer, if you want to get technical. "Make more money on welfare."

"I guess you won't be wanting a steak, then."

"I didn't say that. Poor man's gotta take what he can get."

"Keep talking and you won't be getting anything."

"Tight-fisted shrew," he muttered. "You picking Samson up today?"

"Samson's with Marjory. I thought of asking them over, but…" I shrugged.

"But you're not ready to watch octogenarian dry-humping," he finished.

"Victor! That's a visual I don't need!"

"Seeing it live is even worse, believe me."

"Yuck." I stood and stretched. "I need a shower."

"Praise the lord," he pinched his nose. "I was trying to be polite, but I *am* sitting downwind."

"Hardy, har, har," I said again and punched him in the arm.

"Tight-fisted and abusive," he said as the kitchen door swung closed behind me.

After a cool shower, I felt a little better, but my thoughts were still plagued by Winter and Jenna. I dressed in jeans and a Violet Vineyard T-shirt and went down to finish dinner.

The steaks were marinating nicely, so I put them in the refrigerator and headed out to the garden. The weed invaders were hard at work, crowding around the tomatoes. I ignored them and quickly picked six beefy tomatoes and two purple onions and took them back inside and sliced them up. I put them in a plastic bag and placed them with the steaks in the fridge. By then it was a little after five and time to get the grill going.

The grill was set up at the edge of the patio. Victor had wheeled it over from the barn, hungry and helpful, as always. I loaded it down with mesquite chips and fired up the gas. As the wood crackled and burned, I went inside and poured myself a short glass of Glenlivet over ice. With a smoldering cigarette, I sat down near the grill and plopped my feet in another chair. I watched the fire, sipping my scotch and puffing away. When the mesquite was glowing cheery red, I closed the lid. The steaks were going to be great, and I was starving.

"Bread!" I yelped as Victor came down from the guestroom, his hair still wet from the shower.

"Butter!" He said.

"Slice the bread," I told him, pointing at the knife rack

"You are lucky that I crave steak," he said. "You tight-fisted, abusive, domineering—" he shut up before I threw something at him.

CHAPTER 37

By the time Victor was done with the bread, Jessica and I were on the patio sipping drinks. Victor chose cabernet, and Jess was having a Coke. We watched twilight settle like a silk curtain over the valley. A cool breeze was seeping down off the mountain and the sun was a mellow gold. If I could have gotten thoughts of Winter out of my mind it would have been very pleasant.

"Food!" Victor suddenly proclaimed. "Steak, steak, steak!"

"Light some candles," I told him. Night was coming on fast. The valley below was as black as the sky above. House lights and headlights resembled stars and supernovas from this distance. If you squinted.

I slapped the steaks on the grill and lowered the lid. The meat sizzled and its fragrance competed with the wisteria.

Victor asked Jessica how her arm was. Jessica said it was itching like crazy.

"Coat hanger," Victor said as he knelt to light a citronella candle, one of a dozen scattered around the patio. "Gets right down in there."

"That helps until you stop scratching and then the itch is right back," Jessica whined.

While the steaks cooked, I went in and gathered plates and forks and had Victor take them to the patio while I fixed the salad. I arranged the sliced tomatoes and red onion in a circle on the platter, sprinkled blue cheese over it all and then doused it with raspberry vinaigrette. By then the steaks were ready to come off the grill.

The food was dished up and we fell to with an appetite. I could tell they were enjoying it by the lack of conversation. It seemed like a matter of minutes before the steaks were gone and we were groaning over full bellies.

Jessica started to get up, slipped and banged her injured arm on the edge of the table. Glasses sloshed and Jessica dropped back in her chair moaning and cradling her arm.

"Are you all right, babe?" I asked, half out of my seat.

"I was going to help clear the table," she moaned, "But now, I think I'm gonna scream. It's been killing me all day."

"Why don't you get a couple of pain killers and lie down for a while," I told her. "I'll take care of the dishes."

"It'll be more than a while," Jessica said. "Those things knock me out." She stood and kissed me and Victor goodnight.

"Steak good," Victor said when we were alone.

"And now you have to pay for your supper," I said, rising and gathering dishes. "Pitch in, buddy, or no dessert for you."

"Dessert?" he said hopefully. "Dessert?"

208

We ferried the mess inside and I offered Victor a Dove bar for dessert. He wasn't impressed. He muttered something about being tight-fisted, then fixed us both another drink. We went back outside.

For ten minutes we sat silently in the candlelight, sipping our drinks and looking at the stars.

"Still can't believe he's dead," Victor said, looking toward the Harlan's fields. The vines looked wan and abandoned. "And that she got away with it."

"She won't get away with it," I said, more hopeful than certain.

"She already has," Victor replied quietly.

Again the silence dragged out until Victor spoke.

"Remember when we planted the willow?" he asked wistfully, looking toward the tree two hundred yards away. "That was a good day."

"One of the best," I replied as the memories flooded in.

"She was a beautiful little girl," Victor said and I nodded.

"Why do you think Kevin was in the rows the night he was killed?" he asked.

I shrugged, still looking at the willow.

"With a shovel?" Victor added and a light popped on inside my head. Everything I had learned came together in that moment. All the pieces that had seemed so unconnected fell into place. Kevin, with the shovel, entering my vineyard in the dead of night. His belief that his daughter wasn't the girl identified by Laurel and Dr. Perry. Michelle's guilt-ridden demeanor and the mini-shrine she had created. And the tiny crucifix on its broken chain that had been lying at Kevin's feet. A crucifix just like the one Winter had proudly worn day and night, a gift from her grandparents on her baptism.

"Holy Mary," I gasped, shooting out of my chair, heart lunging into my throat. Winter had been kidnapped only weeks after we had planted the willow. The ground beneath it had been soft, freshly turned. I knew then that the photo on Michelle's dresser was much more than a shrine. It was a tombstone. Kevin had come to my vineyard to look for his little girl.

"What?" Victor asked, standing and following my eyes. "What?" He said again, stepping closer.

I didn't reply. I couldn't speak. What I was thinking was so awful that it couldn't be true. But I knew it was. I trotted to the wine cellar door and all the way to the back of the cool cave where the hand tools are kept. I took a shovel from the standing rack and rejoined Victor.

Victor's eyes took in the shovel and the color drained from his face.

"The willow," I said, brushing at the tears that streaked my face. I almost choked on the words. "Kevin came for his daughter. He came to dig up Winter."

"No," Victor said, turning pale. He shook his head. "No."

209

I didn't reply. I led the way to the willow.

"The crucifix they found was hers," I said. "She never took that necklace off. Never. So, how did Kevin have it when he was killed?"

Victor said nothing. I stopped at the willow and jabbed the shovel into the ground. I turned over the rich black soil and pitched it onto the grass. I made two scoops before Victor took the shovel away. I stepped aside and he attacked the grass around the tree like treasure was buried below. But we knew what we were digging for, and both of us hoped we wouldn't find it. Our hopes went unanswered.

"Oh, God," Victor said after ten minutes of furious digging. He pitched the shovel aside and dropped to his knees, pawing at the earth like a wild animal. "Oh, God," he said again. He turned his head and vomited on the grass. The acrid stench of stomach bile and half-digested steak filled my nostrils and I gagged. I knew what he was seeing and I didn't want to look. But I had to.

Victor stood shakily and looked at me, tears streaming, his whole body shaking.

I stepped around him on rubber knees, light headed, stomach churning. At the near end of the shallow pit I saw a pink blanket wrapped around something. I knelt beside it.

From the top of the bundle a lock of blonde hair stuck out, catching the wavering moonlight. I touched the hair and the blanket fell away revealing moldering skin stretched tight over a child's delicate facial bones. I retched and skittered back on my hands and knees, gagging. Victor tried to take my arm but I slapped him away, stood and rushed to the edge of the lawn. I vomited into the weeds until there was nothing left in my stomach.

Victor put his arm around my shoulders. He didn't say anything for a long moment. His eyes looked hollowed out and dead. I hugged him, thinking sadly that while we had searched the fields, rows and hills for Winter she had been just a few hundred yards from home. Kevin had found that out and it had cost him his life.

"We have to call the police," he finally said. "We have to call Ben."

"I'll do it," I said hoarsely, throat raw. "Stay with her."

Victor nodded and I walked/staggered back to the kitchen and got my purse. I took the cell phone out and dialed 911, but hung up before the phone could ring. I dialed Hunter Drake's number instead. He answered on the third ring.

"Hello?"

"Are you drunk?" I demanded.

"Who the hell is this?"

"Claire de Montagne," I croaked, brushing away tears. "Are you drunk?"

210

"No," he said. "And what business is it of yours? I was just about to have a drink, and—"

"Shut up!" I screamed into the mouthpiece. "I just dug up Winter Harlan in my back yard."

After a protracted silence he asked, "Have you called the Sheriff's office?"

"No," I said, trying to get my breathing under control. "I called you."

"Call them now," he said, "I'm on my way." He hung up. I dialed 911, gave the dispatcher my name and told her what we had found. She seemed uninterested. In a monotone worthy of a machine, she read my address back to me and asked me to confirm it. I did and she said the police were on their way. I hung up and went back to the willow. Back to Winter.

CHAPTER 38

The police arrived half an hour before the reporters, and five minutes after Hunter Drake.

Hunter drove around the house, parked his white Chevy and came across the grass to where Victor and I stood, thirty feet from Winter's grave.

"Claire," he said, looking beyond me at the trench beneath the willow. "Is that where she is?" I nodded and he stepped grimly around me. He walked over and knelt beside the pink bundle, turned aside the blanket and sat on his haunches staring for several minutes.

Police sirens suddenly cut through the night. As the first car barreled around the house, blue strobes flashing, Hunter stood, brushed dirt from his hands and joined me and Victor.

"Looks like Buford gets a walk," is all he said.

"And Laurel gets to fry," Victor added, eyes on the grave. "I'd like to pull the switch."

"They use gas in California," Hunter corrected absent-mindedly.

"Even better," Victor said as a pair of deputies exited their car and came running, pistols drawn.

"What's going on here?" the first one, a tall brunette with an officious manner and a peach fuzz mustache, asked. Then he saw Hunter.

"Hunt?" he said.

"Hey Billy."

Billy holstered his revolver, but his partner, a fat man with wobbly walrus cheeks, kept his in his fat fist. Both uniformed deputies looked toward the grave, but Billy asked the questions.

"What's goin' on here, Hunt?"

"Found the Harlan's little girl," Hunter nodded at the grave.

"Buford dumped her in the river," Billy said. He glanced at the grave and back at Hunter. "We found the Harlan girl, Hunt. Must be some mistake."

"She's over there," Hunter said. "No mistake."

"Christ," Billy muttered. He spoke over his shoulder to his partner. "Gary, call Ben and get Midge out here, too." Gary trotted off, belly jiggling. Billy looked at Hunter.

"Guess I better check it out," Billy said reluctantly. He looked at the grave and then back at the three of us.

"Nothing to see," Hunter said. "Leave it to forensics."

"No," Billy said, rubbing his chin with the heel of his hand, "I gotta look." Hunter shrugged and Billy went over to Winter. He came back after a quick glance. He looked queasy.

"Little kid," he said and Hunter nodded.

"Winter Harlan," Hunter said.

"Christ," Billy said again, looking at his shoes. "You Claire de Montagne?" he asked.

"Yes."

"You found her?"

"We did," I said, titling my head at Victor.

"Victor Gonzalez," Victor said before he was asked.

"We'll need statements," Billy said. "You too," he added to Hunter.

"Got it," Hunter said with a touch of annoyance. I guessed he was used to being in charge at crime scenes.

"Maybe you guys should come up to the house," Billy said looking around. "Midge gets crazy about crime scene integrity."

We walked back to the patio with Billy. Victor and I sat down at the table under the wisteria, awash in the swirling red and blue strobes from the police car. Two more sheriff's cruisers arrived at the same time and Hunter joined the deputies back at the grave, shaking hands with two of them. I sipped my drink as they looked at the grave.

I had just lit a cigarette when a Channel Four news van whipped around the corner of the house and ground to a halt in the loose gravel just inches from the bumper of one of the cruisers. A spike-haired redhead with a brusque manner and fake boobs leaped out of the van. The cameraman was right behind her. I started to rise, an outraged yell on the edge of my tongue, but they were already bolting across the field trailing cables. The van's driver was dragging a rack of lights out of the back. The woman and her cameraman didn't make it twenty feet before Hunter and two of the deputies rushed her.

She tried to skirt the three men, but ran into a trellis, bounced back into the row, tripped over her microphone cable and went down hard in the freshly tilled earth. The dew was already settling, so, by the time she got up her knees and butt were streaked with mud and she was cursing. Hunter blocked the cameraman, waving his hands in the air like a basketball player trying to block a shot. A scene of furious cursing and hurled insults followed as I settled back and watched. They had to tow the woman back to her van. The cameraman filmed it all. Hunter alone was calm, smiling and laughing as he herded the cameraman back.

"I want her off my property," I yelled at Hunter as he deposited the reporter at her van and started back toward the grave.

"I told her she could stay right there," Hunter said. "She just needs to stay out of the way."

"This is my property," I reminded him, my eyes shifting form Hunter to the redhead. "If she doesn't leave immediately, I want her arrested for trespassing."

"Claire," he began, but I cut him off.

"Get her out of here. Move her to the road or to jail, your choice."

"Wait a minute," she shouted, coming toward me at a trot. "Freedom of the press has a greater priority than your property rights."

"Off." I said again, looking at Hunter. "Now." Hunter intercepted her and turned her around. She yelled something about police brutality and freedom of the press as Hunter ushered her back to her van and inside. More arguing took place through the open door, but I didn't pay any attention because Ben Stoltze had just pulled up. I walked over to meet him.

Ben got out of the car, took in Hunter arguing with the anchorwoman with an indifferent glance and turned to me.

"What the hell's going on here?" He demanded. "And what's Hunt doing here?"

"I called him," I said.

"Ben!" The woman yelled over Hunter's shoulder, but Ben ignored her. His eyes were on me and they weren't friendly.

"Why did you call him?" Ben asked, a trace of irritation, maybe jealousy, in his tone.

"He was the lead detective on Winter's case," I said lamely. "He was the only one that would listen to me."

"The only one who hates Laurel as much as you do," Ben finished coldly.

"That's not true—"

"Enough," Ben cut me off as he looked toward the grave. "You sure that's Winter out there?"

"Yes."

"What's happening with Sheila the she-devil?" he asked, jerking his head in the anchorwoman's direction.

"I ordered her off my property," I explained.

"Same old Claire."

I didn't say anything to that.

"Seen Midge Tidwell?" Ben asked as the channel four van backed up with a spurt of gravel. The back wheels went up on the grass as the driver spun the wheel and punched the gas, throwing more gravel in a rooster tail. Jerk.

"No, I haven't," I told Ben, watching the van through narrowed eyes.

"Sit on the patio," he told me, "I'll need to talk to you." His voice held no affection, just resignation.

"Guess you were right about Laurel," he said as I turned away. "Logan claimed he dumped the body in the river. Must have been the Valdez girl."

214

"I'm not happy about it."

Ben grunted, turned and walked away.

Hunter walked over.

"What'd Ben say?" he asked.

I shrugged. "He's mad at me."

"You have that effect on people," he said, smiling. "Some of us are just better at hiding it."

I ignored the jibe. "Thanks for running her off."

"She's kinda cute," Hunter said.

"Not to me," I said with annoyance. "Unless pit vipers are cute."

Hunter laughed and that annoyed me even more.

"Why are you in such good spirits?" I asked nastily. "There's a little girl dead over there."

Hunter's smile thinned, but it didn't disappear. He shrugged. "Been a long time since I was at a crime scene," he said. "Gets the old juices flowing. I'm gonna talk to Ben."

"Fine," I said shortly and rejoined Victor on the patio.

CHAPTER 39

When detective Priest arrived in his personal car, a burgundy Corvette, he parked it on the grass and joined the crew around Winter's grave without so much as a glance in my direction. Victor and I gave our statements to a deputy.

I explained my discovery to him, detailing the connections I had found. He looked at me like I was crazy. At 12:30 A.M. the police finally left. Ben threw us a wave, but didn't stop to speak. He looked ten years older than his years. Priest crossed to his Corvette. Momentarily, I thought of stopping Priest to explain how I had come to the conclusion that Winter was buried under my willow tree. But I was too upset to bother with him. My mental images of Winter as a bubbly little girl had been replaced by the mummy swaddled in dirty pink. I felt like crying but the tears wouldn't come. My anger was too great, an anger that Laurel's arrest and conviction would only ease, not relieve.

Thankfully, Jessica slept through it all, knocked out by her pain medication. I checked on her at 1:00 A.M., and she looked like a frail angel sprawled under her sheet, her blonde hair splayed across the pillow. I watched her for ten minutes with tears in my eyes for Kevin and Winter. I eased her door closed and rejoined Victor on the patio. Hunter Drake was still standing in the darkness at the edge of Winter's grave, his back to Victor and me.

"I'm ready to try to go to sleep," Victor said, rubbing his eyes. "Probably won't be able to, but..." he shrugged pathetically and looked at me with bloodshot eyes. "Are you okay, Claire?"

"No," I answered honestly, "But at least it's over."

Victor nodded. "You going to bed?"

"I'm going to talk to Hunt first," I said, standing and stretching. "Then I'm going to smoke ten cigarettes and cry in my scotch. Maybe then I'll be able to sleep."

"Want me to stay up?" he asked with almost totally concealed reluctance.

"No," I told him, shaking my head, hands on my aching lower back. "You go ahead."

"Call me if you need me," he said and disappeared inside.

For a moment I stood at the edge of the patio and watched Hunter's black silhouette against the lighter purple of the night sky. Hugging myself against the cold, I walked over and stopped beside him. Neither of us spoke, but his presence beside me was a comfort.

"Coffee?" I finally broke the silence.

"No thanks," he said and another three minute silence began.

"They put out an all-points for Mrs. Harlan," he told me.

"They'll catch her," I said and Hunter nodded.

216

"Lot of blood behind her," he said. Hunter seemed as down as I was.

"She was a beautiful little girl," I said and the tears finally came, gushing out in a sob I was unable to swallow. Wordlessly, Hunter hugged me. I didn't argue - I needed to feel close to someone at that moment. I gripped his shirt and cried. He held me a long time, until my tears had become mere sniffles and then for a long time after that. Each of us seemed hungry for the closeness. Finally, I stepped back a quarter-step and looked up into his shadowed face.

"I want to kiss you," he said, his voice husky, his hands on my waist.

"Don't ask," I said and his lips came down hard on mine. Our bodies clashed in a needy embrace. Only the shame of standing beside Winter's grave made me break away.

"I'm sorry." Hunter said. "Sorry."

I shook my head and took his hand. Silently, I led him up the rows to the house. I locked the kitchen door behind us and he kissed me again.

"Claire," Hunter began after the kiss had ended, but I put my fingers to his lips. I led him upstairs to my bedroom and locked the door behind us. I was acting shamelessly, but I didn't care. I had been attracted to Hunter from the moment I met him. And I needed someone right now so desperately...I didn't think, I acted.

That night we comforted each other without words, without awkwardness or pretense. Each took from the other and gave in return, a bittersweet dance. That night I began to fall in love with Hunt, and no thoughts of Ben or Roger entered my mind.

CHAPTER 40

Hunter shook me awake at 5:00 A.M.

"I have to go, Claire," he whispered, leaning over the bed, already fully dressed. I sat up and rubbed my eyes.

"Okay," I said, feeling awkward and shy. Last night I had fallen into Hunter's arms and he had fallen into my bed and it had felt so perfect. This morning I didn't know how it felt. Hunter must have been feeling awkward too.

"Well, uh, when can I see you?" he asked, standing above me, shifting his weight from foot to foot.

"When do you want to?" I asked with a sleepy smile. He laughed and the tension was broken.

"Breakfast?"

"Lunch?" I replied.

"I'll cook," he said, with a grin that had me thinking chili and chips. "My place, One o'clock." He stooped and his lips brushed mine. His beard scratched my cheek. "One o'clock," he repeated and stepped to the door. "I'll let myself out," he whispered. He pulled the door softly closed behind him and I fell back into my bed with a silly little smile on my face and a blissfully anxious sense of anticipation. I was back asleep almost instantly, thinking about Hunter and wondering what he would make for lunch.

When I came downstairs a little after 8:00, I could tell from the looks I got that Victor and Jessica knew that Hunter had stayed the night but neither of them said anything. Jessica had obviously been crying, and I assumed Victor had related the previous night's events. I got some coffee and joined them at the table just as Victor rose to head out to the vineyard. When he was gone, Jessica asked if I was okay and I asked her right back. Neither of us mentioned Winter. The events of the last week had left me, at least, mentally and physically drained. I couldn't take anymore. I guess she felt the same way. Jessica went to her room and I settled lazily into my chair with a vintage wine catalogue. I had to restock my cellar, after all, and it was a welcome distraction.

At 10:00 I was browsing the champagnes while thoughts of Hunter Drake danced at the edge of my mind. Good and bad thoughts. He was a great looking guy with a lot of personality, but a hard drinker too. There was no way I wanted a relationship with a drunk. But then again, who was I kidding? After all, I had slept with the man; if that wasn't the start of a relationship then I'd better start looking closely at my moral barometer.

218

"Never mind that now," I told myself. "Just enjoy the moment." My whole life had been carefully thought out and planned, maybe now was the time to fly by the seat of my pants?

Jessica came down, a pink sweater draped over her cast, and told me that she was going to see her father and might not be back until tomorrow. Victor was dropping her off. I knew she'd probably tell her father about me and Hunter and I grinned at the idea. It was about time my infidelities were reported to Roger instead of the other way around. Let's see how he liked it!

At 11:00 A.M. I suddenly panicked over what to wear to Hunter's. Something casual, I thought, but how casual? I finally settled on khaki slacks and a Violet Vineyard polo shirt. Then I changed my mind. I went through three ensembles before settling on a pale blue dress with a white sash and a modest above-the-knee hemline. I didn't bother putting on makeup, but I did take time to tame my hair into a windswept look just this side of deranged. At 12:00 o'clock I was climbing into Sally after informing Victor that there was lunchmeat and bread in the kitchen.

"I'm disappointed that this new love life of yours is interfering with my food supply," was his dry reply as I walked to my car.

I listened to Golden Oldies on the way to Hunter's. By the time I got there I was feeling a very girlish shyness. Considering I had slept with the man the night before, it seemed silly to have my palms sweating and my breath coming harder as I walked up the sidewalk to his front door.

I knocked and Hunter came to the door in khaki slacks and a white polo shirt, the heavenly sent of roasting chicken oozing out around him.

"Hi, Claire," he said and actually blushed. He wouldn't quite meet my eyes. That made me feel a little less foolish, and a lot flattered. He held the door open, trying to stand aside in the narrow opening, but there wasn't enough room. A bit of bumping and squeezing took place, both of us laughing, uncomfortably aware of the other's nearness. I could smell after-shave of the cheap variety. That took me back to high school dates and dances. The chaste kiss he planted on my cheek after closing the door took me back even farther.

Hunter led me through the kitchen to the back patio.

"Whatever you're making smells wonderful," I told him as we stepped into his back yard paradise. The scent of flowers and wet grass didn't quite obscure the smells coming from the kitchen. A pitcher of iced tea, slices of fresh lemon floating on top, and two glasses sat on the iron table. I sat down across from Hunter.

"Roasted chicken with mushroom sauce and pan fried potatoes," he said.

"Sounds great," I said to cover the growl coming from my stomach. The coffee and cigarettes I'd had for breakfast hadn't been very filling.

219

"The mushroom sauce is really cream of mushroom soup," he said with an apologetic grin. "Chicken's free-range, though."

"I'm glad to know it was a happy chicken," I said and he laughed.

"Until the axe fell."

"We're all happy chickens up to that point."

"Probably a little nervous right there at the end, though," he said. "Iced tea?"

"Love some," I said and he poured us both a glass. I was glad that he hadn't offered me a drink. That would have been the pinprick for my good mood. Today, I just wanted to enjoy the meal and his company without thinking of any deeper issues. Issues that might have already marked this relationship for disintegration. Issues like my marriage and his drinking problem. Little things.

"Can I bum a cigarette?" I asked, and he fished a pack out of his pants pocket, handed me a cigarette and lit it for me. He lit one for himself and we settled back in the chairs, enjoying the sunshine and the breeze. Out front I could hear the occasional shouts of children, a dog barking and the rumble of passing cars, but we might as well have been a thousand miles away in Hunter's personal Garden of Eden.

We sat in silence, comfortably, like an old married couple, smoking and sipping our tea. I felt so relaxed I could have slipped my shoes off and gone to sleep. Hunter must have felt the same way. He yawned then stood and stretched hugely.

"Better check on the chicken," he said and disappeared inside. I heard pans clatter and silverware jingle for a few minutes and then a crash as glass hit the floor. I got up and stepped inside, but not too quickly. I know when I break something I need a moment of private cursing.

Hunter was sweeping up a pile of white glass slivers that had been two dinner plates. He grinned at me as I stepped inside and said; "Chicken's fine, don't worry."

"Let me do that," I said and grabbed the broom from him. "You get dinner on the table," I added with a grin, "I'm hungry."

"Your wish is my duty, fair lady," he said and handed me the broom. "Especially when it means you take the broom."

"That's not an antifeminist jibe, is it?" I asked as I swept the glass into a plastic dustpan.

"I am anything but anti-female," he said over his shoulder as he eased a glass pan filled with chicken breasts and bubbling mushroom sauce (soup if you want to get technical) out of the oven. He looked darned cute as he inspected the chicken. I couldn't remember the last time a man had cooked dinner for me. Probably because no man ever had!

220

I emptied the dustpan in the trash as Hunter transferred chicken to two new plates, ladled on the sauce and then eased a lidded casserole out of the oven. The smell of browned potatoes joined the smell of chicken and I almost swooned. Hunter fumbled through a drawer of loose silverware for a large spoon, which he handed to me. I ladled up the potatoes and we carried our plates out into the sunshine.

"Oh, wow," I said after the first bite. "Either this is fantastic or I'm starving."

"Maybe both," Hunter said after he swallowed. "Enjoy, it's all I know how to cook."

"Mom's favorite recipe?" I asked.

"My ex's least favorite, actually. Probably why I like it so much," he said around a mouthful of potatoes. Such manners.

We were interrupted by a knock on the front door.

Hunter looked up in surprise. I guessed he didn't get many visitors.

"Be right back," he said, wiping his hands on his calves. I just nodded, my mouth overfull. I stopped eating abruptly when Hunter returned with a visitor.

Sheriff Ben Stoltze stopped dead in the doorway, his eyes on me. I was suddenly flustered, like a wife caught cheating. Ben's stare didn't make me feel any better. His expression seemed to be caught between betrayal and surprise, but that lasted only a second before he stepped down to the patio and smiled tightly at me.

"Hello, Claire. What are you doing here?" Ben didn't seem to notice the garden around him or the view of the mountains beyond.

"Having lunch," Hunter said with forced joviality, looking from me to Ben. "Want to join us?"

"Can't." Ben didn't look at Hunt, his eyes stayed on me. "Just had lunch with the District Attorney. He got a subpoena this morning from Buford Logan's attorney. Gonna need you to come in and go over the file with us, Hunt."

Anger flashed across Hunter's face. "I had nothing to do with Buford Logan's arrest," he said. "It was *your* case by then."

Ben turned to face Hunter.

"And I was wrong about it," Ben said flatly, without apology.

"That wasn't the only thing you were wrong about," Hunter said. "You were wrong about Laurel. You were stumbling over your dick."

Ben looked at me, then back at Hunter. "This isn't the time, Hunt."

"I warned you back then," Hunter persisted, his lips a flat line. "Nothing I can do now."

"You can help me keep Buford Logan in jail," Ben barked. "Or do you want another murder on your conscience?"

221

"My conscience is fine," Hunter replied.

"A few drinks cleared it right up. That right, Hunt?" Ben said viciously and I thought Hunter might punch him. The two stared at each other like dogs straining at their leashes.

"Should I leave you two alone?" I asked, starting to rise. Hunter waved me back down. I really wanted to go. To run and hide.

"I'll come in later this afternoon," Hunter said. "Good enough?"

"That'll be fine, Hunt." Ben stuffed his hands in his pockets and looked like he wanted to say something else. Hunter didn't give him the chance.

"This afternoon," Hunter said and it was clear that the conversation and the visit were over.

"See me before you go to the DA," Ben said. "I'd like to talk before we go in."

"Won't change what I have to say," Hunter bluntly told him.

"Damn it, Hunt!" Ben exploded. "I'm not asking you to lie."

Hunter shrugged.

"This afternoon," Ben said and opened the kitchen door. Halfway through, he paused and looked back at me.

"See you, Claire," he said with a feigned indifference that made me cringe. I tried to shrug it off, but I felt as if I had done something wrong, whether I had or not.

"Bye, Ben," is all I said, wondering if he could tell by looking at me that I had slept with Hunter? A silly notion, but sometimes I can be very silly, especially, it seemed, when it came to affairs of the heart.

Hunter dropped into his chair, propped his elbows on the table and put his hands together, like he was praying. The mood of sexually-charged companionship had evaporated. And so had my appetite.

Hunter and I sat in silence for five minutes, our food growing cold.

"Damn it," Hunter said then his eyes flicked up to mine. "Sorry about that. This isn't the way I wanted the afternoon to go."

"That's all right," I assured him, and then the nosy part of me kicked in. "You think Buford Logan will get out?"

Hunter scowled as he dug out his cigarettes, offered me one and then lit them for us. "Yes. Shouldn't happen, but it will. They'll make him out to be a victim of injustice. A damned hero."

"What's going on between you and Ben that you can't discuss in front of me or the Assistant DA?" I asked Hunter.

"You really think that's any of your business?" he asked in a tone so cool that I felt like I had been demoted from lover to nosy busybody. I would have said something sharp in reply, but something I had heard in the two men's brief and bitter conversation finally struck home.

222

I sat up straight in my chair. "Ben was the policeman who had an affair with Laurel," I said, a statement of fact not a question. "He covered for Laurel because he was sleeping with her." That bastard!

Hunter winced and looked away. "Now, Claire," he began. "You've got to under—"

"I think I finally *do* understand," I said, getting to my feet. "Ben had an affair with Laurel and helped her to cover up Winter's murder. And you just sat by with a drink in your hand and let it happen." All the anger that had been churning inside me rose up in my throat. I had just been feeling sorry for Ben and now this! "That bastard!" I roared. "*You* bastard!"

"Claire—" Hunter stood and came toward me, but I circled the table in the opposite direction.

"You let it happen, didn't you?" I said, seeing him with new eyes, ashamed of myself for sleeping with him. This, I felt, is exactly what I deserved for letting my attraction to Hunter overwhelm my good sense.

Hunter held his hands out, palms up. "I warned Ben about—"

"And then Kevin found out and Laurel killed him." I was on a roll now, my anger building with every sentence. I wanted to run after Ben and choke him. "Answer this for me," I said. "Was Ben's wife still alive when he started screwing Laurel?"

"She was very sick—" Hunter began and I held up a hand to cut him off.

"Buford Logan killed Jenna Valdez," I said and Hunter quit talking.

"Probably," he conceded, slouching into his chair. "But—"

"She's dead," I snapped. "Buford Logan confessed to killing a little blonde girl in the valley and dumping her in the Napa River, and it wasn't Winter. It was Jenna. And I think you knew that. Now, thanks to you and Ben, he's going to walk out of prison and do it again." I slung my purse over my shoulder and crossed the patio to the kitchen door.

"Mrs. Harlan and her doctor identified the body," Hunter said defensively. "Besides, I was off the case and off the force by then. I didn't suspect any of this until Kevin came to me a few months ago."

"But you knew that Ben was sleeping with Laurel," I accused. "And you knew that Laurel was lying."

Hunter slumped into a chair and stared up at me morosely. "I didn't know about any cover up. I was drinking a lot back then," was all he said.

"Well, have one on me," I said and slammed the door behind me. Hunter didn't come after me. I grabbed my purse and left, boiling inside. All of this could have been avoided. Kevin would still be alive if Ben had done his job and Hunter had followed his instincts.

I climbed in Sally and gunned the engine, peeling off fifteen feet of rubber as I sped away from Hunter's home. That's when the tears came. Tears of shame, shock, anger and betrayal. I could barely see to drive, but I didn't stop. The only consolation I could find in this mess was that finally Laurel would be made to pay for at least *one* of her crimes. But that wouldn't resurrect the dead, or erase the blood from Ben's hands.

Damn it, Ben, why?

CHAPTER 41

When I arrived back at Violet, Victor was in the rows pawing through the vines, checking leaf color and bud count. He waved at me as I walked to the kitchen door. I waved back but didn't stop. I was too drained to talk. I put coffee on and sat at the kitchen table to brood. My mind was so overwhelmed with anger at Ben, I couldn't even think about Hunter. It was too painful and too close to get any perspective. He had done nothing to me, really, but he had shown himself to be less than I had hoped. And that I could not forgive, no matter how irrational it sounds. His negligence had caused two murders. And the murderer was still free. But what Ben had done was even worse. I had trusted him. I may even have been halfway in love with him. He had betrayed me. Even worse, he had betrayed his wife while she lay on her deathbed. And he had betrayed the trust of the entire community.

I poured a cup of coffee and lit a cigarette. I had finished half of it when I heard Victor shout angrily from the back yard. I leapt out of my chair and rushed to the window to see Victor racing across the grass toward the shed I call a garage. Standing beside the garage was a man dressed in jeans, a blue jacket and a baseball cap. The man looked up sharply, his face shadowed by the bill of the cap. He fumbled something out of the jacket pocket as Victor barreled down on him.

As I watched dumbfounded the man struck a match. That's when I noticed the gas can sitting at the man's feet. It took a split second to make the connection. My eyes leapt to all I could see of Sally, her taillights poking out of the shadows of the garage.

I screamed, "No!" and bolted out the kitchen door just in time to see him toss the match, turn and sprint toward the rocky slope beyond the lawn. Behind him there was a *Whumph!* as flames raced up the walls of the shed and roared into the eaves. The ancient, bone-dry wood sucked up the flames and the garage erupted in a fireball. The edges of the roof joined in furiously and sparks and burning scraps of tarpaper bloomed into the sky like fireworks.

"Sally!" I screamed as I rushed toward the garage.

Victor had reached the garage. He looked back at me, his eyes wild, then threw his arms up to protect his face and raced headlong into the garage.

"Victor!" What was he doing? Was he crazy? Suddenly Sally didn't seem all that important.

Victor jerked the driver's side door open, and leapt inside. Unfortunately, the keys were lying on the kitchen table. I screamed "Victor!" again as a piece of burning tarpaper fluttered down from the rafters and landed on Sally's hood and the old Mustang lit up like a barbecue pit on wheels, flames engulfing it. I realized then that Sally must have been doused in gasoline. I screamed again, and kept running toward the garage, only dimly conscious of the arsonist disappearing over the edge of the slope.

I reached the garage door and stopped dead at a wall of flames. I screamed Victor's name, covered my head with my arms and rushed forward. The flames singed the hair off my arms and the heat tried to slap me back, but I barely noticed. My only thought was for Victor. I made three steps before Victor plowed into me, knocking me sprawling then ran right over me, his hair and shirt on fire. He dove to the grass and rolled, slapping at the flames.

I jumped on top of him, trying to smother the fire as I ripped at his smoldering shirt. I tried to wrench his shirt up over his head but he shoved me away.

"Get off of me!" I flopped on my butt, and looked at him in horror. His hair was singed to black scrub on the right side and so was his ear. That side of his face was red and already puffy and so was his right arm. He coughed and spit into the grass.

"I'll kill him," he said and coughed up black gunk.

"Are you okay?"

"Yeah," he said, nodding at the grass. "I'll live." He looked at his right hand and winced. Slowly, he got to his feet and shrugged off the remnants of his shirt. "I wish I coulda caught him," he said through his teeth. "Damn, this hurts."

"I'll catch him," I swore bitterly, my fear for Victor instantly replaced by rage and bloodlust. Victor could have been killed! And my garage had been turned into Sally's funeral pyre. I was up and running before Victor could try to stop me.

"Claire!" He yelled. "Call the police!"

"You call them," I yelled back. I hit the top of the rocky slope and skidded through a mass of boulders, gashing my knee on a jagged outcropping of porous black lava. The razor-bright pain made me move faster. I leapt over a boulder, skidded around another then slipped and slid on my butt down a river of loose shale, throwing up dust and shards of gray stone. I caught a glimpse of the arsonist up ahead, making slow time, cautiously picking his way through the maze of boulders and brush toward a dirt farm road six hundred yards below my property. A car was parked down there, but he wasn't going to make it.

I covered ground like a jackrabbit, mindless of the spiny brush that slashed at my face and the rocks that tore at my hands. The arsonist heard me crashing down the slope and started moving faster. That was a mistake. I had grown up playing on slopes just like this, battering myself in the name of fun. I closed the gap quickly, getting to within fifty feet. The arsonist's car was still a couple hundred yards away.

A thundering explosion came from the top of the hill and caused the arsonist to look back, taking his eyes off where he was going. He stumbled and went down hard, screaming. I screamed back, bellowing like a Viking. A wave of heat rolled down the slope and slammed into my back, but I didn't turn. I knew exactly what that explosion meant; Sally was gone.

"Bastard!" I roared. I stooped and grabbed a hand-size chunk of rock with a wicked edge. The arsonist scrambled to his feet. Only fifteen feet of slope and five feet of elevation separated us. As the arsonist skirted a lava outcropping, I launched myself at his back like a tackle on Super Bowl Sunday.

My shoulder caught him dead center and he folded, air whoomphing out as my weight drove him into the edge of the lava bed. He bounced off with a fleshy thump and the cap went flying. Brown hair spilled around his shoulders and he flopped to the dust like a bundle of sticks. I landed on top of him, rolled off and got to my feet fast. I squared off with the arsonist, the sharp edged stone clutched in my hand, arm cocked and ready to drive it into his skull. Her skull, actually.

Laurel Harlan gripped her side and kicked at me as she scrabbled away on her haunches. The clothes she wore were men's and far too large for her. The fall had left her dusty and ripped a hole in the knee of her jeans. Her always-perfect makeup was smeared and her hair was a tangled rat's-nest. Blood leaked down her cheek from a scratch under her left eye. I watched her warily, the rock ready in my hand. I wanted so badly to use it! Then Laurel did something crazy. She laughed at me.

"Enjoy the barbecue?" she asked. "A little idea I stole from Michelle." She grinned cruelly. "I know how much you loved that stupid car."

"You almost killed Victor," I panted, sweat dripping down my face, streaking through the dust and grit, stinging my eyes. The rock gouged into my hand, the weight of it begging to be brought down on Laurel's skull. I blinked away the salt, not daring to take my eyes off her.

"Oh, my god!" she clapped a hand to her mouth and arched her brows. "How terrible! I am *so* sorry!" She dropped her hand to reveal a leering grin. She looked absolutely deranged. Her pupils were pin pricks and I could smell gin from where I stood. I wondered what she had downed with the booze? Whatever it was it had pushed her off the edge of sanity. "You're next," she said. "And then your little slut."

"You've done all the killing you're going to," I promised, inching closer, lifting my rock. I thought of Winter's mummified corpse and rage poured thick blood into my brain. My temples throbbed and my vision warbled. "How could you kill your own daughter?"

227

Laurel scooted back another foot. Her smile slipped off. "It was an accident. A terrible, horrible, terrible accident," she said without a hint of sorrow, just an empty string of words. "An accident." Her shoulders hit the boulder and she drew her knees up. Her eyes searched the barren spot we had landed in. I was smart enough to realize she was looking for a weapon.

"You buried her on my property."

"Michelle did that," she said, the rage flooding back into her voice and eyes. "I told her to get rid of her and she buried her fifty feet from my backdoor!"

"Winter," I said. "Her name was Winter."

"*Winter!*" Laurel screamed at the top of her lungs. "I never wanted her. That was Kevin. *She was Kevin's!*"

"And you murdered her," I cut in flatly. I couldn't work up any more indignation. How can you be indignant with a snake?

Laurel glared at me. "She fell. Down the stairs." Her eyes never stopped probing the rocky scrap of ground. "I didn't mean for it to happen. But I knew what the police would think. What people like *you* would think."

"Was Kevin an accident?"

"You really are an idiot," Laurel said with a laugh. "I didn't kill Kevin. Oh, I *wanted* to bash his skull in when I found out he was banging your little slut. What he saw in that airhead I'll never know."

"Who did?" I wasn't buying any of it. I was just waiting for Laurel to make a move so I could bash *her* skull in. I realized with a start that I wanted to kill her. That I would do it without remorse.

Laurel laughed, shrill and crazy. "You think this is a movie? Mystery of the Week? You'd be surprised, oh I can guarantee you that. You'd be *so* very surprised."

"You're not bright enough for a Mystery of the Week," I told her, taking a step closer. "The prisons are full of trash who thought they were clever." The flesh on Laurel's face went tight to the bone and her teeth flashed like a dog's. She snapped a kick into my bloody right knee and pain wrenched me out of my body. Laurel was wearing steel-toed boots. I wasn't even conscious of falling until the ground knocked the wind out of me. I tried to stand, but my leg howled like an abscessed tooth and buckled under me.

Laurel didn't give me time to recover. She rolled to her feet, stooped down, and threw a punch at my head. I don't know how I managed to get a forearm up in time, but her fist bounced off my arm sending a shock wave up to my shoulder and then she was on top of me, digging her hands into my hair, her knees on my chest, pinning me flat.

"Perfect little bitch!" she screamed as she jerked my head forward and then slammed it back, bouncing my skull off the rock. Starbursts and comets

228

streaked through my vision. If Laurel had been stronger the fight would have been over and I would be dead. Luckily I was a hell of a lot tougher than she was. When she jerked my head forward to do it again, I punched her in the face, flattening her upper lip and snapping her head back. My second punch made her nose crunch and blood fly. She toppled off of me taking a double handful of my hair with her, ripping it out by the roots.

Laurel rolled over and pushed herself up to her knees, driven by fury. I know that because the same emotion was driving me. The pain in my knee was forgotten. The cuts, the bruises, Sally, it would all be worth it if I could wrap my fingers around that woman's throat. I rolled to my knees and swung my rock at Laurel's head. My aim was off, and I clipped her shoulder. She yelped and fell away, kicking at me. A steel toe hit my jaw and I was on my back again, dazed, tasting blood in my mouth.

Laurel used a pile of rocks to push herself up. We were both covered in dust and dirt and splattered with blood from Laurel's now crooked and bleeding nose. Laurel's lips were moving but no words came out, only a keening wail that sent shivers down my spine. Her eyes were sunk back in her skull, blood streaking her face and neck. Stupidly, I watched her pick up a wedge shaped chunk of rock. She took a step toward me, lifting the rock high. I gripped my own rock tighter and waited for an opening, waiting for Laurel to swing at me so I could get my own shot in. Not a good idea. I forgot about her feet. She kicked me in the ribs and I screamed. I lost my rock when she kicked me again, knocking the breath out of me, the pain freezing my right side.

Laurel looked down at me, blood dripping from the tip of her nose. It splattered on the rocks beside my head and started to puddle.

"You're dead," She said, lifting the rock high above her head. I threw up my arms, knowing she was right, wishing I had one more chance. Wishing I could take her with me. That's when I saw Ben standing on the slope above us, his pistol in his hand.

Ben didn't say anything. He took careful aim and shot Laurel in the side of the head.

Laurel lurched like she had been hit with a baseball bat. Blood and brain matter splattered the boulder behind her and her eyes went huge. She had a hole in her skull as big as a softball. For a frozen moment she stared down at me, the rock held in a loose grip, then she fell straight down like an imploded building. Her chin hit the rocks and she flopped backwards, her legs tucked under her. She twitched twice and then lay still, the rock still in her hand.

I scrabbled away from the spreading pool of blood and vomited, my eyes locked on Laurel as if she might jump to her feet and yell 'April-Fools.' I gagged and choked and vomited again as Ben calmly picked his way down slope. He stopped beside Laurel's corpse, his revolver loose in his fist.

He stared at her a long time before glancing at me, eyes blank as dinner plates. "You all right, Claire?" he asked.

I didn't answer him. It took all I had to climb to my feet, doubled over by my battered ribs. I staggered past Ben and started climbing, thinking only of Victor.

I remember Ben yelling at me, but nothing more of my ascent to the vineyard. Pain was everything. Pain and fear for Victor.

I stumbled onto my lawn, sweat running down my twitching flesh. My hands were bloody and shaking, my legs felt like rotten toothpicks. I didn't think I could take another step. Then I saw Victor lying in the yard where I had left him, not far from the incinerated tin-can jumble that had been my car and garage. Black smoke was boiling off Sally's tires. A ring of burnt grass surrounded the garage, but Victor lay clear of the fire. He wasn't moving.

I ran to him, almost falling with every step, and dropped to my knees. His face was blistered, his arm as well. Big ugly blisters that were surrounded by raw flesh. I felt for a pulse in his neck and almost screamed with joy when I found it. I laid my hand on his shoulder and screamed; "Call 911!" at Ben, who had climbed up and was crossing the yard. Ben's clothes were dusty and a scratch on his forehead was sending blood down his right cheek. He didn't even look my way.

Samson pulled up in his jeep at that moment and he climbed out, eyes bugging at the still smoldering garage. He came toward Victor and me at a shambling run.

"Call 911!" I yelled at him. Ben had stopped walking and was watching us with complete detachment. Samson kept coming, running like an animated scarecrow.

"Is he—" Samson began as he slid to a halt, wheezing, hand on his chest.

"Damn it!" I screamed at him, out of control. "Call 911!"

"I will call," he said, his voice calm, knocking my own fear back a step. "Stay with him, de Montagne." Samson ran back to the house. By the time he got back I was shaking uncontrollably, teeth clacking.

"They are coming," he said, and then, "Your face! Are you fine?" He lowered himself to one knee and put his hand on my shoulder. I jerked away reflexively. "Are you all right, de Montagne?" he asked, his voice steady. He touched Victor's shoulder and there were tears in Samson's eyes.

"No!" I sobbed. "No." Samson hugged me close. I fell against his chest mindless of the blood I was smearing over his green hound's-tooth jacket. He stroked my hair and told me it would be fine. I didn't believe him, but I felt comforted. Like a child again, seeking protection in my father's arms.

CHAPTER 42

Minutes after the fire trucks arrived, the ambulance took Victor away with a blast of sirens and flashing lights. There were tubes in his arms and nose. There was no ambulance for Laurel. She remained on the slope below. I argued desperately to be allowed to ride with Victor, but by then a pair of deputies had arrived. They told me I had to stay, and when they brought out the handcuffs I relented. I limped over to the patio where Samson was sitting. My knee throbbed and my side was killing me. My hands were battered and bloody, but I didn't even think about medical attention for myself. Nothing seemed broken. I eased myself into a chair beside Samson.

Midge Tidwell had arrived before the trucks, and only minutes before Priest drove up. Both of them went down slope where Ben waited near the body. More cops followed. Twenty minutes later, Priest came back with Ben and Midge. Priest looked green around the edges. He strode over, rigid as an infantryman and stopped in front of me.

"Guess you were right," he said but it wasn't a compliment. "And I guess Stoltze came along just in time," he added. Ben was right behind Priest.

"What the hell does that mean, Doug?" He snapped and Priest spun on his heel to face his boss.

"What exactly were you doing here?" he asked with hostile sarcasm. "Checking up on old girlfriends?"

"You son of a bitch," Ben breathed. It was the first emotion I had seen from him that day.

"You had to kill her?" Priest demanded. "No other choice?"

"She was about to kill me!" I butted in, anger running like electricity through the words. "She had almost killed Victor!"

Priest glanced at me, then back at Ben, waiting for an answer that didn't come. Ben just stared at the younger detective.

"Did you give her a chance to surrender?" Priest asked. "Did you even try?" Priest swallowed hard. His hands were shaking. "You killed her," he said and I thought he was going to take a swing at Ben.

"I had no choice, detective," Ben said flatly.

"Sanctimonious bastard," Priest snarled. "Everything's wrapped up now, huh? You two," his eyes flashed briefly on me, filled with hatred, "can sip wine in the sun, but a woman that never had a chance is dead."

"Detective—" Ben began, but Priest wasn't listening. He brushed past Ben and strode toward his county car.

"This isn't over," he yelled as he opened the car door. "Not by a long shot. You think you've won, Stoltze, but I'll see you out of your job by the end of the week. About the same time Buford Logan walks off death row." He climbed into his car and slammed the door, backed up, and peeled off as Ben watched in stony silence.

"De Montagne, what is happening here?" Samson whispered, but Ben heard him.

"He was screwing Mrs. Harlan," Ben said. "I followed him this morning. He had her shacked up in that seedy little Windjammer Motel on the other side of the Mayacamas. He's the one that's out of a job. I filled out the paperwork this morning."

"Why the hell didn't you arrest her?" I said, repelled by Ben's coldness.

Ben closed his eyes and shook his head. "I wanted to give Priest a chance to bring her in. A chance to save his reputation, if not his job."

"And now Victor's in the hospital, maybe dying. He—" I tried to continue but choked up again. "Damn you, Ben," I finished, barely able to see him through the tears.

Ben stared at me a long moment, then turned his back. "Take her to the hospital, Samson. We'll get your statements later," he said and walked back to the smoldering garage where Midge Tidwell and the forensics team were looking over Sally's burned-out corpse. Sally's tires had been doused, and the whole mess was sodden from the fire hoses, the grass rutted by the big trucks. I watched Ben go with a sinking feeling in my gut and a sense of desolation. My whole world was falling apart, and Ben was at the center of it all.

"Damn you, Ben," I whispered as Samson's arm encircled my shoulder. I reached up and squeezed his withered hand and he tried to smile at me, but his smile wasn't working.

"Let us go to Victor, de Montagne," he said in a gentle voice I didn't know he possessed.

232

CHAPTER 43

Samson drove us to the hospital in his Jeep. I didn't even wait for the wheels to stop turning before I jumped out and ran gimpily on my injured knee through the emergency room doors. Victor was in surgery, the officious nurse behind the desk told me. She asked me about next of kin and my knees went weak.

"It's a standard question," she reassured me with a thin smile. I explained that Victor's mother and father lived in the Rio Grande valley in Texas so I was probably the closest thing to a relative within 1000 miles. In response to that she handed me a stack of papers attached to a clipboard and a pen. I was getting good at the hospital's forms. I could probably fill them out blindfolded.

Samson stayed with me, feeding me endless cups of vending machine coffee and bitching about the hospital staff. Victor was in surgery for three hours. He had suffered third degree burns on his neck and arm. When the doctor came out to the waiting area she looked waxy and tired, deep circles ringing her eyes. She gave me a tremulous smile and yawned, covering her mouth and blushing.

"Long day," she said. "On top of a long night. Flu's got half the staff out and the other half working doubles." She gave us a wry smile. "Lucky me, I'm healthy as a horse. You look awful by the way. Do you need medical attention?" Her eyes went to my hands and concern washed away the fatigue etched into her face. "You need those cleaned and bandaged. Even minor cuts can get infected."

"I'll do it myself," I assured her quickly. "I've had lots of experience. How is Victor?" I asked while Samson breathed raggedly down my neck. I should probably have checked him back into the hospital while I was there.

"He's going to be in a lot of pain," the doctor said cautiously, "but he's strong. He'll pull through just fine."

"Thanks be to God," Samson said and my legs went wobbly.

"Can we see him?" I asked. The doctor was shaking her head before the words left my mouth.

"Not tonight. He's heavily sedated and we don't want him disturbed. Why don't you two get some rest and come back tomorrow? He'll be fine, trust me."

"Thank you so much," I told her and squeezed her hand.

"Get some rest," she said and left us to trudge down the hall, shoulders slumped, feet dragging. "And bandage those hands," she called back over her shoulder.

Samson stayed the night in the guestroom, his snores echoing down the hall, driving me nuts. I tossed and turned for an hour, images of Laurel and Victor, of blood and bullets playing across my mental drive-in. Finally I gave up and got up.

I rinsed my face in cold water, pulled on a pair of jeans that were hanging over the lip of the hamper and slipped into a clean T-shirt. I went down to the kitchen and put coffee on. I made it weak, still hoping for a little rest. With a cigarette and itchy eyes I waited for it to perk, watching the clock's second hand spin, trying desperately not to think. It was almost 5:00 A.M. I winced. There seemed little point in even thinking about going back to bed.

As the pot spewed and steamed, I pulled my cellular phone from my purse, and dialed the hospital. I gave my name and asked for an update on Victor's condition. The reply I got was 'stable and sleeping'. I thanked the woman, hung up and poured a cup of coffee. I'd drive down there later. But for now, there was nothing to do.

It was still hard for me to believe that Laurel was dead. Probably because my hatred for her burned even hotter and brighter now, hatred that was pointless, and maybe borderline crazy. And that frightened me. I shook myself and lit another cigarette, stuffed the pack and the lighter into my pants pocket and went out on the patio. The view of Winter's grave only added to my grief. I stared at the hole under the willow for a long time, too tired to cry, then took my coffee cup into the rows, trailing cigarette smoke like a freight train.

The green vines stood above my head, their tendrils reaching out to brush my arms. I stopped and did some rearranging, though I could barely see. A calming tide seeped up from the fertile earth and into my blood. This was my place. Where I belonged. I would be okay. And Jenna and Winter…well, Laurel was dead and that was the only comfort I was going to find there. And very poor comfort it was. I continued down the row, dragging my toes in the tilled earth.

I stopped at the end of the row, stooped and stubbed out my cigarette. I tucked the butt inside the cellophane of the pack, and shook out another cigarette. As I dragged my lighter out of my pocket I also dug out a shiny slip of something that fluttered to the ground at my feet. I knelt and picked up the purple foil capsule I had taken from Laurel's kitchen. I had forgotten it, never checking it against the bottles in my personal stock. It was pointless now, Laurel wouldn't be charged with vandalism in this life. Without reason other than the need for a distraction I turned and went back up the row to the cellar. The cellar door was padlocked again, so I went back through the kitchen and down the stairs, carrying my now cold coffee. I crossed the cold floor and unlocked the door to my private cellar.

234

This area of the cellar is one of my favorite places on earth. Sometimes I go down there just to sit and think. The room's only furniture consists of a small table and two tall chairs. The rest is all racks and shelves. The smell of the cedar racks and the dusky, sweet smell of wine has a calming effect on me. This time all I noticed were the missing bottles and the purple splatters. I looked for the excess bottles Samson had hand-corked for the lady's brunch. It took me several minutes. Nothing was where it should have been. I was about to give up when I spotted them on the bottom of the far rack. Both of them. I knelt and drew the two bottles out of the rack. The gold lettering was clear to read, there was no mistake. 2008 V.R. in Samson's handwriting.

I sat there cradling the two bottles like a mother with twins. Samson had bottled five bottles of wine for me. Two had been drunk with Marjory and the ladies at the brunch and two were still here. And the other I had given to…My heart sank and my head reeled as the memory hit me. Numbly, I slid the bottles back in the rack, stood and dusted off my knees. I had to be wrong. I had to be!

I climbed the stairs to the kitchen and glanced at the clock: 5:45. She wouldn't be at work yet.

"To hell with it," I said and dialed information. I couldn't wait. I had to know. I asked for Midge Tidwell's home phone number and was relieved that it wasn't unlisted. I dialed and waited doggedly through a dozen rings before the sleepy deputy picked up.

"Hello," she said and then coughed and cleared her throat in my ear. "Excuse me. Who is this?"

"Claire de Montagne," I said.

"Mrs. de Montagne? What's up?" She yawned loudly. "I didn't order a wakeup call."

"It's about the unidentified print on the shovel used to kill Kevin Harlan," I began.

"A palm print to be precise," she cut in, suddenly alert. "Still unidentified."

"Do you have access to fingerprints for the deputies and detectives on the force?" I asked, knowing I was on shaky ground.

"Who are you talking about?" she asked cautiously.

I quickly explained who and what I was talking about, and then told her why I suspected him. She didn't like what I had to say any more than I liked saying it.

"I like you Mrs. de Montagne, but that's a load of crap. I can't believe you'd even say that!"

"Just check it out," I begged. "If I'm wrong, so be it, but if I'm right…" God, I hoped I *was* wrong

"I'll check," she said, "but I'm telling you, you're crazy."

"Thanks—" I began, but Midge had hung up on me.

235

CHAPTER 44

Midge didn't call me back, Detective Doug Priest did, an hour after my conversation with Midge.

"Mrs. de Montagne, my hero," he said, officious with a touch of sarcasm. "I wanted to thank you for *all* your help. The print matched. Thought you'd like to know."

Energy left my body in a flash flood and I had to grab the back of a chair to keep from dropping. I had hoped so much that I was wrong that the news hit me like a punch to the chest. I couldn't reply, I just stood there in shaky shock, eyes pinched closed, phone to my ear.

"Did you hear me?" Priest said, grinding the knife into my back.

"It was him," I said idiotically and tears burned my cheeks.

"Damned right! I knew the son of a bitch was crooked," Priest was gleeful in his triumph. I could almost see him clicking his Gucci heels and dancing around his desk. "Couldn't have done it without you."

"Is Ben under arrest?" I cut in, swallowing hard.

"Not yet. It takes time to get the DA off his ass to issue a warrant for the Sheriff's arrest. But it's coming. Any minute now and it'll be on the wire. We'll need a statement from you and—"

"Thank you for calling," I cut him off, barely able to choke the words out. I sat down at the kitchen table, hung my head and let the tears come. "Oh, Ben," I whispered into my hands. "How could you?"

CHAPTER 45

Eventually I managed to get myself together and get in the shower. I dressed in faded jeans and a sweatshirt because the day had turned misty and cold. I drove Victor's truck to the hospital, barely aware of the road. I felt wrung-out and old. My knee was purple and screamed bloody murder every time I put weight on it. My side had a yellow-green boot-print where Laurel had kicked me, and my ribs felt creaky but I didn't think anything was broken. I had four large adhesive bandages on each hand, and my knuckles were bruised. I was so stiff that it took me a few minutes to climb out of the truck. I limped into the hospital and took the elevator upstairs.

Victor was sleeping, looking thin and vulnerable swaddled in hospital sheets, only his straggly mustache hinting that he was older than fifteen. Careful not to wake him, I eased into the chair at the head of the bed. The doctor had assured me on my way in that Victor would be fine, but seeing him there almost broke my heart. This was the third time I had visited someone I loved at this hospital in *one week*. It was too much. Much too much. I couldn't stop the tears from welling up in my already bloodshot eyes. I took a tissue from my bag, sniffling quietly.

"Why ya crying?" Victor whispered. "Somebody die?"

"Oh, God, Victor," I wheezed and wiped my nose.

"What's wrong?" he asked, trying to rise. He winced and eased back into the bed. "What is it?"

"It's Ben," I said. "He murdered Kevin."

"What?!" Victor tried to sit up again, grimaced in pain and fell back, out of breath.

"Don't do that," I ordered sharply. "You'll start bleeding again!"

"Ben?" Victor asked through ashen lips.

"He was having an affair with Laurel," I explained, watching Victor, concerned by his color and labored breathing. "He helped her cover up Winter's death. He killed Kevin when Kevin figured it out."

Victor didn't get a chance to reply. The door burst open and a heavyset nurse with a long black braid slapping the middle of her plump behind hustled in. Her eyes glued themselves to the heart rate monitor.

"You'll have to leave," she told me in a tight voice as she hurried to Victor's side. She grabbed Victor's wrist and then looked at me again. "Now."

"Is he all right?" I asked as I gathered my purse.

"I'm fine," Victor said before the nurse shushed him.

"He'd *be* fine without this aggravation," the nurse snapped. "Now go. Come back later."

238

I said a quick goodbye and hurried into the hall, anxious for Victor and feeling guilty. I should have waited until he was feeling better. In a half-daze I left the hospital by a side door and went to Victor's truck. I started the engine and sat there as it ran, slumped over the steering wheel. My whole world had fallen apart. Things couldn't be any worse, I thought.

I was wrong.

A tapping at the truck window snapped me out of my fugue. I wiped my eyes with the heel of my hand and stared up at a shape made fuzzy by the tears. I blinked and the shape solidified into a disheveled Ben Stoltze. Before I could react, he jerked the door open and shoved me across the seat, sliding in right behind me. I grabbed the passenger door handle, but Ben snatched me by the hair and jerked me back. He had his revolver in his hand. My mouth formed a scream but my lungs had clamped down tight and wouldn't supply the air.

Ben spoke in a curiously calm voice. "Hey, Claire," he said, "Don't rush off. Hate to have to shoot you." His face was covered with thick stubble and his breath smelled of whiskey. His clothes were rumpled and dirty, his eyes bloodshot. He didn't look like a sheriff, he looked like a prison escapee.

I stopped struggling.

"Move your feet please," he asked politely and I dragged them over to my side of the truck. "And lock your door."

I clicked the lock and Ben let go of my hair. He put the revolver between his thighs, slipped the truck into reverse, checked the mirrors calmly and backed out. Unhurriedly, we left the parking lot and turned out on the foggy highway. He turned on the headlights and snapped off the radio.

"Wh—where are you taking me?" I stammered after five minutes of silent driving. By then my heart had settled down to a life threatening thump.

Ben shot me a glance. And it wasn't friendly. "Why, I'm gonna answer all your questions, Claire," he said. "Isn't that what you want?"

"I don't have any questions." I said stupidly, hating the fear in my voice.

"Sure you do," Ben said. "Don't you want to ask me anything?"

I truly believed that he was going to kill me. But, if I was going to die, I wanted to know the truth.

"Why did you kill Kevin?" I asked.

"You know why," he said. "He found out about Winter. From Michelle."

"He found out that Laurel had murdered Winter," I said with the reckless anger of the doomed.

"I didn't think it was murder," he snapped. "Thought it was an accident. And Buford Logan deserved to go to jail. For Jenna..." Ben trailed off into silence. "I loved Laurel," he added after a protracted moment.

239

"Enough to kill Kevin and send an innocent woman to prison?" I demanded.

"Michelle isn't innocent," Ben said. "She's trash. The world will be a better place without her."

"And Kevin? What about him, you arrogant bastard? You beat his head in with a shovel!"

"I wasn't trying to kill him. He punched me and I hit him with the shovel. Instinct. I didn't plan it. He fell back but didn't go down. So, I hit him again. I don't know how many times I hit him before I realized he was hung up on the grape trellis." Ben blew out a long breath and ran his free hand through his hair. He shook his head once. "I'm sorry about Kevin. And Jenna. About all the suffering her parents went through," he admitted. "Things got out of hand." Ben flipped on the blinker and exited the highway. He turned north on black asphalt and began the climb out of the fog. "But I'm going to set it right."

I laughed a short, unbelieving bark. "By killing me?"

"I'm not going to kill you," he said, giving me an amused glance. "I like you, Claire, but after all the trouble you've caused I'm half tempted to shoot you. But, I need a witness. Besides, I know you'll want to see the ending."

"A witness?" I said, not believing he would let me live. Not after all he had done to hide his secret. "A witness to what?"

"You'll see," Ben said. "Loose ends need to be tied up before I go."

"The only place you're going is prison," I snapped at him and he laughed good and long.

"You've been right about a lot of things, Claire, but you're wrong about that."

We drove in silence for fifteen minutes, climbing higher into the sun, into the mountains. The tops of the peaks shimmered with clouds while the valley below was slowly shedding its misty shroud to reveal the green of fields and the mini-forests of trees in the unincorporated areas.

"Why did you have to frame Michelle?" I finally broke the silence, though I thought I knew the answer.

"Michelle buried Winter," Ben replied matter-of-factly. "Laurel called her the day the accident happened. Bad idea. Michelle didn't know when to stop. After she ran Jessica off the road, I knew she was out of control."

"You told her to blow up the truck," I interrupted.

"Hell no!" Ben said. "I'm not that stupid. I told her to get rid of it, but I didn't tell her to blow the thing up with a hundred witnesses watching."

"You really are a bastard," I said, and Ben shrugged and scratched at his grungy cheek.

"She feels guilty about Winter. She wants to go to jail," Ben told me, wiping his hands clean with a few casual words. "She used to visit Winter's

240

grave. Late at night," Ben said. "Bet you didn't know that. Wouldn't stop going, no matter what I said. Crazy."

"And what about Laurel?" I asked. He didn't reply, but I didn't let it drop. "Why did you kill her?"

"I had no choice," Ben scowled. "I had to kill her."

"Bullshit. You killed her because she was sleeping with Doug Priest," I said and Ben flinched.

"She was using him."

"Like she used you."

Ben didn't speak. His eyes remained grimly fixed on the road winding between farms and fields as it climbed higher and higher into the mountains.

"She loved me," he finally said. "Things just didn't work out."

"You killed her because she was with Priest."

"I saved your life."

I laughed at that. "If she hadn't been sleeping with Priest, you'd have let her kill me."

"We'll never know, will we?" Ben said.

"I think—" I began but Ben cut me off. He grabbed the revolver and pointed it across the seat at me without taking his eyes off the road.

"Shut up, Claire," he said through clenched teeth.

I shut up.

Ben turned on a narrow, pot-holed asphalt road that wound up the mountains, almost circling itself at points. I knew this was the road that led to Bethel Fields Cemetery, where Kevin Harlan now lay under six feet of rocky soil. I had buried both of my parents there, and my grandparents before them. I was unsurprised when Ben turned in under the rusty wrought iron arch wilting under the weight of a mass of creeper vines. The Falconè family plot, containing a dozen of my ancestors, was near the front entrance, surrounded by a wrought iron fence. I needed to come up and pull weeds and wipe down the stones; it had been too long since I had tended it. Would I ever get the chance?

The cemetery was small and looked more like a park with its trees, flowering shrubs and untended tulip beds thick with weeds. Most of the headstones were weathered and crumbling with a few newer additions scattered about. Ben drove to the back of the cemetery and stopped on the grass under a copse of elm trees. He turned off the engine.

For a long moment we sat in the shade listening to the engine tick while Ben stared straight ahead at a plot surrounded by a rust-red iron fence. The wrought iron gate had the word STOLTZE in fancy script at its center. The plot was large enough for twenty, but held only four gravestones, one of them fairly recent: Sarah, Ben's wife. Why had he brought me here? I could think of

241

only one reason for coming to a graveyard: to bury someone. That thought kicked my fear up to bone chilling levels.

"My mom and dad are buried there," Ben startled me out of my thoughts. He indicated the plot with a tilt of his head. "Sarah too," he referred to his wife. "She died hard, Claire. She died and there was nothing I could do."

I didn't know what to say. Somehow I was sure that none of this would have happened if Sarah had lived. No, that's not true. Laurel would have killed Winter, but maybe she would have gone to prison for it and Kevin would still be alive.

"I should have pulled the trigger," Ben said. "Every night while she lay dying in that hospital I'd sit with this gun and try to think of reasons not to put it in my mouth. Then I met Laurel." Ben shrugged. "I'm sorry for my kids."

"Ben," I said, trying for a placating tone that was hard to produce with fear clotting my throat. "It doesn't have to be like this. We can—"

"Shut up," he said sharply, gripping the door handle, eyes on the rearview mirror. He stepped quickly out of the truck as I craned my head around to see.

A Napa Valley Sheriff's cruiser was turning in at the gate, the driver just a shape behind the sun-glare bouncing off the windshield. Ben slipped behind one of the elms, out of sight from the patrol car, but where he could still see me. He held a finger to his lips and tipped the gun barrel in my direction. I got the point.

The patrol car crept slowly toward Victor's truck, gravel popping and churning under its wheels. Whoever was driving wasn't in a hurry, or they were being very cautious. Not cautious enough. The car rolled to a stop twenty feet behind the truck. The car's engine died and Doug Priest stepped out, squinting into the sun.

The next few seconds passed so quickly I didn't have time to think, which was probably a good thing. I jerked at the door handle, a mewl squeezing through my fear-constricted throat, and shoved the door open. My leg went out from under me, sending pain up my thigh. I flopped out onto the grass screaming, "Gun! Gun! Gun!" My mind couldn't form clear sentences. It seemed to be frozen on that one word. "Gun! Gun!" I shouted as I shoved myself up and ran on my half-crippled leg for the Stoltze's family plot, the nearest form of cover.

A gunshot fragmented the silence of the cemetery and a bullet whipped past my head as I dove over the rusty fence, forcing my hobbled knee to work. I had barely cleared the low fence when Ben's second shot ripped through my left heel. I slammed into the ground, pain scorching up my leg as hot blood flooded my shoe. My fear made the pain a tiny thing. And compared to death it was. I scrambled on all fours for the cover of the pink granite monument carved with Sarah Stoltze's name.

242

A half dozen gunshots echoed and overlapped like rolling thunder. I heard a muffled scream followed by a curse and glass shattering, then a volley of shots so tightly spaced it sounded like one long roar. I had to look, had to know what was happening. Gripping the cold marble for support, I peeked around the side of the headstone, careful to keep as much of myself as possible hidden.

Doug Priest was stretched out beside his car, his arms straight out from his shoulders, right leg crossed nonchalantly over the left. His tie was lying across his face, covering his eyes. His pistol was on the gravel beside him and brass shell casings littered the gravel, glittering in the sun. His white shirt was rapidly turning red. I didn't have to look twice to know he was dead.

Ben laughed in a curiously muffled voice and my heart tried to climb my throat and take flight. Ben was sagging against the elm he had hidden behind, his hand pressed to a hole in his stomach that was leaking blood down his pants leg. More blood dribbled down his face from a gash over his right eye, but he was grinning.

Ben glanced my way and I ducked back down.

"Come on out, Claire," he said. "Sorry 'bout the foot."

I didn't move, didn't speak. I stayed huddled behind the monument, breathing hoarse and fast. His mention of my foot brought my attention back to the throbbing pain. I looked down and saw that the heel of my shoe was ripped half away and there was a ragged hole at the toe. It was a horrifying mess. The blood scared me almost as much as Ben did.

"I'm not going to kill you," Ben said. I didn't reply. "Said I was sorry about your foot. Don't hold a grudge," he laughed at that, then coughed wetly. "I got him, Claire," Ben said, his voice much closer. I looked over the top of the monument, my foot screaming at me as I put weight on it. Ben was unlatching the plot's rusty gate. His eyes caught mine and held.

"How's the foot?" he asked, actually sounding concerned.

"It hurts," I said, surprised that my voice wasn't shaking the way my hands were.

Ben pushed the gate open and the hinges squealed in protest. He left it open as he walked to Sarah's grave and stopped. He looked at the headstone and then glanced up at me.

"She was a good woman," he said. "Too good for what happened to her." He looked down, the gun hanging slack in his hand.

"What are you going to do now?" I asked Ben, still concealed, from the neck down.

"Now?" Ben asked, looking up at me. "Now?" He looked confused for a moment. He wiped at his face with his free hand then ran his fingers through his hair. "Why, it's over now, Claire. Nothing *to* do."

243

"Why did you bring me here?" I asked, leaning my weight against the cold stone, lifting my injured foot. "You're going to kill me." I answered my own question and the words sent a chill through my veins.

"I'm not going to kill you. This is where it ends," Ben said, his eyes on the ground.

"Where what ends?" I said, wondering if he had taken the final step off the ledge into insanity, and fearing that I was going to be his next victim.

"Sarah always took care of me," Ben said, nodding at the ground before him. "And I couldn't do anything for her."

"Sarah?" I said idiotically, talking an involuntary step back that made my foot howl. I grabbed the headstone again.

Ben nodded but didn't look up. "You're a smart one, Claire. Gotta give ya that. Couldn't fool you."

"If you hadn't arrested Jessica—"

"I didn't," Ben cut me off. He jerked his head at Priest's lifeless sprawl, "He did. And look what it got him."

"You would have let her go to prison," I pressed.

"Would have made it pretty neat," Ben agreed. "Didn't work out." Ben winced and touched his side where blood was flowing in a steady stream. He looked at the blood on his hand.

"And now you're the one going to prison," I said.

"Nope," Ben said with a seasick grin. "That's one thing you're wrong about."

"You're going to kill me," I said again.

"Damn it," Ben barked, "would you stop saying that! I'm *not* going to kill you and I'm *not* going to prison. You're a smart girl, you can figure this out." He was right; it only took me a second.

"You're going to kill yourself," I said with disbelief.

"Nope," Ben grinned. "Care to try again?"

"I give up," I said, feeling lightheaded from blood loss. "And, I really don't care anyway," I added in disgust, fully believing now that he didn't mean to kill me. What he had in mind I couldn't guess, and I wasn't going to try.

"Guess we'll just have to wait and see, won't we?"

I shrugged and limped from behind the headstone. Gingerly, I lowered myself to a sitting position beside the slab of granite and slipped off my tennis shoe. Blood spilled onto the grass.

"Pretty bad?" Ben asked but I ignored him. I stripped my sock off, grinding my teeth at the pain, and inspected the wound.

The bottom of my foot was gouged a half inch deep from heel to toe, but all of my digits were intact. I took the bloody sock and tied it around the worst of the damage, then closed my eyes and leaned back into the cool stone.

"You'll live," Ben said then paused for a long moment. "I said I was sorry."

"Leave me alone," I barked at him, opening my eyes and fixing him with an ugly glare. Ben didn't notice, he was staring at the cemetery's entrance. At the car passing under the iron arch and heading our way. A white Chevy with paler white circles on the door where decals had been peeled off.

"Oh, God," I said. "No, Ben," I pleaded. "No."

"Figured it out, huh?" Ben asked, his back to me. "This makes a clean sweep. And your boyfriend gets to be the hero. Though he might not live to enjoy it."

"Ben," I said as Hunter's car accelerated down the drive. It slowed briefly as it passed Priest, then came to a stop beside Victor's truck. Ben was facing the road. He ignored me. I pushed myself to my feet and stood leaning against the headstone.

"Hey there, Hunt!" Ben yelled as Hunter Drake stepped out of his car.

"Call the police!" I screamed at Hunter. "He's going to kill you!"

"Hello, Ben," Hunter called back, his eyes flicking on me for the briefest of moments. "Having a little trouble here?"

"Nothing I can't handle," Ben called cheerfully back. "How far are they behind you?"

Hunter shrugged. "Not far. Five, ten minutes. Might as well put the gun down and let the lady go," he said. From this distance I couldn't read his expression, but he seemed calm.

"Chivalry is not dead," Ben said with a laugh. "Come and get her," he motioned with his pistol, urging Hunter closer. Hunter didn't move.

"What are you trying to do, Ben?" Hunter asked. "Why'd you call me out here?"

"Wrapping it all up for you, Hunt," Ben said. "You and Claire started all of this, figured you had a right to be here when it ended."

"Why'd you kill Priest?" Hunter asked. "Because of Laurel?"

"Because he was an asshole," Ben snapped, his good humor slipping. "Nothing to do with her."

"She was a bad one, Ben. Not worth dying over," Hunter said as he eased his hand inside his jacket. Ben didn't miss the move, his smile returned and he chuckled.

"Gonna draw on me, Hunt?" he asked. "If I remember right, you're pretty good with that pistol."

"District Champ," Hunter nodded. "No fast draw, though."

"I'm going to kill you, Hunt," Ben said affably. "If you don't kill me first."

"Let Claire go, Ben," Hunter said. "She's got nothing to do with this." Hunter's eyes flickered on me, but I couldn't read anything in them.

245

Ben laughed and shot a glance at me. "She's got everything to do with it. She started it."

"You started it," I argued like a petulant child.

Ben shrugged. "Whatever," he said, then turned his attention back to Hunter. "I'm not going to jail, Hunt. It ends here. Today."

"And if I don't play along?" Hunter asked, easing a large black pistol out from under his coat. He let it hang at his side.

"Then I'll kill you," Ben replied simply. "Then Claire." My head snapped up at that. Ben winked at me.

"Put the gun down, Ben," Hunter said. "Let it go."

"Not gonna happen," Ben said and started to raise his pistol.

I dove at Ben's legs as Hunter's pistol swung up. A single shot echoed off the mountains and Ben lurched as I tackled him behind the knees. He fell face first on to the grass and rolled over. His pistol went flying. It clanged off the iron fence into the grass. Quickly, I rolled away from him. My foot was throbbing and leaking blood.

Ben didn't move. His hands were at his side, eyes open to the sky. I sat there looking at him dumbly as Hunter walked over. Hunter knelt beside his old partner and friend and felt for a pulse in Ben's neck. He shook his head at me without saying anything. I didn't need him to tell me Ben was dead.

Hunter picked up Ben's pistol and tucked his own back under his jacket. He flipped open the cylinder of Ben's revolver and ejected the shell casings.

"Empty," he said.

"Empty?"

"Empty," Hunter repeated.

"He wanted to die," I said. Hunter nodded, looking down at his friend. "It's not your fault."

"I know," he said.

"He wouldn't have killed me," I said, looking at Ben's corpse, at the blood pooling around his head.

"I know that," Hunter said, shaking his head. He looked at Sarah's headstone. "None of this would have happened if Sarah hadn't died." I didn't have anything to say to that. He was right, but that didn't absolve Ben. He had made his choice and had chosen the illusion of love over everything else.

Hunter's head came up and he cocked an ear toward the road. I heard it then, the wail of a distant siren, a sound I had grown used to in the past week. A sound I never wanted to hear again. I peeled off the bloody sock and squeezed out the blood.

"Oh, Christ," Hunter said when he saw my foot. He dropped to a knee beside me, shucking his coat. He ripped the sleeve off his shirt with a quick motion.

246

"He would have killed himself if you hadn't," I tried to comfort Hunter as he wrapped my foot in his shirtsleeve.

Hunter merely grunted, tying a raggedy bow. He looked up and there were tears in his eyes. "It was the last thing I could do for him."

I gripped Hunter's hand and he squeezed back. He sat beside me and put his arm around me and I leaned my head against his chest. I said a silent prayer for Ben's soul and the souls of Jenna, Winter and Kevin as my tears soaked Hunter's shirt. He hugged me tighter and stroked my hair. We were still sitting like that when the deputies arrived in a fury of dust and sirens.

247

Made in the USA
Coppell, TX
10 December 2025

65333427R00152